Robert Newton Peck

Hang for Treason

Books by Robert Newton Peck:

A DAY NO PIGS WOULD DIE
PATH OF HUNTERS
MILLIE'S BOY
SOUP
FAWN
WILD CAT
HAMILTON
SOUP AND ME
BEE TREE
HANG FOR TREASON

ROBERT NEWTON PECK

Hang for Treason

Doubleday & Company, Inc., Garden City, New York   1976

ISBN 0-385-07337-2
Library of Congress Catalog Card Number 75–14836
Copyright © 1976 by Robert Newton Peck

To the Green Mountain Boys . . .
Good old boys who sang a hillbilly's yell, shooters and skinners of squir-
rel, lean as a fiddler's tune. Plowboy soldiers, who left a half-turned fur-
row to capture the cannon of Fort Ticonderoga, and to yank those
bloody teeth from a British lion's jaw.
And to Verdmont, before it was Vermont.

Hang for Treason

Prologue: *The 1745 Massacre*

"Oh, my God."

Israel Booker was not a man to defile the holy name of our Benefactor. And once, Noah, his son, had even seen his father kicked in the leg by a neighbor's bull, yet he did not crack an oath. Noah remembered the day. It was a year ago, 1744, on his birthday when he had reached the age of nine years.

Noah stopped pulling the two-man saw to see if his father had ripped his hand on the teeth of the blade.

Noah could not understand his father's oath. Puzzled, he looked at him. Israel Booker was still as a frog, so still that young Noah could read the drops of summer sweat that were standing in the lines on his father's face. Israel's eyes narrowed, then widened, not believing what he saw. Following the line of his father's big arm as he pointed across the north meadow, young Noah saw the naked brown bodies tumble over the top rail of the Bookers' fence.

There were too many to count.

On the yonder side of the brook, the tall grass was moving in place after place as though a dog ran through it. Beyond the grass, the bodies kept pouring over the fence rail like a brown waterfall.

"What is it, Father?"

Noah knew the answer to his question even before he asked it, but he just wanted to hear Israel Booker's deep voice tell him that it was just a dream and that they really weren't coming to kill the Bookers. Then Noah felt his body whip through the air, like a toy being thrown by a child. His father's big hands were pushing him back into the root cellar which was only a spit away from where father and son had worked the saw. Noah didn't like the root cellar as there were always spiders spread out on its roof like big black stars; and when he looked up, they were so

1

close to his face, he could see the shine of their eyes. He knew they were looking at him. Noah never went into the root cellar unless his mother or one of his sisters asked him to fetch something, like a butter tub and some apples, or a wheel of cheese.

But now Israel Booker was closing the door and the root cellar got darker and darker.

"Noah," he said, "stay put, boy. Don't come out until one of us comes to get you. And make not a sound."

Noah heard his father's big feet running toward the house, knowing his father would fetch the musket that always stood on its butt just inside their cabin door. He heard voices, his father yelled to his mother and then to Jenny and Grace.

Noah Booker prayed: "Dear God, please don't let the red people hurt us. We don't want to hurt the heathens, so don't let them do us harm. And don't let there be any spiders in here in the dark. Amen."

He heard the shutter on their cabin window slam tight, and with it went the hum of voices. Jenny and Grace usually talked all the time, but now they weren't saying a word. And he heard footsteps. Not big and dust kicking like his father's, but instead they were light and rabbity. Noah heard the puff of his father's flintlock discharge, which sounded less like a gun and more like a soft little cry for help, and from just outside the door to the root cellar came one gosh-awful whoop. It made Noah jump, hitting his head on the earthen roof. Some dirt fell down and into the neck of his shirt. But he recalled how his father had charged him not to speak or to cry, so he held quiet, smelling the dampness.

A musket went off again.

But to Noah it didn't sound anything like his father's piece. Did Indians have firearms? The noise of the gun was followed by grunting voices and more footsteps. Another gun spoke, from nearby. His father had said that one musket will speak higher or lower in pitch than another, like notes on a harpsichord. As he now heard more than one piece discharge, he knew his father had been right. Each gun sounded in a different way. Just outside the door to the root cellar, another musket was fired. Very loud. Its noise must have been heard all over the territory of Verdmont. He wanted to cry out, but he knew the shake in his stomach would not allow it . . . and also he remembered what his father had said.

Noah was hoping that their good neighbors, the Cotter family, would hear and come to help run the red devils off their land. But he recalled James Cotter lived over the ridge, more than five miles to the eastward and would nary hear a shot. Sometimes if Mr. Cotter and his sons were hunting up on the near face of the ridge, the Bookers could hear their guns, if the wind was kindly. And sometimes Israel Booker would answer with his own gun, firing it off without lead, just to say a howdo and let them know they had hearing neighbors. Noah's mother, Mary Booker, always said her wish was that when evening came they could see the fire from the rim of Cotter's chimney. But they couldn't. There was too much high ground betwixt Cotter's place and theirs, and too much forest. There were trees all about their cleared place, except to the westward toward Lake Champlain and beyond, where the Yorkers lived.

Noah heard a man's voice.

It was no Indian, as he could hear the grunts of the red men outside. This voice, although it did not speak English, spoke in Christian tones, even though it talked through its own nose. No Englishman, not even a New Hampshire man like Mr. Cotter, spoke as nasal . . . nor did the Dutchies from down below Skenesboro who spoke English as though they had stomach distress.

The man who spoke was French.

There seemed to be an argument between a Frenchie and one of the heathen. The Frenchman seemed to bark out an order and the Indian's grunts became sour in tone. Noah did not like what the Frenchman said. He wondered what was happening to his family, until he smelled the smoke. The cabin was burning, or one of the outbuildings. Then he heard a woman's scream. Except for his one trip south to Skenesboro, the only women Noah knew (other than Mistress Cotter) were his mother and sisters. But this was surely a woman's cry, high and piercing to the ear. Noah started to open the door to the root cellar so as he could run and help, but then the thought came that he was but ten years old and half growed and could commit little service to aid his family. Perhaps he would be more trouble than help and be only an extra soul for his father's one gun to defend.

He prayed to be back home in England.

Again he longed to see the open countryside where people lived without guns and there were fewer trees, and where you could hear the church bells ring on a Sabbath morning. And no red men.

Noah had not wanted to leave England.

He hated that ship they sailed across the ocean on, and all those weeks they slept on her wet boards under damp quilts, among all those people who never took a bath and who talked all night long and said the hateful words about King George. They were the same persons, Noah remembered, who drank too much rum and then puked it all up for the rest of them to smell, as if the toss of the ship was not enough to sicken every man jack aboard. He could not eat, nor could Grace or Jenny. His mother ate very little. Israel made them eat, bowls and bowls

3

of boiled oats with brown sugar atop that was poorly enough to behold with the eye without partaking by spoon. In a mass of five, they huddled together and prayed and sang, Jenny and Grace both having been blessed with silver voices. One of the drunkards attempted to add his own sotty voice to their song, and tried to place his arm around Grace's shoulder, pretending all the while to adjust her shawl, and breathing his foul breath upon them. His father stood up and had to fist the man until he fell back into a herd of like fellows who were city men, according to friends around them, and, lacking the arm of a farmer, were able to administer no more than sour glances.

Again Noah heard either his mother or one of his sisters scream. Burying his head in his hands, he wept for himself, ashamed that he lacked the courage to defy Israel's word and run to their rescue. He knew not what to do, so he did nothing but listen in the darksome to the cries of his family.

He took a real jolt when he felt the door to the root cellar move.

Someone outside was trying to pull up the Y-latch that worked from inside or out. Backing away from the door, he retreated until his butt was against the other side of the tool-shed wood, as the root cellar and tool shed were back to back, separated only by a wall of rough slabs. His hands tore at the bark, trying to pull three or four slabs loose enough for a door to squeeze through to escape out through the tool shed. As he pulled hard, one slab cracked loose. But the others wouldn't budge.

Light suddenly split the darkness.

A brown hand was forcing the door in, breaking the latch push by push. A big shoulder heaved against the plank, widening the thin line of light. Reaching a hand into the tool shed, Noah tried to touch the ax or the mattock. Both were out of reach. His fingers closed on a long handle, and by felling it, he hauled it into the root cellar. It was a pruning hook, a long-handled pole with both blade and sharpened tip, that his father used to trim the nine apple trees in their modest orchard.

The door opened.

Noah looked up into a screaming brown face, painted white from the mouth up, which made the face appear to be half cut away. The head had no hair, except for a crude topknot placed well back, around which had been wound some strips of red cloth. As the savage tore away the shattered door, Noah saw a giant scar that slashed across his naked chest like a silver snake. The Indian smiled a mean smile, showing that most of his teeth were missing. Throwing back his head he howled again, the cry of a mad dog.

Turning his head away from Noah, he yelled to his companions, beckoning with his hand for them to come and see what he had found.

4

Once again he started to enter the root cellar. In his hand was a hatchet, the blade of which was red with fresh blood. His other hand held scraps of cloth that had once been Jenny's blue dress. He looked down at Noah as the boy huddled in the half darkness. The hand that held the blue cloth pounded his chest, beating his brown body as if it were a drum. Again and again his hand thudded against his skin, a gesture of warlike pride.

"Iron Knife," he said in English. As he said the two words over and over, Noah guessed it was the only English he knew and probably was his name. The Indian grinned an ugly grin, raising his hatchet, wanting Noah to know the name of his slayer.

"Iron Knife," he again said.

Beholding the brown stains of blood on Jenny's dress gave Noah more courage than he had ever felt heat of. He didn't want to cry, but the tears came in a hot rush of hurt feeling that couldn't be held back, spilling down his face.

"Noah Booker," the boy yelled.

Almost like a dream, Noah saw the sharp tip of his pruning hook pierce the hide of Iron Knife's belly. The hateful look on the Indian's painted face changed from pride to pain; as his red body fell forward upon Noah, his stomach swallowed the hook until there was no more blade. Hot blood spurted out, running down the pole and over Noah's hands. Up went Iron Knife's arm, high in the air, his hand gripping a hatchet that never could strike again. His body fell, kicking and bucking in the earth-well where Noah had been hidden, until the boy too went down under the weight of death. Noah had once smelled the carcass of a black bear that had half rotted in the summer heat. Iron Knife smelled in like fashion, a stink strong and cruel. He moaned, a singsong sound that Noah hoped was his last, a tiny cry that pleaded for its mother.

Other red men came.

Grabbing his ankles and screaming, they pulled Iron Knife's bloody body out of the root cellar and free of the pruning hook. Noah still held its shaft in both hands. But from its hook there remained a short loop of Iron Knife's bowel. One of the men's faces told a tale of horror as he recognized that Iron Knife was dead. Drawing his knife he cut two fingers off his own left hand, waving them into the air. Blood poured from his injured hand. Scooping up a handful of dirt, he dropped it on his own head, moaning in genuine sorrow as he let the dirt sift into his eyes, as if the sight of seeing Iron Knife dead made him wish to be blind. What the boy saw turned him dumb.

Other members of the tribe of red men rolled around on the ground, screaming in the agony of their loss. More Indians came. One bit his own hand until his teeth bore blood. Another straddled the fallen body of Iron Knife as if to guard it from further misfortune, pointing at Noah and yelling until his lungs might burst, shaking his fists. Looking down at the dead man between his feet caused the warrior to close his eyes tightly, throw back his head, and wail to heaven.

At his back, Noah heard the door to the tool shed open, making its usual dry squeaky-squeak. His father had instructed him only this morning to lard the hinge, to place a tuft of wool betwixt the two pieces of leather where they effected to rub and squeak. Now, at this moment, he was grateful he had not yet done so. Behind him, a red arm reached through the gap that he had newly created in the rough slabs, grabbing Noah's leg betwixt ankle and knee. With his other leg which was at liberty, Noah came down hard on the brown wrist, bashing it against the rock floor and causing the red man worthy pain. Yet again the hand reached for him, pulling at the seat of his britches in an effort to seize his belt and hold him fast and helpless.

Despite what Israel said, Noah could remain in the root cellar no longer. Out he charged. With the pruning hook, he smote one red savage a blow against his throat. The cabin was burning. No members of his family were in view. The corner of his eye caught a glimpse of the bee hive that Israel brought from Skenesboro. "Bees and a Queen from England," he had said, so that their apple trees would breed themselves and bear fruit. At that same moment, Noah recalled what Mr. Cotter had said, that the one thing red men feared was a bee. There had been no honeybees in Verdmont until the white settlers came and brought them along the route from Boston.

With his long hook, Noah gave the hive a stout smack.

Over it tipped. As it tumbled to the ground, a black cloud of bees emerged in an angry hum. A warrior slapped himself, yowling more in fear than pain. Bees were all around, more than two thousand, according to the tally his father had paid for, although some were away from the hive gathering sweetness from the flowers. Yet in that instant it appeared to Noah that all two thousand of their bees were busy stinging the brown hides of their enemies, as well as stinging the boy.

He had earlier been afeared of the bees, that they might sting. One did such an act to Grace and her hand had swollen up to a puff. It was a day or two before the pink and sting of it began to stop . . . due, Israel said, to the retreat of the poison. But now, as Noah held the prune hook in his hands, taking his share of the stinging, he no longer held any fear of the bees. The red men, however, screamed in horror, as though the insects loosed upon their persons were possessed of tiny evil spirits bent upon doing them in.

6

"Noah Booker," the lad screamed at the red man closest to him, clouting him smartly with the hook. "Noah Booker, Noah Booker!"

Israel Booker had instructed his son, now that he was ten and had two figures to his age, that he must no longer show fear of things, and that courage was indeed a manly and English virtue. Grace had said it was also a womanly one. In fact, because females were smaller it meant they must possess greater courage. Jenny had said that was true; so had their mother. Israel nodded that the two of them (he and his son) were outcounted in the matter. So, therefore, Noah now concluded that, because of his small size, he must act with fortitude equal to the tiny honeybee, her size being no drawback to the intensity in the sting of her little sword.

A man yelled out in French.

Turning, Noah saw the man's musket leveled at him. Bees were at the man's eyes and ears as he fired, just as Noah threw himself to the ground. The man swatted at the bees and did not reload his piece. Jumping to his feet, Noah charged him with the pruning hook held well forward like a lance of the knights of old and with all the English bravery he could muster, remembering the tale of how King Henry had battled the French knights on Saint Crispin's Day and forced them to give quarter.

"Noah Booker," the boy screamed at him. He fled.

Wheeling about sharply, and swinging his hook in a great circle, he did crack an Indian in the shinbone to the point of felling him like a weakened tree. As he tumbled, the boy yelled his name at him, to make certain he would mark well the lad who had given him a smarting. Bees were on the Indian's face and Noah could perceive that the savage was now, at both ends of his body, in more than just mild discomfort.

Two of the red heathens were lifting up the body of Iron Knife, and they carried him away to the northward from whence they did come. One of the bearers took a sting on the face, dropping a leg of Iron Knife in order to swat at the honeybee, slapping his own face and neck a number of times without being able to hit his mark. "Noah Booker," the savage said, as though he had given voice to an oath or some other demeaning term.

"Yes," the boy yelled after them, "Noah Booker, and best you remember."

There were too many bees around to remain in that spot, so he fled for the fire of their burning cabin. Israel had taught Noah that bees detest smoke.

The cabin was blackened and the heat lashed his face. Rounding a corner, he came to the doorway on the southern exposure and there lay

7

his mother, bloody and dead. Her clothing had been torn, her white legs and belly exposed, and he could see that cruel liberties had been taken upon her helpless body. A bee was stinging his face but he felt no hurt. Pulling his mother's clothing down to counterpane her nakedness, he then entered their cabin to find his younger sister Jenny (she was only a lass of twelve years) in a like state. And nearby, the body of his elder sister Grace lay white and still against the brown of their earthen floor. The air was very hot, and a part of Noah's shirt had begun to catch fire. He could not understand why Grace no longer had her long golden hair.

He then found his father.

Noah's lungs were in a cough, and the smoke smarted his eyes to the point of seeing little. Yet he saw Israel Booker sprawled on the dirt floor in a heap of broken crockery that they had brought all the way from England. A shaft of wood, no longer than his arm, had passed through his father's face, on the end of which there had been bound a sharp head of stone. More shafts were buried in his chest. His great shock of brown hair, which he tied at his neck with a leather bow, was missing. So were his stockings and boots. His big feet were white and still. There was dirt between his toes.

Noah's shirt was burning.

Tearing it off, he threw it to the floor where it persisted to burn. He felt the heat of the fire from the roof beating against his face, as though his cheeks and eyes and mouth were being slapped. It was hard to breathe, and his lungs had to labor. The gun that Noah tore from Israel's hands was warm, the metal barrel quite hot. He also grabbed the powderhorn and the pouch of shot. As he was about to leave the burning house, Noah saw a toy, Jenny's doll. He took it. The timbers of the roof started to cave in, so he fled the cabin as small bits of burning wood and blackened sod began to fall on his head and naked back. Smoke was all about him, setting him to choke, but there were no more bee stings. He heard only the ire of their hum.

Running south away from the cabin, he nearly fell over the fallen body of their brown and white spotted cow, Softy. She lay still, her throat cut, shafts of wood growing from her great side like a stand of evil weeds whose heads sprouted with feathers. The ground beneath her was dark with dried blood. Dropping the gun and powder, Noah fell to his knees beside her, throwing his arms on her big warm body. A few flies were on her, as always they were, and they buzzed at his joining them. Curling up against Softy's great underside, he held Jenny's little doll in his arms, in the same fashion he had seen her do, and tried to weep. But no tears would come.

"Noah Booker," he said, trying to say that he was still alive, to the

8

doll; then up to the sky. And to the earth, in which he would bury his loved ones, land that he would somehow hold no matter how many more Frenchmen came with their Indians.

Noah closed his eyes, and saw England.

Chapter 1

"It really happened?"

"Yes," said Papa, running a rough hand along the carved top of the wooden headstone that marked my grandfather's grave. The name he had carved on it was Israel Booker, and below the name were the years 1703–1745. "Yes, boy, it really did happen. Thirty years ago."

"Were you scared, Papa?" asked Phoebe.

"I surely was, daughter. I was just a lad of ten, two years younger than you."

"What kind of Indians were they?" I asked Papa.

"Saint Francis, from Canada. The Cotters happened to gun one down that same day. They knew it was the bloody Saint Francis."

"And they killed all but you?" asked Phoebe.

"All but me."

"I'm thankful they spared you, Papa."

My father reached out his hand and touched my sister's freckled face. I was right proud to be Noah Booker's son, but Phoebe was a girl and special to him. I was near eighteen and clear to grown up, while Phoebe was still Papa's little girl. She still sat in his lap after supper so they could read Scripture together. She was only twelve.

"The Cotters come and found me, right over there, huddled up forlorn against the flank of a dead cow and holding a doll in my arms. Found me and raised me up." As Papa told us his story, my eyes passed to the other headstones. Mary Booker, Jenny Booker, Grace Booker. Four in all. Papa had spoke little of the massacre, not until this day. Phoebe and I had seen him walk from the hill where he had cut some forsythia flowers, rows of little yellow bells, and carried them to our family plot. We followed him over. His knees touched the snow as he said a prayer at his mother's grave. Waiting for him to finish his meditations, we then had asked him to relate how he had lost all of his family on the same day. So he had stood the yellow flowers up in the April snow and told Phoebe and me about that most frightful day of his life.

"I hope the Saint Francis don't come again," said Phoebe, wrapping an arm around Papa and around me. "It would be dreadful, Papa, not to have you and Able and Mama."

Looking again at the grave markers, I knew that one day I'd be making one for Papa. I'd have to chisel out Noah Booker, 1735 and then the year of his death. I want to be buried here, too, I thought. I want to have a son who will carve *my* name, Able Booker, into a pine slab and mark my resting place with it, so there would be a line of us by generation . . . Israel, Noah, Able . . . on and on.

"No, the Saint Francis won't come south again," Papa said. "Times have changed. The year they come to massacre was 1745. This is the year of 1775, and we got British soldiers now to help us hold our land."

Shading his eyes, Papa looked westward across the lake to Fort Ticonderoga, the great star of gray stone that we could see from our farm in Verdmont.

"Look yonder," he said, pointing west at Fort Ti, "and see our Union Jack. It's good to witness the noble flag of England fly from them battlements. Whenever your mother is afraid for us here, I point west to the English fort. The French come south and built it, but General Montcalm couldn't hold it against Amherst. We won the French War. Drove all them Frenchies and their bloody red hides north to Quebec. That's what I tell your mother, and that's what I always tell you. English settlers have precious little to fear as long as we got Redcoats so nearsome. I know the heathen can hear the roar of British cannon, just as we can."

"Good," said Phoebe, "because I don't reckon I could kill an Indian with a pruning hook the way you killed Bad Knife."

"Iron Knife," said Papa.

He had been leaning his back against the trunk of the big elm that grew near one corner of our family plot. The April buds were too high up to see and the branches were naked as they scratched the sky, stiff as a witch's broom. He gave one last look to the yellow flowers that he'd stood up in the snow, a little clump on each of the four graves.

"Verdmont," he said, "is a long way from England."

"What's it like to be born in England?" Phoebe asked. The three of us walked slowly back toward our house and barn.

"It's a fair place," said Papa. "I was shy of eight years when we left England to sail for Boston. I thought England was the biggest place in Christendom, until I caught a look at the ocean."

"Was the ocean as big as Verdmont?"

"Bigger, girl. Bigger by a durn sight."

"Big as Verdmont and New Hampshire?"

"Bigger still. So big that a man can stand in the spray of it and ponder at the vast imagination of the Almighty who created it. My father said it made him question his own size, and his own wisdom for crossing it with a family, as if the Lord had forged it so big that He intended no one to cross. Father said it was to defy the will of God."

"I don't believe that," I said. "Meaning no disrespect and all, but I believe that God made us strong enough to cross anything—an ocean, or the great prairie to the west. Even the sky."

"Able, how could a body cross the sky?" said Phoebe.

"I ain't studied that out yet," I said.

"When you do," said Papa, "be sure to let the rest of us know. Because I sure got one heck of a hanker to see the contraption you aim to do it in."

"Me too," said Phoebe.

"As for now," said Papa, "the only bit of traveling you can do is travel to the barn. It's chore time."

"It's chore time," said Phoebe, giving me a stern glance.

With my hands suddenly under her arms, I lifted her up high in the air and swung her around, pretending that I was going to drop her. Phoebe was giggling and screaming her head off, because my fingers dug in a tickle spot; and if there was a soul on this earth who had a funnybone, it was Phoebe Booker.

"Able, Able, Able," she was laughing. "Set me down, Able. Please, please."

"Not until you promise to help me do chores."

"I can't. I have to help Mama fix supper."

"What?" I said, digging my fingertips into her ribs.

"Yes, yes, I promise. Oh, Able, please stop. Papa, make Able stop before I split."

"Leave me free of this," said Papa. "Able, I'll see you in the barn and proper soon, hear?"

"I hear, Papa."

"You're a man of eighteen now, or near to be. High time you weren't told it was chore time."

Only moments later I was squatting on the milk stool, wiping off Esther's big pink bag that was heavy with milk. I made sure her udder and teats were all clean before I put the bucket under her. Papa didn't hold to having anybody "milk dirty" as he called it. I'd been in a rush once, and had skipped the wiping. And the milk was full of tiny brown specks. Cows aren't too fussy about where they lie down, or what they lie in. So if you think about it enough, as you're fixing to swallow a mouthful of fresh milk with flecks of dirt in it, it makes a body wish he'd wiped ahead of milking. I also made sure the bucket was clean.

It had been a long day and the ache of work was heavy on my back. As I began to milk I leaned forward to rest my head on Esther's flank that was as warm as a morning pillow.

Esther was a cow that always turned her face to look at whoever was milking her. But she wasn't turning now, because I had tightened the stanchion on her neck. Not so tight as to hurt her, but snug enough up to keep her from trying to swing her big old head back and lick my ear.

Nobody ever pailed a cow that was as friendly as Esther. If anyone stopped by at our house, one of the first things we did was bring the person out to the barn to see how I'd teached Esther to shake hands. She wouldn't do the trick for anybody but me. Not even for Papa. Phoebe tried most of a morning once, but Esther wouldn't lift her hoof. She wouldn't offer up her front right hoof to a soul but me.

As I was milking, I heard Phoebe come in the barn, trying to sneak up behind me and startle me enough to fall off the milking stool. I could hear her little feet step lightly enough to only rustle the straw. Esther heard her coming, too. But I guess both of us pretended that we didn't, in order to let Phoebe tippytoe in until she was right close by. Just as I was about to point a teat at Phoebe and squeeze a long white stream of hot milk at her, that was when old Esther thought *she'd* get in the game. With a big wide swish of her tail, she caught Phoebe full in the face with a healthy lick. The tail tassel whipped her a good one and she let out a gasp of surprise.

I laughed, and so did Phoebe. I even had me a hunch that Esther laughed, too.

"Supper's almost ready," said Phoebe.

"How come you ain't helping Mama?"

"I did help. I peeled the apples for the turnips and then I shelled the beans."

"Good girl. Someday you'll make Lyman Shelby a fine wife."

"I hate Lyman Shelby and you know it."

"Why do you hate him?"

"His nose leaks."

"So did yours when you took a cough."

"But I wipe mine."

"Probably on your sleeve."

"I do not. I use the hanky that Mama made me for Christmas."

"Well now," I said, strip milking each teat to make sure Esther was dry, "look at all them white bubbles. I fancy you'd like to take a dipper of this here milk over to the Shelby place and share a sip with Lyman."

"Able Booker, you heard Mama tell you are not supposed to tease me about boys. Mama said it weren't proper."

As I dumped a good portion of Esther's warm milk into the calf pen, Phoebe watched. She leaned over to run her hand along the backbone of the new calf, who was now getting weaned on milk and water.

"April is so soft."

"Just like Esther," I said.

"How old is April now?"

"I reason about five weeks. She got herself early born."

"Why don't we bed her with Esther?"

"Time she was weaned. Soon as the snow melts, we'll turn both out to meadow where April and her mama can chomp the new grass."

"Able?"

"Yes."

"Is the grass green under the snow right now?"

"I sorely hope so. Winter here is long enough. Papa and me are itching to plow."

"Is winter in Verdmont longer than other places?"

"Reckon it is. You heard about the old farmer by the name of Colrain who homesteaded south of here?"

"No. What about him?"

"Well, it seems like the surveyor come to plot out Mr. Colrain's property."

"Then what?"

"He found out that his house was three rod further south than the old man had supposed. So he told Mr. Colrain that he weren't in Verdmont after all. He had been living all his years in Massachusetts. Know what the old man said?"

"No."

"He said he was relieved to hear it. Said he couldn't of took one more Verdmont winter."

When the look on Phoebe's face changed from wonder to a smile, I knew she'd got the wit of the story. She gave me a push. Then she helped me throw down some hay into the outside manger for Simon, our big ox.

"Why doesn't Simon sleep inside with Esther and April?"

"He did all winter. But one thing about Simon, he's always the first in our family to smell spring. Even when there's still snow on the ground, he wants to be outdoors. About two nights ago, just before bedtime, I heard Simon snorting in his stall with a want to get turned out. So I turned him out before he got pesky."

"*I* didn't hear him snort."

14

"You were asleep. Mama heard him and looked at Papa and said that spring was here for sure and certain."

"I'll be glad when winter's over," said Phoebe, hunching up her shoulders inside her coat. "I don't think I can take one more Verdmont winter." With that, she poked me a good one in the ribs and run like a hare toward the house before I could catch her. We washed up real proper, without being told, and took our places. Bowing our heads to give our thanks, we heard Papa say the blessing at the table. As I always did, I peeked up just once to see his hands. Noah Booker had big hands, and when he offered his gratefulness at mealtime, he always locked his hands together in prayer. His fingers were thick with work, and the way he held them reminded me of the rafters of a church. Whenever he spoke the blessing, he pressed his thumbs against the top of his bowed head and then he sort of built a church with his hands.

"Molly, those are proud turnips you and Phoebe cooked up," said Papa.

"It's the apple that makes 'em so sweet. And the sugar. Phoebe puts in a bit more sugar than what's righteous."

"They're real good, Mama," I said, "for vegetables."

"Nothing ails a good turnip," said Mama, "whether it be plain or all frilled up with sugar."

"I hardly think I would eat a turnip without sugar," said Phoebe.

"If you were starving, you would," I said.

"I would not."

"Yes you would."

"Would not," said Phoebe.

"Able," said Papa. There was a wisp of soft severity in his voice, but not real temper. Yet I knew I'd pushed the subject of turnips and sugar and starvation to where his ears were full. Then to even up things a bit, Papa looked at Phoebe.

"Don't make sense," he said, "to give thanks for a turnip on the table and then make talk like we won't down it."

"It be affrontary to the Lord," said Mama.

"To sass a turnip ain't the same as to sass the Lord," I said.

"Able," said Mama, "on occasion there's a breath of blasphemy in you, boy."

"I meant no disrespect, Mama. Maybe I got a turnip where a brain should be."

"Maybe," said Phoebe.

"Corn bread's right good," said Papa. As he said it, some yellow crumbs fell from his chin and freckled the table around his plate.

"Yes, Mama," I said. "It would be a sin sad and sorrowful to blaspheme agin' your corn bread."

"I don't care to hear too much more of this talk," said Mama.

"Able," Papa said again, "you will make an apology to your mother."

"Sorry, Mama. I was only cutting up. There weren't no malefaction in it."

"No *what?*" Mama looked up.

"Malefaction. It's a new word I picked up the day I went up to Shoreham with Luke."

"Well," said Mama, "if that's the kind of thing that you and Luke Shelby pick up, best you stay closer to home."

"What's it mean?" I said.

"I'm sure I don't know," said Mama.

"Then how come it's such a calamity? Luke says it, too. We both said it aplenty all the way home so's it'd stick in our craws. We were planning to say it at a dance some night to a bunch of girls, just to see . . ."

"Able!" Mama said. Her hands went halfway up to her head, as though she wanted to cover her ears.

"Just as a lark," I said. "We wasn't aiming to *hurt* anybody."

"Phoebe," said Mama, "stop giggling and eat your supper."

"It's only a word," I said.

"Words can be a tribulation, boy," said Papa, "and that's why *silence* can be so blissful."

"Yes, sir."

"I thank you," said Papa.

"Samuel Adams says that words are weapons," I said, "and that words can put fire in a man's heart."

"Fire in a man's soul, more like," said Papa.

"And a man's soul in fire," I said.

"Able Booker!" This time Mama's hands did cover her ears, as if to pretend she hadn't heard her own son speak of roasting in hell.

"Sorry, Mama. Somehow I always trip myself up when I try not to shame the Lord and yet still talk respectful about Sam Adams."

With that, I busied my fork to the work of hefting Mama's red beans up to my mouth, not saying a word and trying not to fetch a look at Papa. He seemed to be doing the same, but I knew his thoughts sunk deeper than beans. He was minding what had happened recent in Boston and all the ruckus that got itself caused by Samuel Adams. His was a name I couldn't mention without Papa and me taking sides on the matter. I don't guess I knew as much about politics as Papa, but every trip I took up to Shoreham, the name of Sam Adams sure could stir up tempers.

"If you was to ask me," said Papa, "I might say that some of them notions of Mr. Samuel Adams could be set down as malefactions."

"Luke Shelby says Sam Adams is a patriot."

16

"A patriot or a fool," said Papa.

"Since the shooting, I guess there's a passel of patriots down Boston way. They formed a militia and they drill in formation, just to show them Redcoats that they better not open fire on innocent people ever again."

"Patriots," Papa snorted. "It's dang easy to be a patriot in Boston and to throw a stone or a rotted apple at English soldiers. Let some of them Bostonites come north and cast rock at the heathen, and they'd be bloody glad to have Redcoats to soldier at their side. City folks and their city ways ain't for us Bookers."

"And the goings-on in Boston," said Mama with a nod of agreement, "is no concern of ours."

"I don't blame them Redcoats for what happened five years ago," said Papa. "All them Whig journals give it a fancy name, calling it the Boston Massacre. The worst scum of the streets of Boston was throwing garbage as well as insults at our boys and they opened fire, they did."

"Our boys?" I said. "More like *their* boys."

"Were they really boys?" said Phoebe.

"Some were, yes," said Papa. "Some of the Redcoats crosslake over at Fort Ti are just lads, no older than Able here. Boys."

"Funny thing," I said to Phoebe, but really meaning it all for Papa's ear, "when it be chore time or plow time or the season for haying, I'm supposed to be a man. But at *politic* time, I'm a boy."

Mama was clearing the dishes and she hugged my neck with her free hand. I could feel the rough of her dress against my ear, and the might of her arm. For a thin woman, Mama had her share of gumption. "Growed up and all, you be still a boy to me," she said, kissing the top of my head.

"And still a boy to me," said Phoebe.

"Manhood comes soon enough in this life. So as long as you be under our roof, no harm in holding to a few boyish notions," said Mama as I hugged her.

I didn't want Mama to think there was hard feeling betwixt Papa and me, as we meant it to be only sport. So I kept further thoughts about Sam Adams of Boston bottled inside my head. Adding wood to the fire helped make me think of matters dearer to home. Watching my family move around inside our house, I saw the shadows on the three cold walls that were cast from the one source of light, our fireplace. The shadows were thicker and taller than people, as though three black giants lived with me, darting over the log walls from corner to corner, their heads bumping up into the dark of the rafters above.

Phoebe was upon Papa's knee.

He was whispering a bedtime story into her ear so neither Mama nor

I could get a wind of it. Papa's tales that he told to Phoebe had to be private, according to my sister, for her ears only. Mama and I didn't make a fuss over it, though sometimes we pretended to, just to put Phoebe on so she'd think she was sharing a real secret. It was Papa's ritual with my sister and no one else was allowed to intrude. That was what Mama said. I figured I'd be wed someday and settled to a place of my own, and if the Benefactor saw fit to send us a little girl, I reckon I'd have to tell her stories the way Papa related them to Phoebe.

Banking the fire was a chore I did with righteous care, to be certain that come morning we'd have live embers to kindle into a fresh fire. Not that we didn't have flint and steel to light a cold one. But it was a painful business, as it took me often as many as a hundred strikes before a spark would catch the tinder.

Phoebe went uploft first, her being the youngest. And it wasn't much after that Papa and Mama climbed up to theirs, hauling the ladder up after them. Papa couldn't go to sleep at night unless both ladders were up. Phoebe and I had one, too, which was cruder than theirs; ours being just a single pole with notches on the sides to set your feet on, with a wing rung top and bottom so the ladder wouldn't buck.

By the time I pulled up our ladder, Phoebe was still as the night. The dry crackle of cornhusk, as I lay down on my half of the tick, didn't even make her hatch an eye.

Bed felt good after a day of work. Papa always said that labor was a fast pillow, but I never fell asleep right sudden. As the fire died down, the timbers creaked and the cold set in on us. An owl hooted. Up on the ridge I heard what sounded like the deep black bark of a bear, another omen of spring. Phoebe rolled closer to me under the goose quilt. Her little hand was near and I gave it a good night touch.

"Good night, Able," she said in her sleep.

Chapter 2

"Papa! Papa!"

Phoebe was screaming and running toward us. She was always early up in the morning, first dressed, and the first one in the Booker family to be out the door.

My father and I had just begun our work, facing a new timber to replace a weak one in the barn. Esther had been milked and watered and her calf had been fed. Phoebe had strolled off across the meadow where the late April morning had already burned the first few brown holes in the snow. She said that she wanted to see if the new grass was really green. Papa's hand went to his gun, which was always by him, except when he was plowing or broadcasting seed. Even then, it was never too far distant, always leaning against a nearby stump between his work and the cabin.

"Able! Papa! Come quick."

"What is it, girl?"

"I saw Simon. He's down and there's blood on the snow."

Papa and I both looked where she was pointing, but all we saw was the gentle rise of the east meadow that climbed away from the house and ended at the stump fence at the foot of the ridge. Beyond that was the wooded mountain, with snow among the brown leafless trees.

"You sure?"

"Yes, Papa. Gospel sure."

Phoebe was always storytelling. Her make-believe world and fairy-tale people were common talk. She had no one to play with, except the calf or Esther or Simon, so the rest of us put up with her tall tales. Yet the look in her eyes told me that this weren't no fib. Papa was a step ahead of me, spraying the thin wet snow as he ran. Throwing a glance over my shoulder I wanted to see if Phoebe was running along behind

19

us; but no. Instead she scooted like a squirrel toward the door of the house to tell Mama.

Both of us was breathing heavy as we mounted the rise in the meadow. Then we saw. Lying on his side, like a great rock in an island of white snow, was our ox. Simon's big black body was still and I knew, as did Papa, that he was dead. Slowly we walked across the spotted land, sometimes on snow and sometimes on the brown muck of spring, to where he lay. All around him, the heat of his dying body had melted the snow, almost like a moat around a great castle, things I'd heard Papa tell about, things his father had once told him about England. Beyond the rim of melted snow, the grainy whiteness was stained brown with Simon's blood. It was everywhere; the snow had kept its redness wet and shiny.

I felt him. He was cold.

"Last night," I said to Papa, "I heard a bear."

"No," he said. "Weren't that."

"Wolves?"

Bending down on the snow I saw paw prints. They had not been clear to the eye at first. But as I bent closer to the kernels of snow that looked like a mash of white corn, the paw prints were many and they were not of a dog or a bear. The prints looked like a whole flock of stars. On one there was a tuft of gray fur.

"Papa, it was wolves."

He didn't answer me. Instead he walked around the dead ox to look at Simon's throat and belly. He shook his head.

"It was wolves, wasn't it, Papa? Look here to the paw prints, common as sin."

"Wolves be here. But it weren't no wolf that done our ox. No wolf done this. That bit of fur was dropped."

There was an illness in my stomach, like the frits and pork and fresh milk we'd ate at sunup had sudden turned sour and hateful. I was afraid to ask my next question. But I did.

"Indians?"

I hated to say the word. It just sort of come out of my mouth instead of my brain. Papa never said he was afraid of the savages, but we all knew about how he'd lost his family when he was only a boy of ten. Mama had give us warning years back one time when Phoebe and I were dancing around with feathers in our hair and some red clay streaked across our faces, pretending to be Indians. Mama said that there'd come a day Papa would tell us. Yesterday he had, after he'd rested flowers on the graves of his departed.

"I don't know," he said. "I regret that Phoebe had to see it. She'll be

20

afraid from here on. Best we conjure up a story about Simon to ease her mind, else she may fret on it."

"What done it, Papa?"

"It weren't Indians, boy."

"How can you be so certain?"

"I ain't certain. Not about this, and not about a cussed thing."

Standing at his side as he stared down at the dead animal, I was trying to read his thinking. It *had* to be wolves. Most of the Indians had gone north, or west like a spate of white folks. Maybe it was a catamount who'd done the killing and the wolves come after to sniff the carcass. Or maybe it really was the Saint Francis, and Papa couldn't admit that they'd come back. But there was no word from Shoreham, no bell ringing. And nobody riding up from Skenesboro to the south. No Indian sign.

"No," said Papa, "it weren't the heathen."

"What'll we do?"

"Maybe we can put-by most of the meat. We can freeze some if the winter holds. And if it turns hot, we'll smoke it."

"We'll need to trade for a new ox," I said.

"Yes, we'll need."

"You know what done this, Papa. You know and you're not to tell it."

"Only to you, boy."

"You really know?"

"Yes. Else I got me a close guess."

"Please tell me, Papa. I got to know, too."

"It weren't the wolves, boy. Certain the wolves come after, but it weren't a wolf. Look here."

Where he pointed was a mark in the bare mud, the imprint of a boot heel. My heart raced as I looked at it. I couldn't imagine who of our neighbors would come in the dark of night and slaughter our ox. Yet there was a man's mark, staring up at us from the wet earth.

"Who'd do us evil, Papa?"

"No one close by. No neighbors of ours would deed a thing like this." He shook his head, as though he couldn't face it.

"Who then? Why?"

"I don't know who, boy. I only know why."

"You know *why?*"

No man tells all he knows. Papa was forty years of age, and it ain't easy to live all that time and not make an enemy. But I could see nobody hating Noah Booker. He was too good a man, too loyal a neighbor, too dear a friend to every man's family in the valley. Papa didn't

21

have one enemy in the whole territory of Verdmont. Except one, I thought, as I looked at Simon. The man who done our ox.

"Go get the knives and meat saw," Papa said.

"What can we tell Mama and Phoebe?"

"Wolves."

"It won't be honest, Papa."

"No, but it might do them a better turn for now. Truth is a painful thing." As he said it I saw the hurt on his face. Someone knew that Simon was his ox; and to do Noah Booker a meanness, he'd killed. It was hard for Papa to take. Fetching the knives and meat saw, I returned to where Papa was standing over the dead animal like he was its watchdog.

"Poor old Simon," he said.

I thought of the work the three of us had done together; me and Papa and our black ox. For a moment, I thought I was going to have to wipe my eyes. It weren't easy to blink away the hurt.

"Simon was a good good ox," I said.

"He pulled true," said Papa. "Real true."

"It don't seem right to eat his meat," I said.

"Indeed it don't, boy."

"I told Mama."

"You tell her it was wolves?"

"Yes. But old Phoebe's heart is broke."

"You want to know a fact? So's mine," said Papa.

"It's like losing a friend, sort of."

"Simon was better than some friends I've had. Not that I ever had that many, and now it looks like I got two less."

"Two?" I asked.

"Simon, and the one who done him."

"Oh."

"You bring cloth?"

"No. I didn't think to."

"I'll start cutting. Maybe you'd go back for the wrap and fixings. And bring salt."

"I'll go," I said.

For an hour or more, Papa and I worked the meat into portions, saying nothing to each other, wrapping each cut in cloth as we removed it. I took a roast to Mama who had the pot on the fire and would boil it for a midday stew, adding onions and carrots and some wildroot.

"You said you knew why," I said to Papa.

"I know."

"Tell me, Papa."

"I will."

22

"Right now. I got to know."

Papa let up on his work and looked at me, the way he usual did when what he had on his tongue was worth wording. Wiping his sleeve across the sweat of his face, he let out a sigh.

"Able, you know what Tory means?"

"I heard it used."

"Where?"

"Up in Shoreham, the last time that all four of us went to see the Painters and to go to vespers."

"You heared someone say Tory?"

"Yes. More than one man said it."

"Do you know its meaning?"

"No," I said. "Not exact." I sort of did, but I knew I'd get the straight of it from my father.

"Well, it's a funny word, Tory."

"What's so darn funny about it?" I said.

"Sometimes a man can get called a Tory by his neighbors, and there can be a sickness in the way the word is spoke," Papa said. "Other times, a man can be proud to be a loyal English subject. Even here in New England, a man or a woman can feel the joyness just to say . . . I am British. To look a Frenchie in the eye, or one of the Dutchmen from down-country, south of Skenesboro, and tell the man you're English. It's a good thing, boy. It hastens the heart."

"England is a long way off," I said.

"Yet as close as human spirit."

"Papa?"

"Yes?"

"Are you a Tory?"

He nodded. "Yes, boy. Reckon I be, if the time comes to take sides on the matter. Some folks push you into a corner. They got to know whether a man is one thing or another. They want to mark you, like cattle. Lots of us is a mix of persuasions. No man is any *one* thing. Or no woman. If he is, then I say he's a sorrowful critter, and I hold naught but pity for his poverty."

"You mean when a person is all one way?"

"Yes," he said, "yes. But if it comes to blows," he nodded his head toward the white bones and tatters of hide that had once been an ox, "and it looks like it already has, then I'll take sides along with the next man. But I'll not fire a musket on British soldiers, nor on the flag of England."

"That's what a Tory is?"

"Yes," said Papa. "Nor will I speak ill of our king."

23

"Maybe things are different in Boston than they are up here in Verdmont."

"To be sure," said Papa. "Ain't easy to speak what's right for another man. Easy, hell. Ain't even moral."

"What do you mean?"

"I mean that I can't say what's righteous living for folks down Boston way. We don't have Redcoats in our dooryard, or anyone else. Praise the Almighty for that. We got neighbors only miles away and even that's too nearby for my liking. I'd best sleep alone in my own barn than share a palace with a sovereign."

"Gets lonely sometimes," I said. I guess I was thinking more for Mama than for the rest of us. Sometimes most a year would go by and Mama not see another woman, except for Phoebe.

"The more alone we are, the more we shall cherish each other. When a man is alone, he discovers the good company of his own nature," said Papa.

"When you were a boy, you folks were really alone up here, weren't you?"

"Alone in the dark, my mother used to say. It was a line from a poem. 'Alone in the dark, I shall listen well for the voice of God to hear. Alone in the dark, I shall never feel alone if He be near.'"

"I guess your folks were real Godly," I said.

"They had to be," said Papa. "To leave England takes a cut of courage. But to leave Boston and come north through a wilderness, to a plot of land you bought and never set your eye on takes more than courage. It takes spirit."

"How long did it take, from Boston to Verdmont?"

"Days and days," said Papa. "At first there was a road to follow, and then no road at all. We got lost more'n once. Worst of all was when the animals started to die, one by one."

"Why did they die?"

"No grass, boy. A cow or an ox will down fifty pound of grass a day. But grass don't grow in forest. Weren't nothing to chomp oft the forest floor but a few fern. Horses and cattle and oxen are grazers. They don't browse off a tree like a deer, or wade to water and eat lily pads like a moose. One by one our animals starved. We'd hit a marsh and my mother and father would take kitchen knives and stand in ice water to cut enough marsh grass to keep our beasts alive for another day. Our oxen got too weak to pull the wagon. My father, my mother, my elder sister Grace hitched themselves to the leather and pulled. Israel Booker had a back, that man. And someday, he said, this forest would be cut and cleared away and it would soon look as bonnie as the English midlands."

24

"When did the grass come?"

"Soon as Father cleared away the trees. It was slow labor; one man, one ax. But as each tree fell, it opened up the sky, and then the grass come. Like a rush of morning, everywhere you looked in the open there was that new quilt, like the Lord above had painted the land with grass. Green as England."

"You love England, don't you."

"No man can tell another what do leaven his soul. I was born in England, in the town of Cornwall. Sometimes when my heart is heavy, I close my eyes and there I am, back home."

"How old were you when you come to Boston on the sailing ship?"

"Seven year, I reckon it to be. I didn't like America and I was homesick as hell. How ill we were for England."

"Are you still?"

"In ways," said Papa. "I shall be until I die. A goodly place, England. The Lord must love that land as He made her so fair."

The way Papa spoke of his homeland made me swallow the sadness in my throat, knowing he'd never again walk on British soil. His loyalty was more than to a flag or to the British regulars, the Redcoats. It was deeper than that. I guess what made me saddest of all was the fact that I felt nothing toward the country for which he felt so much. But soon he would have to know how I felt about Verdmont. I was about to tell him about some talk I'd heard when I was with Luke Shelby, and about what the two of us might plan to sneak off and do. But maybe this weren't a proper time.

"This land of ours could be another England," Papa said. "Like they say, a *New* England. All a man needs is an ax, a gun, a plow and an ox to pull it, a cookpot and a few needles for his woman. When we come here, years back, we Bookers didn't have much more. What we had most was hard work, and yet at the end of the day we saw Israel and Mary Booker humble their heads at supper to give thanks that they had the backs to do it. My mother used to say that we were supposed to bite our bread through a sweaty face."

"That's a good say."

"It be true, boy. We got things easy now. We got open land, a cow and a new calf."

"Too bad," I said, "that April ain't a bull calf. Then we could cut him for an ox."

"April's fine as is. Just like Esther, she'll be a proud milker. But now we got to trade her."

"We got to trade April?"

"We must, boy."

"It'll bust old Phoebe open."

25

"Maybe so. But when she sees the new ox, she'll hang to him the way she done on Simon. Up on his back and all."

"Phoebe's got a way with her," I said.

"So have you." As he said it, I thought he was going to fist me in the shoulder like he sometimes did, just for the play of it. But on this day his heart was near empty of merriment. Turning back to his work, he said, "This ox meat will be tough on the teeth."

"Not too tough for a Tory like you," I said.

"How about you, son?"

"Me?"

"Where do you stand on matters of the day?"

"You want me to say I'm a Tory, just like you. Well, I don't hold no hatred for England. I don't know where England is or what it's like to live there. I don't guess I'll ever walk the place. All I know is right here, and this is Verdmont. This here is home. We ain't part of New Hampshire, and we don't cotton to hear it said."

"We don't," said Papa. "And we ain't Yorkers."

"We ain't Englishmen," I said, and took a big breath to wait on his word.

"What are we then?" He looked up at me, his hands white with salt from rubbing the blocks of meat. "What are we, boy? Are we beasts of the wilderness? No flag and no roots? No song to sing that stirs the human heart? I can't be a cloud, boy. I won't drift free in the heavens and have no halter. No tether. I got to have something to hold to, like a shelter for the soul. Until you bury me, boy, I will look other men in the eye, stand toe to toe if they force me to, and say by damn I am an Englishman. And if they wish to cuss me for it, and mark me with a word like Tory, then I shall spite them all and wear it like a banner. And it will take more than one dead ox to strike my colors."

"You got a right," I said.

"When a man says that, he means his own self. It means *you* got a right, too," said Papa.

There weren't no getting around Papa. I was his son and he could read me like weather. Face to face, his eyes looked through me like I weren't even born yet. He was a big rock, my father. Day or night, you always knew where he stood and how his mind rested with a thing.

"I won't show no disrespect to the British flag, any more than I could to you or to Mama. But to tell you honest, Papa, I got mixed up feelings inside about it all. It's enough to stir your stomach."

"Agreed," he said. "These are mixed up times."

"You aim to stay a Tory?" I asked him.

"I aim to be what I be. And it seems logic that I'm harnessed up to

26

be Noah Booker and not nobody else. A man who don't know who he is or what he's good for is a sorry sight."

"I know what I be," I said.

"And what's that?"

"I am Able Booker and a Verdmonter."

"That's fair."

"But if it comes to war . . ."

"If it comes to war," Papa said, "best you and me stay to our own barnyard and tend the milking. Henry Cotter says the same."

"How do you know?"

"He so said."

"I believe it," I said. "You and Henry Cotter are near to same in age. Me and Luke Shelby are the new generation."

"With new ideas, eh?"

"Luke and me and some of the rest of us were all born here in Verdmont."

"So was Henry Cotter," said Papa. "Born up over that ridge a good many years before you was, and before Mr. Luke Shelby was. Henry Cotter stands true."

I wanted to tell Papa about Jake Cotter, but it wouldn't of helped. Henry Cotter's boy, Jake, had told me he was going to join the Green Mountain Boys. That was a month ago. He said they'd promised to give him his own musket if he joined up. Boy, what I wouldn't give to have *my* own gun. I felt like telling Papa right to his face about Jake, but then it might get back to Jake's pa, which would do Jake no good. He said it was all a secret and not to be breathed to a living soul. Jake had probably done the deed by now, probably already joined the Boys and swore the oath. That was what Luke said. He told me that when you join up, it's at night and you have to swear by all that's holy not to *divulge* . . . that was the word he used . . . any of the goings on, or repeat any name in public or private. It was all secret.

"Some of the boys are joining up," I said, pretending to scrape the hunk of hide I was laboring on, not looking Papa in the eye.

"Is that so?"

"That's a fact," I said. "They're throwing in with the Green Mountain Boys."

"Who's joining?"

"Luke didn't say."

"Well, if he didn't," Papa said, "then best you mark the day right well. Because it be the only thing that your friend Luke *didn't* say. Sounds to my ear like he said everything else."

"Maybe so."

27

"And if you're thinking on it, joining that bunch of rowdy good-for-naughts, you can best *stay* joined up and not bother to come to bed or board. You can let Mr. Ethan Allen put up your keep."

"What you got against the Boys?"

"Boys?" said Papa. He shook the meat saw at me like he want to nag his finger. "Some of them *Boys* has got grandsons. If'n you ask me, they named that there outfit after conduct instead of age. It ain't fitting to commit a crime and then call it patriotic. To me, it begs a pardon to raise Cain. Bunch of tom fools."

"They got a cause," I said.

"Yes," said Papa, pointing at what was left of our ox, "and here it lies. Your dang Boys done this. And so help me, God, I hope they hang for treason."

Chapter 3

"No! No, Papa, please don't," yelled Phoebe.

It was the morning that followed the day of Simon's death. Papa and I had done with the rendering of the meat. It was smoked and put by. And this was the day we'd have to go crosslake to Fort Ti and swap April for an ox to help with the plowing and the burdens. Papa and I told Mama that we were going, but we kept it distant from Phoebe as we wanted to surprise her with a new young ox.

Quiet as prayer, we lead April out of the barn. Heading down the west slope toward Lake Champlain, we heard Phoebe's hollering. Looking back, we saw Mama's arms around her, but she'd struck up a struggle to set free. Suddenly she got loose and run to catch us.

"Papa, you taking April to the fort?"

"Yes, girl. We got to."

"Because we need a new ox, Mama said."

"That's reason."

"April isn't going to slaughter, is she?"

Papa put his arm around Phoebe, nodding his head at the calf. "A good milker like April don't get to slaughter. She'll ripe and calf and grow to a merry old age, just like her ma."

"Just like Esther?"

"Yes," I said, "like Esther." Yanking the tail of my shirt out my britches, I wiped Phoebe's face.

"Mama says you're to lead home a new ox," she said.

"True," said Papa.

"I'd preferenced to keep April."

"Understand," said Papa, "we all would like to keep the calf. We would if'n it was a bull calf. But it ain't. So we got to swap, and you got to be a growed-up gal and not cry."

29

Phoebe's arm went around April's neck, her little hands petting her silky hide. "Oh, April," she said, "I can't abide it."

"Hey," said Papa, his hand touching Phoebe's rusty colored hair, "it ain't like April's going to be afar off. I wager on a clear morning, if we all look sharp, we can walk down to the edgewater and see April graze on the grass right in the shadow of Fort Ti, happy as Heaven."

"Can we?" Her face was sober as Sunday.

"Sure enough can," said Papa. "And if'n you behave, why maybe you can boat over to the fort come summer, and pay April a call."

"Can I come *now?* Today?"

Everything always had to be right now with my sister. It was a blessed thing that Mama didn't name her Patience as she had studied on doing, as that wouldn't of made a fit name for Phoebe. No, sir. Not hardly fitting at all.

"Another time," said Papa, "yes. Best you linger here with your mother. Able and I have to walk April across the ice to the York side. I got enough to look after."

I knew what Papa meant. Anytime we ever took old Phoebe with us, she'd probably be away out in front so's to get there the first. And the lake ice in spring ain't all that solid.

"Please, Papa. I don't ask often."

"No, you don't. And that's the reason that when summer comes, we'll raft over and fetch you to see April. But today you best stay to home."

"Good-by, April," she said, giving Esther's calf a final hug around her head. She didn't bother to bid a farewell to her father or to me. Instead she just turned and flounced off in the direction of the house.

Out on the lake there was water on the ice. And when I felt the icy feel between my toes I knew my boot had a hole. April wasn't quite sure she liked the whole business. Twice we had to pick her up and carry her through a puddle. Papa carried her the first time. As we neared the fort side of the lake, I lifted her up. The ice cracked! April kicked in my arms. Both my boots were wet now, which brought the unpleasant vision of sinking into that icy water with the calf still at my chest. I took just one step at a time, real careful. Nearing the bank, one foot did break through to the knee, and it felt like the cold had sawed it off.

"On the way back," Papa said, "best we take the long way. I ain't fit to carry no ox." The way he said it made me smile. Papa was fair company.

The big gray wall of stone grew bigger and taller as we climbed up the hill. I'd been to Fort Ticonderoga on a number of trips, but each time was fresh. It sure was hard to believe that Frenchmen come south from Canada and built the fort, according to Papa and to Mr. Cotter, in

30

less than a year. Fort Ti sure was sizable. Coming closer to the wall, I read the stone in which a man had knocked out 1755. Fort Ti was now twenty years old. I touched the ciphers with my hand. They were smooth and hard; but still cold, even though the wall looked east and the morning sun was hitting full on. My back felt the heat; and the warm of it was righteous welcome, seeing as my feet were so cold and soaking.

April looked back east across the lake and bawled, as if to bid a good biding to her ma. Squinting into the east, I could see our farm. The house weren't more than a wee speck of brown against the white of the snow.

"I wonder if Mama and Phoebe can see us," I said.

"Probably be they followed us with their eyes clear across the lake."

Up on the short wall, a group of British soldiers were laughing at another group below. In all, no more than seven or eight. They were playing a game that I had seen them play before. A man above pushed a cannon ball off the wall, and soldiers below took turns in trying to catch it. Wagers were exchanged. And as the wall ran on a slant, getting higher, it got harder and harder to make the catch. I saw the fall of the heavy black cannon ball. Hitting the man's chest below, it knocked him flat on his backside. As he said a rude word in Scottish, all the men roared.

I wanted to try. So as Papa watched, a soldier dropped a ball to me, which grew bigger and bigger, crashing into my arms like a charging boarhog, and landing on my foot. I jumped around a bit. The soldiers laughed, but one clapped my shoulder with a friendly fist and said, "Stoutly tried, lad."

At least, I hadn't put down a wager.

Keeping close to the giant gray wall, we lead April by the huts and outbuildings on the south bank until we come to the gate. A soldier, his back to the wall, sat on a small powder keg; his musket leaned on the stone in a posture as lazy as the man who should have toted it. Looking at us, he said nothing as we passed by the huge gate without entering. There were stains on the front of his white britches and on his knees. His red tunic was in like condition. On one of our trips to Fort Ti, years back, a British corporal had let Phoebe wear his red coat, and it had really made her day. She talked of nothing else for a month after.

The soldier's jaws were moving as he chewed something. As we walked by him, leading April he spat out a yellow stream of tobacco juice. Not upon our feet, but close by, as though he resented the duties of his post and his calling as a private in the king's service. It give me the feel that he'd like to spit on Papa and me; or even upon his own person, as I told at a glance that there was little joy in him.

31

"You see that, Papa?" I said as we continued on our way with the calf.

"Take no offense, boy. The lad's a far piece from home and ill for the sight and smell of England. Soldiering is a lone life, so best we excuse his manners."

"He looked dirty."

"Yes," said Papa, "my eye caught that, too. It makes me ponder where the officers are, as they should take the man to task."

"You mean flog him?"

"If all else fails," said Papa. "Oft a lick of the leather can wake a man to his duty."

"You never put the switch to Simon."

"No," he said. "Simon walked taller than the lad at the gate."

On my father's face I could read the disappointment. His pride was hurt. Not so much about the spit, but about the spitter. To see a British soldier at the entrance to a British fortress in such a sorry way did not please him. And even more, to have *me* see the same.

As a boy in England he had once seen a parade of soldiers marching in a town along with a band of men who made music with fifes and drums. To see it, Papa had said, made all who watched wish to march also, and to tap a foot in time to the din of the drums. And as the flag of England was carried along the street, even the flag itself seemed to dance to the tune. All who watched had removed their hats with respect, leaving their heads bare until their ears no longer heard the music or the beat of boots on the cobblestone.

North of the fort was an open space where a number of cows, more than a dozen had been turned out of their barns. The cows walked slowly over the patches of melting snow in search of the early grass. Seeing a man he knew, Papa waved an arm and the man did likewise. I stayed with April and let my father do the trading. But his talk was brief as the man had no ox to trade.

"No luck," said Papa.

Then he spoke to another man whose name I knew was Peabody and who was a farmer north of the fort. As they talked, Mr. Peabody looked at April and I could read the fondness on his face. When it come to a trade, Papa had said, "April's good looks won't be no drawback. And even April added her mite to the dickering, poking her nose agin the leg of Mr. Peabody like they was old friends. From the smile on the man's countenance, I knowed he'd took an early-on shine to our calf.

"See that?" I heard Papa say. "Just like her big old ma, she'll milk gentle."

We owned a hard milker once who kicked over the pail on more than one morning. She'd been a caution to handle, and Papa's shins had took their share of smarting from the lift of her hoofs. I remember one healthy kick in particular she'd planted on him.

Henry Cotter was there at the time and had asked if it hurt, and Papa said, "It sure gets your attention."

Mr. Peabody said he didn't have an ox to trade, but he had a neighbor who did. If Papa was willing, he would take April home to pasture right now and be back by noon with an ox. Papa said no deal until he saw both the ox and the price. We tied up April and went back to the fort, walking to the same private who had spat our way. He said not a word, but stood up, seized his musket and leveled it at us.

"Soft," he said. "Right where you stand, or you won't be standing anywhere."

Never before had Papa or I been challenged at the gate of Fort Ti. Any day we had ever come, the entrance was always open to English civilians like ourselves to enter and depart at our own whim. There was a look of surprise on Papa's face.

"My name is Noah Booker, and this here is my son, Able."

"Do you bear arms?"

"Only what you see," Papa lifted up his hands. It made me chuckle. "What is all this nonsense? My farm is in plain view of this fort, on the Verdmont side. I come here often."

"State your business."

"We come to trade, to converse, and generally see the sights . . . like always."

As we talked, he slowly lowered his musket, as if to tell us we could enter the fort, but there was precious little warm to his welcome. Walking past him, I noticed the squint of his eyes. His face had a smooth look, except for a light stubble of beard, making me conclude that he weren't much more aged than I.

"See the sights, eh?" he said. "Well, you'll see your penny's worth on this day."

I wondered what he meant by his last remark. Looking at Papa, I could read a bewildering on his face. Through the gate we walked and into the outer ground of the stronghold. The gate was just a break in the great outer wall of the star. Sky was still above us, and ahead of us lay the three large buildings at the star's center that served as barracks for the Redcoats.

"Good thing he let us in," I said to Papa. "I sure wouldn't cotton to come all the way over here and not walk inside."

"It weren't his decision," Papa said.

"What do you mean?"

33

"If I read him right, he got orders to stop folks before he let them in, and it weren't left to *his* judgment."

"Whose then?"

"One of the higher ups. I got the smell of trouble."

"What kind of trouble?"

"Hard to say."

Walking, we climbed up a slight rise, the south bay of Lake Champlain on our right, barracks to our left. The short wall that looked south to the lake was about waist high, with notches for the cannon. Gun after gun, big and black, so big a man could almost straddle one like a horse. Beside each, cannon balls were piled up like a small black hill, nine on the bottom, then four atop those, with a single ball atop the four. There were fourteen to a pile. There were no kegs of powder, no ramrods, and no artillery soldiers to man the guns. Along the wall, I counted seventeen cannon on the south wall alone. On the upper walls close by the barracks to our left, I counted the mouths of others, as their black holes pointed over our heads to the south, the east, the west.

Following the curve of the muddy path which was one wagon wide, we come to an arch, a dark tunnel that bore through the south barrack. Something was happening inside the courtyard. A rumble of voices told us so. Four soldiers guarded the arch but we passed through without a threat. Some of the stone was solid, I noticed. But other bits of the fort's walls had crumbled and fallen from position. It appeared to me that little effort had been applied to set the loose rock right again.

Nor were the four soldiers we walked between smartly uniformed. Their white stockings were a soiled gray, with holes. Buttons were missing on their tunics, and only three of the four wore a hat. The bareheaded private handled a musket that did not appear to be oiled or even at the ready. It bore rust. How strange, I thought to myself, that as a younger boy I never took note of the slipshod. All I saw was the high-flying Union Jack that fluttered on its pole, and the red of the coats. But on this day I saw the ragged truth, and what I learned by eye agreed with what my ears had heard.

Fort Ti was a sorry place, rundown and ramshackle, fallen into rags and rust. Entering the courtyard, which was as long as a man could throw a stone, not one soldier appeared to be proudly adress. They looked to be as poor in spirit as in costume.

Never had I seen so much folks.

I counted more than thirty civilians like ourselves, clad in humble brown or gray; farmers, mostly, with wives and children. Two woodsmen in buckskin leaned with their backs to the wall, saying naught to each other, holding their long Kentucky rifles. On their feet were Indian mocs. Every other person seemed to move about, but these two stood without motion. A pair of trees. Woodsmen, I thought, carved of wood.

Soldiers were everywhere.

I tried to count the soldiery but as they all moved about with business, it was not to be done. The noise of voices, like wasps, put a hum into the air, a growing grumble that seemed to come from the farmers. Officers yelled orders to the soldiers, several of whom put up a crude framework composed of two upright timbers with a crossbeam for a roof. An odd structure to be sure, appearing as if it would house not a thing. No one seemed to be trading. Usually you could hear the dicker of one price rubbing against another, but not on this day. Even the air was different, and I knew why as we closed ourselves to a group of civilians who were not farmers but did chores at the fort. It was a mix of men and women, and not one of them had a decent smell. Not even the young.

We moved away.

My father was a man who keeped to himself and who did not take joy in thick company. To Noah Booker, a family that lived closer to us than miles crowded him. There were far too many souls in the courtyard for him to take comfort. There was hardly no free space to do our standing, but we found a place distant enough to afford us a breath of air that did not reek of rancid humanity. We stood near the door of a small shed of stone and wood that jutted out northside from the south barrack like a wart on a face. Here we thought was a tidy place to hunker down. We sat. Papa fished his pipe out of his pocket and stuffed it full. No fire was near at hand to light up, and Papa looked toward the fort's ovens which were east of the courtyard and to our right as we sat in its southeast corner.

A soldier suddenly ran to us and kicked the pipe from Papa's mouth. Shattering on the stone, the bits of clay pipe lay like a pile of bones, as though a small man had died there and his busted-up skeleton had been bleached to white.

"Fool," said the sergeant who had kicked Papa's pipe. "You want to blow us all to Kingdom Come?" His head nodded at the small building at our backs.

The sergeant was a man of goodly size, but I knew Papa could have got to his feet and fisted him proper. I wanted him to so do, but I figured he wouldn't. You'd have to pummel more than a pipe to get up the dander of Noah Booker. He'd said to me that once he'd been in a fight and didn't care too much for the sport of it, as his hand had swelled up after busting the other man's teeth; for most of a week he'd had to milk one-handed, and that made his arse end go numb to sit the stool for so long. Then he'd said that *knowing* you could fist a man was as merry a feel as doing it. And the more I studied that statement, the sounder it grew.

But the look in Papa's eyes as the British sergeant turned his back to us and walked off was not a friendly look. I felt the hot of his anger, and saw his face redden. His big hands curled up to a tightness that made me ponder if that English sergeant would ever know his own luck. Maybe my father was thankful that the sergeant, in his own rude way, had safed our lives, so there weren't much point in working up a het.

"Are you mad, Papa?"

"I'm dang grateful," he said.

Reaching back his hand, he rubbed the stone we both sat on, his palm frosted black with powder. Seeing the gunpowder on his fingers made my own hands fat with sweat. An ember from Papa's pipe could have fell at our feet and, in less than a quick breath, eat its way under the door and ignited the whole blessed powder magazine. We'd a been goners.

"No man cottons to be name-called a fool," said Papa. "But what cuts deepest is the fact that I was."

We put some distance between ourselves and the place where the gunpowder was in store. A good distance. And we both made cock sure to dust the black powder off'n the seats of our britches. Just to see a few sights, we moved about. Good thing, too, on account we saw a woman making candles six at once. She didn't dip a wick in the wax the way Mama done, but instead poured out the wax into a metal geegaw that had six holes. There was a stem in each tube to leave room for the wick which she pulled through after the candle took a form.

"Darndest fandangled thing I ever see," Papa said.

"Six to once," the woman said with no small amount of pride. "Isn't that a caution?"

"Sure is," said Papa. "I'd like to git one of them bobs for my woman. Is that thing for barter?"

"No," said the woman. "All the candling I do for this here place, I'd be up to know-what in tallow. This your boy?"

"Yes. I am Noah Booker."

"I'm Able Booker. We come from crosslake."

"Verdmont folks, eh? Never been over yonder," she said, "and don't hanker to go."

"We come here to trade," I said.

"Huh," she snorted. "That's what they all say on *this* day. But you can't tomfool me. You folks come for the same reason as the others. You come to see the justice done to the poor soul."

Papa shifted on his feet, as if he was thinking how to pose the next

36

question. His fingers went into his hair and scratched an itch that I figured he didn't even have.

"What they building over there?" Papa tossed his head to mean the timbers that the soldiers were giving a tussle to.

"A shameful thing if you ask me," the woman said.

"What is it?"

"A scaffold."

"To do what?"

For a moment the woman didn't answer Papa's asking. All she done was to chip away at the beads of wax that was clinging to her hands. Sweeping the crumbs of wax into a pile on the table, she dumped them back into the melting pot. Then she spoke.

"It's a foul shame to hang that boy."

Chapter 4

"Did you say *hang?*" Papa asked her.

"I did," she said, "and what's more, I don't care who hears me. It's a crying shame to knot a hang rope around the neck of some youngster who ain't hardly been weaned."

"What'd he do?" I said.

"Little enough to swing for," she said, "though I grant he's a wild one. Sure, he's got a bit of the Old Harry in him. Most boys do. But the Captain wants to make an example out of the lad. That's why this cussed place is got visitors thicker'n flies. Captain wants 'em here to tell the tale to them that miss it. Sedition they call it."

"Come again?" said Papa.

"See-dition," she repeated slowly, "and don't ask *me* what the name of nobody it means. All this over a cannon."

"A cannon?" I said.

"Him and two cronies of his. The other two got away, but the word is one of 'em is wounded. The three of them boys come to steal a cannon. Just as a lark, boy fashion; but they darn near done it. They drug it down to the lake and then swore when it cracked the ice. Dogs started barking and turned out half the garrison. Probably woke up everyone but the sentries. Most of *them* sleep like the dear departed, and keep the rest of us awake with their snoring."

"And they're to hang the lad?" said Papa.

"Guess that's what sedition means. Just some fancy word for a cannon thiefery. Harsh, I call it. Bloody harsh justice for a lad that's probably never got up the gumption to kiss his girl."

"What's the boy's name?" I asked.

"Don't know. I heard it spoke and forgot it, but you folks probably know the young colt, seeing he's from over your way."

"He a Verdmonter?" Papa said. The two of us looked at each other, but no word passed. But the justice of the matter was ringing closer to home. I was wondering just how near a neighbor he was. Papa's face grew dark and there weren't much mirth in his eyes. I didn't have to say "let's find out" to him.

"Thank you, sister," he said to the woman.

We walked out into the sunlight of the parade grounds or courtyard. Yet we saw no one that we knew by face or name, and the man who had wanted to trade for April had not returned. Again we saw the two woodsmen who appeared that they would oblige to speak to narry a soul, not even to each other. They had not moved from their earlier position, not a foot or a finger. Not even their long Kentucky rifles had moved. Talking to them would make as much sense as talking to the wall they leaned against. The only person we saw that looked at all familiar was the sergeant who had kicked the pipe from Papa's mouth. I was surprised when my father addressed him as though nothing earlier had took place.

"Sergeant," Papa said, "am I to understand there's to be a hanging?"

"On this day at twelve of the clock," said the sergeant. "And all too soon if you ask me." He too spoke as if he had more on his mind than a broken pipe.

"A Verdmont boy, is it?" asked Papa.

"I heard said," the sergeant nodded. "And some of us aren't too happy about the matter. I say flog the boy. Yank down his britches, give the lad a smarting, but let him run home and cry on his mother's lap."

"How old is he?"

"Seventeen, sir, is my guess," said the sergeant. "And if you will permit me, I must express my regrets about your pipe. This hanging business has us all a bit frisky."

"It's forgot," Papa said. "We are Noah Booker and son, Able."

"Mine is Ketter. Sergeant Joseph Ketter, and I owe you a pipe, farmer."

"And we owe you our lives. Even?" Papa held out his hand.

"Even enough," the sergeant shook Papa's hand. "I have a boy myself, in Coventry. Back home in England. Bit of a bother, aren't they?" He gave my belly a punch, but there weren't no malice in his fist.

"More'n a bit," said Papa. "I'd trade mine for a sack o'meal and a shilling to boot. You?"

"Aye," said the sergeant, "and I'd give a month's army pay to stand as close to my son and punch him as I now done to yours. A year's pay and more."

"I got born in England," Papa said.

"Did you now?" asked Sergeant Ketter.

39

"Town of Cornwall."

"You have lost your speech. Now you sound of these parts," the sergeant said.

Papa said, "My people died when I was ten. I got raised up by a Verdmont family who'd been our near neighbors. Name of Cotter."

"Did you say Cotter?" The sergeant's eyes went narrow as though he'd took a bother at the issue.

"Yes," said Papa.

"Aye, that is the name of the lad that's to hang this day. He gave his identity to us in a proud manner. It is Jacob Cotter."

Jake!

I almost spoke his name aloud, but being too hit by the hurt of it, no sound come forth. It felt like I'd got smitten in the chest by a maul.

"No," I said. It was a sorry thing to say but it got said straight out with no help from me. Because I couldn't believe that Jake Cotter was going to die and that I was to stand in the shadow of his gallows and watch it happen. I'd never seen nobody hang. And there weren't much easement in the knowing that my first hanging would be Jake Cotter. The sergeant looked at me.

"A friend of yours is my guess," said Sergeant Ketter.

"They can't do it," I said. "They *can't*."

Papa said naught. But his big hand that quickly rested on my shoulder added enough heft to have words of its own. Steady, his hand was saying. Stand fast, son.

"You can't hang a man without a trial," said Papa.

"They say that's a truth in peace time," the sergeant said, "but this was considered by the tribunal held here last night to be a hostile act of war. Stealing a cannon was judged as sedition, as a cannon is a weapon of war."

"Whose law is that?" I said.

"Right," my father said. "The House of Commons would puke at the travesty. Can you hear William Pitt sponsor such an act? Nay, never. Someone had better remind your officers that Jacob Cotter and all his family pay taxes to the crown, and he is by birthright a citizen of England. And if the lad be a mischief maker, deal with him in accord with English justice in a civil court."

"He was tried and found guilty," the sergeant said. "We couldn't believe our ears when we heard the verdict of our officers, that the youngster would hang for an act of sedition."

"Where are your officers?" said Papa.

"Yonder," the sergeant nodded at the west barrack, "and still asleep as the clock is not yet noon."

"It's time they were wakened," Papa said, "to more than a Yankee morn. Come, Able."

"What do you intend?" I asked Papa as we headed toward the officer quarters with big strides.

"I intend," he said, "to stop this action, to warn them of English law and the rights of all Englishmen. By damn, they won't dare do other than spare the boy. Able, go find the lad. By now he's sick with fear. Tell the boy I am here and there is no cause for his torment."

I'd seen where the dungeon was, on many a visit to Fort Ticonderoga, so I run right to it. The dungeon entrance was down a ramp, located on the south side of the south barrack. The soldier who stood with his back to the large black door made me pull up short before he saw me. One look said that he weren't real ready to crack open that big wooden door just so's me and Jake could strike up a chat. Making tracks to the yonder side, I searched out a window. It was more of a slit between two of the wall rocks, size enough to stick a hand through. I could see the wall was a foot thick. Solid stone.

"Jake," I yelled in a whisper, my mouth close up to the slit. My nose got a whiff of the dungeon and it was sure a sorry fragrance. If a smell could be dark as well as damp, it was this smell. And it stank like a backhouse.

"Jacob Cotter, you in there?"

All I heard was a moan and then a voice spoke, but it sure weren't Jake's. Moving along the wall, I tried another slot.

"Hey! Hey, Jake."

"Yeah?" came from inside. A boy's voice.

"Jacob Cotter?" I said.

"Yes. Who's there?"

"Me. It's Able Booker."

"Able?"

"Yes. Me and Papa come crosslake to trade for an ox. We just heard you was here."

"I'm here for certain. Them unwed mothers got me in irons. I'm shackled to the wall. They even got a chain around my neck."

"What's it like in there? Can you see?"

"It's dark as a pit of sin. Able, you got to help me."

"How?"

"Tell a friend of mine. His name is Ira Allen, and he's just west of Shoreham."

"Ethan's brother? Papa knows him."

"Yes. Go back across the lake and git word to him. Tell him I'm going to hang and hang high. I can hear the hammers."

41

I didn't mention the scaffold, but I figured that Jake had already heard his sentence, according to Sergeant Ketter.

"They can't do this to you, Jake. It ain't right."

"They can't, eh? Well, I ain't scared of any bloody Redcoat that ever walked. They don't give me no fright."

There was a shake to his voice, unsteady and uneven, the way you get when you're trying not to cry. All of his brave talk was just as phony as paint. Underneath he was scared skinny.

"Hey, Jake . . . you really rob that cannon?"

"Sure did. Me an' . . . ." His voice stopped.

"Don't tell me, Jake. Don't tell nobody, because maybe mine ain't the only ears that can hear you in there."

"I won't tell. They ask me plenty and I never said mud. It got 'em right sore, too. That's why they're pretending they's to hang me, to scare me to tell. That and the surveyor who identified me as a Verdmont troublemaker."

"What surveyor?"

"That there Yorky fellow that we caught near Cornwall who was drawing up a map for the damn tax collector. We rode him off on a rail. He's here at the fort. Pointed his finger at my chest, he did, and called me an outlaw. So they got me for more than just trying to swipe their old cannon."

The kick crashed into my ribs and made me lose breath. I was trying to hear Jake so I don't guess I heard the soldier who caught me with my ear to the slit. The kick he give me rolled me over on my back, and I could see his foot was fixing to dish out a second helping. So I got up in spite of the hurt and ran like hell. From the look of him, he was too sloven to give chase.

I found Papa.

He was making talk with one of the officers. But more, he was listening. The British officer did the telling and Papa was shaking his head as if to say no to the whole golly business, like he couldn't believe what the officer was saying. I come up just in time to hear the tail end of it.

"He will hang," said the officer.

"It ain't fit," Papa said, "and it sure ain't English law."

"Look about you, farmer. Do you suppose that this is England? No matter. The lad will serve an example if he is executed. And hang he will."

"I know the boy," Papa said. "I know his father, Henry Cotter."

"Do you now?"

"Yes, and he's a loyal Englishman. I say to you that Verdmont is a land that flourishes with Cotters, and they are no clan to have for enemies."

42

"Soft," said the officer. "Best you not cast a threat at our feet. The boy is bitter against the crown."

"And since when," Papa asked, "do Englishmen hang for the sin of bitterness?"

"Beware, farmer, lest you yourself bear the taint of treason." Turning his back to us, he entered his quarters, closing shut the heavy door upon his heels.

"Jacob is lost," Papa said. "Lost. Did you seek him?"

"He's in the dungeon. He thinks it be all a big bluff on their part, to fright him enough to squeal on the other two."

"Did he say who they were?"

"No. Not to me and not to them," I nodded my head at the door that the British officer had just shut in our faces.

"He has courage," said Papa. "More belly than I, were I in his shoes. And perhaps more belly than brains."

Somewhere from inside the fort, near an open window, a clock struck the hour of twelve. Papa and I stood like a pair of dumb beasts, each of us counting the chimes, not wanting to hear the twelve rings that one-by-one we finally heard. Others among us listened as well, with sober faces that denied the hour.

"What can we do?" I asked Papa.

"Perhaps they only play at a hanging, as players act out a scene, making their performance seem real. They dare not really hang the Cotter boy. England is not a heartless nation, son, and it would rub us all raw to see injustice."

The first beat of the drum hit my ear as if my own soul was beaten. The second beat was followed by a roll to take the place of the third. Then a fourth. The drum sounded the same pattern over and over. Our heads all turned. A drummer stood alone beside one of the uprights of the scaffold. From the high crossbeam, a rope hung loose; in coils, like a vine that had wound itself about an unseen tree. The rope was new, and its tallow shined silvery in the noon sun. I wanted to move, to escape, but my feet were frozen against the brown hard-packed earth of the courtyard as if my toes were made fast to the ground by pegs. My body was rigid, unfree. Breath came hard.

A boy screamed.

Our faces all turned to see Jacob Cotter. His eyes were blinking as he was dragged by two soldiers from the dungeon into the bright sunlight. He looked small between the pair of privates who held him, forcing him to walk by tightening the chain about his neck. As my father and I stood between Jake and the scaffold, he was being dragged our way, closer and closer. Other soldiers, using the flat of their muskets, herded all of us to the side to allow the three to pass.

"They can't," Papa said. No one heard.

Jake passed by so close that I could have reached out and touched him. I heard the chains ring that had been placed on his ankles. His arms were bound behind his back. Several times as he bent his body, the two soldiers yanked his head up again. I read the terror on his face. He stumbled and fell. Getting to his feet, his eyes found mine. Despite the links of iron on his neck, he spoke.

"Pray for me, Able."

He knew. It was no bluff, and Jacob Cotter knew his end was at hand, that he was going to die. His face said that he knew. His eyes were already dead.

Without thought, my arms reached forward in an effort to touch Jake. There was no plan to free him, but the musket barrel that pressed against the side of my neck said as firmly as the Redcoat who owned it that I was not to interfere.

"Stay back," the soldier said. His voice was as hard as the iron of his musket.

Jacob was walking away from us now, his back to us, between the bigger backs of the two privates on either side, growing smaller and smaller. The drum kept up its cadence as he was forced to mount the stairs. Over his head they pulled a small white sack of muslin, tying the drawstring about his neck. Then the rope looped under his chin like an evil serpent. There was no sound in our ears, save for the drum. The drummer looked straight ahead as he performed his duty.

"No," Papa said. "No."

His voice was small and weak, as helpless as the blind boy who now stood in chains alone on the platform of a gallows made of unbarked timber. Jacob Cotter's head was bowed forward, looking at feet he could not see, at a trap that would be taken from under him. I wanted to yell, to say something to someone in protest, to say nay to the death of my friend. But there were no words to say.

The drum stopped.

The officer who'd spoke with Papa mounted the stairs, stood at Jake's side, and unrolled a small scroll of paper from which he read:

"Hear ye all present. Jacob Cotter, you have commit trespass on the military installation of Fort Ticonderoga on the night of 28 April in the year 1775, and did so with the intent of converting one of His Majesty's cannon of war, one 50-pounder, to commandeer such cannon and to depart with it eastward toward the territory of Verdmont along with two other outlaws presumed to be also residents of that said territory. Jacob Cotter, you have been tried and found guilty of the treasonous crime of sedition against your country, that being England; and your reward for such earlier stated acts of hostility, along with your refusal to divulge the names of the other two outlaws that were in your company as you performed this seditious act and acts . . . is to be executed. By the authority of King George of England and by the Grace of God's forgiveness, prepare yourself for your most grievous payment, to be executed in the hanging by a rope until you are dead. And may God grant you favor as He doth now, on this 30 day of April in the year 1775 . . . take your soul, Jacob Cotter."

No one said a word.

The drummer, on a signal from the officer who had read Jake's sentence, begun a long roll on his drum. The officer climbed down the stair, and drew his sword. Waving it high in the air, he held it still for a moment. Then lowered it real quick. There was a flicker of action as a soldier beneath the platform pulled a lever. I saw the frail form of Jacob Cotter fall. We heard a sharp snap of the rope, as though a giant teamster had cracked a great whip. A moan came from the mouth of all who witnessed, soldier or civilian. My father shook his head.

The drum died.

All was deadly still. Jake's body twisted beneath the rope which was now straight as a tulip tree. One of his legs kicked with a temper for several times and then hung as loose as its mate. What had once been Henry Cotter's son now dangled as dainty as a doll. He seemed so small and yet so big.

"So die all traitors and enemies of the English throne," said the officer in a hoarse voice. "Amen."

"God take his soul," Papa said. His arm went around my shoulder and he let out all his air as if he'd held it since Christmas. There was a tremble in his hand.

"Who claims this body?" the officer asked the crowd. No one spoke. Papa looked around but, like me, saw no Verdmonter to step forward.

"I do," he said to the officer.

"State your name."

"Noah Booker. I know the boy's family."

All eyes looked to Papa as he stepped forward, walking toward the scaffold until his head was almost touching one of Jacob Cotter's shoes.

"You a Verdmont man?"

"Yes," said Papa. "*And* a citizen who works a farm that rests in English soil. So I say to you, brother, and to all that are assembled here . . . we hold no pride for this day. Nor should you."

Hearing a sob, I looked to my left and up into the big pumpkin of a face that belonged to the farmer who stood at my side. His name was unknown to me. His body shook with real grief. With him were a brood of five children, the eldest being no more than Phoebe's age. Reaching out his big arms as the wings of a matron hen, he seemed to try to touch all his children at once, herding them closer under the shadow and protection of his big body.

"Cut down the prisoner," the officer said.

"I missed it," came a voice behind me. Turning I met the face of the man who wanted April and had gone to fetch an ox in order to seal a trade. "I missed the whole durn shebang. They really hanged him, eh?" said Mr. Peabody in a whisper.

"Yes," I said. "They hanged Jacob Cotter."

"Pity," he said. "A young buck like that. Know him, did you?"

I nodded. "Our farms are almost within the sound of a musket. We know all the Cotter families."

"A damn shame," he said. "Where's your pa?"

"Claiming the body."

"He ain't kin, is he?" asked Peabody.

"In a way, yes. Cotters raised my father."

"What's your name, boy?"

"Able."

"Well now, Able, you can tell your pa that I'll be outside the gate with an ox as fair as his calf. And I'm frisky to dicker. But he's not to hurry. I can wait."

"Yes, sir. I'll tell him."

"Good," said Peabody as he left me.

Outside the fort, we bargained with him for almost an hour. He'd brought us each an apple, as he said, to sweeten the deal. Papa and I had brought food with us which we ate without tasting as we did our trade. The ox was about half growed, a black and white beauty of a Holstein.

"Fresh cut," said Peabody, pointing to the pink scar under the tail. "His owner cuts late so's he'll bull up through the withers and size up big in the haunch. Why he bulled up almost near to breed age. If'n they hadn't dropped his balls a week or two back, I bet he'd near to have himself a heifer."

I sat on a stump and let April poke her sweet little face into my hands, to let Papa do the dickering with Mr. Peabody. Usually my father bid his bargains with a good deal of gumption, but on this day I could tell by his gestures that his heart weren't in it. I wondered what he thought of his beloved British soldiers now. The bargain finally got spit and sealed as the two men shook hands in agreement. Papa paid Mr. Peabody all of 20 shillings, counting the silver into the other man's palm a clink at a time.

The soldiers at the fort supplied us with a tarp sheet to wrap up the body of Jacob Cotter. Between us, we bore the corpse, leading the new ox by a twine halter and a lanyard to around Papa's waist. I walked in front, carrying Jake's feet. He wasn't heavy. Toting him made me feel better. But then, once outside the fort, we packed him on the back of the ox.

Instead of crossing the ice, we used the rest of the daylight to go south, near to Skenesboro, and cross by the floating bridge. The ice was soft from the warm of the day and I wouldn't have cherished walking it, not with the heft of a half-growed ox. So we had to go home the long way. We both were silent on the way to the Cotter farm, and then during the way home. I kept seeing the British flag on its staff over Fort Ti. They always flew the Union Jack hauled up as high as it would fly. But as we'd left the fort, the flag had been lowered to half mast.

It was as though the entire garrison had bowed its colors. We repent, the flag said, for the death of Jacob Cotter.

We repent.

Chapter 5

"Whoa!"

No tonic and no herb could ever perk us up quicker than the holler we heard at our dooryard that May morning.

"Whoa back, you hackbone heathen."

"First she's heard and then she's seen," said Mama.

The smile on my mother's face was real as she most flew to throw open the bolt of our house and wave a welcome. All four of us tumbled out in a bundle on account we'd not miss the mirth. The horse hadn't seemed to hear the "whoa" yelled by his driver. Chomping on the bit like a last meal, the white horse trotted circle after circle around our cabin, hitting every bump and stump along the way. All four wheels of the buckboard never seemed to touch the ground at one time, and twice the rig appeared fixing to fall on its side.

Widow Starr screamed her "whoa" still louder, but it seemed to serve to only hasten her wild-eyed gelding. The rig hit the edge of a stump, knocking her bonnet down over her eyes. She made an effort to cuff it back, but to no avail as the reins were knotted round her hands and arms halfway to the elbows.

The rest of her family clung to each other and to the edge of the rig for dear life. After some heavy hauling on the ribbons by the Widow Starr and two of her six riders, the white gelding seemed to be winded enough to cut his last lopsided loop around our house. Planting his forehoofs into the dried mud, he stiffened his legs, hurling Mrs. Starr forward against his rump. She tumbled to the ground in a heap. Papa helped her up, asking where she and her family were bound for.

"Cussed animal," she yelled. "We're bound for Skenesboro, now that the road's dry."

According to Papa, the Widow Starr had learned to whisper in a saw-

48

mill. The beller of a bull was near to silence compared to every letter that passed her lips. Getting to her feet, our small and birdlike neighbor rubbed her backside, and let out a big sigh. Her daughters, all six of them, leaped lightly to the ground. They sure wasn't the plainest gals in Verdmont, looked at as a bunch. And one was a real beauty, as pleasing as poetry. She was getting so doggone plump and comely that to see her was half pleasure and half pain. I sure hoped they'd come to linger.

"Morning, folks," screamed the Widow. "Say *good morning,* girls. Cat got your tongue?"

"Morning," the girls said in a chorus.

"Cream of the crop," hollered Widow Starr, "and every one a peach. You know my girls, don't cha, Able?"

"Yes'm."

"Propagate, Fruitful, Comfort, Ardent, Mingle and Nocturnal," she rattled off in full voice, as she always did on every visit. "Nocturnal means an animal that's active at night," she said, winking in my direction.

"Morning, all," said Papa, holding the horse.

"That son o' yourn," she screamed at my father but looked my way, "is reached high time to produce a brood for himself. Ought to git that boy wedded and bedded."

The red in my cheeks was bubbling up for fair, and I did my best to think of some way I could change the subject. But I don't guess that a widow with six unwed girls of an age to marry could stand by and see ripe go rotten. Since I turned thirteen, almost five years back, the Widow Starr had begun my courtship with all half-dozen of her daughters, stopping by the house almost every month to see if I was ready to pick or choose. Luke Shelby told me he got the same treatment. Luke and me weren't ready to settle down, but I sure had to admit that one of the Widow Starr's girls looked sweet as an apple.

"Ought to hear them girls o' mine recite the Bible," yelled Mrs. Starr with a nod of her head as a cue.

"Thy two young breasts are like two young roes that are twins, which feed upon the lilies," said Ardent.

"Songs of Solomon," shouted the Widow Starr.

"I have put off my coat," said Nocturnal, or maybe it was Propagate, as my mind would oft mix up the two, seeing as they was twins.

"My beloved," said Fruitful, "put in his hand by the hole of the door and my bowels were moved for him."

"I rose up to open for my beloved," said Comfort, looking my way as she spake it.

"I am my beloved's and he is mine. He feedeth among the lilies," said Mingle. "And then he . . ."

49

"*Yes,*" said Mama, sending Phoebe back inside the house to fetch her shawl, which I figure she needed about as much as I needed a wife. Or a second belly-button. "My," said Mama, "that's real Scripture for sure. You folks had breakfast?"

"Before sunup," yelled Widow Starr, "didn't we, girls? No need for *me* to cook, not with *them* so skilled with a skillet. But I might rest a spell. Tugging away at that blessed beast sure tuckers a body."

I was right glad for Mama to have some womenfolk for company, as most folks who stopped by were males, in a wagon or a saddle. Lady talk was in order, but the Widow Starr wasn't about to let either Papa or me make a getaway.

"My," she yelled into my ear as if I was a mile off, "you sure are growed to the prime of manhood." Walking around me, she give my shoulder a squeeze as if she was like to take purchase on a horse.

"Thank you," I said, not knowing what else to say and feeling like a ninny for saying it.

Her hand found a gap in my shirt, and before I could duck away, her boney old finger poked its way through the cloth faster than a weasel to his hole. I grit my teeth and took the jab as well as her comment on how handy her daughters all were with a needle and thread.

"Are you going to get wed, Able?" Phoebe piped up. A big help she turned out to be; but seeing as I was usually giving her a twit about Lyman Shelby, being sweet on him and all, I don't guess I had a kick coming.

"No," I said. A real mistake.

"What?" screamed Mrs. Starr. "Course he is. Big strapper like this can't go to waste, can he, girls?" she proclaimed to the whole territory.

The Starr girls all giggled and goshed and I just stood there and prayed that Mrs. Starr would take her finger out the shirt hole, because it was in there doing its darndest to tickle me enough to smile at one of her daughters. So I smiled in spite of myself; and so did Phoebe and Mama, and even my father who wasn't one to smile every year. All the Starrs smiled back, but the dearest come from Comfort.

With six girls around, and seven to count Phoebe, the only one I saw was Mary Comfort Starr. Even her name was pretty as pie. All she had to do was look at me sideways and I took to torment. It weren't much of an easement to fess up to, but I had to admit that I ached for Comfort like a sore tooth. Pretending not to take notice when she was walking my way, I play-acted busy with a busted bucket.

"Look at there," I said. "Spring ain't come yet. Never leave water in a bucket in winter lest you want a busted bucket." I was thinking how poor I was at making conversation.

Papa and Mama and Mrs. Starr went inside, and the girls all followed.

All except Comfort. Never till now did I know that a split pail would hold her interest, but she come up close for a look see. She had on a pink frock, smelling as fresh and as fragrant as the May morn.

"Able?"

Hearing her say my name was like getting hoofed by a horse, in the belly and on the backside both to once. It was hurt and it was heaven. I couldn't even muster up the gumption to glance at her face. I just stood mute and looked at a tomfool bucket that I see'd every day of my life, staring at the doggone thing like it was the family heirloom that somebody's grandmother had lugged all the way from England or Boston or someplace as distant.

"Yes'm," I said, in my smooth-talking way.

"You fix to look at a pail or are you going to have yourself a look at me?"

Her voice was soft as music. Each word that passed from her lips reached out and touched me all over. Not just on the ears, but everywhere. It was a feeling to rub the reason out of a man, and it sure made its way with me.

"I want to look at you."

"You know what I really want to see?"

"What?" I said.

"We heard tell you Bookers got a new ox."

"True enough do."

"Can I see him?"

"He's just a dumb old ox."

"Please, Able."

It was the way she said things. Every letter went through me like a sword. I swear, Comfort Starr could say a fool thing like "pass the pickles" and make it sound like hugs and kisses.

Short of the barn, there be a muddy spot and she pulled up her dress so's not to drag the pink cloth through it. Up come her dress, a lot higher than the mud could go unless mud had learned itself to high jump, and I saw her ankle and the start of her leg. Her stockings were white, but inside . . . inside . . . inside I could see the outline of her ankle and shin and the swell of her calf. I wanted to see all the way up to her knee, up up up to the end of her stockings. The thought made my face hot. In fact, it turned me hot all over, except for my feet.

"Able, why you standing in the mud?"

Because I am thinking about your legs, Comfort Starr. And I can picture you sitting on a bed, pulling the white stockings oft your legs. Real slow. I wager you got a thigh that's as soft and full and white as a pillow, and I sure would like to rest my face on you. But I don't think it would be at all like resting on goose feathers on account I wouldn't feel

51

a mite like falling asleep. That's what I wanted to tell her. That was why I was standing in the mud, because I was a bit touched in the noggin. If I ever get into bed with you, Comfort Starr, you will be touched everywhere else.

"It keeps my feet cool," I said.

I was so doggone heated I wanted to take off my clothes and roll around in the mud and be pleased as a pig in August, but all I did was tread the mud like a crazy person. Comfort was laughing at me as if she didn't even know that all of this foolery was *her* fault, because she had to heft up her skirt so that her ankles would show. I knew she was thinking that anyway, and I was hoped she didn't imagine what *I* was thinking . . . about her body which I knew would be pink and plump.

"Let's see your new ox," she said.

"Sure," I said. Entering the barn, I pointed to our cow Esther and said, "Well, there he is."

"Able Booker, you certain are a one for game playing."

Without my pointing him out, Comfort studied our new ox, which didn't take a whole lot of looking for as he was nearby. Our barn was only three stall.

"He's beautiful," she said, reaching her hand inside his pen to stroke him.

Oh, please, Lord, let Comfort Starr pet me like the way she pets my ox. Make her hand run along my back the way it now travels the spine of this here beast who don't care two ways to Sunday whether or not he ever gets a female to touch to. Oh, yes, Lord. Even if you got to turn me into an ox. What am I saying?

"What are you saying?" she said. And for a minute I didn't realize that maybe I'd done a mumble, and a good thing Comfort didn't get full wind of it.

"Nothing," I said, being so right gifted in conversation. A natural-born orator, that's me.

"You are such a game player," she said.

"Not me. I don't know any games at all. Besides, games are for kids."

"Not the game I know," she said. It almost turned my breakfast. I don't mean it went sour or anything like that, but it sure did a flip flop. Jumped right up inside my gullet and clicked its heels.

"What game?" I tried to be real casual, so I lifted up my foot so's it would rest easy on the bottom rail of the ox pen; but instead, I hit a rail higher up and give my knee a crack.

"Hide-an'-go-seek," she said.

"Aw, I played that lots of times."

"Not the way I want to play it," said Comfort.

She said it soft and very slow, like she was sort of sleepy and wanted to lie down somewhere. Her big eyes were as blue as a chicken gizzard, eyes that left looking at me and wandered round our barn. Her eyes seemed to climb the ladder up into the hayloft, rung by rung.

"How do you play it?"

"With just *two* people. It's more fun."

"You and me?"

"Just you and me," she said, "Able Booker and Comfort Starr. We'll be a pair."

"A pear?"

"How old are you, Able?"

"Eighteen."

"No you're not."

"Darn near. How old are you?"

"Fifteen. But in some ways I bet I'm older than you are. Mom says that girls are always older than boys."

"That's a lot of feathers," I said.

"I know a new way to play Hide-an'-go-seek."

"How?" I said.

"I'll teach you."

"Aw. I don't have the time for game playing. I got work to do."

"What do you have to do?"

It was good that Comfort asked me that question, because I had the next thing to say already on the tip of my tongue. "Well, I got to check on things."

"What things?"

"Now that the month of May is here, the loft needs cleaning. A wet spring will mildew hay and best not run out of feed. You want to come along and watch?"

"I'll come."

Walking over to the ladder, I was about to start up it, but then remembered my manners. I even had one foot up on the first rung but then hauled it down again, gesturing for Comfort to go up ahead of me.

"Ladies first," I said.

"I know why you said that."

"To be polite."

"You just want me to go first, Able Booker, so you can be underneath and look up my petticoats."

I thought she was going to back off and make me go up ahead of her. And that's when I got jolted, because without as much as a "beg your pardon," Comfort went up that ladder like a treed coon. All I saw was a lot of white frills, as her skirts were bouncing all around her legs, and that was all. Except for the bottom of her shoes; mud on one and cow dung on the other, both of which I reckon I already seen my share of.

So I just followed along up. When I got up to the loft, Comfort was already lying in what was left of the winter hay, looking so dogged pretty it was near to painful.

"Get a good look?" she said.

"I got better things to do," I said, "than look at petticoats."

"Oh!"

"What's wrong?"

"A hayseed's in my eye." Her hand covered up half her face like it was hurting.

"Gee, I'm sorry."

"It's not *your* fault. But maybe you can see it and help me get it out."

Her eye wasn't wet or anything. She just blinked it a few times, and I couldn't see if'n there be a hayseed in her eye or whether there weren't. It was dark up there.

"Hold still," I said.

"It hurts, Able."

"I don't see anything in there. Your eye just keeps rolling around and there ain't too much light."

"Maybe," she said, "you could kiss it and make it better."

As I kissed her eye, Comfort's eyelids fluttered against my lips in a real tease.

"Better kiss my other eye and make sure," said Comfort. "You wouldn't want me to go to Skenesboro with a sore eye, would you?"

"Sure wouldn't."

But this time, as I bent low, she moved her face and gave her lips to me. Her arms went around my neck and held my mouth on top of hers for a very long time. I didn't know what to do with my mouth, but Comfort sure knowed how to handle hers. We didn't talk. We just kissed and kissed. Her mouth was open and soft, and her breath would come and go into mine, sweeter than candy. Her mouth seem to suck on my bottom lip and then on the one up top, drawing me inside of her. Her tongue rose into my mouth like a flower reaching for sunlight. Everything she did felt so clean and beautiful, like her mouth was washing my soul.

She loosened the top of her dress.

Then she took my hand and let it rest on where she was really warm. Her breast was soft and it more than filled my hand. I wanted more of her, and more. I didn't want to tear my mouth off hers to tell her how good she felt. And yet I wanted to tell her everything all in one word. Love. How I longed to say that one word to her, and to hear her gentle voice answer it back to me.

"Comfort!"

There was no mistake about that voice, because whenever the Widow

54

Starr had a mind to make herself heard, she wasn't too easy on the ears. That woman had a voice, Papa had once said, that would swim upstream. Under water.

"Mary Comfort Starr, you come."

"I'll be, Mama."

Comfort righted her dress and her feet hardly touched the rungs on the way down the loft ladder. We brushed off the hay so's folks wouldn't guess how we'd been pastiming.

"I want for you, Comfort," I said, kissing her cheek one last time. "I want to come and court on you, meet and proper." I sure hoped she'd prosper to the idea.

"Able Booker, you'll be more than welcome. And don't be shy about it. We only live eight mile north of here." She lightly touched my face.

"I'll come."

"When?"

"Soon. I promise."

"Cross your heart. But only if you want to."

"Honest. I'll come and court you to death. I wonder what we'd a been up to if'n your ma hadn't of called."

"You'll know soon enough," she said as we ran out of the barn. "But I got to be courted first."

"I can't wait," I said. "I guess I'm a growed man."

"We're both as ripe as a grape," she said, "and there's no feel in the whole world like it. I could sing."

"And I could whistle."

As we rounded the corner of our cabin, heading for the dooryard, Comfort Starr squeezed my hand and I did likewise to hers. My girl. I never thought about anything like that before but it sure was pleasant to think on. I could of danced across the sky.

"Where you been?" bellered her mother.

"Looking at Able's new ox."

"Well," shouted the Widow, "guess a gal would be hard put to get herself troubled by an ox." But as she said it, she looked me up and down, pulling a straw out of my hair. "Where is he, up in the loft?"

I sort of stood there, trying not to look anybody in the eye, shifting my weight from foot to foot. Papa didn't look too happy, but then he wasn't the type to smile for no reason when there was no call to. The Starrs piled back on the rig, and their mother took up the reins, bracing her feet on the shinboard as though she was fixed to wrestle a bear. Giving me one last look, she turned to Mama.

"Pity," she said.

"What's a pity?" said Mama.

55

"Sure is a pity you folks didn't raise that there son of yours in the ways of polygamy."

"Polygamy?" Mama raised her eyebrows.

"Then he could wed up with all six of my girls and give you Bookers half a hundred grandchildren."

"Is that true?" Phoebe asked Mama. "Could Able really do all that?"

"Able," said the Widow Starr, "now that's a fit name for that young stud of yours. Wish I had a son of my own instead of this herd of hens. Well, we be off for Skenesboro."

"Stop by on the way home," I said.

"Why? So you can roll around in the straw pile and look for an ox? Noah, too bad you didn't raise a Christian out of this lad of yours. What *are* you folks, anyhow? If you can't be Baptist, you ain't much good for breeding me a grandson. You folks Baptist?"

"Shame to say we ain't," Papa said.

"We go when we can," Mama said, "and when we can't we pray."

"What's your faith?" the Widow yelled, holding back her horse from hoofing up turf.

"Church of England," said Papa.

"Pity you can't find one closer," the Widow Starr hollered.

The white gelding reared high in the air, striking with its front hoofs. He hardly touched ground before he bolted, and the heads of all seven of the Starr women cracked like whips. Some horses will walk, trot, canter . . . gaining speed in a smooth way from gait to gait, but not Widow Starr's.

"That fool horse knows naught," Papa said, "but go and whoa. And narry a lash mark on him."

Mud flying, the ground was almost a scorch spot where the rig had rested. The departing buckboard grew smaller and smaller as it rattled down the road, heading south toward the town of Skenesboro, the white horse stretching his speed with every pace. The last we heard was not hoofbeats, but the distant screech of the Widow Starr as she threatened her horse with punishment unless he slowed to a gallop.

"Some woman," Papa said.

"She's fair company," Mama said. "Always makes me hold my sides."

"I ain't sure I'd seek her as a mother-in-law," said Papa as he looked my way, "but you could probable do worse."

"Able," said Phoebe, "are you sweet on Comfort?"

"Shucks, no," I said, lifting Phoebe up so high in the air that both her feet pranced almost clear above my head. "You're the only girl for me."

But that night, just before I went sleep, I closed my eyes and saw the fair face of Mary Comfort Starr.

Chapter 6

"Too big," Papa said.

We didn't even bother to put the work yoke that had been Simon's on our new young ox. He just wasn't up to it. His neck was starting to thicken, but it sure was plain he'd do with a smaller yoke.

"Will he be as big as Simon?" Phoebe asked.

"For certain," Papa said. "Maybe even bigger."

"He needs a name," I said, trying not to look at Phoebe. I knew, as well as my father knew, that my sister would want to put a name to our ox. I give a wink to Papa as I said, "I wonder who we can get to help us give him a title that's proper."

"I will," said Phoebe.

"Before we turn him out to meadow along side of Esther," said Papa, "I want to notch his ear."

"Will it hurt him?" Phoebe wanted to know.

"Not if you help to handle him."

"I'll help."

I got hold of his head, leaning his body to the wall of his stall, and slipping the loop of the twitch over his nose. Papa put a plank under his ear and made sure his knife blade was free of dirt, but the ox shook loose before I could tighten the twitch so I had to take another purchase on his head. Then I took a turn on the twitch loop.

"What's that thing?" Phoebe was stroking his back from over in Esther's stall where she'd not be under foot or get herself hoofed.

"A twitch," I said.

"To do what with?"

"Well," I said, "all it does is pinch his nose a bit, for two reasons. First being, so's he'll stand still. And second, it'll add a small hurt to his nose to take his mind off his ear."

57

Papa cut one big notch and two small on either side of the ox's ear, just like the way he done on Esther and Simon. The three notches with the center one tallest was our sign that this was Noah Booker's animal and no one was to trespass with him. His ear bled the way it should.

"Does it hurt?" Phoebe asked the ox.

"Not no longer," said Papa. "Only for a breath and then it's over forever more. I heard a fellow tell that some folks put a hot iron to the flank and hold it long enough to scorch away the hair. Seems wrong to me."

"And to me," I said, loosening the twitch.

"Done," said Papa. "Now what shall be his name?"

"Something out of the Bible," I said. "Seems to me it ought to be a name that's as big and strong as Simon."

"How about *God?*" said Phoebe.

"That sure is an ambitious name," said Papa with a slight wince on his face, "but I don't guess it's fit for a dumb ox. What say you, son?"

"Agreed," I said. "We'll all study on it."

"I know," said Phoebe. "Let it be Festus."

Papa nodded and looked my way, as if to prepare me for her next question. There was a blank look on his face that hailed for help.

"Festus," I said, stroking his shoulder, "how do you like your new name?"

"He says it fits real fine," said Papa.

"Festus it is," I said, talking fast as a fury.

"Papa, who was Festus in the Bible?" said Phoebe, asking the question that I knew for certain she was pondering.

"A friend of Paul's," said Papa. "Now I recollect."

"But what did he *do?*"

"Well," Papa ran his fingers along the tiny bow that tied back his hair, "I do believe it was Festus who helped old Paul write all them letters. Yes'm, that's what he done. It was Festus who kept the pens all sharp."

"Oh," said Phoebe. She seemed satisfied that the real Festus was noble enough to have his name passed on. Papa let out a breath and looked sideways in my direction. I hoped he was accurate. Phoebe ran out of the barn, yelling back over her shoulder that she was going to the house to try the new name out on Mama. And no doubt to trip her up on just who the real Festus was. She was some girl.

"Let's turn him out," Papa said.

So we let Festus out of the barn. He shook his ear, and sure enough, he walked as calm as could be over to where Esther was grazing on the new grass, right close to the block of salt where she'd take a lick every while with her rough old tongue. Festus smelled the salt and sampled a lick or two for his own self.

"Salt keeps a cow to home good as a fence," Papa said. "That and a friendly rub on the rump to let 'em know they're neighbors. Never owned an animal that run off, because with us it knows it's to home."

"Papa, you reckon Festus knows?"

Our young ox was already near to Esther, and the cow seemed to welcome the company, just like people.

"Yep, he knows. And he'll pleasure in the labor of the land, with us, same way Simon did. He'll welcome the work."

"Do you think animals get stale with nothing to do?"

"They certain do," said Papa. "Ever see teethmarks on the neckrail of a horse stall?"

"Sure. Lots of times."

"Well, when a horse'll crib . . . that is he'll bite the wood and suck wind down his gullet, it probably be he's bored. A beast is like a man. He don't cotton to open his eyes to a vacant morning and have narry to do. It ain't right, and even a dumb animal knows it."

"Seems all we do is work," I said.

"Be thankful for it, boy. We can't beg the Almighty to grant us furlough from it. But we can give thanks we got the belly to bridge it on our own."

"That we do," I said.

"Lazy folk get nowheres in the world. Starving is too good for most of the lazy louts."

"You mean like the men at the fort?"

"You took note of that, eh? So did I. Become a tumble-down place, Fort Ti. A shame, too, as once it was run tight as a drum. You could hear the drills clear across the lake and even see the shine of their bayonets, sharp as silver. But not no more. You saw for yourself their slipshod ways."

"We saw more than that," I said. "We carried away their shame and helped to bury him ourselves. Some army that, if all they can muster is to wage war on Jake."

"Henry Cotter is my friend, boy. But that son of his was hard to handle. Some say he was a troublemaker."

"He was plenty wild. But he weren't mean, Papa. Jake Cotter was a bit fisty because of his puny size. We all knew it. As for being a troublemaker, the day he hung at Fort Ti will cause the British more trouble than they bargain for."

"You know that as a fact?" Papa squinted one eye as he looked my way.

59

"As a guess. Luke stopped by yesterday."

"I didn't see him," Papa said.

"You were in the barn. He said that not a soul in Verdmont will forget the name of Jacob Cotter. He said we should write to Boston about it, a letter to Samuel Adams."

"Best we leave Boston to the citizens there and turn our own soil," said Papa.

"I'll wager that it ain't no easy task for Henry Cotter to turn the soil his son now lies in," I said.

"A shame, yes. More than that. What you and I stood witness to was a crime. But all men make mistakes, boy. Even good men."

"Papa, how in the name of all that's holy can you cite Captain Delaplace as a good man? He's the top officer over there, the commandant. It was his word that hung Jake. Him and his tribunal. Good men don't hang boys for pranks."

"I agree. I know little of the law. I'd be cussed to explain the meaning of sedition," said Papa.

"Means as much as a day-old spit."

"Act not of anger, son. I don't know what's said betwixt you and Luke Shelby, and I dasn't ask."

"Nothing," I said. It was a lie and I hated saying it to my father.

"Every town has its measure of hotheads," said Papa.

"And you think Luke is a hothead."

"Yes, I happen to think so. Except for now, I will keep shut about it. John Shelby is a man that I have known for twenty year and more, so I'll not tar the name of his son. Nor pin the label of treason on him."

"Treason?"

"Yes, that is the word I would use."

"About Luke?"

"About some of his Shoreham cronies."

"Who?"

"I'll not say," said Papa. "We both said too much. What did the hanging learn you?"

"If I were to say, Papa, you'd like to fist me for it. And well I might deserve the thrashing."

"Has it come that we can no longer talk as one man to another?" Papa looked square at me, and his eyes said that although we often played our games of politics, it was now more than sport. More to him, more to me.

"No, Papa. It ain't come to that. But I know you feel strong about certain matters."

"Such as what?"

"Such as England. And there are men in Verdmont, neighbors of

60

ours and even more so, the sons of neighbors, who speak ill of England and talk of . . ."

"Of war?" asked Papa.

"Yes, of war. Not that any of us want to have it out with the Redcoats, but there's talk of independence."

"Independence, eh?" said my father.

"Yes, to be free of England and free from English rule."

"I was here over thirty years ago," said Papa, "and there was no rule, no law, no grass to speak of. There was nothing but ourselves. Naught but five Bookers. Four of them are buried in this earth. And I tell you, boy," his voice softened to near a whisper, "better to face English rule than to face the Saint Francis. And were it not for the flag that flies over Fort Ti, the French and their heathen would come again. They would come this day, to this very farm. And your mother and Phoebe would be . . ."

His voice had shattered in the memory of a day that ended his childhood. I saw in his face the many things he knew that I could never know, and what he could never forget. He had lived one day of such horror that it could not be told of by one man to another. Even now as we stood together in the meadow, his memory was breaking him apart. For a moment I could see what he had seen, only I saw my father dead and with arrows in his body, and then I was fighting a picture of my own mother and Phoebe, their clothing and their bodies tore by savages, their dead faces frozen into a dying scream of fear. Here I am, I thought, near to eighteen, and such a scene would cut me open. But my father was ten. Only ten.

"Papa, we must not allow the matters of our time to come between us."

"No," he said. He rested a big hand on my shoulder and I was honored by its heft. Together we walked back to the barn to select some tools to carve a grow-yoke for Festus.

"Ash," said Papa, his hands caressed the word as though it could feel his fondness, almost as if it were sacred. "It's good wood. Soft enough to shape and tough enough to work."

I wanted to read his thinking so I asked him about the wood. "You got a real feel for wood, Papa?"

"We live by it," he said. "It gives us a cabin, chair, fence, bridge, church. We begin in a wood cradle and die in a wood coffin. We yoke our beasts with it."

"And ourselves," I said, holding an ax by its handle.

"Just like a bird," Papa said, "our nest is wood, mostly. It goes to make potash, turp, rosin . . . you could name from now till noon."

Except for our clearing, around us was nothing but trees and the lake

61

to the west. More wood than we could ever put to use. And over our heads was the roof of our barn, built by old Israel before 1745. We took a scraper and some iron dogs for steadying, walking out of the barn and into the morning.

"Trees," said Papa. "I wager a squirrel could go tree-to-tree from the town of Boston and git himself west to the Mississippi and not touch ground. Not even once. Them trees is an army of soldiers, and unless you keep fighting 'em, they march in on a man and take back his land."

"The way a twig will pop out a stump," I said, looking at the big yellow moon where a tree had been. Papa knelt down to touch the tiny twig that was just fixing to bloom out from the edge of the stump. It would have about three leaves and no more.

"Still alive," Papa said. "That old stump is like hope. You can't kill it. You can see how it keeps coming back, year after year, as it is spoke of in the Book of Job. It's sort of like to . . . hope."

"Hope?"

Papa nodded. "Yes, in a way. It makes a man fight back, no matter what fells him. You can be down without being dead."

"You sure can."

"Dog that wood snug now, so's it won't slip."

The dogs held the ash close to the stump so Papa and I could draw the wood. I cut out the neck curve while he did the ends like they was twins, and punched out the holes for the bow to bend through. Scrape by scrape, the ox yoke took form. I carved FESTUS on the thick of it, and I could hardly wait to show it to Phoebe. She never give me a breath of rest until I carved ESTHER inside the barn on the cow stall.

"She'd give a name to a thorn," Papa said, running his hand across the fresh letters.

We soaked a willow for the bow, so's it would bend proper and not split. Each end of the bow took a wee hole for the cotterpins. There weren't a scrap of iron on the whole. It was naught but wood, which was the way Papa built most everything. We never used no nails, not when we could mate a dove joint so snug. Nothing could please my father more than when he saw that I could marry one beam into another; and then the time would do the rest, melting each to each. Papa called it ordaining the timber.

Watching his hands as he worked, I marked how he never seemed to hurry. He was sitting on the stump edge, scraping a last touch to the yoke to twin the ends, so alike you could close your eyes and flip the yoke over and swear that no hand had moved it. He did everything in this fashion, and somehow I felt that he found peace in his perfection. Even when we added trees to the orchard, he made me move a hole after he'd paced off the distance to a neighbor tree. Too close, he'd said, telling me that trees were like people. They need room to breathe. He wouldn't be crowded himself, nor would he pack his trees too near to one another. Nor would he ever overgraze his land.

"Our farm," I said, looking around me.

"What about the place?"

"It really is home, isn't it." It wasn't a question and I didn't say it so.

Papa said, "Not just a home. It's *our* home. And our land, all the property I'll ever need or want. I ain't no Philip Skene, wanting to own every drop of dirt in Christendom. Or like them Allen brothers, wanting to git this tract and that tract."

"I thought Ira Allen was your friend," I said.

"He is. I can stand him a whole durn sight better than some of his kin."

"You mean Ethan?"

"Yes, I mean Ethan. I don't hold with Ethan Allen and his dang Onion River Land Company, that wants to grab all the ground in Verdmont."

Yesterday, when I'd talked with Luke as he rode by, I'd told him to git word to Ira about the hanging. Luke said that Ira already knowed about it. And if Ira knows then Ethan knows it. They eat oft the same plate, Papa said.

"He'd do about any deed, that Ethan," said Papa, "if he thought there was a scratch of dirt to be gobbled up. I don't like it."

"Like what?"

"Being betwixt Phil Skene to the south in Skenesboro," said Papa, "and your friend Ethan Allen to the north. He won't rest until he owns both banks of the Winooski and every drop of water in between. And each beaver that slaps his tail in it."

The way Papa had spoke "your friend" to me in reference to Ethan, I knew he was calling me out. It made me wonder how much he knew about the talks I'd had with Luke, and with Ira. Papa couldn't have smelled out what our plans were. But if he did know, would my father tell it? Tory! The word came back in my mind. Right now it was my main worry, because Papa's politics could spoil it all for me.

"Papa, is that all you got against the Allens?"

"By 'that' I don't guess you mean just their land business."

"No. I mean about politics."

"Politics," Papa let out sigh, "is what all men talk about and no man understands. On the subject of politics, a stand of men will gossip worse than any quilting bee in all creation. Heard tell this and heard tell that."

"Maybe so," I said.

"And there stands my son, Able Booker, just itching to tell one more

63

ear all he heard from his pal, name of Luke Shelby, just yesterday. Am I honest?"

"You're honest," I said.

"What's more, my own son wants to ride oft somewhere with him to raise Cain and bad-mouth the British."

My hands were starting to sweat, and not from just the wood working. Rubbing my palms up my legs, I tried to dry them without Papa's eye on me.

"The wet of conscience," Papa said. "It can worry more than the wet of work."

"It can."

"Well, you want to cough it up?"

"Nothing to cough up."

"My opinion's not worth a tinker, but sometimes a bottled up secret can turn into wine. Or into vinegar."

"Vinegar?" I said.

"Enough to sour your soul. Like a poison inside that won't puke out."

Damn him, he knows. How much does he know? Names? Places? Plans? Did he hear about the meeting in Bennington that Luke had spoke of, the one they held that night at the Catamount Tavern? How did he hear? I've worked at his side since the hanging. Close as two peas we've been. Someone got his ear, for sure. Who? Just maybe Luke Shelby weren't the only one to come this way and spread news, and perhaps the Tories hold meetings as well as our boys.

Does he know about his son; and that, for me, tonight is the night?

My hands were again wet, and I was hoping that Papa wouldn't notice. There was little that missed his eye. He could look at things and see through people. That was just one reason why I never did fib to him too much. Papa could pull truth from the mouth of a liar, and I always felt good inside whenever I'd face him on a matter and tell him the straight of it. The true of it.

"True" was a word he used on a number of stuff; the way an ox would pull, the way one beam fits another. He was a true man, I was thinking, and he was sure enough true to England. He carried a pledge in the deep of him that was sort of the compass of his character, pointing him in the proper direction and along a path to home. Not home in the sense of our farm, but a feel of belonging to an ideal that he wouldn't even forfeit his grip on. The wood we worked on could never be more solid than Noah Booker.

"Done," he said. His hands were yellow with wood dust, almost white, the way Mama's hands got frosted with flour when she was busy with baking.

"A fine yoke," I said. "Real fine."

Phoebe came running our way, and before she got to where we stood, I covered up the FESTUS on the yoke with my hand. I wanted to look at her face when she saw the name.

"Look, Phoebe," I said.

"What's it read?"

"Study it," Papa said. "What word do you see?"

"Festus," she said, and she gave off a smile that broke as sweet as spring. "I still miss April, but the hurt isn't so deep, now we got Festus."

Turning tail, she run off across the meadow. The snow was gone and the grass was greening. We stood like stocks, Papa and I, watching her run to where Festus and Esther was walking, heads down, searching out the new grass. They took small notice of her.

"Ever mark," said Papa, "the way cattle graze?"

"How so?"

"See how they both walk north, going the same way. End of pasture, they'll both turn and walk south together."

"I don't guess I ever took note of that before," I said.

"Well," Papa clapped the sawdust oft his hands, "I hope it be the same with father and son."

"I don't understand," I said. Yet as the words come out, I think I caught his meaning.

"It's a hope," he said, "that you and I trod a like path."

"But in politics, you go east and I go west," I said.

"But if we both turn a bit," said Papa, "we'll walk side by side."

Chapter 7

Phoebe was asleep.

It was a warm night, and she'd kicked off the covers. The white of her foot was a little lantern in the dark of our bed loft. As she rolled over on her belly, the dry cornhusk whispered to us in the night and then was still.

Carefully I lifted the bottle from our tiny window, so I could see out. Our small shutter was propped open; and sitting up, I could look out into the moonlight. Listening to the bugs, I waited for what was near to be eternal before I heard a horse. Closer and closer the rider come, and then all was still until I heard the owl scream. Only this owl had the name of Luke Shelby. I'd already dropped the ladder into its slots and had put my clothes back on, except for my boots. All I wore was a shirt and britches; no stockings, as the May weather had turned warm. I returned the bottle to its slot, hoping that someday we'd afford real window glass to look through.

On my way down the ladder, I heard Papa's heavy breath come and go. Don't wake up, please don't. Silently I slid the bolt of the door and, carrying my boots, sneaked out into the night. Boots on, I ran east to where I knew I'd find Luke. Even before I saw him in the dark, the snort of his father's black mare spotted his location. I saw two horses, both black. Luke sat one, holding the bridle on the other.

"Hasten," he said, with his usual grin, "or you'll be late for your own torture."

Throwing a leg up over the bare back of the extra horse, we held in both mounts, until we'd rode north to where we hoped we'd be out of earshot. Deep in my belly I felt the fear of what I was about to do. But I'd give my word to Luke, and I don't guess Luke was going to listen to me back water.

"Come on," he said, driving his heels to his horse.

Our two blacks shot forward, their hoofs hitting the hard of the road north, hammering a heavy noise. Hoofs was all we could hear. On both sides of the road, the forest was dark and lightless; but up ahead, the moon made the road a white scar that cut north toward the town of Shoreham. After what I guessed was a two-mile canter, we pulled in short to let our horses breathe easy for a while. Luke reached for something inside the pocket of his britches.

"Here," he said, handing me a bit of white cloth, "tie this over your eyes. You ain't suppose to see where we're at. I plum forgot."

"I already know where we're at. We're east of Drury's farm. Besides, I'll ride myself into a low branch that'll wipe me off."

"Don't argue, Able. Do it. These fellows will raise a ruckus with me if you don't."

"Why?"

He stopped his horse. "Do it or get off and leg for home. I got my orders. You want to join, don't you?" He weren't angry; just sort of insistent.

"You know I want to join," I said.

"Then rag up. Nobody goes to the meeting place without a blindfold until he's swore in. Understand? Here I'll do it. Your hands are too shaking." Reaching over, Luke tied the white cloth over my eyes. It sure felt lonely all of a sudden.

"I'll lead your horse," he said. "Hang tight."

My head and upper body jerked back as the horse almost went out from under me. Slightly to the front I could hear the hoofs of Luke's horse. Digging my hands in the horse's mane, I hung hard, gripping my legs around his bare barrel, and tucking my head low. Nothing to do but cling and think. What was I getting into? For a moment I wished to be home in bed.

As we turned off the north road, the hoofbeats were slower and softer on the forest trail. I could feel the woodland cool closing in on me. Shivering once, my muscles tightened as I was breathing harder than my horse. Into the woods, on and on, with Luke in the lead we went. Questions kept itching at my mind, but none of them would get asked. Sure wouldn't do to have Luke think I was afraid of what was going to happen. Even if I was.

Voices were up ahead.

Not loud, but there was plenty of people. Closer now, I could hear that all the voices were male. No women present. It was the kind of talk men made when no women folk were around to hear. Rough laughter. I couldn't understand why I felt so cold. As the horse stopped under me, I was hoping that the dark would hide the sorry way I was trembling.

You are scairt, Able Booker. You are scairt right up and out of your skull, so much that your scalp itches. As they pulled me down off the horse I almost shot out my supper.

A man was on either side of me; and a third was behind me, pulling my hands back.

Bits of rawhide? My wrists got bonded together, crossed and tight. Nobody ripped off the cloth that covered my eyes. I wanted to say "Luke?" but I knew it wouldn't be fit. He didn't seem to be nearby. Strange hands pushed me forward, and it stung when my neck took the whip of a branch. First I thought that I'd been cut with a lash that was laid on by a firm hand. Then other twigs told me it was naught more than a tree branch. My mouth opened to say something, and I felt leaves against my face. Sassafras. The smell was a make-no-mistake smell of laurel leaves.

Another smell run up my nose. Torches. And then I could hear the soft crack of flame.

It sure was spooky not to see nothing. It made me keep on studying what I was afraid of. I wasn't going to be hurt, was I? And just as I told myself how safe I was, a fist or a boot or a rock or the hoof of the biggest bull in Verdmont smashed underneath my belt buckle. Doubling over, I feared for an instant that I'd puke, or that my bowels would move into my britches. Yet I felt that who'd ever done it could of hit harder.

"Take off his clothes."

Hands undressed me, and not in a gentle way. Lifting me up off the ground like I was narry but a child's toy, they pulled off my britches. Every stitch. There I stood, blind and shaking and naked as a skinned rabbit. A voice made some remark about the size or condition of my privates. I was hoping my parts looked manly, big and bold, but then realized how cold I was and how shrunk I must appear. Other voices spoke other things, but nothing seemed to matter except my nakedness and my hurt gut; I expected another kick or blow but none came. Still the expecting was almost as hurtful. So I realize why they'd give me a single shot.

"Who brings this man?"

"I do." It was Luke, but not nearby. He was trying to deep his voice to manly.

"His name?"

Somebody kicked me in the ass and ordered me to speak up good and loud.

"Able Booker," I said.

"Son of a Tory," a voice said. It sure was a mean sound, the way he said it; and it made me ask of myself if this was the man who'd done in

68

our ox. Did you kill Simon? If you did, I'd like to make an ox out of you.

"Are you son to Noah Booker?"

"Yes," I almost whispered.

"Speak up, boy."

"Yes, I am Noah Booker's son and proud of it," I said in a full voice.

My ass got kicked again, harder, making me stumble forward a step. It didn't hurt as much the second time, but it got up my ire. Turning my head, I threw a remark over my shoulder. "And you, you unwed bastard, you are the son of something else." I figured if Papa could use that saying, then so could I.

Men laughed.

I took another stout lick for it, but it made 'em all see I could dish it as well as take. Luke had said that the "swearing in" wasn't no picnic. But the damn bugs were out, and I could hear 'em hum all around me like a choir. They bit my bare backside, but I didn't flinch. What in hell did I care about a bleedy butt. The mirth of the men gave me heart, so I turned around and faced the man or men who had kicked my arse end.

"Kick a man who's blind and bounded," I said. "If that's a sample of Green Mountain courage, I'll not be one of you."

"Face around, boy," a big voice ordered, "and mind your manners, or else. Why do you come here?"

"To join," I said.

"Well," said the big voice, "so best we see what you're cut from. Step forward."

Being barefoot, my right foot trod on hot coals. Backing up fast, I heard the merry guff of the men on all sides of me. My foot hurt like a hatful of hell. Damn if I'd dance to feed *their* fancy.

"Good lad," said Big Voice. "Show him into the Inner Circle, boys, and prepare the *knife*."

I knew a lot of all this was narry more than just a puff of wind, so I'd grit my teeth and ride it out. Nothing abides forever. Besides, I recalled that Luke had said there was a bit of whoop-do-doo to it that every chap got give a taste of. Well, if all of them kickers could stand toe to toe with it, so could Able Booker. I wasn't to spook that easy.

We were walking forward.

I was again betwixt some men, and one of them was Luke. His mouth was up close to my ear when I caught his whisper, "Able, don't git so all-fired uppity. Them old folks just cotton to cook up a little sport with some of the fresh ones. They're good old boys."

I said nothing, figuring that Luke weren't supposed to be talking to me and no sense to get him into the soup. So I just kept silent and walked as guided, and took a kick from the good old foot of a good old boy. I wanted to return the favor right into his good old crotch.

"Doc Young is here," said Luke.

"Who?"

"Doctor Thomas Young. He's a friend of Ira's and they say a real firebrand when it comes to public speaking. Ethan's here, too."

"He is?"

"You been talking to him, or rather him at you. Now best we hush up, so prepare yourself for the upcoming. It ain't bad."

It felt good to hear Luke Shelby's voice, as all the others were strange. We were walking sort of single file among the trees from what little I could make out. Finally we stopped. I felt a hand on my shoulder that said not to press on no more so I stood stock still and waited on Christmas.

"Able Booker," said a voice, "before the sight is returned to your eyes you must swear an oath. Are you prepared?"

"Yes."

"Call me *sir*."

"Yes, sir."

"Are you pure of soul?"

"Yes, sir."

"And are you, Able Booker, clean of body?"

Before I could answer, some heartless rascal threw a bucket of cold water on me. Almost stopped my heart. He must of dipped it up out of a spring because ice couldn't of been any colder.

"I am now, sir," I said. Men laughed.

"Stout lad," said the voice. It wasn't Big Voice. "Now then, boy, are you prepared to swear that on this night, and from the morrow forward, that you will tell nothing of what occurs at this place, relating no name and point to no man whose identity may soon to be revealed to you? Do you so swear?"

"I do so swear . . . sir."

"Give the lad his sight," said Big Voice.

Some men stepped in closer to cut the rawhide thongs from my wrists and also to remove the cloth from off my eyes. I could not much more than blink in the darksome looking from one torch to the next. Other than Luke, I recognized no one except Ira Allen. At his side stood a bigger man, thick in the chest, who held a sawed-off flintlock that he aimed toward the ground but yet at the ready. His face was as broad and round as a skillet, like a man who had a big appetite for all things. Food, drink, song and women, horses and land and power. I didn't have to ask who he was. I just knew it was Big Voice. It was like a

70

painter had lettered a sign across the bull of his chest that said ETHAN
ALLEN.

Ethan looked me up and down. "Give the chick his clothes," he
roared.

My clothes were tossed to me. They were soaking wet and all the men
roared with the wit of it. I held my temper, trying to catch the fun in it
all. In spite of the bugs and the chill, I did manage to coax my face to a
grin.

"So," said Ethan, "you wish to join us then."

"Yes. Yes, sir."

"Bring the knife," he said. "Bring it hot."

Ethan cut my arm and then Luke's. His big hands made me feel the
heat of the steel or the pain clear to the bone. Real deep. I almost
fainted, and Luke weaved a bit at my side. The big man held our arms
together as one, his big ham of a hand stretching around our two wrists
as if they were twigs, crushing one against the other.

"Able Booker," said Ethan, "do you now take your oath, that on the
penalty of death by fire, will you now swear allegiance to our cause and
to this company of Green Mountain Boys? Will you keep silence about
all secrets shared with you? Will you pray to God and ask only that our
cause be just? Can you so swear?"

"I swear."

"Defame this oath and your body will be staked and you will burn in
our sight and in these very woods. If you prove treacherous, or if you
are shortcoming in the line of your duty, you will be entombed in this
earth forever. But, if you be steadfast, you will walk in honor among
your fellows here now assembled and your name we shall regard as a
true brother for as long as you live."

Ethan's big hand gave my face a gentle cuff, then a second. It was not
meant to give pain; instead it was a gesture a father might offer his son.
Then he gave Luke the same treatment.

"You lads will do just fine," he said. "Now I want you to meet Seth
Warner who is to be your group leader. He gets his call direct from Ira,
my brother, so do as he bids."

Seth Warner appeared out of nowhere, shook our hands, and even
assisted me to wring more water from my shirt. It sure was cold.

"You took your medicine well, Able Booker."

"I've took more," I said.

"We have to see what you're made of, to see if you can take orders,
and also whether there is more stuffing inside you than goose feathers.
To my judging, you took the guff well and the oaths with a fervent
heart. Luke speaks no ill of you, even though there could be higher
commendation." Seth smiled.

71

"Thank you," I said.

As we talked, we were joined by Ira Allen, a thicker but shorter man than his brother; and by my assessment, younger by ten years. Ethan was stiff as starch, but Ira had a limber laugh and was easy to be around. He put a hand on my shoulder and spoke directly to me.

"You were there," he said, "at Fort Ti on the day Jacob Cotter was hanged."

"My father and I saw it all."

"A rotten shame. What did your father have to say of it?"

"He tried to stop it, sir."

"The word is that your father's a Tory," said Ira. He didn't look right at me, but busied himself in stuffing a chaw of tobacco into his cheek. "That true?"

"Yes, it's true. But my father's politics belong to my father's house, not here."

"Agreed," said Seth Warner, and Ira nodded.

"I like your pa," said Ira. "Make no mistake on that score. Noah Booker has a fair name in this valley. But he was born in England. Correct?"

"Yes, but . . ."

"You know as well as I how he stands. What would your pa do," said Ira, "were he to know of his son's activities? I can see you respect him and well you should. I do, too. But all it takes is one Tory to upset the boat. These are jumpy times." He leaned closer. "Had I not said that I knew you, and that Luke and you were the thickest of friends, my brother would have washed his hands of you, Able."

"You believe in our cause?" asked Seth, as he threw a blanket around my shoulders.

"Yes," I said, not knowing quite what their cause was or what I believed in.

"Perhaps you should not return home," said Ira Allen. "Must you?"

"I must. Tomorrow my father and I are to yoke-break a new ox. Somebody done in our former animal, and I got a guess who."

"None of us, boy," said Ira. "And you got my word. There be no score for you to settle on that matter. Am I right, Seth?"

"It's true," said Seth. "But the whole truth is that we knew of it, heard about it after the fact. We don't condone it."

"It was a rotten deed," Ira said. "We can't change what's been done, no more than change a man's thinking." He looked at his brother as he said it. Ethan's back was to us and he was talking to a group of six or seven men, none of whom I knew.

"Who are they?" I said.

72

"You ask too many questions," said Ira. "They are men from the north, from up on the Onion River."

From where the three of us stood near one of the burning torches, the light flickered on our faces. But where Ethan stood the night was thicker. The men he talked to were stone still, listening. Their faces seemed to be carved out of wood. One of them faced our torch and his eyes tried my memory.

"Who is that man?" I said.

"Able," said Ira, "I don't know who you mean. And for your own sake as well as ours, ask little. Names are a risk, and no man in this gathering wants to hear his name bantered about, as we meet on midnight matters. For the now, you go with Seth. I have duties to perform."

As Ira left us, Seth Warner faced me and looked me square in the eyes. "Do you have a musket?"

"No, sir."

"No weapons at all in your house?"

"Only Papa's gun."

"Does your father go often to Fort Ticonderoga?"

"No, not often. Several times a year, that's all."

"How about Skenesboro?"

"We don't hardly ever go there," I said. "Papa went last year."

"To see Major Skene?"

It was strange that Seth Warner asked so much about my father. I didn't like it, and it made me feel a traitor to my own family to tell of Papa's comings and goings.

"This here, sir, is the last question I'll answer about my father. No, he don't hold no heart for Philip Skene. He thinks Skene is a land-grabber."

"Skene is also a Tory."

So is my father, I almost said. But for once I held my tongue. I knew why Seth Warner was digging into me about Papa, and I was suddenly angered at myself for saying as much as I said. If the oath I just took meant being a spy on Papa, then to hell with you, Seth Warner and Ethan Allen and all the rest. To hell with the Green Mountain Boys.

"Who are your friends?" asked Seth, in now a different tone.

"Luke Shelby's a near neighbor. I knew Jacob Cotter but not as well." Then a thought hit me, concerning the trip to Fort Ti that Papa and I made the day they hanged Jake. Just maybe it'd be the right thing to say. Sure seemed to be.

"Before they started to hang Jake," I said, "it was my father who knocked at the west barrack, faced the officers, and pleaded to spare Jake. Lots of other plain folks was there that day. But by damn, not a

73

manjack stepped forward to say nay to it all. Nobody except my father."

"Interesting," said Seth Warner. "And now I will tell *you* something. But you must swear to me not to repeat what I say to you. Do I have your word?"

"Yes, sir."

"Guess, if you can, how many men and boys have enlisted to our cause since the hanging of Jacob Cotter. How many would you say?"

"A dozen?" I said.

Seth laughed. "Over a hundred."

"A *hundred?*"

"Yes, and more this night. John Painter in the town of Middlebury will sign up five, Jesse Whiting in Bridport three more, and Timothy Chippen in Brandon a half dozen. Because of the rope on the neck of young Cotter, we are no longer a family affair, meaning the six Allen brothers. We, the Green Mountain Boys, are now . . . an *army.*"

A chill went through my bones; and inside the blanket, I shivered with more than just the cold and the wet. An army! I was part of an army and I didn't even own a gun. Or a horse. But at least I was now a Green Mountie.

"So you see," said Seth Warner, "the tragedy of Jacob Cotter was not his hanging."

"What then?"

"The tragic thing is that we knew they'd hang the lad, and we let them do it."

"You could have stopped them?"

"Perhaps we could have dumped the cat from the bag, got him out, but we did nothing . . . and I hate my own guts for our inaction. Jacob Cotter was a sacrifice."

"You mean . . ."

"Yes. We needed a hero. So we let Jake Cotter hang."

"I don't believe it," I said. "Nobody over here in Verdmont knew he was in irons. Jake himself told me. Nobody knew."

"We all knew. We had men inside the fort when the lad tried his trick to steal the cannon. The night before the hanging, Ira and I and some others met down by the lake, with a plot to spring Cotter loose."

"Why didn't you?"

"Ethan said no. His order was to tarry it. And the death bought us over a hundred men with more to swear in every strike of the clock. Sorry a tale as it is, sorry enough to make us all bow our heads in contrition, it's true."

"You traded Jake's life for an army," I said, almost whispering. The words in my mouth bore a bitter taste.

Seth nodded. "Just that. Now look at the men who are listening to Ethan. Tell me where you have seen them?"

Taking a step or two in the direction of where Seth Warner had nodded his head, I could make out several faces. The first three were strange to me. But the next pair were a second sight. The two wore buckskin, and carried long rifles.

"Kentucky rifles," I said.

"Yes, but made in Pennsylvania. And you saw those men before, Able Booker. Tell me where."

"At the fort that day. The two woodsmen."

"Yes, they were there. So were others of us. Remember the big farmer, twice your weight and more, who stood at your side and wept with his children?"

"Was *he* . . . ?"

"And do you remember a woman who busies herself in the activity of candle making?"

"We talked to her."

"So you did."

"We were watched that day, Papa and I?"

"Every move. We could even tell you the cost of your new ox."

For a moment I couldn't breathe. And then Ira Allen returned to us, handing me a musket. "Here," he said, "you'll supply your own powder and shot. Keep it well hid but handy in case we call to arms."

"It's for *me?*"

"For you. Practice with it, until you can knock out a squirrel's eye from a stone throw."

"Do I get a horse, too?"

Ira smiled. "A horse is not so easily hidden as a musket. Luke will stop for you if an assembly is called. Go home now. But be at the ready. Above all, boy . . . thread your lips." I nodded. "Come," said Seth.

We moved through a thicket of bushes. Had not one of the men held a torch we would have seen nothing. Coming into a clearing, we stopped. The men with the torch walked forward, holding high the flame, as if for me to see a certain sight. And I saw! There before me, staked to the ground, was the black corpse of what once had been a person. The hands and feet were still chained, stretching the body into a charred and blackened star. He had been burned to death, in chains.

"Have you wondered, Able Booker," I heard the soft voice of Seth Warner speak, "why we have this night entrusted you with tales not to be told? Here before you lies the remains of a Green Mountain Boy . . . who talked too much. Now you know why we will trust you to be silent."

75

Closing my eyes tight, I almost fell into Ira Allen's arms. God, I thought, I do so want to puke.

An hour later I was lying in my bed on my back, my fingers locked under my head. Phoebe was still asleep. But I knew that I would be awake for much more of the night, thinking of what I had seen and done. Pondering what would be asked of me by the Green Mountain Boys, and hoping that I could do it. Most of all, praying for the wasted soul of Jacob Cotter, as well as the poor beggar who'd been burned alive.

I was curious to know if all the other Bookers could hear the pound, pound, pound of my heart.

Chapter 8

"You all in, boy?"

"Just resting," I said to Papa.

"Looks like you been rode hard and put away wet. Ain't even noon, and there you set with your hinder smack to a stump and looking plum wore out. Best you bed down in good season, come evening, and be to sleep before Phoebe. Aid me budge this digger."

"Will do."

My whole body was so dog-tired that I was shaking. But with my gumption along side Papa's, we both took a purchase on the twist handle and dug the posthole a hand deeper.

"Fencing," I said, "is a hefty chore. How come we have to do it in such an all-fired hurry?"

"Well, we got Philip Skene to the south who won't want to see heaven until he's titled every piece of land this side of Hades. And we got Benny Wentworth to the east."

"He's the Governor of New Hampshire, not Verdmont," I said.

"To be sure, boy. But he don't recognize the Yorkers' claim to us. He wants our tax money for the New Hampshire purse, the way Billy Tryon wants it for New York."

"Why can't Verdmont be a colony, too?"

"Don't know. We just ain't."

"Ethan Allen says we will be soon." The moment I said it, I marked it as an error. Me and my mouth.

"Ethan's a big-headed fool," said Papa, "and how come you know so much on the sayings of Ethan Allen?"

"Luke told me."

"Just a fount of news, that Luke."

With a deep ram of the dirt scoop, I pressed the two handles close,

77

lifting up a measure of dirt. But as I let up the pressure, at least half the soil dropped back into its hole. What I deposited on the ground was a sorry load. Papa noted the process, looking at me with an asking eye.

"You weak today?" asked Papa.

"Just tired."

"I heard you leave the house last night. I figured where you might be scampering off to," he said.

The choke in my throat cut off my wind. I couldn't take the burn of Papa's eyes, but instead just looked down at the poorly pile of dirt I'd snaked out on the second jab of the scoop.

"I guess you know," I said, trying not to let on about the flutter in my gut.

"I know."

"Does Mama know, too?"

"Boy, there's some things that mothers ain't to know about their sons and all the tomcat that goes with it. Same for fathers and their daughters."

"Tomcat?"

"I know where'd you go last evening. And *why*." His voice had a smile to it. The light way his words come out made me breathe easy. Because if'n he knew the righteous truth of matters, he wouldn't of been so doggone fancy about it. Maybe he *didn't* know. I'd have to go easy and test him out.

"You heared me come home, too?"

"The way you're working this day, don't look as if you come home at all. No, I don't guess your ma did hear you arrive 'cause she'd a spoke up. But I guess I know where you been and what you was having at."

"No you don't," I smiled.

"Sure enough do," Papa smiled back.

"How do you know that me and Luke weren't out hunting coon with that old hound of his?"

"Yes, boy. You was sure hunting coon. And the coon's name was Miss Comfort Starr."

If a person can sigh inside without making no noise, then that was just what I was doing after I heard my father's remark, and knew he was way off the scent.

"Papa, I can't fool you, can I?"

"You tomcat that girl? You know what I mean. Not that your courting is my business. It ain't. You're a man. Maybe not in your ma's eyes, but if you're leggin' it up to Starr's eight mile up as horny as a toad and eight mile back when you're all loved out, to juice that fat little frisky . . ."

"Comfort ain't fat," I said.

78

"She ain't exactly scrawn."

"Ain't no girl by the name of Comfort intended to be boney," I smiled at Papa. "She's just a wee bit fleshy."

"And I reckon *you* know where," he said.

"Reckon I do."

"I figured as much," he said. "The way you was working today over an empty seed bag. I sentenced you'd had at it last night with *little* Miss Comfort. Love by moon and pay by noon."

"I surely am tuckered out."

"She's a widow's child, boy." Papa looked serious.

"Meaning what?"

"If you knock her up and put her in pod, it means that Comfort don't have no pa to come after you and drag you by your ear to the preacher."

"I know."

"But *you* have a pa."

"I know that, too."

"And you catch my mean," he said. "You seed that girl and you'll wed her proper, hear?"

"Yes, sir."

"How long you two been joining?"

"Not long," I said, wishing it was all fact.

"Well, unless you're ready to nest and nurse your young, best you spill your seed outside and not inside. Understand me?"

"I . . . think so," I said, wondering if I really did; wanting it true, that I was having at it with Comfort instead of Ethan Allen.

"Three beats of pleasure," said Papa, "that comes at the end of love-making ain't easy to rip out of. But remember, unless you do, you could give your girl three seasons of pain. It ain't fit nor right to bear an unwed child, and no son of mine is going to kiss and deny. You hear?"

"I hear, Papa."

"If a gal is fair enough to bed, she's fair enough to wed."

"Yes, sir." I wanted him to shut up his sermonizing, but I knew the old boy was right. I promised myself that I'd never put Comfort in a family way. But it sure was a joyful idea.

"Besides," said Papa, "if the Widow Starr ever goes out to the barn in the dark and trips on the two of you, she just might up and bullwhip your white and shiny backside all the way home. Or all the way to Shoreham to see the Reverend Hamden."

"I'll remember."

"Wouldn't be the first wedlock in Verdmont that got glued under a gun," said Papa. "Not by a durn sight. Nor the last."

79

I stopped work and wiped my face with the sleeve of my gray shirt. Would this day ever end?

"Hot?" Papa asked.

"Hotter than the devil's drawers."

"My poor Molly," Papa said, speaking of his wife.

"Why poor Molly?" I said.

"If she only knew," said Papa, "how her darling baby boy spent his evenings, she'd have herself a spasm."

"Well, I ain't about to tell her," I said.

"Nor I," said Papa.

"Don't think Comfort will either."

"Then she's never to know," said Papa, "less you git greedy with your pleasures."

"Boy," I said, trying to heave Papa off the subject of me and Comfort Starr and how I might be spending my time in the dark of night, "it sure is a hot one." My face was fat with sweat.

Papa said it sure was, unbuttoning his shirt as he nodded his agreement, pulling the cloth off his back. He looked at me as though he waited on me to do the same. But I didn't dare expose the fresh cut on my arm. He'd of asked me where I got such a gash and then I'd have to cook up another fib, and try not to fidgit as I give him the false of it. You sure have to have one heck of a memory to be a great liar; as it'll keep you busy, I was thinking, trying to bookkeep what you tell and to who. Truth was starting to look sweeter by the minute, but how could I just spout out that all I did last night was join a band of the local outlaws? A truth like that ain't easy to tell a person like Noah Booker. I'd sooner go crosslake to Fort Ticonderoga and spill all the beans to no other than Captain Delaplace. But not to Noah Booker.

"You'll git a sunburn," I said to Papa.

"Reckon I might."

We ate our midday meal, and afterward I didn't think I'd be able to go back to the fields to work at Papa's side. But I did. I worked at fencing until it was chore time. Then I milked Esther, threw some scratch grain for the chickens, put Festus in the barn and ate supper.

All during the evening meal I listened to Phoebe prattle on and on about how she'd do herself a trip to Fort Ticonderoga to see April. She sure did love that calf, but I was also heartened to see how quick she'd took a shine to Festus. If either Papa or me touched his horn bumps, he'd shake his head free; but he'd let Phoebe climb all over him. Festus had even let Phoebe sit his back.

It was already dark outside, and cloudy, when we heard the nicker of a horse. In less than a quick breath, Papa grabbed his musket. I heard the click when he pulled back the hammer. Not a big noise; but the quick way his thumb cocked that iron sure hatched a sound that meant business. My musket, the one I'd got last night from the Green Mountain Boys, was hid out in the barn under some straw, not too far from where I'd been sparking with Comfort Starr.

Was there going to be trouble?

My body grew the chilly bumps and my backbone crawled up and down like a scairt snake. Mama blew out the candle, so the only light in our cabin was from the hearth at our backs, our fireplace being on the north wall and our door to the south. Papa split the door open a crack, just wide enough to poke his head out. Rain was coming down.

"Who's there?" he said into the mist.

"Hello!" came a wet voice, young and male.

"Who are you, sir?" Papa said.

"Luther Peacham."

Luther Peacham? Who in heck is that? I never heard the name before, and there sure weren't no family in these parts that bore the Peacham name.

"Who is Luther Peacham? Is he your friend, Able?" asked Phoebe. Her hand took a tug on my shirt sleeve.

"No friend of mine," I said.

"Nor mine," said Papa. "State your business, Brother Peacham."

"I am lost, sir." His voice sounded lost in the dark and the rain.

"Maybe you are," said Papa, "and maybe you ain't." He said it real friendly and it could of been read both ways.

"I am a schoolmaster, sir," said Peacham, "on my route to Fort Ticonderoga where I have an assignment."

A schoolmaster? Shoot the bastard, I was wishing I'd say to Papa. My years in Shoreham under Master Pippit was toil enough, and one less schoolmaster would certainly help the world. Old Jack Pippit held the same high opinion of me as a scholar. Phoebe sure was lucky to be a girl who didn't have to endure the torments of Old Jack's classroom and the frequent (as far as Luke Shelby and Jake Cotter and Able Booker were concerned) whacks of his birch.

"Do you bear arms?" Papa asked him.

"Sir, I do not."

"Well then, you can take your wet animal around to the barn. There's a third stall that's free and empty, and give him a measure of oats."

"Yes, sir, and gladly."

"And," my father went on to say, "there be an old quilt handy, so best you rub him down or else he'll be sorely grieved."

"I will, sir."

"Then you can enter the house for a swallow or two of hot broth, if it fancies you, and a dry seat by the fire."

"Bless you, sir."

Papa shut the door. "Says he's a schoolmaster on way to Fort Ti."

Mama put the broth pot back on the fire, and added a cut or two of potato, some sweet roots and an onion. "Poor wet devil," she said. "I wonder if he talks true." She relit the candle.

"He's young," said Papa. "Not much the senior to our Able here. But if he be a schoolmaster, best he learn better geography than to come this far north on the wrong shore."

"And at this time of year," Mama said. I figured she meant it was too late to walk the ice and too early to swim a horse in water that winter still had a freeze on. He sure was dull for a teacher.

"It's the times," Papa said. "We've lost trust in people, and worse, in the process we've lost the know-how to warm a welcome."

"Feel ashamed, Noah?" asked my mother.

"More than a mite." Papa hung up his gun.

"I'm pleasured we didn't turn the boy away. Could have been Able out in the night. I'd want some husbandry lent to him." Mama smiled at me, and I could see Phoebe in her face.

"And I," said Papa. "Hard to say which is the worse, to trust everyone or no one."

"Best we just do what we always do," Mama said, "and that's trust our own judgment."

"We can spare the oats, and feed ourselves on his company," Papa said. "And to tell you the straight of it, I'd be more content to dry him here by our fire and under my eye than out in the barn alone all night."

"Amen to that," said Mama.

"Amen to that," said Phoebe. It was what we all needed and I hugged her for it, harder than usual.

We heard his knock. When I opened to it, in he came as black and shiny as the rain that ran down his cape. I tried to think of the word to describe his hat, and I did. A tricorn. It was a black triangle, and as wet as the rest of him. He was taller than I but by less than a hand, and his face was young and fresh as an apple, yet pale. He was not an outdoorsman.

"I am Noah Booker," Papa extended his hand to the man, "and this is my good wife Molly."

"Howdo," said Mama, with a quick bend of her knees.

"Your servant, mum." Peacham removed his hat, and I could see his brown hair was pulled neatly back and bowtied to the rear of his neck.

"I am Able Booker."

"Good to meet *you*, sir," he said to me, as I took his cold hand. His fingers were quite thin. "And this is my sister, Phoebe."

82

"Miss Booker, I am delighted," he said, bowing low and with a gallant sweep of his triangle of a hat. Water poured from it.

Well, I don't guess I heard the advice of not to get mixed up with strangers, especially in fast places like Skenesboro, but I admitted to myself that I did like the face of this Luther Peacham fellow. And I could tell that Mama was more than pleased with the grace of his manners. As for Papa, it weren't ever an easement to read *his* face, but Phoebe . . . well, it was no trouble reading hers. She was all smiles, as cordial as could be and sweeter than spice. She looked at Luther Peacham like he was a first bite of pie.

"How far am I off my course, sir?" asked Luther, as he loosened his dripping cape, taking the bench near the fire that Papa offered him.

"Well," said Papa, one foot resting up on the bench and his elbow to his knee, "if'n you was a crow, I'd say less than a mile from your destination."

What a word! I never heard Papa come out with a noise as gussied up as that one. I guess he weren't to be second best to no schoolteacher, not with a word like *destination* rattling around in his pocket.

"But," said Papa, before the poor soul's smile was too wide for his face to hold, "you ain't a crow. You be a schoolmaster, so you say."

"Actually," he said, "I suppose I'm really not a schoolmaster, if the truth win out. It's just, sir, that . . . well, I was out of work, and I saw an advertisement for a teacher. I did not know that it was so far away into the hinterland and through such wilderness."

"It reflects well to you, Master Peacham," said Mama, "that of all those souls who applied for the position, only you was chosen."

To the sudden surprise of all of us, Luther threw back his head and had himself a healthy laugh. He chuckled like to choke from the genuine mirth of it, and it was more than a moment before speech returned to him.

"Oh," he said, "oh, that is rare. You good people pay me far more honor than I merit, I assure you. You see," he said, continuing once again to enjoy the joke, whatever it was, "I was chosen for *one* reason only."

"That be?" said Papa.

"I was the *only* applicant," he said, roaring at the wit of it. "The only soul who asked for the job."

"When you see the place," I said, "you'll know why."

"A sorry place, eh?" His face straighted a bit.

"Sorry enough," said Papa, "but once proud."

"That explains," said Peacham, "why the last schoolmaster lasted less than six months."

"So now we know your experience, Brother Peacham," said Papa, "how stand you in the field of politics?"

"Sir, as it is raining," he said, "and my mount is as frail as I from our journey, permit me to say, sir, that my politics go hand in glove with yours."

"Well put," said Papa, but without a smile.

"What are *your* politics, sir, if I may be bold? Are you Whig or Tory?" he asked Papa.

"Tory," said Papa, "and proud to say so. All them Whigs call their-selves patriots. Most of 'em wouldn't know a patriot from a ladle of lard."

"And some would," I said. "Ethan Allen's a patriot. He's a good Verdmont man."

"Can't say I have heard the man's name. At least not in Boston."

"There sure must be plenty going on in Boston," I said.

"To be sure," he said. "Events that will be known throughout the colonies, thanks to the pen of Samuel Adams. Agree with his sentiments or not, he doth prove himself a spirited journalist, week upon week."

"A newspaper every *week*," said Papa, almost as if he couldn't believe his ears. "A weekly paper."

"One? Nay, nearer to half a score!"

"Are they Whig or Tory?" my father wanted to know.

"Whig mostly. You can wager the ones Sam Adams writes for are Whig to be certain. You heard of the tea affair?"

"Yes," said Papa, "we heard. Boston Tea Party, eh?"

"As a result, the British closed up Boston Harbor tight as a tick. The people were without more than tea. There was nothing to eat in the shops, sir. Next to nothing, and the citizens were talking of . . ."

"Of what?"

"Of rebellion, sir. There was no food, not even for the children."

"Hunger hits with a boney knuckle," Papa said.

"It does, sir. But we survived the Act. The Boston Port Bill, they called it. Yet before it even took effect, the other colonies rallied for our sakes. Philadelphia sent flour, barrels and barrels of it. Connecticut sent corn; New Hampshire pigs; and Rhode Island cattle. And hear, sir . . . the good folk of South Carolina sent rice. Rice by the box load, all the way north by wagon. You should hear how they talk, the teamsters from South Carolina who carted the rice to us. Strange voices, yet such good men and true."

Mama handed him a bowl of bubbling broth and the wood to spoon it up with. "You are almost too excited to eat, Master Peacham."

"That I am, sister. These are exciting times."

"Yes, and worrisome," Papa nodded.

84

"I sure would like to see Boston," I said as I watched Luther Peacham spoon down the porridge.

"To git away from work," said Papa, "this here son of mine would foot a mile to see a fool foam at the mouth."

"Such talk," my mother said. "There's another helping of broth, Master Peacham, in the instance you're not filled by the first."

"It tastes good, sister. I am beholding to you all."

"No need," said Papa.

"No need," said Phoebe. Her saying it in the trail of my father made Luther grin again.

"No? Well now," he said to Phoebe, "would it be proper to forget a kindness? Sister, not to appear a glutton, but another spoon or two of your splendid stew would tempt the tallest of Christians."

"You sure can talk," I said.

He swallowed. "Talk you say? Now if it's talk you'd fancy, you all should come south to Boston and hear James Otis. There's a man, sir, who uses every word there is, and then makes up more anew."

"I have heard of James Otis," said Papa.

"A bit more cautious a man than Sam Adams," said Luther.

"Most folks are," said Papa, "from what I hear of Samuel Adams."

"Even his cousin, John Adams by name, says that Sam will hang for treason, ere he stops giving his pen a dip in poison," said Luther.

"John Adams, you say?" asked Papa.

"Yes, sir. A face you'd say was weaned on a pickle, and mostly sour on England. Can't change his mind any more than he can change the subject."

"Some souls are sour on everything, even life," said my father.

"Harvard men, the both, Sam and John. My father says that Harvard College is a breeding ground for treason. He says that General Gage should board up the place. But then my father is a loyalist, and a Catholic."

"I gather you are neither," said Papa.

"If I may speak out, sir . . . there's too much of Europe in our colonies. I want no Church of England and no Church of Rome."

"Better than no church at all," said Mama, with a no-nonsense look on her face.

"Aye," said Papa.

"Not that I'm not a Christian, sir. I have even joined the Congregational Church, as I find its preaching to be more American."

"I see."

"Seems like we now talk religion and not politics," said Luther, setting down the empty bowl and spoon.

"They are one and the same, from what I have seen of the both," said my father.

"Authority," said Luther. "My father says that I am a rebel against all authority, including his."

"Is he correct?"

"Yes, sir. Meaning no disrespect. And certainly not to undermine the control that you as a father must exercise over Able here."

Papa looked my way as he answered. "Coming down to cases, it is not that I wish to control Able as I pray he learns to control himself . . . *and* his passions." I knew he meant more than politics. He meant Miss Comfort Starr.

"Controls are sore saddles, sir. Look at the new law, the Declaratory Act, saying the King has power over all the colonies, to govern as he sees fit. Hah! But he is a wise old George. No mention of a tax. My grandfather, who lives in Lexington, is Irish. Born in Ireland, and he remembers the rebellions of 1720; and the Declaratory Act they had there, issued by the King. My grandpa said it was mud in the face of a conquered people."

"Strong words," said Papa.

"He said stronger when the men fell in Lexington."

"How many fell? We heard only two," said Papa.

"Two! Excuse me, sir, but the count was eighteen."

"Eighteen?" Papa straightened up.

"Three weeks ago, sir. Grandpa saw it all. He was at the Battle of Lexington, and the Redcoats open fire on *us*. And when the smoke from their muskets blew away, eighteen of our boys lay fallen."

"British soldiers don't do things like that, not for no cause. Why did they open fire?" said Papa.

"There was cause," said Luther. "The British regulars were commanded by General Gage who is now the military governor of Massachusetts. They say that Gage was defeated, years back, under Braddock and again under Abercromby. General Gage is a determined man."

"To keep the peace you mean?" asked Papa.

"No, sir, to beg your pardon. Not to keep the peace, as there will be no peace for the keeping."

"What then?"

"War, sir. War."

Chapter 9

"War with England."

As Papa spoke, the sadness in his voice stilled us all for a long moment. He shifted his body, as if he were preparing himself to do battle. Slowly he shook his head, as if to deny his thoughts.

"There's militia now, sir. Almost in every town and village. A year ago they were a sloppy lot. Met only twice a year, but now it's twice or thrice a week in Concord. They have supplies of powder and lead buried beneath every barn and pigsty between Boston and the River Hudson."

"Farm boys with rabbit rifles," Papa said. "They can't see the bloody ground, because they never see'd the Regulars."

"We saw them in Boston, sir. Over three thousand Redcoats. And you'll never imagine such cannon. A boy could hide in one of the barrels and take his dog beside him."

"I'd like to do that," said Phoebe.

"The latest count is even more, sir. Perhaps even four thousand Redcoats; and crack regiments, the Fourteenth Foot and the Twenty-ninth, plus some artillery. Smart soldiers all, and General Gage has them parade every day for show. They make our boys look a mite meager by a comparing. No uniforms for us, no insignia, not even a patch for the shoulder. But rumor has that a patch is being designed. From the looks of the locals, the patches will best be needed on the seats of their britches."

We all laughed.

Luther said, "I wish our troops could look as smart as the British Regulars, just for one day. One hour."

"British soldiers are always a fine lot of lads," said Papa.

"They are, sir. Proud and fair, disciplined to a man. And no wonder they laugh at our Yankee Doodles."

"Our what?" said Mama.

"A name, sister, that the Regulars dub our local militia when they watch them try to drill. We don't even have a flag to fly."

"I'd hate to stand toe to toe with the Regulars," said Papa. "They are a tough bunch, make no mistake. Tell your lads, if you can, to think twice before they try to lock claws with a lion."

"Tough boys, yes," said Luther. "But good lads. Many are Scot or Irish. Peasants, said James Otis. But then he is a man with a big mouth for speech."

"Bigger for booze, I hear," Papa said.

"Peasant lads, yes. But not a bad bunch. I have talked and drunk rum with a few of the British soldiers my own age. They sing some merry songs in the Bunch of Grapes. That's our neighborhood tavern."

"Sing one for us," said Phoebe.

Luther's face went red. Mama reached out and touched Phoebe from behind, her hands on Phoebe's shoulders as though trying to hold in a heady mare. I could see that Mama wasn't about to press Luther into singing army songs. I bet Mama wouldn't of took a shine to some of the songs that Luke Shelby sang. Especially not the one about the Jolly Wife of Bath.

"That's good," said Papa, after a moment of thinking.

"What's good?" I said.

"Singing," he said. "It's the strength of the Protestant Church. Once you sing with a man, it's hard to fist him."

Luther smiled. "The songs are not hymns, sir."

"No," said Papa, "I don't guess they are, by the way *you* took to hearing. Even so, it's good to sing. I wager, when armies meet, if the generals had the pure sense to get all the boys to sing, one side with another, there'd be no battle at all. And every son would march home whole to his mother."

"Or his sweetheart," said Phoebe. Boy, the remarks that kid sister of mine could come out with. She sure was a caution.

"I wouldn't want to be a soldier," said Luther, looking into the fire.

"Why not?" I said.

"They are lonely boys, the ones I've met. Their sweethearts are an ocean away. The accounts of Redcoat conduct in the Whig weeklies are hardly ever just."

"I am surprised to hear you say it," said Papa.

"Well, it's true. If a Redcoat lad as much as winks at a girl on the street at high noon, it journals into a rape. Beg your pardon! Oh, sister, I spoke in haste. Please know my good mom taught me better."

88

"Forgiven," said Mama, "for I know she did."

"My father says he doesn't blame the Redcoats for what has happened," said Luther.

"How so?" said Papa.

"He says that the Regulars took a lot of lip from us Yankees. And more than one stone. It's true, sir. There's things to make both sides a bit contrite. My mother told me she'd seen an English lad, a Redcoat, take a rock on the cheek of his face, thrown by one of our local scum. The boy's face was cut but he never broke from his ranks."

"A sturdy lad," said Mama, "with British cheek."

"True, according to my mother. She wet her hanky at the horse trough and wiped the boy's face. The soldier's I mean. And said her apology for the way some of our Boston folks deport."

"Is your mother a Tory?" asked my father.

Luther sighed. His face looked a bit unsure as he looked at Papa, as though it was an asking that he wished not to answer.

"I withdraw the question," said Papa. "In fact, son . . . questions of that order are out of place in these troubled times. Agree?"

"Yes, sir, I do. And it isn't because I am a guest under your roof. Personally I would just as happily see the wounds heal. Which is one reason I took the job at Fort Ticonderoga as a schoolmaster; to show the British that we are not such bad fellows, we Yankees. I don't want a war, sir."

"No sane man does," said Papa.

"If the folk of Verdmont are like you, sir . . ."

"Some are," Papa said.

"Some ain't," I said. It just up and blurted.

Luther looked from Papa to me, and then back to my father, several times. As if Noah Booker and his son were throwing a ball to and fro so Luther could witness.

"You and your son, Able," he said, "remind me a bit of my father and me. We talk politics, day and night according to my mother, although it can be early said that her opinions are rarely bottled up."

"It's her right," said Mama.

"Every time two souls greet these days," Papa let out his words like they was tired, "seems like that's all we talk about. If words was war, we'd of burned up the earth."

"You people," said Luther Peacham, "are the first Verdmont family that I have the honor to meet. I had heard . . ."

"That we were stubborn," said Papa.

"Mule-headed," I said. "Well, the older ones are, but the new generation is all for fresh ideas." As I said it, I tried so hard not to look at

Papa and to keep a straight face that I just about stared old Luther to a melt.

"You two," said Luther, "are a pair. You talk through me to one another, bouncing your comments off my face to hit your adversary. I feel like a shuttlecock. Well, let me say also how ill-informed people are in Boston about the goodness of Verdmonters. But then not all Bostonians are learned men."

"Some rebels like yourself?" Papa said.

"Not really rebels, sir. Hooligans is the term my Irish grandfather uses. Young punks who crime and then call it patriotic. They think a smashed window is a statement for freedom. Well, say I, if that's what they crave to be free to do, I hope the Regulars crack their skulls. But then there are judgments to be made on both sides. The British officers race their horses on Sunday."

"They *don't*," Mama said in a gasp.

"They do, sister. And to boot, I have seen more than one pound of money exchanged from one hand to another, as they always wager on the race's outcome."

"Well," said Papa, "I'd hate to hang by my heels for every bet that us Verdmonters have put on a horse."

"You'd be upside down until Christmas," said Mama. "Not that I see any fault in it. People like to gamble. It's human nature. I say if men would gamble at the foot of Calvary's Cross for the robe of Our Lord, they'd like to gamble everywhere. But it won't do for the Sabbath. Six other days seem plenty enough."

"My mother would agree with you, Sister Booker."

"It's always best to agree with Molly," said Papa.

"Hush you," said Mama. And as she said it, a look passed between them that was good to behold. I hoped right then and there that Mary Comfort Starr and me would hold such happiness. Only she wouldn't be Comfort Starr anymore. Folks would call her Sister Booker. Or am I dreaming it all?

"Sam Adams had quite a bit to say on the Sunday horse races," said Luther.

"For or against?" I said. If old Sam Adams was contrary to horse racing, then best I'd swallow and say I was, too.

"Against," said Luther.

"That man Adams got pepper on his tongue," said Papa, "when it's got to do with anything that's British, and is probably against any function that's fun."

"There's more than a bit of bitterness in Boston," said Luther. "And it just isn't all the fruit of Sam Adams. Look at this."

Reaching inside his shirt, Luther Peacham pulled out a piece of folded paper. As he unfolded it, his hands seemed white and delicate. He sure weren't no farmer. Smoothing out the crackled brown of the paper, he handed it to Papa. My father leaned toward the fire in order to see; Phoebe, Mama and me leaning with him so's we wouldn't miss the drawing and the words.

"What is it?" Papa said.

"It is called a cartoon, sir. The artist, if he can be called that, is a man my father knows, by name of Henry Pelham. The event is what took place five years ago, in 1770, and has been called the Boston Massacre. See there, sir. A file of seven Redcoats discharge their arms in a volley; and over here, the Bostonians are falling down in death. Note the sign over the shop in the background, sir."

"Can't make it out. What's it say?"

"Sir, it reads Butcher's Hall."

"So it does," said Papa, handing the paper back to Luther who folded it with care, returning it to inside the dark of his clothes.

"Son," said Papa, pointing a finger at Luther Peacham's chest, as if his point was want to go right through Luther's shirt like a dart and pin that paper, "it don't make a nevermind to me or to any of us Bookers what people in Boston tote around. You can carry a dead injun in your shirt and I dassn't much as whistle. But come sunrise, you're on your way to a British outpost. Maybe if I was you, I would give it pause."

"Papa's right," I said. "At least about this."

"Probably little else," my father said, but there weren't no laugh to his lips. He looked as dry as a deacon.

I knew that Papa wasn't going to say anything on the subject of the hanging. Phoebe hadn't yet heard about Jacob Cotter, and I knowed Papa weren't about to tell her now. At least not before her bedtime so she'd be too riled up to even close her eyes. Not after the ghost story he'd told once. Old Phoebe went to sleep that night with both arms around my neck, and she'd also brung along a pitchfork for company. And a cook knife.

"Are you serious, sir, about the cartoon?"

Papa answered "Dead serious."

"Then there's been trouble at Fort Ti?"

"Some trouble?" said Phoebe.

"Time for bed," said Mama.

"No!" Phoebe let out a yell. "I want to hear Luther tell about the trouble."

"Luther hasn't ever been to Fort Ti so he don't know a lick of trouble. It's just a lot of man-talk," said Mama.

"I want to *hear* it," said Phoebe. "I'm somebody, too. I'm Phoebe Booker. Phoebe Booker!"

Papa looked at her in his strange and silent way, as if a word she'd said brought a memory to his mind. I wondered what it be. His face, every so often, had the hurt look of a dying animal; and there was some sort of a suffer inside him, chewing his innards, the way a rat crawls up a dead duck.

"You're somebody, Phoebe," said Papa. "And there ain't a soul who's seen your shadow that'll attest contrary."

"Surely not I," said Luther.

"Nor I," I said.

"Nor I," said Phoebe.

"You are somebody," said Mama, "who is on her way uploft, because we're all as tired as you are. And if I were Master Peacham's mother, I'm sure I'd send him off, too."

"True," said Luther, extending his arms to my sister. "So how about the favor of a good-night hug for a poor and lonely traveler who left his true love in the far-off town of Concord, and who's heart beats a lowly tune."

Never before had I give much thinking on seeing my sister's arms around a fellow's neck. But there they were, hugging Luther Peacham as though they'd growed up in the same pen.

"I just know," she said to Luther's ear.

"*What* do you know?" he said.

"I know you'll be our friend," said Phoebe.

"Oh, if only I had no sweetheart back in Massachusetts. You would be my sweetheart, Miss Booker. Yes, Mistress Phoebe Booker of Verdmont, you would be my love forever more, and for you I would scribble poetry, and in the moonlight steal softly to sing beneath your window."

"My," said Mama, "you'll turn her head."

"Not I, mum. A soaked and sorry suitor I'd make. But to tell you all true, I am genuine glad that Fort Ticonderoga is so nearby. We can say hello often. Able, I suppose you are past your school days."

"Way past," I said.

"You'd never know it," said Papa.

"I don't guess I learned too much," I said.

"He'll make a farmer, though. I'll work the learning into him," said Papa.

"Like salt into a hide," I said.

My body still ached with today's labor, but the coming of Luther was somehow a resting tonic; for me, and for us all. It weren't every night that a body stopped by who was fresh out of Boston and all its news. I felt like things were ajump all around me and I'd miss it all. At least I'd joined the Boys. But I sure did hope there weren't no owl hoot tonight, because I'd be sore tempted to tell Luke Shelby to go along without me. Then I'd miss all the action for sure, and have all the other Green Mounties down my neck besides. Politics sure was getting to be a weary business.

"Well," said Luther to me, "if it will lighten your load of learning, let me say that I have more to learn as a new teacher than any of my pupils do as scholars before my bench."

"Fairly said," said my father. He clapped Luther's shoulder.

"You'll do fine, Luther," I said. "Old Jack Pippit never made such a clean confession. He always thought that he knew it all and had invented most of it hisself."

"I hope to do well," said Luther. "Never have I been a teacher before. The youngsters will probably get me primed up on politics, and I'll rant all day on public affairs instead of teaching them their sums."

"You'll be the toast of Ti," said Mama. "And you won't need to do sums. Every soul over yonder will want to hear the goings on in Boston."

"We hear so much rumor each day in Boston, it becomes a worthless wind. Like the one I heard before I left."

"Which was what?" I said.

"It was about three British generals on route to America."

"Who?" asked Papa.

"Sir, I heard their names were Henry Clinton, William Howe and John Burgoyne. And generals all."

"Gage makes four," I said. "England wouldn't be sending so many of their bigwig Regulars unless they was up to a war."

"Do you agree with Able, sir?"

"I ain't no military expert," said Papa. "Not like my son. I'm just a farmer up here in the worthless wilds of Verdmont. Politics are not made or decided in hills."

"Blessing for that," said Mama who was brushing Phoebe's hair, getting her ready for bed.

"Master Peacham," said Papa, "what think you on the Boston talk? Will they meet the new generals with generals of their own?"

"Not that I condone it, sir, but I can only answer your question so. Earlier the English sent us their tea. And you know where that tea is now? At the bottom of Boston Harbor. The citizens of Massachusetts do not stand alone. There's the Continental Congress now, men from all the colonies united to stick by one another if trouble comes."

"Has it come?" Papa asked. He wasn't really asking Luther Peacham, or any of us. It was as though he asked the Almighty.

"Sir, it may. They say that in Lexington, when eighteen of our boys fell, it started then and there, and the world heard that very round of British shot."

"It would be a blessing to all," said Papa, "if the wounds could heal."

"Wounds?" I turned to my father. "Eighteen wounded would be another matter. You can't *heal* eighteen dead Americans."

"Hear that, sir? We have a name now. No longer are we just colonists. And as we don't live in England, we'd be hard put to call ourselves Englishmen. Agree?"

"This is English soil," said Papa. "It's right outside our door. We walk it and we work it. To think this brings me closer to England."

"For a Verdmont man, sir, you do indeed have strong ties to a land that I presume you have never seen."

"Never seen? Master Peacham, I was born in England. And by damn, young sir, I am a Britisher."

Luther's jaw dropped, opening his mouth in surprise. "You, sir? Born in England? But your accent . . ."

"Come here as a small lad. But my folk was killed off and I got took in and raised up by a near family. So I reckon I speak as they do, Verdmont style, like a Cotter."

Was I imagining things, or did Luther Peacham's eyes widen at Papa's say of the Cotter name? Had he already heard of the Cotter family and about how the Regulars at Ti hanged Jake? His face sure said so, like a spur had raked his flank.

"I see," was all he said.

"There's a lot of talk up in Shoreham," said Papa, "against Grenville, that fellow in England who wants to tax us colonists to pay for the French War. Well, I'm willing to pay my fair share of taxes. We all prayed for the Redcoats to come when the Frenchies come down from Canada along with the red Saint Francis. So best we pay the fiddler. And I say to heck with that bunch of blattering bigmouths who go by the name of the Sons of Liberty. A lot of 'em weren't here when the Frenchies come. Cotters was here, and so were us Bookers. And when the French went back north ahead of General Amherst's guns, there wasn't many Bookers left. So I say we pay our taxes to England and keep the Redcoats." Papa had spoke his piece.

"William Pitt would disagree," said Luther, in a respectful tone. "Sir William says that the Crown has placed too big a burden on the colonist and his purse."

"William Pitt said that?" asked Papa.

"Yes, sir. But there are few William Pitts in Parliament these days. Too few. Most of the Lords are concerned with lining their own pockets with the fruits of their mercantile. All you hear from the English businessman in Boston is the Triangle of Trade."

"I've heard that term," said Papa. "What is it?"

"Three legs, sir. Or three voyages. Ships bring black people from Africa to the West Indies islands. Then molasses to New England, and finally rum back to Africa for more black slaves. English ships, aye . . . but no English ports. So the fat fleet owners are of a mind to be certain that the profits, if not the ships, reach home to England."

"Rum," said Mama. "I see little cause for so much of it."

"The opinion is, sister, that a working man can't stand his existence, say in a Boston rope factory, without his daily ration of rum. And a seagoing man, with no rum aboard, cannot abide the loneliness."

"Huh!" Mama snorted. "Well, I've had a measure of work in my time and years with no near neighbors, and I believe I could weather it all without as much as a thimble of rum, thank you just the same."

"Yes, mum."

"So that's what they have become in Parliament," said Papa. "Just a row of rum runners."

"Perhaps so, sir. But word has it that in Virginia, in an assembly called the House of Burgesses, they are equally concerned with commerce and profit. Except for one. His name is Patrick Henry."

"And how stands he before his fellows?" Papa asked.

"The richer ones, sir, call him . . ."

"Yes?"

"A hillbilly."

"Good," said Papa, snuffing out the candle. "I'm pleasured to listen there's a few of us left."

"So be I," said Mama.

From up in the loft, Phoebe said, "So be I."

Chapter 10

Comfort was naked.

We were out in a field of flowers, all yellow as buttercups. But they were blooms that I'd never seen before, all tossing their heads in the breeze. Comfort had no clothes on. Not a stitch, and she was running toward me sort of slow, with her arms stretched out like she was fixing to hug me hard. She was coming and coming, and I felt my face smile because I was so doggone happy. I wanted to giggle all over, and to tickle Comfort all over. She just looked so pretty and pink. I could have eaten her up as quick as a honey muffin. Until she spoke.

"Good morning, Master Peacham," she said in a voice that wasn't hers. It were a real deep voice, just like my father's. She said it again, as I reached for her, and it was Mama's voice,

"Good morrow, Master Peacham."

Opening my eyes, I saw Phoebe opening hers.

"Able," she said, and smiled. Her hand touched my chin and then she said, "Able's got whiskers."

Looking out through my bottle-glass window, I could see that it was still early, but at least the rain had stopped. Raising up the bottle in its slot, I let a breath of the morning come in wet against my eyes. It was like a face wash, until Phoebe sat up to push me away from the window slot so she could take a turn. One thing for sure and certain about Miss Phoebe Booker, she weren't to take no backseat in anyone's buggy. Not old Phoebe. If somebody built the stair to Heaven she'd be early up, Mama always said. She was the first one down out of the loft, and jumped to the dirt. Didn't even wait for me to drop the ladder pole.

Luther Peacham was curled up on the hearthstone, asleep as a run dog. Phoebe shook him until he moved his body a bit and opened up an eye.

Papa was shaving.

"Papa," said Phoebe, "best you lent your razor to Able on account he's got whiskers on his chin that he ought to crop. Luther's got some, too. Wake up, Luther."

Luther Peacham groaned, moving one leg. "What is the hour?" he said.

"Sunup," said Papa. "Time for good folks to chore and rogues to travel." He smiled as he said it so as Luther would know that he was funning, even though he done most of the smile to the pitcher and bowl. As Papa put a dab of apple pomade on his hair, he watched Luther Peacham from the corner of his eye.

Pulling a gold watch from his britches, Luther squinted at the time. "Gosh," he said, "it's not even the hour of six. Do you people arise each and every morn at this bilious time?"

"Sure do," I said.

"Some of us sleep more than others," said Papa, without a look my way. He didn't have to. I got the point of his fork.

"Are we the first hillbilly family that you give the honor of your overnight company?" asked Papa.

"Yes, sir . . . and if these hours are an indication of the hardy life you lead, then I shall remain in the confines of Boston, content with my lot."

"Just what is your lot, Luther?" said Papa.

"I don't believe I am wakeful enough, sir, to catch your meaning. My lot?"

"Well, I don't guess you're a farmer."

"No, sir."

"And you claim to be a schoolmaster on his way to a first position."

"Yes, sir."

"What have you been doing with yourself prior, to take up the many hours of sun and moon?"

"I . . . I attended Harvard, sir."

"Yup," said Papa, "I heard of it. Harvard College."

"It's in Cambridge, sir, near Boston."

"That where you pick up all that lingo about Samuel Adams and John Adams?"

"Some of us were active in politics as students, and oft we'd hear a visitor who'd come to speak, to address the student body."

"Whose body?" said Phoebe. "Did somebody die?"

"No one died, Phoebe," said Luther. "Honestly, I promise you that no one died."

"Harvard must be *some* place," I said.

Luther smiled. "Indeed. Plenty of tradition and all that, close to the tried and true, yet we cock an eye for the new and true. Fresh ideas. We claim that the Sons of Liberty were founded at Harvard College."

"Is that so?" said Papa. "Well, my young friend, we got a few of them Sons of Liberty north of here, in Shoreham and Bridport, and I believe I just might call a few of them varmits *Sons*."

"Noah," said Mama, "come eat your breakfast."

"Did someone say breakfast?" asked Luther. He got up as though a part of him was still asleep on the hearthstone, and rubbed his hip.

"For them that works his keep," said Papa.

"Of course, sir. In fact, it was my plan to offer you people, if you would honor me by the taking, a shilling for the housing of myself and one more of my horse, seeing as you were so kind as to usher us in when we did beg your board. Would you accept?" Luther reached a hand into his pocket.

"Let's eat," I said. We didn't need Boston money.

"You, too," Papa looked at Luther Peacham. "Nobody goes hungry under a Booker roof, so keep your shilling in your britch, young sir. The pay at Fort Ti for a schoolmaster will be thin enough, so I advise you don't miss a meal. You can later lend a chore hand."

"Most kind of you, sir."

Luther Peacham sat himself down in Phoebe's chair. Now if I'd a did that, my sister would of raised up Cain, but no. All she done was smile real sweet and take *my* seat.

"This here," said Papa, "is a rare treat. We usual do chores before our first meal. But seeing as we got you for company, I guess Molly here took a notion to rock the regimen."

"That's something like a cradle," said Phoebe.

"There's corn bread," said Mama, as she looked at Phoebe and shook her head laughing.

"You can have it with syrup or butter," I said. "Butter's my choice."

"Syrup's mine," said Papa's straight face.

"I would guess," said Luther, looking back and fro from my father to me. "When we were children, we used to play a game like that."

"With corn bread?" said Phoebe. "Let's play."

"No, Phoebe, not with corn bread. But all the youngsters would be asked, in private and in a whisper, which he liked the better, sugar or salt. Those who favored sugar went on one team and those for salt on the other."

"Then what?"

"Then they brought out a rope for a tug-o-war."

Both my mother and father stopped eating as Luther said "war." A breath later, they went on munching but the joyment in our talk had

98

been chewed out. The corn bread tasted dry in my mouth, even with butter. Luther tried to break the quiet,

"This is *maple* syrup, isn't it. And surely good."

"Did you get syrup on your bread at Harvard?" I said.

"Yes, but never this sweet. On Sundays we were allowed honey on our biscuits. Say, how much of the water, or whatever it is that you tap from a maple tree, does it take to make syrup?"

"Forty to one," said Papa. "Sometimes less."

"That means that you have to . . ."

"Boil near to forty gallon of sap to realize a gallon of syrup," I said between two cheeks of corn cake.

"Able talked with his mouth full," said Phoebe.

"You took my seat," I said.

But there weren't any more joy to our exchanges. I guess that we all were thinking about a war. And it wasn't like a war that makes you cut down on just Frenchies or Dutchies or Indians. A war with England would make us kill English or they'd kill us, and it sure seemed wrong to me. It was like the Cotters drawing a sight on the Shelbys, or the Bookers. Or even on the Peachams. And it be all wrong. There weren't a man at that breakfast table, be he Whig or Tory or just plain English or be he of Verdmont or of Boston, that didn't know how sorry a scene it had a mind to be.

I knew that Able Booker's opinion didn't account for squat. But then I recalled the faces of some of the Regulars that day at Fort Ti, faces of British Redcoats whose job it was to hang a young man by name of Jacob Cotter. They hated the work. Hated the sorry justice it was, knowing it weren't proper for a prank. No matter how many words they cooked up, like *sedition,* no word would ever excuse it in the sight of God.

Later, we were out in the barn. Except for Phoebe and Mama who were busy inside carving a design into the earth on our floor. Just as a lark, I asked Luther if he'd pleasure to milk Esther, claiming that my hand was a mite poorly. We'd put both Esther and Festus in the barn because of yesterday's downpour of rain, so she was right handy.

Willing as could be, Luther sat hisself down on the milk stool, and I showed him how to wipe off the udder. Then we put the milk pail under her bag. Luther took a good grip with a tit in each hand and give a yank. Esther turned her head around to see for herself. You never saw such an expression of dismay on a cow's face. If only she'd been able to talk, she sure would have asked Luther Peacham what in the name of nothing he thought he was doing.

Papa saw the look on Esther's face and the two of us near liked to

99

split from the mirth of it. And then Luther got to choke and chortle at the whole business and fell off the milk stool and onto the barn floor. He come to rest with the seat of his britches in something that sure weren't milk.

"I guess I'm not a successful farmer," said Luther, as he stood up to brush off his pants. Some of manure stuck to his hand and it sure soured his face. Had I not hanged on to Esther I would of fall over with the fun of it. Hard to say for certain, but I could of swore that even Festus was chuckling.

"Luther," said Papa, "if'n I ever am a mind to take on a hired hand, you sure would be an attraction. Is that the way the Sons of Liberty do their milking?"

"Sir," said Luther, "I believe I have discovered where the error lies. You forgot to tell me that Esther was a Tory."

Papa hardly ever laughs out loud. To be sure, he will crack open a smile on occasion; but Luther's comment on Esther's political persuasion really widened his face. He threw back his head and let out a whoop that you'd swear had been hiding inside his heart. And then wiped his eyes to boot; he had to use one sleeve and then the other to do it.

"Master Peacham," said Papa when he could finally talk, "I can hardly patient to hear how you instruct the good folk at Fort Ti in the finer arts of milking."

"Sir, if I thought that was my calling, I'd turn my horse south and head back to Boston."

"Well," said Papa who was now sober, "you will have to head south for a way. South to Skenesboro, over the bay on the float bridge which will cost you a penny for yourself and one for your nag. Then bear north, keep the lake on your right and you'll bust Fort Ti wide open. But go a bit upstream to wade the crick."

"A crick, sir?"

"Yes, the overflow from Lake George that carries down to below the south wall of Fort Ti. Just ask anyone you see. They'll point out the crossing. But don't attempt too low a cross. Crick bed's tricky and you'll flounder your horse."

I finished milking Esther while Luther took a manure fork to tidy up the pens. He didn't work too well, but yet he didn't shirk and Papa took note of it all. Then he asked Luther to turn out both Festus and Esther into the meadow. That's when I give a wink to Papa and said;

"Esther, we're sorry we let a Boston man milk you. It just were a dusty trick, and we beg your forgiveness. Are we friends? Can we shake on it?"

I knelt down and sure enough, up come Esther's right front hoof and we shook hands. I got a look at Luther's face and he couldn't believe it. It was too much for ribs to take. He was still shaking the disbelief from out his head when we turned out Festus and Esther to the new grass.

The bay horse that Luther rode nickered in his stall, rolling his eyes as if to see what the three of us was up to. He was a proud looking animal, and tall, well over sixteen hands. Wow, I thought as I slid my hand over the smooth hair of his croup, what I wouldn't give (or give up) to own me a horse like this.

"This your horse, Luther?" asked Papa, rubbing the bump betwixt the animal's ears.

"Yes, sir. I was taught to ride as a youth as my father is also a horseman. His name's Pit."

"Your pa or the horse?"

"The horse, sir. It's a sort of jest one could say. You know, Peacham and his Pit. I've owned him since I was fourteen."

"He's pulled lame," said Papa.

"Oh, no!"

Papa pointed to the manner in which Pit was standing. "See? He favors a hoof."

"But he was sound yesterday, and full of spirit."

"He's grieved," said Papa, moving closer.

"Take care, Mister Booker. He dislikes to have anyone touch his rear quarters. Tends to kick."

"Able," said Papa, "pick up one of his front hoofs."

"I thought, sir, you said his soreness was hind."

"It be. But I don't cotton to take a kick in the head for my trouble, and if Able lifts up a hoof . . . that's right . . . I don't guess I have to."

"That's a Verdmont stunt," I said. "No horse will kick when a front hoof is hefted."

Just to make sure, I saw Papa take a high purchase on Pit's tail, pulling all the long whiphair straight up. His free hand stroked the animal's haunch, then dropped down the thigh meat to check the stifle and gaskin.

"Hold his tail," Papa told Luther.

My father knelt down, his hands moving over the hock, fetlock, and pastern of Pit's leg. Up and down, until he heard what he patiented. Pit let out a little neigh, as if to say that's where it hurts, sort of the way a one person would tell another.

"There's a mite of swelling on his pastern. Just a sprain. But you're right about the animal. He's sound."

"Can he be rode, sir? I have to arrive at Fort Ti on this day and in good season. I *must*."

"No, best you don't ride him for a day. But you can walk him."

"Then walk him I shall. Every step."

"This time of year," I said, "it sure is a long way from here to Fort Ti, even though it's only crosslake."

"How far," Luther looked at me, "if I must go south to Skenesboro and then north?"

"Forty mile. Agree, Papa?"

"Close to. A good thirty or more."

"I despise walking," said Luther, "or any exercise for that matter. The thought of leading my poor Pit with his sore quarter for thirty miles, and more if I lose way, is not an appealing idea. May I leave him here with you, Mister Booker? Please. I'll pay his board."

Papa scratched his head.

"Well, as I see it," he said, "ain't much board to be paid, not if he gets turned out to eat meadow grass. He don't take up that much room."

"Thank you, sir. I am truly beholding."

"You really are fond of this here gelding," I said.

"Pit's a good mount."

"I'd be fond of him, too, if he were mine," I said, and without thinking, I set his front hoof down. No sooner than done, Pit lashed out with his rear hoofs. Papa backed away quick, but Luther wasn't so lucky. The flat of a hoof caught him square in the chest and over he went like a tenpin. I thought sure he'd be wounded, but before either Papa or I could reach his side, up he sat, shaking the sense back into his head.

"Can't . . . breathe . . ."

"Got the wind knocked out," said Papa, feeling Luther's chest for a bone break. "He's lucky. The flat of the shoe was what hit. Some of the frog swallowed the shock. Luther Peacham, you are one lucky soul. You hear?"

"Can't . . ."

"You certain to walk thirty mile in your way?" I said.

"Have to."

"It's a far piece to walk."

"I'm . . . not . . . walking."

"Well," I said, "you ain't about to back-it on Festus."

"How do you aim to go?" said Papa. "Fly?"

Luther smiled. But it was just to quilt over the misery he was in. I could tell there was still a helping of hurt in him, and I sure felt sorry about it, seeing as it were all my doing.

"Able," Papa slowly turned to look dark at me, "you best think before you drop a hoof."

"I'm sure sorry, Luther," I said. And I real was.

102

"When his mind is off on worldly matters," said Papa to Luther, "this here son o' mine can't find his arse with both hands."

With a wince on his face, Luther Peacham got up to standing. If'n he was sore on me, I don't guess I'd question why, and it all made me feel like two pence. Not that I was worth that much. My mind took up the thought that when the time come to nightride with the Green Mountain Boys, I'd probable to spill the whole business and bust it all up. I was starting to long that I hadn't joined up, but with Luke in the membership and all, I sure don't cotton to miss the frolic. Or the fighting, provide that we'd have a go at that.

Best I rehearse with my new musket or I'd just might shoot off my own backside. But how would I carry it off earshot to Papa? And then get it hided again uploft? Politics sure got to be a mud hole. Step in with one boot and you sink to your neck.

"Like I said," Papa asked Luther again, "how do you aim to go crosslake?"

"Sir, I shall try to swim."

"*Swim?*" said Papa and me, as if we'd had one mouth 'stead of two. Looking at my father, I could see plain that we both was dumbfound.

"Master Peacham," said Papa, "this is early May. Only a few days back there was ice on that lake, thick to walk on. You'd be froze up by the time you wade out."

"Since childhood, I have always held a loathing for cold water. Father used to swim in the Charles River and bid me do also. Sir, how cold is Lake Champlain?"

"Ice cold," said Papa.

"Are there any boats around?"

"Will be," said Papa, "come warmer weather. But nobody I know would have his boat in the water this early. Even if it was, the boards would still be shrunk from winter and not watertight enough to ferry. You'd sink."

"I see. Then swim I must."

"Luther," I said, "I live up here on the shore of Lake Champlain, and have all my born days. Some of us used to take pride in being the first to plunge in each summer. But not in early May. It'll stop your heart."

"Perhaps. But you chaps didn't have to reach Fort Ti, and that is the difference. For I must, you see. I must."

"You're a fool," said Papa. He didn't say it mean. "You could get a cramp out there and go under. I knew a fellow had that happen. Name of Sutter, and he tried to swim it in June. And what about your duds and gear and all?"

"We shall see," said Luther. "I have an idea, sir."

He picked up his pack, gave Pit a farewell pat and we walked out of the barn and into the morning. "That box," he said, pointing at a small tote box near our woodpile, "may I borrow it, please? Just for an hour."

"What fer?"

"And that long ball of twine that hangs in your shed," he said, "and one more thing. Your blessing, as the Bookers of Verdmont have shown me shelter and I will not forget your goodness and your grace."

Papa extended his hand. "And to you, son. We welcome the company and we wish you call again. Sure you wouldn't want to give a good-by handshake to Esther?"

Luther laughed. Mama and Phoebe come out the house and said good-by, too. Phoebe said she hoped Luther would come every night, and said so with a bear hug. For a moment, I even thought Mama was going to hug him a so-long, but she restrained.

"Come on," I said. "You got the pack and saddle bags, so I'll tote the box. But only to lake's edge. You couldn't drag *me* into that ice water with oxen."

Walking west together to the lake shore, we looked back and Phoebe was still waving. She'd wanted to come, which made Luther color up a bit in the face, seeing as he was soon to strip down to the white and natural. And he did. His body was thin and pale. He sure weren't no farmer. His pack, clothes, and saddle bags went in the box. Then he tied an end of twine about his waist and we shook. His hand was puny, but there was a mysterious strength to it. He wasn't as frail as he looked.

"Able," he said, "best you find a more secret place to hide your musket."

The remark made me feel as naked as he was. How in the name did he know about my gun? He never went up in the barn loft. My mouth opened.

"How . . . ?"

"You Bookers sleep like the logs of your hut," he said, "so last night, after the rain had abated, I took the liberty of a prowl. Please do not be angered with me, Able. We must never quarrel among ourselves. Our bone is with Mother England."

Turning over his arm, he suddenly showed me the scar, made by a knife. His cut was like mine, only fresher. *He'd joined!*

"Who *are* you?" I said.

"Luther Peacham, your servant and friend and comrade in arms."

"Yes, but *what* are you?"

"A spy."

His back was to me now, as he waded into the cold water. No man could have done that, no man or woman or devil could of took the stab of that lake. Looking back once more over his shoulder, he smiled,

"This is so unfair," he said. "You will never know, my friend Able, how I have always so intensely hated heroics."

He said no more.

Diving in, he swam toward Fort Ticonderoga with a determined stroke. To watch, you'd think it'd been the middle of summer. Not a shriek nor a howl did he give off; I don't know how the poor beggar done it. He just did. Farther and farther he swam, out into water as deep blue as ink and little warmer than liquid ice. When he hit the current, I saw the twine grow taut, as though I'd hooked a great sturgeon. I'd seen sturgeon in that lake, monsters longer than a man's body and with a mouth as full of teeth as a wolf trap. Papa described the sturgeon's jaws as a bucksaw with an appetite. I hoped it was too early for them to be up on the surface and hunting for prey. Henry Cotter had once seen a sturgeon attack a wading bear.

I could no longer see Luther's head. He was now just a tiny white splash, moving west, growing smaller and smaller. He was tired. He stroked slower and slower, and once he even quit. I almost give a yank on the twine to see if he'd answer. But there was little sense in breaking it, as it maybe weren't stout enough to haul him back by. And by the time I pulled him in, he'd be real dead. It was so doggone sad that I wanted to weep. But I give a little jerk of the line, which was now no longer tight and firm. It was slack and lifeless. Then I saw it straighten; and in my hand, I felt a jerk of the twine. Luther answered me. Believe, it said. And pray. So I closed my eyes and asked the Almighty to kick Luther Peacham's legs.

He did.

Somebody must have, because there sure was a splash over west. Weak but kicking. The sun was on my back and I was starting to sweat. Good thing he'd come up and out into sunshine to melt his chill. I saw a man run from the wall of the fort, pointing at Luther in the water. It was no soldier, but one of the locals, who stripped off his boots and stockings and britches. Whoever-he-was waded into that icy water until he reached Luther. I saw the man lift him up like a blue corpse and lug him to land. Others came.

They pulled over our box, emptied it, and sent it back to the Verdmont side. I took it home; with each step of the way, I wondered about who Luther Peacham really was.

Chapter 11

Returning from the east bank of Lake Champlain, approaching our house, I saw a stranger.

He and Papa was at a real jaw. But before I got close enough to listen, he rode off south on the road to Skenesboro. His horse was a buckskin, long-legged and proud. I sure did long to own a horse. And then I remembered Pit. He'd be sound in a day or two and would need be exercised. Even as I toted the box, I almost busted out into a gallop.

"Who was that, Papa?"

"Name of Hessitt. He's a Skenesboro man."

"What'd he want?"

"Good news, boy. We got us an order for chain."

"Hot peppers. It's hard money."

"Good as any money crop we got. Better."

"How much chain did he order?"

"Fifty measures."

"Fifty?"

"Yup, and he wants 'em sudden. He's stocking up a store."

"Papa, that's a lot of links. How many do you say? I don't even think I could cipher it all out."

"Best we do, or get cheated."

"Well, a chain is sixty-six foot long, times fifty is . . ."

"And you won't collect a penny of it less you go fire that bed. Don't spare the charcoal."

"I won't."

Our forge was to the north side, under the house, so as not to waste the warmth. It was usual to make chain in the winter as the heat from the die of the forge could sure cozy a cabin. I shook coals from our house hearth down to the forge bed. Soon the forge fire was red and then white. The bed and bellows was ready for Papa, soon as he fetched the aprons.

"I'll warm," he said, nesting his tools close to the heat.

"But it's May," I said.

"No matter. The metals are still cold from winter. Hit with a cold hammer and you'll foul the steel," said Papa, placing his tongs, chisel, and hammer next to the fire as though they was foundlings. I liked the way he handled his tools, as if they was alive and part of him. As though be belonged to them despite he was their master. But at the forge of Noah Booker there were no slaves. Only partners.

"How much rod we got?" he asked.

"Not near enough for fifty chain."

"How much then?"

"Twenty chain," I said.

"Pity that Brother Hessitt didn't bring us more rod. Means that one of us will have to go to Skenesboro to drag it home."

"We just traded for an ox. I don't guess we got enough coin for more rod."

"Then maybe I will ask Hessitt for an advance, or do you think you can front him?"

"I can do it. I'll go this day." I made a false pass at taking off my apron.

"Soft. This day is a work day and you been social enough, betwixt Miss Comfort and your friend Luther Peacham. Best you work an all day, so's you won't forget how."

"Yes, sir."

"What, no argument?"

"No, sir." I pumped the bellows harder.

"Glory be. Work and manners all in the same breath," said Papa. "How come you're so sudden polite?"

I didn't answer. If I was going to court Miss Comfort Starr, maybe I'd sort of practice up a bit close to home and get real handy at manners, like the way Luther Peacham was. Mama said that Luther was as polished as a boot.

"He dented you, eh?" asked Papa.

"Who?"

"Fetch a rod through. You know who. Our young traveler of yester, that noble young Son of Liberty from the learned location of Harvard College."

"Him? He's just another mortal."

"That he is, boy. But he's a smooth talker, that cuss."

Clank! My hammer cut the length of hot iron for the first link of chain. I flipped the rod and made the counter cut. Using tongs, I pulled the rod up for the next length, the weakened end passed through the header. A kick of my foot on the treadle and the tiny length snapped free of the mother rod. While it was still hot, Papa bent the prime loop and married the ends, butt to. I heard the first hiss from the dunk tub, a real good sound of work well done. "I'd like to talk like Luther," I said, "but I don't guess I ever will."

"And you aim to hang all the blame on Jack Pippit 'cause he didn't turn you into another Harvardite between milkings."

"No. It ain't Old Jack's fault. But I sure would cotton to go see Harvard College."

"To study your lessons, or to attend all them politician meetings and hear all that gossip? Keep that rod crawling."

"Both maybe," I said.

"All that's wind don't always turn a mill."

"I don't guess it do."

"Well then?"

"It just seems, now that I'm near to eighteen, that I ought to see more of the world than just a farm and a forge, or the backside of an ox."

"It's a bug."

"A bug?"

"Bites every manjack of us, and makes us jump up out of our tracks and make new ones. New places, new friends, and oft some new enemies. Keep up your cutting, boy."

"Did it ever bite you, that bug?"

"Sure did."

"Were you living with the Cotters?"

"No, not then. I was living right above your head. I rebuilt this place. By the time I was your age, I lived alone, right here. My father bought this land and lies in it, so I didn't aim to render it up."

"But you run off."

"Just once."

"How far'd you get to?"

"Far enough to wed your ma, buy a supper in Skenesboro, and carry her into this cabin. Hammer that iron! You stand there in a trance, boy, and we won't cut no chain."

"Sorry." With a yank, I cut faster, flipped and recut, and headed off the links. Fast as I could, and said narry a sneeze all the while. I'd cut maybe two dozen links and was continued to cut more.

"Easy, son."

"You said to work. Well, I'm looked to it."

"Neither fast nor slow will git more to a finish. Think how lucky we are to have a trade. Some farmers don't. All the money crop they got can wash away, or blow out, or frost to rotten. My pa was a chain-maker, too."

"What was he like, old Israel?"

"Like the wire in your hand, boy. He was a tough Englishman. As a lad, he'd apprenticed for a blacksmith, but then went to a farmer and made chain. Worked the man's forge on shares. He found a farmer with a cold forge and they spat on the bargain. That's how he squirreled up to buy land himself. That was before he got bit by the wander bug."

"How old was he when he wed grandmother?"

"Young, I'd guess."

"How young? My age?"

"Can't say."

"You lived in the town of Cornwall, in England. And then what?"

"My father got wed, and two girls come along. My sisters, Grace and Jenny. Then they had a son who died. And then me. When I was the age of seven, we sold our house and farm. Israel sold most everything we had, booked our passage on that infernal vessel, and here we come. Smack up to Verdmont, to land we bought that we'd never yet set eyes on."

"Must of been a hardship."

"We laughed," said Papa. "Every day, we sought a something or other to chuckle at. Never a sun went down that we didn't pray and sing and laugh. We were that close to tears."

"And work, I bet." As I said it, I hit the hammer extra hard with a solid lick.

"And work," said Papa. "Not just a day's work. Every wakeful moment. My mother and father never were still abed by sunup. Not once. Come sickness or fever, snow or rain their backs were bent to this place. Grace and Jenny were cut from the same cloth. I remember how we sunk the well."

He stopped talking, stopped bending the links of the chain, as though somewhere inside him he was getting bent up, too. Hurt by something brutal, seen only by himself. Seen or felt or remembered. So I let it worry him a spell, as there weren't no words I knew that could ease his curse. But how very much I did want to tell him that I felt his hurt. A man's pain is personal, and there weren't no way I could help him shoulder the burden. Yet someday I'd know a way to tell him that I understood his pain. Better yet, perhaps even soak up some of the sorry, in order to ease his.

"That well of ours," said Papa, "went through rock and shale and mud. Even gas. But by damn, that well got dug. My sisters pulled up the dirt on a rope, hod by hod, until the fingers of my elder sister Grace were wore raw. Jenny's, too. Mother would set a poltice to their hands before they went uploft to sleep."

Again he stopped his talk, but not his work.

"You know, Able . . . this be a silly thing to say aloud, but late at night, just before I fall to sleep with your mother's head rested close to my shoulder, I can sometimes close my eyes and see them. Clear as day, I can see Jenny and Grace as women, all growed up and in their Sunday best. How fine they look, healthy and alive. I just know they are somewhere, in the sky or beyond it, safe in a haven which our mere minds lack the might to vision."

"I surely hope they are, Papa. I honest do."

"Son, I *have* to think so. As thinking other would be an illness in my mind, too sad a thought to permit in a memory. Instead of the way I found them on their last day, I see them fair and free. Sometimes they sing a duet, and I hear Mother singing along as a third voice."

"Like angels."

Papa nodded. "Yes, like three angels. Sounds that be too sweet to come from earthy persons like ourselves. And their song is high and clear, soaring like sunlight, higher and higher, until the dim is reached and the song snuffs out like a candle. I spoke to them once, but they heard me not. Like a talk to stars. Lights of the night, for a morn to shoo away. That was a verse from a poem we recited. I forget the rest."

"You never told me these things before," I said.

He worked, his big arms curling the iron in the tongs as if it was red taffy, yet handling the tools as though they were of lace. His hands never dropped a thing, but set it down the way you'd rest a cup to a saucer.

"No," he said, "never. And only this once, else I will wear you down with having to listen. These are things I never even told Molly, yet she knows, just as I know *you* know. I always wanted to tell my family of my gratefulness, and how blessed I be to glean such understanding of those lost by those I later found."

Doggone, I ached to say words to Papa, but now I don't guess they're in need. Well, if Mama was righteous when she said that work is prayer, then I'd show Papa real proper just how reverent I could be. My mother said that Lord Jesus was a carpenter, and I always did ponder if He had as much blisters as I got. Well, it sure was good to know that Jesus was a working man, like He could come to share our labor and our bread.

"That's the reason be," said Papa, "I try so hard to hold us Bookers together. I know my own son, Able. I know you, boy, and you got bit."

"By the bug?"

"For certain, and it ain't no sin, any more than to get bited by a horsefly. But it can be just as painful. More so. You look at Luther

110

Peacham, then at your own self, and it pricks you to wonder why you aren't off somewheres, doing deeds."

"Like the Tales of King Richard."

"Aye, like him."

"So you think I want to leave you and Mama, to run off with Richard and free the Holy Land from the Turks," I said.

"In a sense. But your Richard is here in our hills, for you and Luke Shelby repeat his name, to make him your god as though you could nearly have no other. As if you'd forsake the God in our Heaven for the soldier god of Onion River."

"I don't know what you mean," I said.

"Hell, you don't."

"I don't." I avoided his look, yet my bones could feel the burn of his eyes.

"Do you believe there's a single lad in this entire Champlain valley that doesn't ache to night ride at the hip of Ethan Allen? Is there? You and young Shelby get so passioned in your whisperings that you might as well scream out your sentiments to all of England."

"This isn't England," I said, like always when I didn't know what else to say for my own politics, and when I wanted to oppose my father's.

"Little these times be as it seems. Do you honestly believe that your young friend, who gives his name as Luther Peacham, is really a school-master?"

"He said so."

"Swallow it if you're a mind to. Not me. For I felt the ears of his horse, and I know what those notches tell, old as they are."

"You mean . . ."

"Aye, lad, I do indeed. The ears of the animal he so fondly calls Pit were cut by a Verdmont owner, and that horse belongs to the Allens."

"To the Allens?"

"My life on it. Aye, and perhaps so! As we have seen how little the Allens respect of Booker life. Or do you forget Simon?"

"The Allens didn't kill Simon. Did they?"

"You tell me, Able Booker."

"If I lied to you, Papa, I'd choke on the words."

"Worse if you choke on a rope."

"You mean *hang?*"

"I do, son."

"Like the way they did Jacob Cotter?"

"Mark his death, and well."

"I do," I said, feeling my hand sweat the hammer.

"See him kick the air when you prepare for sleep."

"Why are you saying all this?" I asked him.

111

"Remember young Cotter, and how he died, for he will not be the last. Lord take the soul of the next, whoever that is fated to be."

"Who?" I asked.

"Your friend Peacham. Or perhaps young Shelby, or any one of a hundred sons of Verdmont farmers who raise a boy to do more than straight out a rope. I pray the next to hang for treason will not be Able Booker. Yes, and I'll pray for the sons of Irish and sons of Scots, the lads whose mothers wait back home in Britain. I'll pray they don't get no letter from a General Gage or a Howe or a Burgoyne to say their boy died in battle, at a place called Ticonderoga. Because some young hothead in Shoreham said let's go crosslake and bait the British. And because some Allen sees another crop of Verdmont boys that will fight for *his* glory and for *his* fee-hold."

"Ethan's a patriot," I said.

"About as much as Festus. Ethan and Ira and all the Allen brothers look to their own interests. I say this, if the Green Mountain Boys ever ask their own good womenfolk to put their minds and their needles together to sew a flag for Ethan's army, then I know what the flag should say."

"What?" I said, lowering my hammer.

"Onion River Land Company, sewed with gold thread to represent the Allen cause."

"I . . . I don't believe that."

"Don't you?"

"No, I sure don't. Every soul in Verdmont knows of Ethan. He's practically made for a hero."

"Yes, and *self* made."

"Well, ain't nothing wrong with believing in yourself."

"Nay, there ain't. So best you believe in Able Booker, because a time is coming."

"What time?"

"A time to be a man. To plow your own land, seed your soil and your woman so that she bears young, and to be your own boss. Now let's make some chain."

"It sure don't sound to me like *you're* so all-fired ready to quit being *my* boss."

"Well, I am."

"I bet."

"High time you quit cocking ear to what this one says or that one says. Time you told the two fools in your life to hoe their own corn."

"Which two fools?"

"Ethan Allen and Noah Booker," he said.

112

I laughed, and missed with the hammer. Papa sure could come out with a real cooker. He saw my smile and added his own.

"You may be a hog-headed Tory," I said, "but you sure ain't no fool."

"I'm sure glad to hear it. Had me worried."

"Well," I said, "if'n it'll make you the happier, you ain't nobody's fool. Nor you didn't raise one."

"I'm pleasured about that, too," he said.

"Maybe it's the times."

"How so?" he asked me.

"Just maybe they's such a passel of ideas buzzing around a person's head, it's hard to decide which gnat to slap first. Which idea to believe."

"Sound enough said. That's why I want you not to contagion *my* views any more than Ethan's, or Luke's, or Luther's. For the long haul, only the will of Able Booker will serve your purpose. You cutting?"

"I'll cut."

"We make more talk than chain," he said.

"I wonder if Mama and Phoebe talk the way we do. I sort of hope they do."

"How come?"

"I just do."

"You pleasure in the sport of it."

"Yes, I certain do. Don't you?"

Papa nodded. "Even when I'm losing."

We made chain. Link into link, it built up, a snow-drift of silver and gray on the floor of our forge; yet still I'd cut another length. And my father would hook and marry until the tilt of the balance told us that we had sixty-six feet. Rod after rod was fed into our forge, until no raw iron was left to us. Our bodies were shiny with sweat, and I tasted naught in my mouth but the cutting flavor of my own salt. All day we worked, never allowing the forge to go gray on us. Mama come often to feed in more charcoal; and Phoebe, to bring us a noontime meal.

We ate at our work.

Every so often, we would exchange our duties. Papa would cut the raw stock and head it, while I would marry the links, one into the next. It was like a row of Booker men, I was thinking. Israel and Noah and Able and whoever my son would be, and his son to follow. And then the Booker womenfolk, from Mary to Molly to Phoebe. But one day my sister would be wed, to cast away her name and take another. In a way that I longed for Comfort Starr to be Comfort Starr Booker, my wife.

We worked on that day in May as though we would never have another day on which to bend our backs, or wet our shirts. After each

113

cut, my arm would cry out that it could no longer lift the hammer for another blow. Yet up the hammer came; as though my grandfather, Israel Booker, had cursed it with a spell of its own. My father and I made chain until our eyes were blind with the smoke and the gas from our forge, and until Phoebe and Molly Booker came below to us and begged us to wash for supper.

Mother milked Esther.

Pulling as a team, Mama and Phoebe had done all the evening chores. The chickens were in their coop, the pig fed; and they had even bruised a few oats for Pit. The extra oats (unheard of in summer) was a reward, according to Phoebe, because the bay horse would be so lonely for Luther. And to health his leg.

"Are you lonely for Luther, too?" I asked Phoebe.

"Yes," she said. "I believe we all be."

"I believe so, too," said Mama.

Trying to hold my tired head above my supper plate, I could see in my mind the red gash on the thin white arm of Luther Peacham, a most unlikely Green Mountain Boy. But by damn, I thought, there sure was stuff in him. I could see his naked body as he staggered wet to the far shore, being wrapped and rubbed raw in the farmer's coat. Luther Peacham has bowels, I think. Perhaps more than I. Just at that moment, Papa said,

"He really did swim it?"

"Aye," I said, "he did so."

"Was it cold, Able?" asked my sister.

"Cold as ice, and wetter still; and if my eyes hadn't seen it both to once, I'd be a doubting Thomas to the whole event."

"I wonder when he'll come for Pit," said Phoebe.

"Soon," said Papa, "if I know the true owner of that beast."

My father could bounce a rifle ball off a rock and put out an Indian's eye. He was talking to me only, inside and secret, but not to let on to the others about his suspectings that Pit was an Allen horse.

On my way uploft to bed, I wondered if an owl would hoot this night. No, I prayed. Not tonight for a hundred reasons, a hundred aches and blisters. It was hot uploft. The forge heat had sifted up through the cabin and rested under our roof, lingering like the smell in a sick room. The black stink of iron was still strong on my hands, and I burned all over. In my ears the forge still roared, even though it had long been banked. Phoebe said a word or two to me, in her sleep, but I was too hot to give her back an answer.

My body was a cinder.

114

Chapter 12

"Wake up, Able."

I didn't cotton to wake up. So all I did was just roll over on my other hip, pulling the quilt up over my head. But a sudden hand give it a yank, so I opened my eyes a crack, to defend my person from the punch I knew would come from the small but forceful fist of Phoebe Booker. It come!

"Able Booker, best you wake yourself up, Mama says, or there'll be no hotcakes for stayabeds."

"Go away, Phoebe."

"Wait'll you hear."

"Hear what?"

"I'm going to Skenesboro."

"You?"

"Papa said."

"I don't believe it." I closed my eyes.

"Papa said we're *all* to go. Our whole family, Mama and me and everybody."

"It's a far piece, Skenesboro. Did Papa say how we was to git down there and back? Festus can't cart us yet. He ain't full growed." All this I said with my eyes tight up.

Trying to move enough to sit up, the stiffness hit me like a load of lumber. My arms and shoulders were cut from wood. There just weren't no give in any of my muscles. It sure sounded good, a trip to Skenesboro in place of another tour at the forge; that is, if my bones would git me as far as the cabin floor. Papa always said that an honest day's work would do me in, and by golly it near did. Luke said his pa told him the same. Pulling on my britches was a slow process, but I could see

115

Mama's good breakfast wouldn't fix to wait. Molly Booker set an impatient table, as Papa put it, so best I hasten.

"Should of named that boy Molasses," said Papa, taking note of how dreadful slow I was moving. I sure was sore boned. Even my hair hurt.

"Hurry, Able," said Phoebe, "or we'll miss Skenesboro."

"No we won't," I said, coming down the ladder a notch at a time, "unless they moved it."

Papa looked at me, and said it! He couldn't resist, so out he come with it like he'd been ordered to by the Almighty,

"Always knew an honest day's work would kill that son of mine."

"If you ask me," said Mama, "it neared to wipe out the pair of you. Should of seen your pa rising up, groaning like a ghost, and looking like the dregs of the demon. We always knew that an honest day's work is *every* day to a woman. We don't have to talk politics, do we, Phoebe?"

"We sure don't," said Phoebe with a nod.

Papa never answered a word. He just went out the door, probable to go to the barn where Esther would be waiting. Phoebe went, too. So while he milked, I ate.

"Mama," I said, "them's real good jacks."

"No finer than you deserve," she said. "You and your pa did double yesterday, so I put an extra egg in the batter to lift 'em light. Here's the last three."

Mama's arm was around my neck as she served my plate, and along with an extra egg, I got an extra hug. "My sweet Able," she said, giving the top of my head a quick kiss.

I must of looked surprised, but I didn't stop chewing. Mama sure could fry up jacks, kind enough for a king. And I sure was beholding to her for a breakfast this good, but it was the hug that threw me. My face must of said what I was thinking. It was rare that Mama ever sat down to rest, but suddenly she done just that.

"Last night," she said, "I dreamed I was somebody else."

"Who?"

"In the dream I was Emma Cotter."

"Jake's ma."

"Yes. Jacob Cotter's mother. And I stood in a doorway, watching and waiting for my menfolk to come home. I was all alone."

"That's a funny dream, Mama."

"Well, I wasn't laughing. Not one mite. I kept wiping my hands on my apron, that I recall, and wanting to bring the apron up to dry my eyes. But I couldn't lift that apron. Like it was lead. My eyes was all a blur of tears, and I couldn't make out who was coming uproad, right toward the door."

"Who was it?"

116

"A man and a boy, bringing home a dead son that was throwed over the back of a young ox. The dead boy was wrapped in fresh muslin, all tidy. And when they pulled back the flap for me to see the face . . . it was you, Able."

"No, Mama. I'm right here, alive and kicking."

"It made me lie awake for a spell," she said, "and wonder about how Emma Cotter felt, only a few days back. One day you have a boy, and then the next day he's dead and gone. Cold and still, and belly down over the spine of an ox, no more than a sack of sorghum."

"Why you telling me this, Mama?"

"Just because." Her voice that was usual strong suddenly went puny.

"Are you weeping?"

"Trouble is, I don't know whether it's for Emma or for myself. Or for you."

"You don't have to weep for me."

"It could of been you, boy. For real."

"No, it couldn't of."

"Could of been Henry Cotter and Jake coming to our door with my dead son they packed home to bury. That was a dream. Curse my soul if I don't get to Emma's to shed a measure of kindess. And even cry with her a bit, if it'll relieve her some."

"Women cry too much," I said. But the moment the words come out, I wanted to touch Mama's hand. So I did.

"And men fight too much. Argue too much. Something's happening betwixt you and Noah."

"No, nothing's . . ."

"Don't deny it, son. Even if you do, I feel it. Phoebe feels it to, on account she asked me about it, like it's a plague in the air. It's come to haunt this house."

"That's not true," I said, knowing full it was.

"I say it is. Truth, every word, and I feel it all the way inside of me, clear to the bone. A woman can be haunted like a house, and maybe my mind is leaving me." She smiled a real soft smile.

"Not you, Mama."

"I'm lonely," she said.

"Why?"

"Even with Phoebe here, and Lord knows she's a fine daughter. But the day you and Noah left to go crosslake to trade for the ox, it was like some great hand fetched me up and dumped me out like a bucket. Like I was empty. I cut my finger on a pare knife, then burned a knuckle on the oven and dropped a good dish. Busted to bits."

"We're home," I said. "All safe as sanctity."

"Promise not to chide me, but I'm afraid."

117

"Afraid?"

"I don't even want to go to Skenesboro. Maybe I'll let the three of you go, or just you and your pa."

"Daft talk, Mama."

"Aye, daft enough to worry even me."

"We'll have a time in Skenesboro. There just ain't no holding that place down. No, sir. I can't wait to go. What made Papa decide of a sudden?"

"Same reason I dream," she said.

"I don't understand."

"Your father wants to hold to his family. Keep us all together. Not so close as to choke a growing lad, and cut off his air, but to hold us near and dear."

"He will. Ain't nobody leaving home."

"Nobody but you," she said.

"I ain't going to go nowheres, except to Skenesboro."

"That's this day. What about the next, and the one that comes after? What about when they bring you home face down? I can see it in mind's eye. See it all, as if I could look through Emma Cotter's heart."

"You ain't Emma Cotter. You be *my* ma."

"Maybe she held her tongue. Said nothing when *her* son snuck out in the dark of the moon. Well, I'm not holding mine, Able Booker."

"You know. You *heard* me."

"Aye." Her hand that was red and shiny from scrubbing went up over her mouth. Her head nodded little nods.

"Only once, Mama."

"Where'd you go?"

"Just out for a coon hunt with Luke."

"You ain't no liar, Able."

"Well, I suppose I am. Can't a fellow sneak out once a year to go court his gal?"

"You walk to Starr's?"

"Eight mile up and eight mile home." I smiled.

"Hard to believe," said Mama.

"Well, she sure is worth a trek to see."

"Comfort, you mean?"

"Nobody else. I just had to go see her. Papa knows I went. I got his blessing, and I certain hope I got yours."

"Fine girls, every one. Thank the goodness they all don't inherit their mother's voice. But that's harsh said. Widow Starr's a good woman and their place is homey. Cared for."

"Please don't talk about this with Papa and Phoebe."

"Why not? It's good news, a courting."

118

"Yes, but they'll like to twit me on it until heck won't have it. You know."

"I know. Some matters hold personal."

"You can't get more personal than the way I feel about Mary Comfort Starr."

"She feel the same?"

"I believe she does. It's . . . well, it's sort of like the Songs of Solomon."

"Religious, you mean?" Mama laughed, and the sparkle come back to her eyes.

"Not exact."

"No," said Mama, "not exact. Not at all. I so dearly recall," she looked around the cabin as if she never seed the place before, "the night Noah Booker brought me here. I was eighteen, just wed, and so frightened my teeth was a chatter."

"But you loved being his wife, I bet."

"Sure did, and sure do. He's a good man, your father. And the things he holds dear ain't to be trod on by the foot of nobody. Not you, and not me. He's a rock of a man."

"He is that," I said.

"It would wound him more than a bit, if you was to . . . defy King's law."

"I surely don't intend doing that," I said.

"Boys do these days, so I hear. Must be the darkness brings out the mean in a male. Like a hungry wolf. Some of those outlaws ride at night, and cover their faces when they do their deeds."

"What about it?" I asked her.

"Men who mask their faces, by night or by cloth, are shamed of what they do to people. They can't plight their position in light of day, in the open. Not those men. It would hurt, son, if you become a man who hides his face because of your doings. Hurt your pa, and me. Mostly hurt you."

Just then, Phoebe and Papa come through the door, making both Mama and me jump up from the table.

"Horse is ready," said Papa.

"I get to ride first," said Phoebe, "with Mama."

"Fair enough," I said.

We all slicked up a bit, and hit the road to Skenesboro before the sun did. Heading due south. What a day it would be. Papa and I walked in the lead. My father carried his musket. Mama and Phoebe sat on Pit's big back, and rode along behind us as proud as pie, Phoebe in front.

"What was you and your mother so busy about?" asked Papa.

"She was upset."

"Over what?"

"Me, I reckon."

"You'd upset an ore wagon."

"Well, not exactly *me*. It was more over Jake."

"Your ma's fond of Emma Cotter."

"I know."

"She don't want you to be another Jake Cotter, brought home on the back of some animal, or in a cart with a blanket over your face or with holes in your shirt."

"Holes?"

"Bullet holes. We Verdmont men ain't the only ones who can point a musket. Best gun shot I ever knowed was an Englishman."

"What was his name?"

"If I was to say"—Papa smiled—"the rabbits would jump to their holes."

"I bet."

"Name was Tidwill."

"I never heard of him," I said.

"Reckon he's heard of you, though, seeing as you be such a night-hawk, so full of daring do."

I held my breath and let it out real slow, thinking for sure he'd found the musket I'd hid up in our hayloft. But he didn't mention the gun.

"Was he a farmer like us?" I asked.

"No, he was a British officer. He taught marksmanship to the Regulars over at Fort Ti. His name was Lieutenant Charles Tidwill, as I recall, and he sure could shoot sharp. Matter of fact, he showed me up in a match one time, over here on the Verdmont side. I asked him what his secret was."

"What'd he say?" I asked.

"Trigger squeeze."

"Any fool knows that. Can't discharge a musket without pulling the trigger, once you cock the hammer full back."

"He don't mean that," said Papa.

"He don't?"

"Nah. What he meant was that most chaps give the trigger a yank. Quick like."

"And it ruins your aim."

"Right, according to Tidwill. He said what worked for him was to hold the sight bead smack on the target, and ease back the trig so dang slow that the report of the discharge'll come like a shock."

"And he was a crack shot?"

"Best around. He sure cut a spate of bull's-eyes. Never seed a Yorker or Verdmonter who could outshoot the man, soldier or civilian."

"How come you're tellin' me all this?"

"No reason," said Papa.

"Just making conversation?"

"That be all. And probably ain't even making sense."

"You always make sense," I said.

"And you say that like what you been up to lately don't."

"Maybe I'm ready to leave home. You know, to sort of go it on my own hook."

"It's that bug."

"Trouble is, I don't know where to go. Or what to go at."

"Could be a problem. Baby birds don't know either. All they know is they got a notion to get free of that nest, so out they tumble. Some fly and some fall."

"You want me to go?"

"Aye, when your time cometh."

"You sound like the Bible."

"A man could do worse."

"Will we go to vespers in Skenesboro?"

"Plan to," said Papa.

"How long will it last?"

Papa looked at me as we walked. "Why? You made other plans? I'd be right sorry to have you be absent at some political meeting."

"What made you say that?" I asked him.

"Yesterday," he said.

"What about yesterday?"

"Molly said that your friend Luke Shelby rode by our house more than once, looking for you."

"How come Mama didn't tell him we were down in the forge to make chain?"

"Probably 'cause he never asked."

"That's funny."

"I don't guess," said Papa, "that what Luke had to say was intended for me to listen at. Do you?"

"I couldn't say."

"Guess old Luke couldn't either," Papa smiled, and shifted his gun to a fresh shoulder. The hickory stock rode behind him, as his hand held the barrel.

"It was probably about a coon hunt," I said.

"That's what I thought, too." Papa looked me a squint.

"Sure is fun, a coon hunt."

"Certain is," said Papa. "Small wonder there's such a mess of coon hunting going on these days. I should say these *nights*. Didn't know they was so much coon in Verdmont."

121

"Better than coon," I said, "I certain would like to go court Comfort Starr."

"Nobody to stop ya."

"I surely would."

"Well, it only be eight miles to her place. You could a gone last evening, seein' as you got all that energy."

"Papa, after a day at that furnace, I don't guess I could of paid a call on Comfort Starr if she lived out behind our own cowshed."

"Huh. You don't sound too much like an ardent swain."

"What's an ardent swain? It don't have to do with Comfort's sister, Ardent, does it?"

"No, sir. I'd say an ardent swain was a lad who'd swim a cold lake, or leg it up a steep climb, or wade in snow up to his whiskers . . . just to be by the side of his beloved."

"You got to do all that to be an ardent swain?"

"At least," said Papa.

"All that after a forge day?"

"After a forge day, and with another to follow."

"Sixteen miles is a lot of weary steps."

"Not for Pit," said Papa.

Pit! I don't have the brains of an old muley cow, I was thinking. Looking over my shoulder, I saw Luther Peacham's bay gelding carrying Mama and Phoebe and stepping along as pleased as punch.

"You think Pit's sound now," I said.

"We wouldn't be takin' that nag to Skenesboro if'n I thunk otherwise."

"Then some night soon I can go pay a call on Comfort, on horseback."

Papa nodded. "But he ain't to be run all the way. Today we're only to walk him. The swelling in the pastern's all gone down and he don't no longer favor a foot. He's sound. The walk this day'll nurse him good, but you ain't to strain him."

"I won't," I said.

"I don't guess you can wait two days, but *she* probable can. Pretty gal like that gits a passel of callers." The way Papa spoke out, I figured he was trying to bait me a bit. "But pay that no mind," he said. "They's always her sisters."

I only wanted Comfort, I said, but just to my own self. Oh, how I do hanker after Miss Comfort Starr. Papa must have seen the misery writ across my face.

"Love," he said, "it's a bit like lumbago, on account it can sort of hurt all over."

"And feel good all over," I said.

122

"Hell and Heaven."

"Was it that way when you were courting Mama?"

"Worse."

"How far away did she live?"

"Fourteen mile."

"And how often could you go pay call?"

"Three time," he said.

"Three time in a week? Or a month?"

"Just three time and that be all. Three visits in two years. And on the third I asked for her hand. Had to face her father."

"What was he like?"

"George Saxbe was his name. A big man, and Molly was his only daughter. Apple of his eye. It was like to snatch away a she-bear's cub."

"What'd he do?"

"First thing, he told me (Papa almost laughed) was to stop scratching myself. Asked me if I had lice."

"Did you?"

"Not more'n a couple dozen."

"What were you scratchin' at, your backside?"

"No, just my head."

"Then what?"

"Before I could sum up the louse bites and give old George a counting, he'd held my head under the water spigot and pumped away for glory be."

"Was it summer?"

"Not quite. It was end of February."

"Did it stop you scratching?"

"Ain't easy to scratch when you're froze to death. I guess the lice thought I was dead. Or drown. At least they moved on to a warmer host, and I ain't seen 'em since."

"What did Mama have to say about the animal life in your hair? Her being so doggone keen on soap and water."

"Well," said Papa, "when your beau lives fourteen miles away and comes calling once a year, I suspect Molly would of took me whether I had lice in my hair or pigs between my toes."

Walking along to Papa's hip, I got to ponder if Comfort Starr would latch on to me the same way. Maybe I already did smell not too distant from a pigsty. As to lice, I reckon most everybody's got a few of them to contend with. Except for old Phoebe. Never did see a louse on her. I guess she kept 'em at bay by being so ornery. A louse ever up and bite her and she'd probable to bite it back, just to git even. Well, if Phoebe could keep clean, so could I. Maybe if I court Miss Comfort, I'll swipe a lick or two of Papa's pomade to plaster my hair with. Guess anyone

123

would be preference to smell an apple instead of a pig. Or a cootie. I was wondering if a louse could smell another louse. Now there's an important question. So doggone dull that Phoebe wouldn't even ask it, though it sure sounded like her type of asking. She'd even asked me once if there was anything in a hole. Not if it's empty, I told her. But before you dig it, the hole's full up with dirt. Less than an hour later she was in the meadow, whacking away with Papa's spade, trying to dig a hole to see what was in it. I thought Mama would split.

"Noah," said Mama, from up on Pit's back along with Phoebe, "why don't you or Able ride for a spell. I'm partial to walk a ways."

"Me, too," said Phoebe.

"Rather walk," said Papa. "You want to ride, Able?"

"I don't guess I do. Let Phoebe stay up."

Mama slid off easy, as Pit was without a saddle, and adjusted her skirts, to shake out a wrinkle here and there. Phoebe was alone on Pit, looking smaller than I'd ever see. And prettier. I took notice of the new yellow frock that she'd made for herself, with some help from Mama. My sister was growing up. Soon we'd have a few boys turning up at our place, come evening, just to hold hands and sweet talk. Funny, but I just couldn't picture Phoebe in the company of an ardent swain. She'd probably git to a giggle, and then the poor suitor would have to limp along home. But I bet more would come than stay away. Already my sister was turned out to be a good-looker. That is, if she'd sit still long enough to get seen.

"Whee! Look at me," Phoebe was yelling.

"Easy, girl, or you'll spook your mount."

"Can I make him gallop, Papa?"

Turning around, Papa got a grip on the bridle so Pit wouldn't take to run off, just to test either his leg or his rider.

"Well," said Papa, "you easy *could* make him gallop. The worry is, could you make him stop? Horse as sleek as this one, pent up for a day or so, once he's out the barn he might get a notion to run from here to breakfast."

"Are we to Skenesboro yet?" asked Phoebe.

"No," said Mama, "we're not there yet. The town isn't even in sight."

"I can't wait," said Phoebe. "I can't wait to see it."

"It's some place," said Papa.

"Do they know we're coming, Papa?" asked Phoebe. "Do they?"

"Well," said my father, "I got me a hunch that by time to leave, they'll all know you been there."

"I don't think I can hardly wait," said Phoebe.

Papa shook his head. "Me neither."

Chapter 13

"Gee!" said Phoebe.

Her voice carried over the hollow clumps of Pit's hoofs on the wooden boards as we were all walking over the little bridge that lets people enter Skenesboro from the north of town. And it sure was some place.

I saw new stores, businesses that wasn't here on our last trip, which was more'n three year ago. There was a saddle maker, a tannery, blacksmith shop, cobbler, dressmaker and tailor, livery stable, harness maker, general store, dry goods, feed store, wheelwright, a smithy, and a tavern called the Golden Eagle. Its door was open so Phoebe thought she'd look inside; but Mama give her arm a stout yank which rightly quick changed her direction.

The four of us Bookers walked all the way through town, leading Pit, so as we wouldn't miss any of the sights. Papa spotted a fresh-painted sign that said Thomas Hessitt, underneath which there was printed the word "supplies." Papa pointed at the sign to say that this here place would be his first stop.

"Able," he said, "you mind the horse. I suppose," he said to Mama and Phoebe, "you two ladies got better things to do than listen to talk about chain."

"We surely have," said Mama, and took a step toward the corner where we'd see the dry goods. All it looked to me was just a lot of rolls of cloth, but there's no accounting for how people want to squander a morning. I sure weren't about to stand on one foot and then the other while Mama looked through a ream of ribbon.

"You come along with me," Mama said to Phoebe.

"No," said Phoebe, "I want to go to the tavern and hear all the politics."

125

There was a horse trough handy, so I give Pit a long cool drink. My hand went to his throat so's I could feel the water go through his neck, swallow after swallow. Then I tied Pit in a shade spot under a big elm tree, and took myself a quick look to see how they made saddles. There was a smell of fresh leather in the place as fragrant as flowers. You could almost eat the odor.

"Smells good in here," I said to the man who was pulling a thong through a cantle. He looked up.

"Don't know," he smiled. "When ya work in a place like this here, ya don't smell it."

"I don't guess you do."

"Funny thing," he said, "how a tannery can smell so sorrowful, but leather ripe so sweet."

Even though I could of stayed to watch the saddle get mended, I didn't dare to tarry and cause Papa to search me out. So I hotfooted over to the Hessitt store and there he was, still bargaining. The store was chuck up on stuff to look at and smell, so I paid no mind to what they had to jaw about, until I chanced to hear Mister Hessitt say a word.

"Troops," he said.

Then Papa said something in a low voice and I got to wondering what. On a pretend to look a squint at a fox trap, I done a sidestep closer on to where the two men were making their mumble. I heard the word "troops" said again, and "Whig." I knew Samuel Adams in Boston was one of them Whig fellows. It meant a patriot, but Papa said it was another name for rebel, or outlaw. As the talk went on, I fingered the jaws of the trap, to play-act that I was testing the sharp of it . . . and all the while, edging nearer to the conversation to pick up a word or two.

"Outlaws and freebooters," said Thomas Hessitt. "That's all they are. Scum, doing no more now than years back. Only these days their foul play is out of the shadows and into the open, defiling property of a Loyalist and calling it patriotic."

"I'd like to give 'em a dose of salts," said Papa, as he give a pat to his musket.

"They don't dare to make too much mischief, seeing as Philip Skene is of a Tory mind. Lot of us are, but not all."

They sure weren't talking much about chain, either one of them two, like they never heard of the stuff. Like old Hessitt never ordered and the Bookers never sweated out a link of it.

"Band together, I say. Force is all they respect," said Hessitt. "I was born in the town of Fitchburg, south of here and to the east. But I say we're still British."

"Brother Hessitt, so do I. Some of the young punks don't know what it be like in the early time. They don't have an inkling."

"Take care," Hessitt whispered, nodding to me. Yet his remark was for Papa's ear and not mine.

"This here's my son. Able, come shake the true hand of Brother Hessitt."

We shook. "Howdy, sir."

"New word they use up our way. Howdy," said Papa.

"Means no disrespect," I said. "Honest."

"No offense took." Hessitt smiled. "Howdy yourself. See? I keep up with the times."

"Yes, sir," I said. "Good to meet you, sir."

"Polite boy, your son. So many are rude these days. Town's full of galoots. Drifters. Don't know where they come from and they never say. Come and go, them lawless. And not a lick of work in a dozen."

"That's a caution," said Papa. "Well, I can say I got a worker here. Able put in more than a day on the forge yesterday. Burn's still on his face. We'll have your order less than a week."

"Stout lad," said Hessitt. "I can see he's not a rummy-dummy like some around here. Gamblers, that's what they are. Betters, and racers of good horses."

"That a fact?" said Papa. "Be there a race this day?"

"Wouldn't surprise me none. You don't know what all goes on in this town. Best you don't, not when it comes to . . . *scarlet women.*"

"Never see one that color," said Papa.

"This very morn," said Hessitt, "there's a cockfight to be held back of the tavern."

"At what hour?" said Papa.

"Noon." And then Thomas Hessitt lifted his eyebrows. "Don't tell me, Brother Booker, that *you* would entertain attending such an event." He looked over his glasses at the both of us.

"You dassn't think I would escort my wife and young daughter to watch a bloody sport of cocking, do you?" said Papa.

"I should *hope* not," said Hessitt. "Now, back to business."

"One week," said Papa, "if your wagon brings rod. Can't pull chain out a milkweed."

"On the morrow, sir. I'll send my nephew . . . my wife's nephew, to be true about it, as I'd not claim the lazy loaf to be akin to me. And a week hence, I send him again for the whole wagon, the complete order of fifty measures of chain, well married and well made. Good day, Noah Booker."

"Good day, Brother, and we thank you."

As we left the store, I asked Papa if he got some advance money from Mister Hessitt on the chain. "Sure did," Papa pat his pocket. "But that's a secret betwixt Noah Booker and son, and not to be shared with no other."

"You mean . . ."

"Not even your ma or Phoebe."

"Sure. But how come?"

"Son," he said, "how'd you like to leg it over yonder and take in that cockfight, and maybe even put us down a wager or two?"

"Honest?"

"Why not? I ain't seen a good cocking match in ten year."

"Doggone if I ever seen one at all," I said.

"Then what are we standing here for? Molly'll think that we're still to Hessitt's bartering our business. So if that's what she thinks, why we'll just let her keep on thinking, as there ain't a lick o' hurt to it."

"Gosh," I said, as we rounded the corner of the building to duck out of sight, "I don't guess it's much short of noon right now, so I do hope we get to take it all in."

"Aye," said Papa. I took notice that he weren't walking with no modest a stride. Like he couldn't wait to see it for himself, and his powderhorn even danced on his hip.

The noise up ahead told us that something sure as shooting had took place. Hollering, laughing, and some strong talk. Papa pointed at the location as if to say that's where all the excitement is and let's git there. Behind the tavern, the structure we approached was round and high up, near to thrice my height. Up on the top we could see the backs of men sitting hip to hip. Really packed in hog tight. There was a mumble of male voices that growed louder and louder the closer we got to the place. We had to walk to the yonder exposure to find the door.

Inside, it was dark.

We claimed the last two seats, but not side by each. Papa sat behind my back. Men made room for us, but not too much, as it sure was hot in there. And smelly. Smoke was all around, as the pipes were many, and also I saw a long brown object. I pointed it out.

"Cigar," said the man who smoked it. "Want one?"

"Sure do!" I said, and Papa nodded.

Reaching into his shirt pocket, the man pulled out a spare cigar, smiled, and gave it to me. I'd took a puff or two on Luke's pipe, but never did cotton to the habit enough to purchase a pipe of my own. But a cigar! I sure wished Luke was here to see it, as the man passed his own cigar to aid me give a lit to mine. Took a few puffs, but I got the bloody thing to glow. "Thank you, sir," I said. It had a brown taste.

"Sure you can handle it?" he said.

"Easy," I said, choking, the cigar causing me to cry. As the man had a laugh, Papa laughed too.

In front of us there was a ring of sawdust, like a pit, not much bigger than a horse stall. I heard a rooster scream, but couldn't see any of the game birds. That cry sure didn't sound like any of our roosters. A man stood up way down in the ring, holding up a cock for the crowd (of maybe forty men) to see. The man who give me the cigar seemed to know all about cocking.

"See *him?* Boy, that's a Law Gray, name of Lancelot. Tough bird. I seen that big gray before and he shuffles real good."

The owner took off the cock's blindfold.

"There's another," I said. "It's a red."

"Redshackle. I know the handler. Breeds 'em himself. Runs 'em to and fro in a lidded trough until they be too tired to stand. Toughs up the legs. He calls it roughing. Runs them cocks back and forth with a switch, and if'n they stop they get a whack with it."

The second man held up the red for all to see. The gray cock saw him, too, and started up a real kick. The red cock screamed at the gray. I saw some green feathers around the neck of the Redshackle.

"I never see green on a rooster before," I said.

"Egyptian," said the man beside me. "Kings of old Egypt used to breed them cocks. Five thousand year ago. You believe that?"

"No," I said, but smiling so he'd not think me rude.

"It be true."

"Aye," said Papa. "I heard that. Ancient sport, this."

"Best there is," said the man. "Look at the natural spur on that gray. Over two inches."

"Is that what they fight with."

"You fun me, boy?"

"No, sir. I just never seed a cockfight."

"Wait'll you git a look at the battle spurs they lace on them birds. Hey! I got ten on the gray. Ten gray! Who'll fade? You a better, boy?"

"Not usual. Guess I'll just sort of witness a scrap or two, before I wager ten pence."

"Ten pence? Boy, I'm to bet ten *pound.*"

The man laughed, as I don't guess my mouth stayed shut for too long. You could a hid an apple in it.

"Ten pound?" I said, when my breath come back.

"That ain't nothin', lad. Nothin' but Continental money, and if'n the right be known, it probably ain't worth as much as your ten English pennies. Ha!"

All the men laughed a good laugh. I laughed, too. But then I wanted to twist around and ask Papa what he'd be paid in for our chain. If colony paper was so poorly and worthless, it meant we busted our backs all day on that forge for next to naught. Yet I didn't want these men to know that Papa was in town to pick up a bankroll of bills, on account one might try to pick his pocket. Nor did I want 'em to think that Papa got cheated.

Another man said, "Money ain't no good these days, less'n it be English pounds." I marked him for a Tory.

"Aye," said Papa from behind, so I decided right then what his posture be on matters of money.

"Hell you say," said a voice.

"Hell I don't," said Papa. His musket stood straight up between his knees, muzzle up; and his big hands slided down the iron real slow . . . toward the stock end. The trigger end.

"Same goes for York money as New Hampshire," some man said.

"And the same for counterfitters, no matter where from."

Papa always said to take a man's temper, just bring up the subject of money and it'll bubble all the elixir in his blood.

"It pays to be honest," I heard someone mutter.

"But for most folks," his neighbor said, "it don't pay enough." This bit of wit got a belly-burst of a laugh. Everywhere I looked, rough faces enjoyed the ways and manners of mirth. Then some man started a song about the Governor of New Hampshire, and others joined in with their voices. The words of the song started out "To hell, to hell with Benny Wentworth."

Down in the pit, the two handlers were on their knees on opposite sides of the ring. Near one man I saw some stains on the sawdust, which I figured was blood. I couldn't see what was going on, and nobody seemed to pay attention. The handlers were busy putting spurs on their birds.

"Counterfitters," a voice nearby said, "oughta hang. Men who pour light metal git what they deserve."

"Brand 'em, I say. Burn a C on their brow."

"Or cut off the right hand and throw 'em in jail for keeps. Quartering's too good for 'em."

I decided then and there that I sure and certain weren't going to be no counterfitter, and it also made me ponder about all the money that I saw getting counted on all sides of us. How much of it was good? I heard bets being offered and took behind me, for both pounds and shillings. Everyone was at a wager.

"Look there, lad," said the man who'd give me the cigar. "See the gleam of them spurs? Made of steel they be, three inchers. *Now* you'll see a scrap. Who'll fade me ten on the gray?"

"Ten red," said another man.

"Done and done."

"There's a third man down there," I turned around to Papa. "But I don't guess he's got a bird. What's he do?"

"Umpire," said the man on my right. "He don't care which cock bests the other, or least-wise he ain't suppose to. He'll stop the scrap a time or two to give a breather to the birds and a break for the betters. See? He's got his arm up now, and when he brings it down, them two handlers'll turn loose the gamers."

So much was going on, I could hardly think. Swallowing that last gulp of cigar smoke had been a mistake, my stomach knew that for sure. I could taste the wet of that tobacco all the way into my bowels and it sure was sorry. Down in the ring, there was some sort of an argument, and plenty of yelling. Men were pointing at the spurs of the red cock.

"Looky that! That there Redshackle's wearing saw-spurs. See them teeth? Look on the underside of the blade. Unfair! Unfair!"

I looked sharp; and sure enough, there was a jagged edge along the three-inch blade, like a little silver saw. The umpire did not drop his hand, as the gray's handler worked on his bird.

"Changing," said my cigar friend. "Now they're to even up. The gray'll get saws. Lad, you's about to see one Hell of a scrap. You watch that Law Gray shuffle when he drives."

"I sure will," I said.

All the terms were new to me and I got to pondering what a "shuffle" was. The man in front of me was fat and when he leaned back under my nose, I got a healthy whiff of a body that I don't guess had got itself a helping of soap and water since Jesus washed the feet. He sure was gamey. The man next to me didn't seem to notice it much, and I decided that could of been the why that he smoked those dang cigars. So for reasons of self-defense, I took me another deep drag of the weedy thing, and another, until my head went into a spin.

"Fight," yelled the umpire, dropping his arm.

Both cocks screamed at each other, circling, the feathers around their necks all puffed out. Our rooster back home, Thistle, would of been lost for sure in a scrap like this here one promised to be. I never see two meaner-looking creatures in my born days as that red and that gray.

"Sick 'em, Red!" somebody yelled out.

Before I could even blink, both birds charged, flying up about three foot in the air, feet up and the tips of them spurs pointed dead on. Feathers flew. There was lots of screeching and flapping of wings, as the two birds beat at each other. Again they jumped, and I saw the spurs of

131

the gray disappear into red feathers. When the spurs withdraw they was no longer silver, but shiny red with blood.

The cocks locked beaks, rolling over in the sawdust, and the umpire yelled, "Handle!" As each handler reached for a cock, more bets in the seats where we were took place. More wanted to bet on the gray than the red, and odds were offered and accepted. Three, four, five to one. As the umpire's arm raised and fell, both cocks were released to scrap.

"Get'im, Reddy."

"Shuffle'm good, Gray."

"Sick'im, cocky. Spur that Redshackle."

The men made more noise than the roosters and it sure was exciting. I near to swallow my cigar. But I did manage to gulp down some of the brown juice. Cigars sure git soggy.

The red cock's pain must of made him go mad, because he jumped higher than the gray and got on his back. He pecked out an eye, and when the Law Gray got to his feet, he was half blind. His head had to turn to one side to see the Redshackle. And now the red cock's saw-spurs dripped with blood. Everywhere in the ring, the red drops freckled the yellow sawdust.

"Kill! Kill!"

The betters on the Redshackle wanted their bird to press the attack, now that the gray got woozy. The Law Gray stumbled and fell, but regained his feet before the two met spur-against-spur in the air. The spurs sawed upon each other and made a gritty sound of metal on metal. A mean sound. Again the red drove both spurs into the gray, but as they went down in a fly of feathers and blood, I could see the gray had also scored. The Law Gray still looked sidewise with his one good eye. Their beaks locked again, their bodies too close to spur.

The umpire yelled, "Handle!"

Before the handlers could reach for the cocks, the Redshackle was on his feet ready for another strike, but the gray cock laid on his side, coughing like he was to choke. The Law Gray's handler picked up the bird, shook him, and patted his breast several pats. He still coughed out drops of blood.

"Draw him," the cigar man said. "Draw him!"

The handler placed his mouth over the bird's bill; sucking and sucking, the man's cheeks caved in. Then the handler spat out the cock's blood on the sawdust. I was so shocked I couldn't even speak. Yet it worked. The Law Gray checked his cough and seemed near as ready for the next round as the red.

"Fight!" hollered the umpire.

Spurs up and forward, the gamecocks met again in the air. We heard the clacky noise of steel upon steel, until the tips of the tiny swords found their feathery targets, plunging through into bodies and blood. Both spurs of the Law Gray took a deep plant into the breast of the Redshackle, high up. The gray did not withdraw his spurs to strike again, but instead jabbed his twin weapons in and out, in and out; as one spur lifted, the other sank deep.

"Lookit'm shuffle! He's got that devil red."

"Git up, Red. Git up."

"Kick him off, Red."

"Bleed'm, Gray. Bleed! Bleed!"

"Blood'im good!"

The sweat was pouring down my face, just as the juice of the cigar was pouring down my throat. The salty drops from my head and hair ran into my eyes, smarting, so I could hardly see. It sure was exciting, but my stomach started to kick up. For some dumb reason, the cigar juice in my mouth tasted like rooster blood; which was sort of strange, on account I never tasted the stuff.

I wanted to spit.

The gray was shuffling the red and the blood splattered until both birds was the same color, bloody red. I could see the Redshackle was going to die. The man who'd supplied me the cigar was up on his feet, yelling for the Law Gray to kill the Redshackle. It was plain to see the red couldn't of got any deader, but the man kept yelling.

"Kill! Kill! Kill!"

Only the men who'd bet on the Law Gray were hollering, as the other half of the crowd was real silent, just staring down into the circle where the Redshackle was on his back. Yet the spurs on the red cock slashed in a weak way, still trying for a strike at the gray. He was dead, but he wouldn't quit the fight.

"Game," said a man. "He dies game, that red."

The handler picked up his Law Gray, holding the win cock high in the air to hear the men clap for him and yell their praise. I had me a hunch, that gray rooster would of traded it all just to get back his eye.

I spat out some tobacco juice, but it didn't help too much. None at all. How I did urge to puke. Something made me think of Mama's good breakfast in my stomach that was getting closer and closer to my throat. Closing my eyes, I saw the rope around Jacob Cotter's neck. And I saw my mother's flapjacks; only instead of maple sauce, I saw her golden jacks all get poured on with cock blood. It felt like I was going to fall forward into the circle of sawdust.

"You sound, boy?"

Papa's voice come from behind me, deep and booming, above the noise of all the men who were telling each other how much heart the Redshackle had, even though he didn't lick the Law Gray. It made me feel I sort of got beat up myself, or maybe killed. Or half-dead, and the crowd was jeering me to git up and fight some more, but I was too dog-gone sick to even open up my eyes.

My cigar was out. So I let it drop between my feet, where it fell to its death in the darkness.

I wanted to fall after it. Just so I could get out from the smell of the people. Mama always said that townsfolk had a stink that she'd never cotton to, and dogged if I didn't agree with her. I don't guess country people like us are made to be close to folks, leastwise not hip to hip, so near that you could sniff all their smell. What I wouldn't give right now, I was thinking with my eyes closed, to be back in our barn betwixt Festus and Esther. Them two smelled sweet as hay next to Skenesboro folk.

"Come, boy."

Papa's big hands were around me, and I didn't feel very growed up. And I sure didn't feel like to be a Green Mountie, or feel like courting on Comfort Starr. I just wanted to see Mama and Phoebe and go home. Manhood sure did have some rough habits; and right now, I felt like a little boy. Trying to say something only made me gag. It sure would be a joy to throw up, and puke out the whole town of Skenesboro.

Somehow I got up and stumbled along the row of men, stepping on feet and getting myself yelled at, even pushed, until we got down to the ground and out the door. Sunlight hit our eyes like a knife. I'd forgot it was day outside, it being so nightly inside. The fresh air was welcome. Even a whiff of the local tannery seemed fair by comparison.

"Well, son," said Papa, "how'd you like cocking?"

"Sure is sport," I said.

"You put down a bet?"

"No," I said, "I was a bit busy with that cigar. You?"

Papa nodded. "I put one shilling on that gray."

"You *won?*"

"I didn't, but the gray did."

"You won a whole shilling, Papa. That's keen."

"Certain is."

I could tell by the way Papa said it, he was real proud that he'd bet the right rooster. He took a pleasure in letting all them men in there see that a hillbilly's got an eye to bet a cock to win.

"A whole shilling. Gee," I said, "how you planning to spend it all?"

"Well now," said Papa, "I just might buy something for you. A present."

134

We were walking back toward the front of the Golden Eagle, and Papa put his arm on my shoulder, which sort of steadied my walk a bit. Golly, I thought, he's going to buy something for me.

"What is it?" I said.

"What else? A fresh cigar."

Chapter 14

Two more days at the forge made the chain.

Every link of it was married and measured, ready for whenever the wagon come north from Skenesboro to take delivery and pay us our due. No more orders for chain come our way, which was a blessing, as it was time to plow. Winter had at last let loose its hold on the hills.

Days were getting longer. First light come early, even before Phoebe could waken to it. The earth beneath our feet was a soft brown woman that begged for seed. Little clumps of green sprung up here and there. You could see the lacy deep green of daisy leaves; and if you bent over real close, inside the heart of each cluster was a tiny bud. It looked like the body of a green spider that had retreated to its shelter to lie in wait for spring.

During the two days that Papa and I served at the forge, Mama and Phoebe had yoke-broke Festus. He pulled without ever a lick of the wand, according to my sister's smiling report. Pulled her crossmeadow on a stone boat, which was easy for Festus. And then he pulled the wagon, empty, around the house and anywhere Phoebe cottoned to go. Mama said she'd never see an ox broke so quick, and give her daughter most of the credit . . . which Phoebe took. But then she passed on some of the glory to Festus. And back to Mama, which was rightful.

We were plowing.

The sun was just up, we'd ate breakfast, and were already afield with ox and plow, ready to turn the master furrow. One look at Festus told us we really had an ox again; not as large as Simon, but equal willing. Sort of the way I am, I thought, compared to my father. My hands were still black and my body baked red from the days at the furnace, and it sure be welcome to work in the sunlight. Festus give a snort as much to say he thunk the same.

136

Papa had said he'd let me plow the north field this spring, just me and Festus, so I don't know why he come with us . . . unless it was to see we got off to a square start. He sure was a sticker when it come to exact measurement. He never sold 66-foot chain that was even a half link short. Right now he was on a pretend to look at the fence, but Festus and I knew different. Noah Booker wanted to eye his son and his ox to see if they worked true. And in chorus.

"Hah!"

That was all Festus needed to hear. Head ducked low, his strong body yanked the plow forward, but in the wrong direction. We was plowing, but on a slant.

"Ho!" I yelled.

He stopped. Papa come over to walk the first furrow, as a guide to all the others that would lean against it.

"Let him see the fence," said Papa. "He'll follow it like an ant on a twig. Talk to him in a low voice. Can't let every word he listens on be a command. Stir in some conversation."

"Like sugar on a turnip?"

"Like that. You best holler only the commands to him. Otherwise, you got to court him a bit with low talk if'n you want Festus to be a worker."

"I'll remember," I said. "Good boy, Festus."

Papa walked the master with us, end to end, and it was straight as virtue. Then he turned us loose, picked up his musket, and went off about other business, leaving Festus and me and the plow to do our darndest.

Plowing with an ox was easier than with a horse, even though it was slower. You can't hustle an ox. Festus had one steady speed and that was all. With a horse you had to knot the reins around your back so's to hold the plow handles. But with an ox, there weren't no ribbons to take charge of; just a yoke and the lead lines that run back from the wings of the yoke to the rack of the plow.

It was hard work to pull a plow through Verdmont land that was so spiced with stone but you'd never know it to witness the way Festus leaned to his yoke. Looking down, I could see the steel claim its bite into our land, as the share swam through the brown earth like a silver salmon. In the handles of the plow I could feel all the might of Festus and his brawn.

"Share," I said to him. "That's a good old word, Festus," as we ended a row and was taking our turn to go back. "It's like we share the work, you and me, sharing the land and what we plant in it. Oats for you and corn for us."

Festus snorted as if to say he blessed the whole business of sharing

137

the works and wonders of the earth. I knew he didn't understand a word of it, but he did respond to my voice, good as a rub down. Beneath us, the land was a dark brown and rich with rain. Spring water and melted snow made the May ground seem so alive and motherly, like it wanted to bear babies, to raise up to be tall and true and green.

"Corn children," I said to Festus.

"Oat's is better," I pretended I heard him answer me back, like a real conversation with a friend. I sure wished Luke was here, so's we could have a chat. It would be a glorious thing to tell Luke Shelby about our trip to Skenesboro, and about the cockfight, and how I'd smoked a cigar and how Papa'd bet on the win cock and pocketed an extra shilling.

If old Luke asks me how I enjoyed the cigar, I don't guess I was going to give him the straight of it. Best I'd rehearse a sentence or two, just to be ready if he asks.

"Luke," I'd say, "a man likes to go to town every so often. Yes, sir. And he likes to have a cigar when he takes in a cockfight. What say, Luke? You mean you ain't ever seed no cocking up your way? Well, my boy, best you listen to old Able Booker, because I been places and done things up right proper."

I was talking out loud to Festus who seemed to imaginate that he was Luke Shelby and was hanging on to my every word.

"Luke," I said, "I don't usual take in a cockfight less'n I got a good big cigar to lit up and chaw down on. It's grander than spit."

"You smoked a *cigar?*" Luke would say, on account of some of these Verdmont hillbillies don't get around or do much. Lucky he had a traveler like me to show him a new step or two or he'd be way behind times.

"Yes," I'd say, "the betting was right heavy on the first match-up. I didn't know to put my ten on the red or the gray."

"You bet a ten pence?" he'd ask me, his voice away up high in all his bewilderment.

"Ten *pence?*" I'd look at him, then throw back my head and laugh fit to split. "Why, no my dear lad, when you go to a cockfight in Skenesboro, ain't nobody there going to fade (I'd be sure to say *fade* instead of cover) a small-tune bet like a ten pence."

"You don't mean . . ."

"Sure do," I'd say. "All the chain we busted our backs on loaded up our pockets so fat that we was dropping pound notes as we walked along the street." No, not that . . . "as we strided along the walkway."

"Are you saying . . . ?" His mouth would be wide open.

"Ten pounds ain't nothin' for a cockfight, Luke. Why on just one match-up, I seen more money change hands than you seen horse turds."

"How much?" he'd probably say.

138

"Well, that depends."

"On what?"

"Luke, there's money and then there's money, if you catch my meaning. Continental money ain't worth chicken feathers these days. And that includes the New Hampshire currency them fellows to the east think is so high and mighty."

And before Luke could catch up, I'd go on and on, "To hell with Benny Wentworth."

"What made you say that?" he'd ask.

"Now don't tell me you ain't never heard that? It's from a song, and a merry air it be. *To hell, to hell with Benny Wentworth,*" I'd sing.

Festus looked over his shoulder, wondering which hurt the worse, pulling a plow or hearing my song.

"Some sport," I'd say to Luke, "cocking."

"I ain't never seen a cockfight."

"You ain't?"

"No, not even one."

"Well," I'd say, being a bit watchful with my words, "I sure have seen more than one of them birds, and they sure are game."

"Are they big?"

"Oh, I see a Redshackle go about six pound, or seven. Maybe eight or nine. Law Gray'll run about the same."

"Is that their names?" he'd ask.

"It ain't the name of the bird, it's the name of the *breed*. I reckon it might stem from New Hampshire or Egypt or someplace in that there vicinity."

"Egypt?"

"Them old fairies used to cockfight, that's for sure. Don't you know *anything* about the sport?"

"Not much," Luke would say.

"Well, if'n there's anything you ever fix to know, I'll study on it and fill you in."

"You will?" His voice would be chuck with admiration.

"Course I will. Fellows who don't know a straight spur from a saw ought to git educationed on the whole she-bang. Why, you'll be at a cocking sometime yourself when you git a little older. You don't want folks to think you're a bumpkin, do you?"

"No, I sure don't."

"So listen tight. A saw spur's got teeth just like a tiny old saw. Make sense?"

"Yeah. Reckon it don't to the poor devil bird who's gittin' hisself sawed."

139

"It's bloody business. Why, I seed strong men near to faint when the blood starts to flow."

"That a fact?"

"Gospel."

"Do they kill each other quick?"

"Luke, it sure is plain that you never been to a good old cockfight. They's an umpire who starts and stops the going-at-it."

"What's he stop it fer?"

"Give the birds a breath of rest. And, oh yes, to sweeten up the wagers a few pounds."

"Pounds?"

"Sure as likely. Course, I mean the money some of which might easy be counterfit."

"Counterfit?" he'd ask.

"Ought to horsewhip them counterfitters, if you want my notion. Cut off a hand, or maybe burn a C on his cheek. Rail 'em out of town or throw 'em in the irons. I sure would hate to win a ten-pound note and learn later it was counterfit. Sure would."

"So would I," he'd say.

"Especially after I'd sized up them birds real close and picked out a real shuffler to ride."

I could just see Luke Shelby's face, with a real lost look in his eyes. As if he didn't know a mule from a hinny. He'd want to ask me what a shuffler was, but his pride would possum it already knowed. So I'm stick it to him again,

"Can't whip a bird that'll shuffle."

"Reckon not."

"More so if'n he's saw-laced," I'd say. And if'n *this* didn't get his goat, I'd give up. But right then he'd ask me to explain away a shuffle, so I'd have to tell him about how the Law Gray brung the fight to that Redshackle and really done him in. Poor old red.

It sure would be a handsome thing, I was thinking as I followed the plow which was following Festus, to tell it all to Luke Shelby. But handsomer still to tell Comfort Starr.

What a girl.

Her face was like it was right in front of mine, looking up into my eyes, and her eyes all shiny like a brace of June bugs, and her mouth clean and sweet as a freshet. Gee, instead of my hands on plow handles, I sure would like to handle her. Wonder what makes girls so doggone delicious to look at, sort of like a cupcake. Like you'd want to haul off and bite into her, knowing she'd taste sassy as sap.

"Comfort," I'd say to her, "I meant to come calling on you sooner, but have been pressed by matters of business."

140

"What business?"

"Chain making," I'd tell her, only that didn't have too high-toned a ring to it. Naw, I'd have to say something like . . . "the steel business. Yes, and commerce demands I go to Skenesboro to do a dicker or two." Dicker? Sounds like I went down to purchase a pig. No style. Let's see now, how would Luther Peacham say it in all his wonderous says?

Sure weren't easy, pretending that big backside of Festus was the face of Miss Comfort Starr, and at the same instance imagining that I was Master Luther Peacham of Boston Town. But I did,

"Miss Starr," I said, "would you honor me by being my partner for the next dance? Who am I? Well, around here in my palace, I answer to Prince Charming, but you can just call me Able, or Luther.

"Yes, Miss Starr, I do dance divinely, and so do you. There's a bit of manure on my boots, on account of I been plowing all day, but you'll notice how little it affects my fancy footing.

"Would you care to stroll out on the (what in heck's the name of that contraption they put on houses?) on the *porch,* Miss Starr? The two of us could look up at the stars and study 'em all as long as we're a mind to. What? You'd prefer a scamper out to the barn so we could go uploft and hide in the hay and take off all our clothes and do just about any old thing that comes to notion. Oh, I say, Miss Starr, that does sound like a suggestion I'd cotton to. But what about your mother?"

"Oh, she won't ever find out, Luther-Able."

"Very well then, my fair lass, I shall sweep you away in the night, off to the barn or the stable or the hay mow, anyplace where it's dark enough for the Devil to do his work, if you understand my meaning."

"I do. I *do,*" she'd say, her voice almost breathless, like she'd run in mud from Hell to Shoreham. "And we won't have to go out to the barn, as there's a hayloft above our heads, right over the palace ballroom."

"After you, I'd say, watching the flutter of her pink petticoats as she climbs the ladder to the loft. Then, light as a hungry cat, I would leap up the ladder in a single bound, and there in the darksome I would spring to her side. How quickly she would disrobe. So would I. How pink her body would be. And we'd lie together on pink hay, smelling pink cows and pink horses, and doing such pinkful things.

An ox snorted!

Blinking, I saw Festus in front of me, standing stock still, munching on the leaves of a tree. We were way off furrow, and nowhere near the master. Festus had just wandered off into the field until he'd come to a tree at the far end. Looking behind me, I saw our tell-tale trail, crooked as a cowpath, like we'd both been plowing on raw rum. It weren't even

141

a furrow. Looked more like a bolt of lightning, a jig here and a jag there.

"Festus," I said, "we're in one heap of a mess. And if Noah Booker comes by, he'll about tan your hide well as mine." How could I of done such a mess of it?

A horse nickered from beyond the trees, jerking up my head.

It was Luke.

His big black rounded the curve of the road, cantering easy, and Luke waved his arm. I wanted to wave back, but my hands stuck to the plow handles and wouldn't turn loose. Luke pulled up to rest his horse.

"Hey, Luke."

He didn't answer. His eyes were too busy looking at the furrow Festus and I had just cut in a crazy way that went hither to Hell and back in six ways.

"What the deuce you doing?" he said, standing up in his stirrups to view how I'd cut a crooked brown scar across that tan field. Then he looked at me like he wondered if what I got was catching.

"Plowing," I said.

"If that's a furrow, I'm Queen Bess."

"Your majesty," I said, bowing low and with a majestic sweep of my arm, like I'd seen Luther Peacham do. Luke slid off the back of his black, and come over to lean his hands on the fence that was between us. Eyeing the furrow again, he shook his head.

"You got a fever?" he said. "Or a blind ox?"

"First day ahead of a plow," I said, trying to smile.

"Yeah, and your last behind one if your old man gits a squint at that ragged rut. Where in Hell are you going . . . China?"

"No."

"Old Noah seed it yet?" he asked me.

"If I ain't limping, he ain't seed it yet."

"Able, you're the only plowboy I know who gits lost in his own pasture."

"Papa once said I couldn't find my arse with both hands. I don't guess he's too far off the mark."

"I sure hope," said Luke, "you can shoot straighter'n you plow. You'll gun down old Ethan, or hit his backside square between the buns."

"I can shoot," I said. Inside, it give me kind of a queer feeling. To cut down on a rabbit or a turkey was just for food, and righteous I suppose, seeing as us Bookers was partial to have meat on the table. But to squeeze off on a Britisher would be like some other boy taking his aim on my father. Or at Luke's father.

"Luke?"

142

"That's me."

"You think there's going to be a war?"

"Going to be? Already *is* down Boston way."

"I mean here in Verdmont."

"Why? You anxious to draw down on a Redcoat?"

"If I could get the one that decided Jake was going to hang, yes," I said. "I'd sure cut down on him."

"So would I," said Luke.

"Jake was a good old boy."

"And funny."

"He could make a dog laugh."

"Remember the dead cat in old Pippit's desk?"

"Not as long as he will." We both laughed.

"Hey! Here comes your pa."

Turning around to look south, I saw Noah Booker coming our way. He sure weren't walking like a happy man, looking at my wayward furrow and then at Festus and me. The closer he got, walking that crazy furrow, the gladder I be that Luke was here. Not that I was that glad. Turning around, I took a quick notice of the scar on Luke's arm, and it durn near stopped my heart.

"Luke!" I wanted to scream, "pull your dang fool sleeve down," but there wasn't no time, Papa being too neighborly, and getting closer with every kick of his boot. Noah looked at me, then at Festus, then at Luke.

"Used to be," said Papa, "a fellow in Shoreham years back, name of Charlie Ledder. Charlie didn't have all his hay in the loft. He sure was one to talk, that Charlie. But he had a problem. Every sentence he ever made had naught to do with what got said earlier. Sort of like a crazy quilt sewed up out of words, none of which made a lick of sense. Howdo, Luke."

"Howdo, Mister Booker."

"Well, one time Charlie got into a conversation with a traveling man who was just passing through Shoreham but who made the mistake of asking poor befuddled Charles for directions on how to get to the next town."

"What happened?" I said.

"Charlie Ledder's words just tumbled out his mouth, like usual, and making no sense. Some of us was there, and just as a lark, we let the poor stranger listen to it all, nudging ourselfs in the ribs. The look on that traveler's face was more'n a mite confused. So finally, when Charlie quit talking about the corn on his toe in connection with how high the fish in the crick would jump, along with a few quotes from his Aunt Idy, the stranger got in his one observation."

"What'd he say?" said Luke.

143

"Mister," he said to Charlie, "talking to you is like plowing with a blind mule."

Luke and me, we just about split our britches. It was the way Papa told it that made it so mirthful, like he took a joy in the telling because he wanted to hear it all again himself.

"Able."

"Yes, sir."

"I never thought I'd live to witness one of Charlie Ledder's conversations right in my own dirt."

"Sorry, Papa. It was Festus. Must of been a bee in his ear. There weren't no holding him. Maybe I talked to him too much."

"Boy," said Papa, "I seen plenty of plowing in my time, but ne'r a cut like this one."

"It's a bit crooked," I said.

Luke was still leaning on the fence, his chin on the stop rail and his boot on the bottom, taking in all my torment like it was a medicine show. (I never seed a medicine show, but one came to Skenesboro once.) I was hoping he'd linger a bit, so's I could tell him all about *my* trip to Skenesboro, and about the cockfight and the cigar and all that money. Nothing was working out the way I'd hoped it would. I was supposed to git the laugh on Luke, but instead of that, here he was resting on my fence in the shade while I stood in the boil of the sun, at the new end of the silliest furrow a fool ever dug up, waiting for Papa to decide what to do about it.

"No harm done," said Papa. "It ain't always an easement to drive an ox, real proper."

"Sure ain't," I said, making sure I sounded as agreeable as a heart could make it.

"For one thing," said Papa, "the plowman's got to know more than the ox."

Luke almost had himself a spasm, laughing until I thought he'd bust. It wouldn't do a whit of good to wish he'd not say anything to anybody as I knew he would. Well, I done likewise to him, so let the lout have his merriment. Papa had his hands on his hips, looking that furrow up and down like it was the Hudson River or the Nile or something. I knew he was cooking up an idea that I probably weren't going to cotton to, like not being allowed to ride Pit some evening and court on Comfort Starr. He sure was studying the matter.

He just shook his head.

Luke seemed to want to hear it all, so he climbed up and sat the rail of our fence, like he was just waiting for the next piece of amusement to take place, all at my expense. Me and Festus. Served me right, I suppose. All that day-dreaming, and I was liked to tag the blame on Festus.

144

"Yes, sir," Papa said at last, "I know now where I made the mistake."

Here it comes, I thought.

"What was it, Mister Booker?" said Luke. Oh, he was a big help, that boy.

Papa nodded his head again, looking at me then at Festus, and at the mess I'd dug that went nowhere. Looking from me to Festus and back to me.

"Yes," said Papa. "I should of put the yoke on Able."

The only joy in this whole morning happened right then, when Luke laughed and fell off the fence.

Chapter 15

I pretended to be asleep.

But when I sat up to look out of our bottle window, the whisper I heard in the dark come from my sister. Her hand touched my shoulder.

"Able?"

"Be quiet."

"I won't be quiet."

"You want to see outside? Then keep still and I'll give you the lie beside the window."

"That's a bargain," said Phoebe. She spat on her hand and made me shake on it to close the deal. "I don't see anything except moonlight," she said, after she yanked up the bottle to look out. Our bargain was soon forgot.

"Phoebe," I said, "go to sleep. Please."

"I'm not sleepy."

"You certain are. I took notice of your face during supper, and when Papa was telling you a story. You could hardly hold your eyelids up."

"Well, I'm not tired now. How come you want me to go to sleep so sudden?"

"No reason." I whispered low as possible.

"That's a fib. I bet you and Luke Shelby are going out to run coon."

"No we're not."

"I want to come."

"You can't."

"Why, because I'm a girl?"

"That's not the reason. And who said Luke an' me was fixing to coon hunt?"

"I can tell, by the way you fidget."

"Phoebe, for the last old time, will you please lie down and go to sleep. I plowed all day and into evening. I'm as wore out as Festus. Honest I am." That part was true enough.

"Then how come you got the gumption to run off and coon with Luke?"

"Only place I'm going is to sleep."

"I'm going to lie awake and watch you sleep. And if you get up, I'll yell that I hear Indians."

"Phoebe, what makes you so doggone ornery? It's like you graze all day on thistle. Every word you say's got prickers."

"I want to go, too."

"You'll just get in the way."

"Then you *are* cooning tonight?"

"No, I'm going to sleep."

"Good. I'm going to watch."

Closing my eyes tight, I pretended to go to sleep, but I knew that Phoebe would be up as an owl. My body ached from plowing. But the other ache was worse, and it started when Luke had told me why he'd rode by.

Papa had left me to finish the plowing, and that was when Luke had told me the message from Miss Comfort Starr. According to Luke, she was going to sneak out of the house, so's I could meet her near Hobb's Mill, which was near the Starr place. I was to be there, Comfort told Luke to tell me, an hour after dark. And I told Luke to tell Comfort that I'd be there.

Unless I got into my britches right away quick, I'd be late. And then Comfort will think I weren't going to show up, go back home to bed, and hate me forever. All because old Phoebe wouldn't go to sleep. Damn her! I sat up again. The rattle of cornhusk would of woke up the dead.

"I'm coming, too." Her fingers curled to fists.

"Phoebe, please. I'll make you a present if you go to sleep and say narry a word."

"I don't want a present. All I want is to coon hunt with you and Luke. Please, Able."

"Can you keep a secret?"

"*Yes!*" Phoebe whispered like a cannon.

"If you can't even keep quiet, how you going to keep a deep-dark secret like I'm going to tell you?"

"Tell me."

"If I tell, will you go to sleep?"

"So you can go coon hunt?"

"Phoebe, listen. Tonight, I'm not going to run coon with Luke."

"What are you going to be up to?"

"It's a secret."

"Whisper it then."

"You have to promise to keep it."

"I promise."

"Swear."

"You mean like God-damn-it?"

"No, not that kind of swearing. Raise your right hand." She did. "Now promise you won't ever breathe a word of all this."

"Narry a word. I swear."

"I'm to meet somebody at Hobb's Mill."

"Who?"

"Miss Comfort Starr."

Phoebe's mouth popped open and I thought for sure she was fixing to holler out so's every ear in Verdmont would know it. But all she did was let her air out real slow. Her right hand was still up.

"You're to meet *Comfort?*"

"Yes. I should of took leave long ago, if only you'd a drifted off. Put your hand down, and your head."

"Can I come?"

"You have to go to sleep."

"Are you and Comfort . . . *lovers?*"

"Sort of."

"Will she have a baby?"

"Phoebe Booker, who put such dreadful notions in your head?"

"Babies ain't dreadful."

"True enough, but Comfort and me . . ."

"Are fixing to get *wed.*"

"In a way."

"Are you going to get wed this night?"

"Of course not."

"But you're going to be lovers."

"That ain't proper, Phoebe. I got half a mind to wake up Mama and tell her what you said so's she'll soap your mouth."

"No you won't."

"How do you know?"

"I know," said Phoebe.

"What makes you so certain?"

"Because you want to run off in the moonlight and be sweet on Comfort Starr."

"I sure do." I got my britches on.

"Then go." She gave me a push.

"Remember, you promised not to give me away."

"I promise. Now git."

"Will you go to sleep?" I pulled on my shirt.

"I'm too het up. I'll just lie here and think about you and Comfort."

"Girls your age shouldn't be thinking on matters such as love."

"I bet Comfort did when *she* was twelve."

I'll just bet she did, too, I was thinking. Why do girls always seem to know more about love than boys? Instead of me going off in the dark to moon-love, I ought to stay uploft and send Phoebe to meet some boy. She'd probably do a better job of it.

"Here," said Phoebe, "let me fix your hair."

"What's wrong with it?"

"Turn around."

Her fingers pulled a lock here and yanked one there until my hair seemed to Phoebe's liking. She untied the bow at the back of my neck, and then tied it up again.

"There," she said, "hog tight. You have to look proper to be a lover."

"Won't matter in the dark."

"If I was Comfort, it would matter to me."

"Well, you ain't. You're just little-old Miss Phoebe Booker who ought to be nigh to snoring."

"How you fix to get to Hobb's Mill?"

"I'll ride Pit."

"Sure wish I was coming."

"Well, you're not. Someday your turn'll come, so be patient." Working real quiet, I hung the ladder into its notch, and started to leave. That was when Phoebe leaned over and put a light little kiss on my cheek.

"I hope Comfort loves you, Able."

"How come you said that?" It was a question I didn't have to ask, and I don't know why it even got asked.

"Because *I* do."

My hand shot up under the covers and caught her leg just above the knee where I knew she could tickle right good; and I give her one heck of a pinch. Her fist come back with a punch, and then I was off and gone.

Easing a bit and bridle on Pit, I walked him out of the meadow and headed north. Once over the hill, I threw my leg across his back. Without as much as a heel in his ribs, he took to a quick gallop that ate up distance. Several times I wanted to pull in and rest him, but he just wanted to run. That big bay was some animal. Small wonder that Luther Peacham took so fond to him.

Pit was hardly puffing when I had to rein him to a stop at Hobb's Mill. And as my leg swung across his back to slither down, I saw Com-

149

fort Starr running my way. Before I could even take a breath, she was in my arms, sweet as sassafras. I kissed her and kissed her for a long time, neither one of us took bother to say a word; on account there weren't no words to need. Besides, our mouths were powerful busy. Her lips were crawling all over mine and it sure was a joyful experience. Every breath or two, our teeth would sort of grind together and our tongues would touch. It all felt so righteous and clean. To kiss Comfort was something near to holy.

"Able, Able, Able."

"Here I be."

"Oh, I missed you so much."

"I miss you, too."

"Do you?"

"Ever day."

"Honest?" Her voice was so soft.

"Honest to Peter. I even dream about you when I'm pushing a plow. Sometimes I'm out-to-barn on one end of a manure fork, and my heart is writing you a poem, or else I'm singing you a song."

"A love song?"

"No, a hymn."

Comfort's fingers went into my ribs, and for a breath, I'd thought to holler out. But instead, lifting her high in the air, I slowly bent my arms, bring her face down to mine, closer and closer until she could bite my mouth. It hurt, yet there was no pain to rip away from. A hungry hurt that I wanted to have hurt me even more, giving me desire to hurt her, too. The pain she gave me said, "Be aware of only me."

"Oh, my dear Miss Comfort Starr," I said.

"Mister Able Booker. I like your name. It's so strong and honest. And clean, like somebody washed and scrubbed it. Fits you like a used boot, it truly does."

"Ought to. I wore it long enough."

"And I been wearing Comfort Starr long enough, I say. *Too* long. Sometimes I wonder if I can wait another day or month or year for *you* to poke along."

"For me?"

"You're so pesky *slow*."

"No I ain't."

"You blessed are. You said you'd come to court me soon. Well, in my book *soon* is right away. It's come and gone."

"I'm here, ain't I?"

"Not until I had to tell Luke Shelby to go fetch you here. It shameful made me out like a hussy."

"Good. Can't beat a hussy for fun."

150

"That old Luke Shelby!"

"What'd he do?" I asked her.

"He said he'd probable have to hogtie you so's you'd come."

"Luke's a caution."

"And he said that if'n you refused, that he'd come in your place."

"He say that?"

"Then he tried to kiss me."

"Luke's got good taste." I was too happy to be hetted up.

"Aren't you mad?"

"At old Luke? Shucks, no. He's a good old boy."

"Well, you ought to be, Able Booker. If you'd stayed to home, maybe I'd be standing here with Master Shelby 'stead of with you."

"Maybe you'd preference it."

"Just maybe I might." Comfort give her head a little nod.

"No, you wouldn't. You're *my* gal."

"Not yet."

"What do you mean, not yet?"

"I mean . . . not yet."

"Everybody in Verdmont knows you're my girl."

"Everybody but you."

"Me?"

"You big ox. Yes, you."

"I ain't no ox. I'm a *bull*," I snorted.

"Well, if you're a bull, Able Booker, you certain are the shyest bull ever seen in this valley. God show mercy on the dried-up milkcows."

"I been busy."

"Doing what?"

"We had to make chain."

"Is that what I smell on your hands?"

"Probable. If you marry up with a farmer, best you get used to it, 'cause he'll smell worse'n iron."

"Nobody said a thing about *marry*. Is that all you're going to do, once you get wed and settled, is to make chain?"

"What should I make?"

"Love." Comfort kissed me.

Without another word, she turned and pulled me by the hand toward the downhill door of the millhouse. We were still in the moonlight, and the silver danced in her hair. Her hand was strong, and it felt that she'd done her share of work. Inside, it was dark. The dry dusty smell of grain was everywhere, but at last we were away from the bugs of night, in a spot that was quiet and peaceable. I was glad that the mill weren't grinding.

"Over yonder," she said, pulling my arm toward a corner beneath a

151

south wall where moonlight come sifting through the large slits between the logs. As we stopped in the light, we were striped as a pair of skunks. Beneath our feet was a pile of empty sacks. We both sort of fell on the pile, arms around each other, feeling the rough burlap against our hands and arms. I kissed her. And then she brought her body close to me, head to toe, which made the hugging and kissing a lot more pleasured.

Comfort sure was a comfort.

"Do you think I'm fat?"

"No," I said. "You're just ripe. Like you're full of juice, the way a red apple is in October, the kind of Jonathan apple you want to bite into and swallow down until it's all inside."

There was laces in the bib of her dress. I took one of the lace tips in my hand. Comfort just looked up at me, saying nothing. So I pulled the lace real slow, to untie the bow that held her goodies in, and the dress fell open. Underneath was a white undergarment that also had laces, which I untied in the same slow way. The slower I pulled the string, the faster Comfort breathed. She was young, but she sure was growed.

One of her breasts popped up to fill my hand with softness. Arching her back, she pushed both her breasts toward me, against my face. It was a sudden feeling that busted inside me, making me know I couldn't live the rest of my life with anybody except Mary Comfort Starr.

"Kiss me, Able. All over."

I didn't know which of her breasts to kiss first, as they both were billowing against my hands and face. Rolling my head from side to side, one to the other, I heard her moan with pleasure given and pleasure got.

"All over," she whispered.

Her hands were up under my shirt, moving and moving, her fingernails clawing against my flesh. It sure was a tidy time. Everything she did felt so joyful and so righteous. God sure knew the business when he created love. It made a day of plowing seem worthwhile. I was glad my body had worked hard to deserve the pleasure, happy that my arms were hard and strong enough to hold Comfort Starr the way a woman ought to be held, hardness to softness. Through the layers of clothing I could feel her young body thrusting against me, inviting me, teasing me to the point where I couldn't even think of anything except her body and all its freshness.

"I never want to do this," she said, her voice halting as if to gather strength to complete her saying, "with anyone else. No one but you, Able."

"I'm real happy."

"So am I."

"Let's take off our clothes," I whispered.

"I'll get in trouble."

"No you won't."

"I sure will. My whole body feels fertile. I could give birth to an entire family. Like somewhere deep in my insides there's an unborn clan of kids, just waiting for seed to grow on. I bet I can born a hundred children."

"You should. You're a strong girl. Inside you're strong. Outside, you're all soft and pink and sort of like strawberries."

"Do you like my body?"

"Boy, do I." I had a hand on each breast.

"I love *your* body, Able. I want my arms around you and my legs around you, so's I can own it all."

"Let's strip down. Want to?"

"Of course I want to. Don't mean I will."

"I'll be . . . gentle with you."

"I don't want you to be gentle. I want you rough as a stallion. Bite and kick if you want to."

"I will."

"I want to feel how heavy you are on top of me, and hard inside of me. But not this once. With me, it's got to be always. Love is as much a prayer as it is pillow."

"I want to do it to you now, Comfort. Right now."

"I know you do, and don't think I don't want you to do it to me. I'm as ripe and as raw as I'll ever be. I could outlove a giant. And if I ever get you inside of me, Able Booker, I'll never let you out. Just keep you there all night and all day and forever more, I will. Like a bear trap."

Her voice was strong, like she knew what she wanted from me, and would demand to be loved as tight as she could love in return. Rolling over on my back, I pulled her on top of me. She sat my belly like she'd sit a horse, a leg on either side. Sliding my hands up under her skirts, I felt the warm meat of her thighs. It almost burned my hands.

"I'm not wearing any petticoats. Or stockings."

"Oh, Comfort, you do feel so awful good."

"I wanted you to touch my legs to feel how much woman I be. I'm the youngest of us girls, but my legs are as full as any of my sisters' legs. Feel how big my thighs are."

I felt her.

"Higher up, where my legs are biggest." She made a forward motion with her belly, bring her legs to my hands. My fingers reached all the way up her legs and almost met behind her hips where she was big and round and soft; like her breasts, only bigger.

"You're a real woman, Comfort."

"I want to be your woman."

"You truly are."

"I want to live with you and cook for you and bear your children. We'll lay naked together every night, and we'll do it until we drop off to sleep. Then I'll wake you up in the night and make you do it to me again." She was bouncing on top of my belly.

"You sure are pretty in the moonlight," I said.

"I feel pretty."

"You certain are a picture."

"Right now, I feel so pretty I could sing to the night and wake up everything and everybody."

"So could I."

Her face came down and kissed me, her mouth moving under my chin, kissing her way to my ear. I felt the soft stab of her tongue as she whispered,

"Take off your shirt."

"I can't with you on top of me."

"Here, I'll help."

Once my shirt was off, her head rested on my chest, like she wanted to taste the salt of my sweat. Her lips moved lightly along my flesh until I wanted to yell for murder. Her hands never stopped moving along my shoulders and arms.

"You are one beautiful boy."

"Thanks." I sure had a way with words.

"You must be Adam. The first man God ever created must have looked exactly like you, and felt to Eve like you feel to me. She couldn't have hungered for Adam any more than I for my Able."

"You sure do talk sweet as Gospel," I said.

"It's you that's so sweet. You're the candy and I'm the mouth."

"Eat me up."

"I will. I will eat your face," she said, giving the tip of my nose a tiny bite.

"And I yours."

"You are so different than other boys around here."

"How so?"

"You just are. You're so pure. Nothing you say or do is ever dirty. It's just clean and strong, even your manly want is pure as Sunday. I feel this feeling every time I look at you, or smell you, or touch your curls. The way you grip your legs around the barrel of that horse. Say! Where'd he come from? You Bookers don't own him, do you?"

"Belongs to a friend of mine."

"Better not be a girl friend."

"It ain't. I only got one girl."

"Who?"

"Well, let's see now, she's about post high, blue eyes, full breasted and soft legged. She's a woman fit for a king's chamber."

"Do you feel like a king?" she said.

"Don't know. Feel me and find out."

Bending low, she drew her breasts to and fro across the meat of my chest and belly, teasing and tormenting with every speck of distance. At one moment, only her nipples touched me and I could of kicked that old millhouse plumb over. There's something about a light touch that makes it more jolly than a grab.

"I sure feel like a king," I said.

"King Able."

"And good Queen Comfort."

"I'm not a queen yet. Only a princess. And you're still a knight. Did you ever read all that stuff? I can read, you know. We all can. Mama gives us a book on every Christmas Day."

"What book's your favorite?"

"Holy Bible."

"Mine, too, I reckon. It's the one blessed book we Bookers got. We ain't very booky. I weren't much of a scholar, according to old Jack Pippit."

"I heard tell he's a Tory."

"So's old Noah," I said. "He's to England like tree bark."

"Are you a Tory or a Whig?"

"Whig. I'm a patriot."

"I know I'm not supposed to ask, but did you join up? You know, with the night riders?"

"Womenfolk don't have to bother their pretty heads about politics."

"You mean their *empty* heads?"

"I didn't say that."

"You certain did, or might as well said it. Men give me a pain. They're so all-fired uppity."

"No we ain't."

"Well, when you tell me not to bother my pretty head about matters . . . that's *uppity*. And I don't cotton to it, not a whit."

"Sorry. No offense meant."

"I don't want any man of mine to be in politics. Or to night-ride all over Verdmont with a dumb mask over his face, burning out Tories."

"What have you heard?"

"Nothing much. Except that boys up this way are sneaking downloft at night and riding off to meetings by torchlight. We saw one once. Must have been two or three score torches, all burning up on the ridge. Riding by the house at night to frighten decent folk."

"Who are they?"

"Nobody I care about. It's you that worries me. You admit you're a patriot. Well, so did Jacob Cotter."

"Now look, I ain't no Jake Cotter."

"Aren't you?" Her face was sure sober.

"For sure I ain't. Honest."

"Honest my foot. You're smiling at me, like I was some little child who can't understand patriots and politics. Look at me."

Sitting up, her hands held her own breasts and her face was dead serious, as if she wanted to swear an oath, or make me swear one.

"Breasts like these," she said, "you won't find on a child. I'm a woman. And I have the right to know if the man I intend is going to get musket-shot, or maybe hung for treason. Are you Able Booker, or just another Jake Cotter?"

I couldn't answer her. The truth was stuck somewhere in my throat like a lump of pork that wouldn't go up or down. My hand reached out to touch her hair, but she pushed it away. Both of her hands caught my wrist, and I was surprised how strong her fingers were. She pinned my arm down against one of the meal sacks where the moonlight would show it up.

"There's a scar on your arm," she said. "You're one of *them*. One more fool who can't wait to aim a squirrel rifle at British cannon. And for what? To hold Allen land for Allens to get rich on? Well, go ahead. Bad enough we all lost *our* pa years back, and you know how?"

"No," I said. "How'd he die?"

"Over *land*. He went against the Allens and their might up along the Onion River. Deed papers and claims and seals all added up to a grave for Thomas Starr. I was just seven, but my sisters remember how he'd hated Ethan Allen and all his brothers. My father wouldn't sell out, and he got in the way of Ethan's empire. An accident, they called it. So we buried Tom Starr, sold out for half what the land was worth and come to Shoreham."

"I'm sorry, Comfort. I real am."

"Don't be. It's over and done. And tears can't bring back Thomas Starr or he'd come back long ago. I've heard my own mother cry late at night, when she thinks none of us hear the wail of a widow."

"I didn't know," I said.

"Now you do. So best you choose."

"Choose?"

"Me or Ethan Allen."

156

Chapter 16

Pit took up an easy trot.

He didn't seem to be in much of a hurry, as the night was warm, and above our heads the black sky was a freckle of stars. By now, Comfort would be home in bed, but I bet she weren't asleep yet. I was wondering what her thoughts would be this very moment. About me? Or about her pa and his run-in with Ethan.

People just don't understand about Ethan Allen, I thought. Down in Boston they got important people like Samuel Adams and Paul Revere and James Otis. Away off in Virginia there's the fellow Luke was telling of, by the name of Washington, who'd fought at the hip of General Braddock against the French out west at the Ohio Fork. And then Mister Benjamin Franklin from Philadelphia who was over in England, or so they said. Or coming home.

We got Ethan.

We want somebody, too. And he can't be no Yorker or some Hampshire man. He's got to be a Verdmont soul. Ethan is ours. Big and brawny, like King Henry in the story. Sure, we all know Ethan's a land grabber. Well, why not? All this wilderness was redskin land before us whites come to take it, without as much as a by-your-leave. Boy, if I was a red-hide Indian, I'd be sore as a boil on a horseman's arse. Small wonder all them heathen is so blessed ornery. I'd feel the same way, I certain would. They say all them Mohawk over in New York is loyal to the British. Red fools. Ain't no Redcoat alive that would help an injun. No white man gives a spit about the red. Never did and never will, and suppose it's the Good Lord's way.

We're all in one tribe or another, that was what Jack Pippit used to teach. Maybe the old boy was honest. Us Bookers sure don't cotton to bed down with Canada French or the Dutchies in Skenesboro. What

157

was the name the Whigs down there called it? Whitehall, instead of Skenesboro. Bet big Phil Skene won't cotton to that idea. He's another Ethan, according to what Papa always says. Another grabber of land. Wants to hog it all for his ownself.

I wish I was somebody like that. Why didn't old Israel Booker or Noah ever think to go north to the Winooski and form the Onion River Land Company? Papa's as smart as Ethan. Why can't he see that it don't pay to be so humble and so doggone stay-home. Hoe the corn and slop the pigs and do chores. Plow, plant, hay, reap, lug and tug away at a crotch of earth that ain't no bigger than a mouse turd, compared to what's to be had in all Verdmont.

Ethan says we'll be no annex to nobody, not to New Hampshire or New York or even to England. We could be a kingdom. And I certain wager who Ethan plans to rest a backside on the throne. Nobody but himself. Yes, indeedy. King Ethan of Verdmont. What was it he said? I recall. Ethan said that if'n he ever goes to England to the Court of King James, he will shake His Majesty's hand but he will not lower his head. And when they ask Ethan why not, he'll say . . . "royalty does not bow to royalty."

King Ethan!

Sure he's a bastard, but he's *our* bastard. And by damn we need a sovereign of our own. Who else could do it but Ethan Allen? No one. Without him, Verdmont is just a pack of plowboys with mud on our boots and straw in our hair. So it's got to be Ethan, on account we ain't got nobody else to fork a horse and say, "follow me." If I said it they'd think I was headed for the barn and needed a hand with chores. Not even Ira could command us, even though they say he's got a shrewder head for trade. Not even Seth Warner, or Luther Peacham; or Luke or me or Papa.

Tories will follow Major Skene.

He's like Ethan. There's a presence to him, they say, to make others give ground as he passes by. A quiet Englishman who is never known to holler. Ethan sure can roar it up. When *he* talks, even the birds in the trees stop their twitter. Of course, it was night when they joined me up, and all them birds was asleep, but they'd a been hark still to hear the voice of Ethan Allen. He's a leader. Ain't nobody else in these hills to favor him in that respect.

Thomas Starr stood up to him. And now old Tom ain't standing to anyone.

How would I feel if I thought Ethan was at blame for my father's death? Bless be, I sure hope that dreadful day don't ever come. And now I got to choose life's way and take up with Ethan or stay home with the Bookers. Ride with the Greenies or go spoon with Comfort.

Dang it, I haven't even poured powder into my new musket. I didn't get to make love to Comfort . . . we come awful close . . . and I probable don't farm good enough for Papa. Maybe I'll do 'em all a good turn and not side with a soul. I'd probable shoot off my own toe, split the plowshare, or get Comfort in a family way. Guess I'll be lucky not to fall off Pit and bust my brains twixt here to home.

I wonder when I'll be a man.

Is there a day, a year, a time in a boy's life when he knows he ain't no longer a kid? I don't see my father as God anymore. Maybe that's a sign we are now man and man. And it sure is certain that Miss Comfort Starr don't see me no more as a boy. Oh, golly, why didn't Comfort and me have at it tonight instead of just teasing ourselfs to death? I just plumb *know* I won't feel like a man until I get into bed with her. No skirts, no britches, nothing but us. Funny thing, I thought, but I feel closer to the Lord when I lie with my arms around Comfort than I do in church; whenever we go, which sure ain't too often. If I offer up thanks to the Benefactor for one thing, it'll be that we live a long way from church.

"Well," I said out loud to nobody except me an' old Pit, "one thing sure. I certain am going to ask for the hand of Miss Comfort, to wed and bed forever more."

Pit didn't answer. He just stretched out his long easy trot, heading south toward home. Ears forward, he held his head real high. And it made me ride tall, just to see the notches that nicked the edge of his ear, and to know that under me I had a horse that belonged to one of the Allens. I wondered which brother's hand had cut his ear, and if Pit was his righteous name.

Some horse, Pit.

My legs held firm around his barrel, taking the full thrust of his gait. To be up on Pit's back was like to ride thunder. I wanted to own him for my own, like I wanted to own Comfort, and as much Verdmont land as I could have and hold. Maybe that's the answer. Just maybe boyhood is wanting and manhood is the *get* of it.

No wonder Ethan wants to be King of all Verdmont. I want to be, too. I want it all, Ethan; just like you, old boy. They say that Ethan ain't too strict about his marriage vows. Well, is any king? You have to be a king to understand a king. And the only king in Verdmont is Ethan and he knows it, just like he knows the rest of the us are serfs.

Golly be, I wish old Jack could hear me recite all this to my lonesome, and then maybe he wouldn't of thunk I was such a putrid pupil. I don't guess we was all intended to be scholars. Jack Pippit's a scholar and what does *he* own? One suit of clothes that ain't fit to wipe slime off a newborn calf. Lives in the back of a store in Shoreham. He don't even own the piss pot under his bed.

So much for the riches of learning.

And then fetch a look at Ethan.

Is there a manjack in the whole territory of Verdmont who can turn a word or pen with the flourish of Ethan Allen? I wonder where he learned *his* lessons. Not from Jack, that's a surety. Jack Pippit couldn't see beyond the rim of his spectacles. Wouldn't know hay from straw. Yet somedays, when he'd forget the lessons and the birching of a bad boy, he'd wander off in his lecturing and into the *why* of things. He was then at his best. Like what he said that one time about kings.

We all come from England, he said, in one year or another, to be free of the crown. Yet is the common man, he asked us all, ever free of some fellow who will lord over him? No, according to Master Pippit. I remember telling that to Papa, who nodded his head, mentioning Phil Skene down yonder and Ethan to the north.

"Only worse," Papa had said, "than a king is to be betwixt two kings in a land that's sized for one."

I don't guess old Israel Booker give a rat's arse for Allens *or* Skenes. He just counted out his coin, put his deed to pocket, loaded his family and his gear, and left Boston, heading for Verdmont and to a land he owned but never cast eyes to. Them old Bookers sure had bowels in their britches. I wager no Allen could match that march. Us Bookers measure up. Yes, sir, we do. And that's what gives me the willies about Papa. He's a Tory, to be sure. Yet he ain't about to give ground to Ethan or Phil Skene or nobody on either side.

Iron Knife was the first.

No one has ever drove Papa off his land. Or off his argument if he thinks his stand on a matter is just. That red-devil Saint Francis was the first to learn the lesson that Noah Booker don't backtrack for red or white. And when Noah says he's an Englishman, it sure hits my hearing with more'n words. More than a flag. These here hills are full of Tories. Under every rock.

"Pit," I said, "I'd give a day's work to hear what Papa was whispering to Mister Hessitt the day we went to Skenesboro. You remember, 'cause you went, too. Only if you're a Whig, you'd call it Whitehall instead of Skenesboro."

To be sure, I thought, the Tories could be just as organized as us Green Mountain Boys, and maybe more so. Hell, we ain't organized at all. Luke don't know what's going on any more than I do. Ethan and Ira ain't about to ask our opinion of even a fart in a strong wind. I can just hear the big boy now, requesting my judgment on the whole business,

160

"Able?"

"Yes, Ethan."

"What think ye on matters of the day?"

"Well, Ethan, as I was saying to James Otis and Sam Adams, if you solicit my position in these trouble times, I must remark that Festus'll make a good plow ox."

"Ah!" Ethan would say, "just as I thought. This is so sober a situation that a special meeting of the Continental Congress should be called at once. Do you agree, Able Booker?"

"Well," I said, "I have earlier met with Washington and Revere and Henry and many others on the matter of how I slop the hogs and shovel out the dung. Needless to comment, they had powerful praise to my ability as a plowman."

"Hard to believe, Able."

"But true, Ethan. And more, the Minute Men of Boston beg me to come and be their general."

"And will you?"

"Nay, I must decline. Instead I have more pressing matters."

"Such as?"

"Best I stay to home and milk Esther."

"Stoutly said, lad. And when we assault the British Regulars who march this way from Boston, we'll need sturdy striplings like you and Luke Shelby to do certain deeds for us."

"Such as what?"

"We'll need you, Able Booker, to stuff your head into the mouth of a British cannon and shout a warning if a ball is coming out."

Even if the jest was on me, I got myself up to a chuckle and dang near fell off Pit. I'd have to tell this to Luke the next time he come this way. Heck to be a goodness, I never got to tell him about the cockfight. Never even told Comfort Starr about it.

"Pit," I said, "how'd you cotton to hear about the sport of cocking?"

Pit never give out with an answer, so I don't guess his interest was peaked a powerful lot. Well, I already told it to Festus, so maybe Esther would hanker to hear it all. Or the chickens. It sure was a blessed long haul from a barnyard to a throne.

Yes, I thought, and a blessed long ways home from Hobb's Mill in the middle of night, with naught on either side of the trail but trees, trees, trees. Verdmont sure was a wilderness. Narry but a doggone endless forest that seemed to have no begin and no end.

Up ahead I heard horses.

Pulling in Pit to a whoa, I had me a loud listen. Sounds like a bevy, coming toward me at a gallop. Tories? Greenies? Shucks, it sure was a gamble to sit a horse and wait for what could be a passel of trouble.

161

Siding the bridle, I kicked old Pit into the brush and beyond a wall of trees. As he stopped, he let out a low nicker. But as it might have been followed up by a loud one, I slide off his back and bent a twig around his nose. Not tight. Yet with enough purchase to worry away his calling to the other horses.

They went by us at a gallop.

I counted a couple dozen torches, and more than two score of mounts and men. Not a word got spoke, so I don't guess I'd ever know who they be. Stride by stride, the hoofbeats melted off and into the night, leaving me with only the sound of bugs and the heavy breathing of both me and Pit. My skin was wet. For some reason, I'm scairt of something and doggone if I know what, my mind kept on telling me. Then I told myself there ain't a thing to be frighted of, and why in the name of nothing was I such a coward.

I remember, as I hooked my left leg over Pit's bare back, a talk I had with my father about bravery. He said it weren't no disgrace to be scairt, on account of which he was plenty nervous near a rattlesnake, and only a fool ain't. Fear, he said, was not a sign of weakness, but a sign of wit. Well, Papa, if you could see me now and hear the drum of my heart, you'd know I had a brain or two on my shoulders. You sure enough would think I was Jack Pippit's prize pupil, I'm so fearful.

Pit resumed his easy gait, as though nothing had happened. Except when we got back on the trail, he had a hanker to turn north and follow the other horses. Even when I reined his head around, his rump went the other way until my heels made him grunt with a brace of kicks. He bolted a bit, then settled his pace. Pit's notion to go north made me wonder if he'd smelled Allen horses, if there was such a smell, and wanted to run with his own pack. I don't guess I know much about horse sense, I thought, seeing as us Bookers never was fancy enough to own one. Two kinds of folks. Horse people and ox people, and we was the heavy end of it, as though we was yoked to the oxen ourselves. Somehow I just couldn't picture Noah Booker up on a horse. He was too much a part of the earth to be separated from it by anything thicker than boots.

I could smell home.

There was a fragrance to our farm that no other place give off. Papa said it could be the stand of bracken ferns northside, but he weren't sure. Mama said it was our own thankfulness for being blessed with a good living. Phoebe said it was Esther. Whatever it was, it was home, a good old Booker smell like Mama had baked it brown by her own hands.

A musket fired!

Pit twitched his right ear to the west in the direction of Lake

Champlain. At first I thought that the night was playing tricks on me, until I again heard a musket, fired from a long ways off. Crosslake, I figured; on the York side, probable from near Fort Ti. After a breath of silence, the muskets sounded again. Night sounds carry like a bird; more so over water, which would explain the fact I heard voices. So did Pit. His ears was flopped this way and that, straining to hear what was going on, as if all them torch-burning nightriders wasn't enough to take a caution at.

The moon was full out.

To the left, I could watch the dew shine on the roof of our house, the roof under which my folks were all abed and resting. I hoped. Curious, I turned Pit to the west and down toward lakeshore. Sure enough, I spotted a boat coming this way, toward the Verdmont side. It held one boatman who worked the oars and he was rowing like Hell wouldn't have him. On the far shore, yellow sparks were silent, and then were followed by the after-reports of each musket. And I thought I heard the noise of a lead ball splinter the wooden stern. The oarsman was no longer erect on the seat. His back was to me, and now he slumped down. Only one oar kept on with its work, the other dragged in the water like a broke arm.

Pit tossed his head, as if to say he wanted no part of the Fort Ti lead, as each musket ball dug up a little splash of white water as it would hit the black surface of the lake. Still only one oar was pulling; and it sure was plain to me that the crossman (whoever he was) either was doubled over with the bellyache or was wounded by British lead. The boat turned sideways, its one oar splashing like a helpless duck whose other leg was in the jaws of a turtle.

Pit nickered.

Something in the sound of his neigh said that Pit knew who the boatman was. Another stroke of the oar and so did I. It was Luther Peacham. Even though his face was looking west and his back was coming our way, the whole manner of the man spoke Luther as if he'd had it writ on his shirt. He sure looked like one beat-up Bostonian. Luther fell down into the boat, and now no oars were pulling. The craft spun around like it couldn't decide twixt York and Verdmont. He was in trouble.

"Luther," I yelled. No answer.

"Able," I thought I heard, but the muskets were still discharging aplenty from the yonder side. Barking like a pack of coydogs.

"Hello, Luther Peacham!" I yelled.

"Hurry, Able. Please hurry."

I could see he weren't about to row as much as another oarstroke, so if he was going to git shoreborn, there was only one way. It took more than a kick and an urging to get Pit into the water, but the big bay gelding finally got the idea that he and I were going out to that little skow in which Luther Peacham lay helpless. So we went. The cold water climbed up my feet and legs, hitting my body like a cudgel. It sure battered the breath. Reaching the boat, I saw Luther. Saying nothing, he just looked at me so I could read the hurt in his eyes.

"Map" was all he then said.

Sliding off Pit, I grabbed the bow line of the rowboat. The water creeped up to my neck, and it felt bad as a beating. It was water but it was ice, and it sure made the moving slow. I remembered Luther's swim a week ago or so, and still couldn't believe it. To make things worse, Pit turned his head back toward Verdmont's warm earth. All I could do was keep my grip on his mane and on the bow line. For a breath, I figured my arms were fixing to rip out of my shoulders like a pair of roots. It hurt enough to wonder which hand I'd hang with, to Pit or to Luther. One was coward, one was brave. Lucky for me, Pit lost his footing for an instant and eased my pain.

We made it to shore.

And with Pit's help, I got Luther to the house. Everybody woke up, even the chickens tuned up a chorus of cackles, and Papa's gun met us at the door. There was water in my ears which sort of made me distant from what was going on. I heard Mama's voice, and then Phoebe's:

"It's Able and Luther! Able, where'd you find him? Was he up at Hobb's Mill?"

That sister of mine could sure spill a bag of beans in just one breath. Said everything but her prayers. Good old Phoebe.

Papa looked me full in the face and said, "You been busy."

"And soaking wet," said Mama. She stoked up the fire.

"Did you fall in the millpond, or did Comfort push you?" said Phoebe.

"You promised," I said to her.

"I'm sorry, Able." I could tell she was.

"Easy with him," said Papa. We were bringing Luther into the house and up on the harvest table. He toted real light and easy, as his bones didn't hang much meat.

Mama lit a lantern. "He's bleeding."

"Luther got shot," I said.

"How so?" said my father.

"Coming crosslake. Muskets from the fort."

"He certain is active for a schoolmaster," said Papa.

Luther's shirt and britches were bloodstained. As I tugged on his clothes, they felt wet and sticky sweet. I smelled his blood, and also felt the fresh heat of it in my hands. Papa helped cut away the cold red rags.

"You a criminal?" he questioned Luther.

"No, sir," Luther whispered. "I . . . think that I might die, sir."

"Luther's not a criminal," said Phoebe.

"He ain't much of anything right now," said Mama, "except a mess. You, too," she shot my way, as I was drip wet and shaking.

"You, too," said Phoebe.

With his shirt stripped off, Luther's body was thin and pale. He sure was shy of muscle. I don't think I ever seen a male with arms so skinny. He weren't used to farm work, that was certain, but I don't guess they had too many chores to do at Harvard. His face was twisted up tight to his pain, and I was wondering if he was about to let loose and cry, but as Papa and Phoebe turned to where Mama was starting to boil some water in the hearth, Luther reached out for me. Taking me by the thumb, he guided my hand to the top of his britches. I felt a folded bit of paper which I sudden knew he wanted me to have. And only me. I yanked it out and stuffed it under the table. No one saw except Luther.

"Tonight," he said in a whisper, his eyes closed and his lower jaw in a tremble. "Hands Cove. Get the paper to Ethan. No one else."

I stood in my wet clothes, shaking like a dropped calf and wondering what I was fixing to do next. Doggone, but all this sure was working my old stomach up into a fret. I felt Mama's hands on my shoulders, so I turned to face her.

"Best you skin down and rub yourself red," she nodded to me, "else you might take a cough."

"Yes'm," I said.

Hanging up my wet clothes to dry by the fire, I pulled on my other pair of britches. I was warm now. As the fire had got stoked up, there was a glow inside the cabin. While I was undressing myself, Papa and Mama washed the blood off Luther's body. As he loosed Luther's belt, my father leaned his face down closer to have a nearer look.

"Mark there," he said.

Phoebe said, "It's purple. Luther, you got a plum buried in your belly."

"Lead," said Papa. "He took a ball."

"He took a ball," said Phoebe.

We were all quiet. I never see anybody who'd got musket-shot before. Once I see the musket of Henry Cotter bury a ball into a tree. Went right through the bark. It sure was a wonder how Luther took the hurt of it. I'd a bust out crying, like most would. But not old Luther. He just lied there on the supping table, white as a midnight spook. Though I

165

took notice how his hands was on a grip to the edge of the planks, holding on as if he knowed what Papa was going to have to dig out the lead.

"Able, fetch the rum," said Papa. "You a drinking man, Master Peacham?"

"No . . . sir. My parents were . . . set against it."

"So were mine," said Papa.

"And thus are we," said my mother.

"I'm not," said Phoebe. It almost smiled poor Luther.

"Luther," said Papa as he pulled the cork with a squeak, "best you swaller down a slug of this good English rum." Luther did and made a face. "Take another for good measure," Papa said. "And another."

"Will it . . . hurt?"

"The rum won't," said my father.

"Phoebe," said Papa, "I want you to play-act for us. Just pretend that Master Peacham is your sweetheart, and he just come back from Canada where he drubbed the French."

"All by himself?" asked Phoebe.

"Him and Robert Rogers," said Papa. "So put your arms around his neck, that's right, and hug the lad for all your worth, daughter, with narry a let up. Whisper words of affection in his ear."

"I will," said Phoebe. Her arms were already about the neck of Luther Peacham, her young face next to his. "I'll imagine that he's Able and I'm Miss Comfort Starr."

Without as much as a twist of my head, I felt Mama's look crawl into my hair, like lice. She'd be asking questions that I rightly won't cotton to answer. Papa took Mama's scissors and a pare knife from out the boiling water. Placing a leather strap between Luther's teeth, he told him to bite down hard as winter. Mama held the lantern closer. Her lips were set firm.

"Hold tight, lad," she said.

I saw the tips of the sewing shears dig into Luther's flesh, the points on opposite sides of the purple spot. The ball sure was buried. Luther moaned, but he didn't move. But as my father pushed the tips deeper, Luther lift up both his legs. So I sat on his thighs, to hold him down until the shear tips could straddle a purchase on that bullet. Underneath me, I felt the muscles of Luther's legs tighten, and his quiet scream sort of gargle into the leather between his teeth. The shears were dipped with red.

"I can't look," said Phoebe.

"It's deep," said Papa, "and into his gut. The belly wall is torn by the hole itself. But I wager he's got a rip in his bowel."

Mama wiped the sweat off Luther's face with a cloth, and then did the same for Papa. "Try again," she said.

166

Again the shears went in, farther, farther. Luther's body was one massive shudder of pain. I don't know how he took the hurt, but he didn't cry out. His face was deep pink. Papa got a grip on the lead, but his shears come up empty. On the third try, the tips come up with a ball of blood between, inside of which was lead and scraps of flesh. Blood poured out the wound. Little riverlets of red run down the white of his body, through the cracks between the table plank and into the dirt of our floor.

"Sew him," said Papa. Reaching for the rum bottle, he dumped a swallow or two into the wound. It was a cruel pain. Luther's face was that of a dog gone mad in the August heat. Yet he failed to cry. He just give a weak little whimper, like a wet pup.

Using the cloth with a tender touch, Papa blotted the blood from the hole, as Mama put a needle and thread to work on the soft white tube that was Luther's gut. Only the tubes were bloody as blood could be. The cloth was red all over. Stitch by stitch, she closed the rent in the bowel, and then in the wall of his belly.

Spittle run down the leather from each corner of Luther's mouth, his head rolling from side to side, even though Phoebe hung on for dear glory. He took it without even one scream. All we could hear was the gargle of agony in his throat. I hoped the rum would pass him out, but he was sober with pain. Again and again, the needle went into his meat and out again; Mama's little hands tying a neat and tidy knot with each stitch. The thread had been white. But now it was red as the tips of my mother's fingers.

"One more," she said.

"Hang on, Luther," I said.

Even with the strap of hide in his mouth, I heard the one tiny word as it fought its way up and out of Luther's lips.

"God!" It wasn't swearing. It was just his prayer.

The last stitch took its bite, and its knot. Mama gnawed off the bloody thread with her teeth. It was done. Bending low, she kissed the face of the boy whose cheeks and brow were awash with sweat. Slowly the pink drained from his face. He was white. Phoebe slowly lifted up his head and Mama put a small chair-pillow behind his neck to ease him. He tried to speak, but couldn't. Then the tears (of his torment that he'd held back) filled his eyes and run down his face, sob after sob. Papa held one of his hands, Mama the other. His eyes had been closed, but he opened them and looked at us all, one by each. He couldn't seem to stop crying.

"I'm . . . sorry," he said, "but you see . . . I never could . . . stand pain."

He passed out cold.

Chapter 17

Everyone slept.

And this time when I left the house, there weren't no games to play with Phoebe. Darn that kid. Well, if Mama was going to fret because I shadow off to pay call to Comfort, she sure would have a Friday fit to see me now.

I was tempted to ride Pit, but as I'd turned him out into the meadow where Esther and Festus was, it wouldn't be practical. By the time I caught him and got the bit into his mouth, I could run the mile or so north along the lakeshore to Hand's Cove. So I got my new musket out of the barn and scampered off into the night on a dead run. Something sure was up. I wondered if the British Regulars was marching on Bennington, fighting their way west from Boston to Albany, as somebody told Luke they'd do. Shucks, old Luke Shelby didn't know where Albany was and cared less about some Yorker town. But if it was Bennington . . .

Run fast with a musket to tote, when you're tuckered out with love and surgery, sure can tire a body. My heart was pounding like fury by the time I heard the voices. Horses was everywhere. But not one single torch. I saw a man start to light his pipe and another warn him to smother the flame. If we was to turn around and march south to Bennington, I'd be blessed if I was going to go without Pit. Poor old Luther wasn't going to fork a horse real sudden, not with all of Mama's thread holding his insides in one piece.

Working my way through the crowd of muttering men and muskets, I heard them bicker in the dark. Then I saw Seth Warner, sitting under a tree. I almost tripped on him.

"Seth."

"Who calls?"

"It's me, Able Booker."

"You were to be here an hour ago. Shelby was to contact you. Where you been, boy?"

"Busy, sir."

"At the midnight?"

"We had to take care of somebody who got hisself musket-shot, sir."

"Who?"

"His name's Peacham."

"Is he dead?"

"No. He's abed at our place, sir."

"With your *father?*"

My stomach hurt of a sudden. Seth Warner said it like he knew Papa was a Tory and not to be trusted, a Tory to be fought or maybe killed.

"It was my father who pulled the British lead out of Luther Peacham's body," I said. "And it was my father who tried to save the life of Jake Cotter."

"Still your mouth, lad. No one's here to fight a war on Noah."

"Why are we here? What's afoot?"

"That's been decided."

"All I hear is arguing," I said. "What's all the differing over?"

"You'll see soon enough. Did Luther Peacham carry anything on his person?"

I didn't know what to say. Inside my shirt, I felt the corner of the map I took from Luther scratch my chest. It was to go direct to Ethan Allen, he'd said.

"Where's Ethan at?"

"Why?"

"I got a message for him, sir."

"From young Peacham?" asked Seth.

"Yes."

"He's over by them trees, probable still at odds with the down-country man."

"Who's that?"

"Benedict Arnold of Connecticut."

"All the way from Connecticut?"

"To be sure," said Seth Warner. "Arnold wants to take command of the march, but the Greenies fix to follow Ethan."

"So do I," I said. "I ain't takin' orders from no Benedict Arnold. Who in the heck is he?"

"He's a soldier. Fought in the French War and did well, I hear. His father was military, too. Arnold's a professional soldier, which is more than I can say for some."

"Like who?"

169

"Ethan's a barrel of a man, with lots of land and as many ladies. But Ethan Allen is no soldier. He's got a big head and a big mouth, but I'd rather listen to what Ben Arnold has to say."

"You seen Luke?"

"Earlier. I told him to be quiet or get hogtied to a maple and miss the whole show. Same goes for you."

"Yes, sir."

"Best you get your message to Ethan if he's got one coming. I hope it's from Washington. Oh God, do I hope it is, and it says that Ben Arnold's in command."

"You mean the George Washington away down in Carolina?" I said. How in thunder did Luther know *him?*

"Virginia," said Seth.

"Is he a general?"

"Everybody's a general in this Continental Army. Booker, you want to be a general? Just go to a tailor and get your body sewed into a uniform. Don't matter what color. Then get a horse and a sword and you'll be General Booker. Hell, I'm a goddam *colonel*. Trouble is, I don't even know what I'm in charge of, less it's to bow to Ethan Allen and salute him every breath. When I think of what'll happen when us Yankee Doodles run smack into the Regulars, it curdles my supper. Come to think of it, I never got any supper. The great and august Continental Army doesn't hold to having supper. Jesus, we got more officers than we got beans."

"We shouldn't be saying all this to each other," I said. "I don't trust nobody no more. And you shouldn't trust me. How do you know I won't blab it all to Ethan?"

"Because you're Noah Booker's son."

"He's a Tory," I said.

"Yeah, but he's a *good* Tory. Not like some. And to tell the straight of it, lad, one more hour in the Green Mountain Boys and I'll be thinking of becoming a Tory myself. At least if you're a Tory, you don't have to listen to all them Allens figuring on how to divide up all the earth in Verdmont once we go independent."

"Best I get this to Ethan." My hand almost touched the map in my shirt.

"Your message?"

"Yes, sir."

"Then git. But come back and tell me if Ethan and Ira and Benedict Arnold are still jawing on the order of command."

"Where's our group supposed to be?"

"Ask the Allens. They know it all."

There was at least four or five hundred men waiting in the darksome.

170

Some were quiet as death, some asleep. A few were drunk, and I saw more than one fisting another. Some army. I wondered if we was going to Bennington to meet the Redcoats under General Gage. I looked for Luke but couldn't see him. It wasn't hard work to settle on Ethan. His big voice was booming through the trees, and I walked to it. Leaning against a tree, I listened to the banter. There was a fire among the men who did the talking. Other faces watched silently, and one of them belonged to Luke Shelby.

"Luke."

"Able?"

"Yeah. What's going on?"

"A lot of talk. Wind sure is cheap tonight."

"Who's them two talking to Ethan?"

"One is Colonel James Easton. He's a Massachusetts Bay man."

"Is he the short one in the red coat?"

"Nope. Easton's the tall one."

"Who's the other?"

"The short one is Benedict Arnold of Connecticut, but he's in charge of the troops from Massachusetts. You git to pay a call on Comfort Starr?"

"Sure did," I smiled.

"Well, tell me about it."

"Ain't much to tell."

"Did you get her clothes off?"

"Come on, Luke, don't ask stuff like that."

"Why not? I'd tell you."

"No you wouldn't."

"Sure I would. Why, the night me an' old Comfort spent in Hobb's Mill together, I had her skirts off her legs before you could say spit."

"I don't believe it." My voice was shaking as I said it. "I don't swallow a word of it, Luke."

"Honest to Gospel. I give that filly a good punch in the pants."

"You . . . and Comfort . . . you *did* it?"

"More'n once."

"You spoofing me?"

"Me? Shucks, no. We're going to war, Able. On the night before a battle, soldiers always tell the true of it, so as to clean their mortal souls."

"Damn you, Luke."

"What'd I do? Oh, I know. You mean you and Comfort didn't make ends meet and it's all *my* fault. Son, if you can't sow your oats into a Starr girl, then you couldn't get off your piece in a bawdy house."

I wanted to kick his face in. Damn, he couldn't of been telling me the

171

straight of it. And now here I was, loving Comfort and hating her all at once, which sure could mix up a man.

"I sure do like doing it with a chubby gal," said Luke.

"You want a fist? Besides, she ain't chubby."

"Ain't you fixing to tell me what you and Comfort did tonight? Wasn't for me, you'd stayed uploft with your sister."

"Come on, Luke, be quiet. Unless you want my ire."

"I never see you lose your temper. Didn't even know you had one. Want me to tell you about Comfort and *me?*"

"No. And if'n you don't hush about it, I'll pound you proper, you hear." He knew I meant it.

"It was only fun."

"Was it?"

"Certain."

"I want to marry her, Luke."

"Honest?"

"Sure do. What's more, Comfort wants to wed me. I just know she does."

"Congratulations. Too bad you're to get shot by Redcoats. You'd made Mistress Starr a fair husband."

"Are we marching tonight?"

"Not until them bigwigs settle on who the ram of the flock is going to be. My brother Will was here for a spell, listening to all the lip. He got bored and took home. Said the only cause he come in the first place is that him and his wife had a scrap. You sure you want to git hitched?"

"I'm sure," I said.

Ethan was raising his voice again, shaking a big fist across the fire at Benedict Arnold, like he wanted to poke him a healthy hit on the chin.

"My men," said Ethan, "follow me."

"You know not what you do, sir," said the man in the red tunic who, according to Luke, was Benedict Arnold.

"God's crotch I don't. This is my land, and my boys are Verdmont men, as am I. We know our enemy, their position and strength, and thus I shall command the undertaking. If not, sir, there will *be* none."

"My forces," said Ben Arnold, "are here to cross either with or without you. I need your plowboys about like I need balls on a mule. Our force is going, and we go this night, by authority of the Massachusetts Bay colony who outfitted us. You are to attend me, sir, as rear guard."

"Hah!" Ethan roared like a cannon.

"It's true, and I outrank you, sir."

"I'm a *general,* sir," said Ethan.

"Among farmers."

"Farmers, eh? Soldiers in the Grand Army of Verdmont we may call ourselves, if the Green Mountain Boys is too humble to go by."

"No name," said Arnold, waving his arm into the trees, "could be humble enough to describe your shoddy collection of backwood scurf. You scrape an army off the backside of a hog and aim it on Regulars? You're daft, man. You'll butcher the lot and end with a lake of blood for your trouble."

"So you say, Colonel Arnold. But in these hills and on these waters, I'll pit my boys against yours and kick the britches off all of you."

"Are we here to battle each other?"

"Yes, if you like," said Ethan.

"Then wage a war among yourselves. We come north to take the outpost, not waste our lead on hillbillies."

"Hillbillies?"

"You heard, sir. Our men are trained in more than weaponry. They are disciplined to a man, and prepared to carry out orders."

"*Whose* orders?"

"*My* orders. Yet I won't have the top spot. The Virginia gentleman has cornered that for himself, I'll wager, as his politics are superior to mine, and he powders his wig more than his cannon."

"You mean Washington?"

"None other," said Arnold.

"Not here. Not in Verdmont, I say. This is ours to take charge of. If the war comes north, we *hillbillies* will meet it head on."

"Against the Regulars of Gage?" Arnold laughed.

"Against the Regulars of King George, if need be."

"Mister Allen, you'd slaughter a passel of plowmen just to earn the braid for your shoulder? For shame, sir. I have few friends in your green hills. Your lads are strangers to me. But by damn, sir, I'd not wish to see them wasted on a charge against British infantry."

"We do not intend a charge, sir."

"And what *is* your intention?"

Ethan took himself a deep breath. "It is our plan to surprise them all. Fire not a shot, if that be possible."

"Not a shot?"

"Not one, sir. Colonel Arnold, we have had our plan for some time. I must insist on taking full command myself. My brothers and I are a close family. I trust them and they me. We are Verdmont men, sir, and used to our own ways."

"God, man! Verdmont has no corner on patriots. Blood for our cause flows as red in Boston as here, and red in Carolina and Georgia and Virginia."

173

"To be sure. But our target is *here,* not there. What does your friend Washington care about Ticonderoga?"

"Enough to want the cannon," said Arnold.

"To fortify his blessed Potomac? Pig's arse! We keep the cannon here to fight the northern war. To turn against Crown Point if we must. But not to guard George Washington's slave huts."

"I agree, *General* Allen."

"Do you now?"

"Aye, I do. I cannot return south to Connecticut and report that I have refused to execute that for which I was employed."

"A compromise, sir?" said Ethan.

"Aye, just that."

"Of what description?"

"A share of command," said Colonel Arnold.

"Split my troops? Half for you and half for me to take charge of? They won't follow your lead, Colonel. They are Verdmonters."

"Not that. You lead your lads and I will lead mine. We share the command as leaders in common. I hope you will agree. More than that, I ask it of you, sir. Please accept."

"Done," said Ethan.

"Colonel Easton and I will back you up, and wage the second assault."

"Fair enough."

"Then it is agreed," said Benedict Arnold. He extended his hand toward Ethan Allen who took it. Easton shook with Ira.

"Agreed."

"Well," said Luke, "if'n you ask me, you and I best decide how to divy up Comfort Starr. You take the right leg and me the left. She sure is fleshy enough for the both of us. Too much gal for just one man to keep happy."

"You're a curse, Luke. You know that?"

"Easy, I'm having a bait at ya."

"Well, cut it out. I got personal feelings."

"Who don't."

"You don't, you banghead. All you want to do is kiss an' tell. You got all the feelings of a froze up frog. So back off about it, hear?"

"Sure."

"Now I got to see Ethan."

"You? What would you see him about?"

"Got a message for him."

"From old Comfort?"

"Dang your eyes!"

"I bet she's still awaiting back at Hobb's Mill for the next lover. Never guessed it'd be Ethan."

I couldn't think of a comeback, so I just give his nose a tweak, and marched over to where Ethan was. He sure was big. They say with his shirt off he was even bigger; and the more he took off, the bigger he grew.

"Ho, boy," he said to me.

"Sir, I got this map from Luther."

"Who?"

"Luther Peacham. You know, the fellow who was fixing to be schoolmaster over at Fort Ti." I took the map out my shirt, unfolding it.

"Ah!" said Ethan.

It was a detailed map of the fort, drawn in straight lines and to scale. There was a gun count for each wall, and it all seemed to add up to about a hundred pieces of cannon plus some mortar and swivel mounts. And a head count of fifty Regulars, sergeants and officers. I took note of the position of two powder magazines, one of which (on the east end of the courtyard) Papa and I darn near exploded with a smoking pipe. It sure was some map, exact in every respect from what I could see. Luther Peacham was as fair a spy as he was a swimmer. I don't know what made me believe that Luther drawed the map by his own hand. I just plain knowed he done it. That map could of hanged on the wall of a mansion, it was such passable artistry.

On the map's edge was a scribble, as if hurriedly added in butternut ink and with a quill not too sharp. It read: "W.G. unbolted. Sentry bound."

As I was still at Ethan's hip, sharing a moment with the mighty, I don't guess I had a thing to lose by asking, so I asked,

"What's the 'W.G.' mean?"

"Here," said Ethan. "It's for the Wicker Gate, a small door on ground level through which we'll enter, avoiding the main. And the sentry already bound. *Let's go!*"

Now was my chance to put in a good word for Luther, to tell Ethan all about his bravery and how he'd come crosslake with British lead in his insides. "Luther Peacham's wounded," I said, "and darn near to be dead."

"Wounded, eh?"

"Yes, sir. My mother and father cared for him."

"At your place? Your name is Booker."

"Yes, sir."

"We'll fetch him later. And give the brave lad his just due."

"Sir, are we really going to do battle over at Fort Ti?"

175

"We'll *take* her, boy. Lock and stock, we'll snatch the whole she-bang before they can even wake up long enough to scratch their arses." Ethan gave me a clap on the shoulder that could have broke Festus's back. "Well done, Booker. Go join your company and be at the ready."

"Yes, sir." I felt proud as punch.

Seth Warner was rounding up his command by the time Luke and me got back to where I guessed we was sort of supposed to be. Ira come up and said a word to Seth who just shrugged it off. Ira left.

"What'd he say?" said Luke.

"Call me *sir*," said Seth. "I'm a colonel, and also your unit commander."

"Sure. What'd he say, sir?"

"We ain't going over until morn. Our company is the rear guard." Seth spat in disgust.

"Rear guard?" I said. "Ain't nothing *here* to guard. All the to-do is over yonder and we'll miss ever lick of it."

"Can't help it. You heard what he said."

"No, we didn't," said Luke, but he didn't say it too public, as account that Seth Warner was knowed to tote a temper. But I guess he got wind of it 'cause he turned on Luke real sudden.

"Shelby, I just might remedy that lip of yours if'n I hear me one more sour note from your whistle. Understood?"

"Yes, sir."

"Sit down and keep silent as a grave, both of you. I got to go see Ethan."

"Rear guard," said Luke, when Seth left.

"I feel like going home," I said.

"Me, too."

"What'd you think of Benedict Arnold?"

"He ain't a Verdmonter," said Luke, "and if you want my notion of the whole business, Verdmonters is the only souls *I'd* lend money to."

"Same here. But he striked me as being a soldier. Ethan ain't. He's a king, maybe. But he ain't no soldier."

"Looks like *we* ain't to be neither."

"Rear guard. I could puke," I said.

"Then puke on me, 'cause that's how I feel. Let's cut out and go visit the Starr girls and give all six a bloom in the bloomers."

"You starting that up again?"

"Me? I thought *you* was sweet on Comfort."

"I am. But I don't guess I want to divide it all up with you and your mean mouth."

"Meaning what?"

"Meaning some things is private."

176

"Like your parts?" Luke chuckled.

"No, but what you do with 'em is. Or wouldn't you understand that, you being such a blessed man of the world. *You* ain't ever see a cockfight."

"Neither have you, Booker."

"Have so. Me and Papa took in a cockfight in Skenesboro."

"Go on." Luke didn't believe it.

"We certain did. And my father put down a bet and *won*."

"Was it good, the fight?"

"Sure was."

"Bloody?"

"Bloody as war."

"Nothing's fixed to be very bloody about *our* part in tonight's fray. Best you stub your toe on a root so's you can tell Miss Comfort you got wounded."

"Getting wounded ain't so gee-dee funny, Luke."

"To mean what?"

"Luther Peacham got wounded, that's what."

"Who's he?"

"He's a patriot. He's a real *spy*. And he's resting well at our house right now."

"Who's he spy on, your pa?"

"Leave my pa out of this."

"If I got old Noah figured, he'll want you to stay out of it, too," said Luke. "Who shot your friend Peacham?"

"British."

"Over across?"

"Yeah. Luther did the map and they must of found him out, 'cause he come rowing like fury. And all them Regulars firing after him. The lake was so full of lead it was near to be a host of mad bees."

"I'd like to be a spy," said Luke.

"Who'd you spy on?"

"You and Comfort."

"*Damn* your hide, Shelby!" I cocked my fist.

"Damn yours," said Seth, "the both of you, if you don't shut your blasted faces before you wake up the whole doggone garrison over there. Noise goes over water as clear as it comes our way. Pair o' dang fools."

"We want to go, Seth," I said.

"*Sir* to you."

"Sir," I said, "send me an' Luke up with Ira and them others."

"Yeah," said Luke. "We want to see some of the thick of it, sir. We certain do, don't we, Able."

177

"Right," I said. But my mind was seeing the purple gut-wound of Luther Peacham, and the blood on the tips of Mama's shears, clear up to the crotch. Like the legs of her scissors wore little red stockings.

Seth Warner had his hands on his hips, looking from Luke to me and back to Luke again, like he was pondering what to do with the both of us. He scratched his ear. His other hand then rested real easy on the handle of the pistol that rode in his belt, and he let out a sizable sigh.

"I'll do it," he said.

"Do what, sir?"

"I'm fixing to git even with Ethan on a few matters, and I can't think of a sweeter revenge than to pack the both of you along with the first wave of boats."

Luke and I looked at each other.

"You mean," I said, "we git to see the show?"

"If that's what you call it."

"Sweet spit," said Luke. "You're a regular guy, Seth. I mean, sir."

"It's dark," Seth said, "so come on. The two of you can mix in with Ira's bunch. Stay low in the boats and above all, try to keep your tongues from twittering all the way to Ti. You wake them unwed bastards up over yonder, and it's one Mary of a damp trip back, under cannon. That water's cold as a witch's spit."

We both nodded to Seth Warner, as if to say we'd be as quiet as a brace of boulders. My heart was beating away inside my chest. Seth sure was a sport to turn us independent and fix it so we'd git to see the frakus. When we got close to the lakeshore, following Seth, we turned south and saw a bevy of rowboats. Men were all over the place. Falling into the water, dropping oars on their own feet, a real hodge-podge of folks moving this way and that. I couldn't see either Ira or Ethan which helped matters some, and Benedict Arnold was nowhere in sight.

Seth pointed out a good size boat. "Get in, the both of you. And don't let me see your faces again this night. Ethan knows you're both assigned to me, so best you don't let him see you. Keep low, keep quiet, and God go with you."

We nodded.

Men were loading into the boats. I held my musket real tight. We were really going to take Fort Ti away from the British Redcoats. If only Comfort could see me now. I bet they'll hear about this all the way to Boston. Oars got fitted into oarlocks.

"How far you reckon it is?" I whispered to Luke.

"Two mile."

"Can you see the fort?"

"No, but I guess we'll see it doggone soon, and from close on."

"I'm so worked up, my heart's like to bust."

178

"So's mine. I sort of wished I'd done something before I left the house tonight."

"Done what?"

"I wish," said Luke, "I'd kissed my mother good-by."

"Same here."

"Leastwise, you got to kiss your fat gal."

"So help me, Luke, less you shut up on that score, I'm going to dump you over the side once we get halfway across."

"It's only sport. Don't get sore. It keeps me from getting the nervous shakes."

"Are you scairt?"

"Sort of. You?" asked Luke.

"I'd like to say no, but I'd be a liar."

"You and me both."

Our boat rocked as four men got in, with oars, and we pushed off from shore. I kept up one swallow after another, even though there was nought in my throat to choke down.

"We're really going," I said.

"It ain't the *going* that worries me," Luke said. "I just wonder how many of us'll ever make it back."

Verdmont got farther and farther away. So I quit looking back over my shoulder. There was some seep water in the bottom of the boat and my britches was mop wet. For the second time tonight, I was soaked and cold.

War sure was a discomfort.

Chapter 18

"There!" said Luke, pointing into the night.

Squinting, I stared through the gray curtain of lake mist to where he pointed. The York shore was coming closer and closer, but it was like we was rowing through smoke.

"I don't see narry a thing," I said.

"Now! Right in among that there nest of birches."

Real quick, I saw what he saw. Indians, maybe a score or more. Hunting party at this time of night? Reaching around, I tapped the big brawny back of one of our oarsmen. He turned his head.

"What is it, lad?" he whispered.

"Injuns," I said. "See there?"

"Don't nobody fire," the man said. "We ain't over here to cut down on a pack of stinking redsticks. So don't nobody pull a trigger, hear?"

The prow of the boat turned south toward the fort, keeping close to shore. Fort Ti would still be a two-mile walk. I wondered about the Indians and if they were the Mohawk, the allies of the British. Not only the Mohawk, but all the Iroquois were friends of the English. Samuel Champlain was at fault for that, according to Papa and Jack Pippit. Both said the Iroquois stand true to England and to Sir Will Johnson, who was their friend. Papa said Sir William was certain a true friend of the red man, and was even a bit closer with red women, which was how come a passel of Mohawk kids seemed to favor Sir William in looks. But some said the likewise about William Penn, from what I heard tell. And also about Robert Rogers. Papa said Major Robert's name should have been Father of the Forest, on account he was so willing to handle his share of sire work.

The Mohawk, or whoever them heathen was, sort of melted into the early mist. Not that it was light yet, but I figured the moon was backing

180

off for good reason. The water was still, except where the bow of a boat split the silent surface into a growing wedge, and the soft work of oars splashed against the night. Maybe them savages was just curious and no more. I don't guess they saw near to a hundred Verdmonters come their direction every day. I listened for the grunts of the Mohawk but heard not a whisper. The men who worked the oars kept twisting around to study the shore. We all waited for the hiss of an arrow. My face was as wet as my clothes. We landed, and drew up our boats, hearing the iron keel grind into the small spread of pebbles at the edge of the water. Other boats landed.

No one spoke.

Ahead in the mist, I could see the dark shadow of Ethan's mighty frame waving us all forward and into the swamp. Water sucked at my boots as I sunk in up to one knee. The bugs in that swamp was dreadful in number, like a host from hell. My mouth was dry enough to chew up wool and spit yarn, but the water we was wading smelled foul as a summer death. Sure weren't fit to drink. On we waded, until I figured we was halfway to Skenesboro and we'd somehow overshot Fort Ticonderoga. That old swamp sure was a mess of misery. I was soaked to the skin and steamy hot, like my body was starting to rot. Still we kept on our parade through that wicked wet until I was wondering if we all was just plain lost. Ethan and Ira was up front and I trusted they knew their cussed way to Ti. At least Benedict Arnold was with us, and he was a professional soldier. So they said.

"Able!" whispered Luke.

"We're supposed to hush up."

"I just heard our count is eighty-three."

"Did they count you and me?" I whispered back. "If not, we make eighty-five."

"You sure got a talent for ciphers."

I giggled. Darn that old Luke Shelby. He sure could be a thorn. Yet he was good company. There was a spark inside him that made Luke different than so many Verdmonters. Most of 'em wouldn't of said fire even if their arse was burning. I was in school with a pack of dull ones. But Luke Shelby weren't boring to be with. Even if he did ride me about Comfort, his friendship was worth the bother. I sure hoped old Luke weren't going to git himself killed.

"Able, where do you think we are?" he whispered again.

"We're in New York, that's certain."

"You're a walking compass, you are. I mean, how close are we to the open field that's north of the fort? My legs feel like we passed it an hour ago. I can't wade another step in this bitch of a bog."

"Then stay here."

"Quiet," somebody ordered us.

Luke stuck his tongue out in the direction the voice of authority come from. He sure weren't cut out for soldiering. All these dogged orders was getting to me, too. Do this and do that. Sure wish I was an officer, and boy! would I make Luke Shelby toe the line and hop to it.

"We're close by," a voice said.

"Up ahead."

"How close are we?"

"Two shots. Maybe less."

"Here we go, boys. Keep in a bunch, on account we got to run like Old Harry was after us once we reach open ground." I recognized the voice of Ira Allen. I kept on pondering about Benedict Arnold's handsome uniform. It would sure be a dreadful shame to wade through mud in a get-up as comely as that.

The ground under us was firming up. Didn't rightly matter, as we was all soaked and soiled from falling. My arms ached from wading through the swamp carrying my musket over my head.

"Steady, boys. We'll rush any moment now."

Rush to what? I could see narry but trees and purple puddles of stink water. But I was blessed glad we didn't see any of them red-hided Mohawk. Can't say I liked Indians a whole lot. Most of 'em was improved by dying, as Papa used to say. Well, he had cause.

"Run, boys."

I could hear the distant bark of Ethan's voice, trying to whisper. His voice just wouldn't go light and airy. It was like asking a bull to dance. From then on we ran and not one Verdmont soul said a word. On my right was Luke, but ahead to the left I saw some of the Massachusetts men, rifles held high. How'd they get so far in front of us? It ain't easy to run in wet clothes, carrying a firearm, when you're tuckered out to start with. Breathing come dearer and dearer. We were in the open and the fort was a giant gray star ahead of us in the misty night. Funny, but earlier it had been clear. I felt a drop of rain hit my face, which I wanted to swallow to put out my thirst. Any moment, I thought. Any moment, them big guns up on that stone wall was going to belch fire and some of us would fly down like chips from an ax. Any moment. How many more steps would I run? I started counting. One, two, three . . . all the way to ten and then twenty, thirty, forty . . . and with each step I expected to see the row of cannon burst out an orange discharge that would spit death among us all. Where were the damn British? As the big north wall got closer, I could not see even one sentry's head against the gray sky. Were they all asleep? That would be too much to expect. Luther had give one of them mother's sons a conk on the noggin, but I don't guess he could of give all them Regulars a likewise

182

treatment. We was running hard, and now about a musket shot away or less. My feet felt like the pair was poured out of lead, like they just won't lift up and set down again for even one more pace; yet somehow we all whipped ourselves forward. Ahead of me I saw a man fall. But I'd heard no musket, no puff of smoke, Luke and I both stopped to help the man to his feet. His hair was gray, and it brung to mind what Papa mentioned about some of the Green Mountain Boys being grandfathers. This man was fifty or more. Old as the hills.

"Come on, mister," said Luke, "or we'll all be lied down."

Somehow we reached the wall. All of us seemed to touch it with our hands, just to feel it was there for real. The gray stone was rough and cold, and it seemed to be so doggone hard compared to our human flesh, like it was a huge rock that could of just rolled over on the bunch of us, to crush us like a clan of ants. The old man stood between Luke and me, but he weren't puffing any harder than the two of us. Down the line, I saw Ira waving us around the east corner. Ben Arnold was with him and so was Colonel Easton. In my mind, I kept seeing the letters W and G, which Luther Peacham had writ in a hot rush on his map of Fort Ti. It meant Wicker Gate.

Colonel Easton was to it first, as he was more fleet than either Ethan or Ira who were big men and who ran like yoked oxen hauling a load. Easton tore open the door. As he did, out fell a British sentry. He was gagged by the mouth; and behind his back his hands were bound with a white rag, and his ankles was likewise tied. Yet his eyes peered wide, looking at all eighty-five of us as if we was ghosts of the night. We was all splattered with mud and sure must of been a spook of a sight to surprise an English lad.

With a sudden scoop of his lean arm, Colonel Arnold set the boy down gently on the wet grass at the edge of the fort wall. He give the lad's cheek a pat.

We went through that tiny gate like shorn sheep. I never saw either me or Luke move so sudden, and Papa would have studied our alacrity with a nod of his head, as he confessed I was a slow hand at chores. The whole durn garrison was still as a church on Saturday night. Not a snore. But maybe they was all hid, just waiting to unload their muskets at us. Inside the Wicker Gate, we run up a small hill and I soon saw (even darksome and mist) exactly where we was at. Ahead of us was the arch in the south barrack, a tunnel leading into the main courtyard. How in the name of nobody them English never heard the rattle of our musket stocks as they clattered against our horns. I toted a pouch of lead pellets and Luke packed our powder. It was an unhandy arranging, but I didn't have the gumption to run off in the night with Papa's powderhorn and leave all the Booker's with no black powder. And maybe at the mercy of Tory-haters who lack the spunk to go against Fort Ti, and instead stay home in Verdmont to cause trouble on sleeping loyalist folk.

"Here we go!"

I heard Luke mutter to my ear as the two of us, hip to hip, ran the dozen or so strides through the black of the tunnel and out into the courtyard. It was like a big parade ground; bigger, now it was empty, and quiet; but all I could think on was how we'd stood on this ground only a few days back to watch Jacob Cotter hang to his death.

"Pray for me, Able" I heard his voice say.

His words were young and pure, like a bud instead of a flower, and I heard the ring of his voice over and over inside the ear of my memory. If I live to crack sixty, I was thinking, I don't guess I can ever forget the hanging of Jake Cotter; how Papa and me stood there, like our souls was carved of walnut wood, and watched Jacob die.

"We're back, Jake," I whispered to my own conscience. Suddenly I wanted to kill me a Redcoat. I was glad both me and Luke had remembered to load our muskets.

A brace of sentries was sitting on barrels, side by side, with no more life in 'em than a pair of blowed-out candles. It certain would be sorry sport to cut down on a sleeping man, even if he was a Britisher. We all saw them two, and I figure the lot of us come up with the same reasoning, on account not a Verdmonter or a Massy as much as raised his musket in their direction.

I saw a flash of red.

Colonel Arnold in his crimson tunic was at a quick run across the courtyard, headed for the officer quarters. The corner of my eye spotted another motion, high up on a balcony above Benedict Arnold's head. A door flung open. A man in white undergarment popped out, a pistol in hand. He give a whoop of a yell, aiming his piece at Colonel Arnold.

Raising my musket, I fired.

My ball took the man in the shoulder, spun his person around. Backwards, he fell off the balcony at Ben Arnold's feet. His body kicked up a puff of dust, but he lay quite still. Before I could even release my finger off the trigger, I got a salute from Colonel Arnold who had not once stopped his run. He leaped light over the fallen Regular, like a fox over a log. There was some ways betwixt Ethan and Benedict Arnold. He threw the salute back at me real easy, like he done it a score of times before, in other battles and against stranger foe.

Some more Britishers yelled out.

The whole blessed garrison was up and astir, as window after window in the barracks went yellow with candlelight. But nobody fired a shot. Except me. My mouth could taste the smell of burnt sulfur and saltpeter from the explode of my powder. I supposed I best stop and reload, but so much was going on, I just sort of run around in a circle like a headless turkey. Luke run, too.

Now the sentries was awake; but as each felt the cold iron of more than one Verdmont musket barrel under his chin, not a sentry made as much as a hiccough. Didn't yelp out a sigh or swallow.

Colonel Easton run up a flight of stairs on the outside of the west barrack. He met a Regular coming down, who had his bayonet at the ready. I thought Easton would be a goner; but pushing aside the point, he delivered a whale of a blow on the Englishman's temple that he fell down the stairs like a trunk.

Colonel Arnold had picked up what looked to be a fullering iron, used by a blacksmith, and was forcing open a barrack door. Shouts come from inside. A lady screamed, using a word that I hadn't yet heard, but I believed it had something to do with the anatomy of Colonel Arnold. The door give way.

Ethan went up the same stairs, bulling his way ahead of Arnold and disappeared from sight through the door. He come out against carrying a man whose shiny scalp had little hair. Yet I recognized the visage of Captain Delaplace, the head one. Never had I see the man without his white wig, and he sure looked a mite puny. His face was as flourly as his billowing nightshirt. Ethan held Delaplace over the edge of the railing as if to hurl the wretch down to his death or destruction. As Ethan's hands held the man's ankles, the poor soul screamed his fear to all of us below. His eyes was wide as two candle trays.

"Look here, boys!"

Ethan yelled down for us to take a view of the frightened devil he'd captured. Captain Delaplace was still upside-down in the grip of a Verdmonter whose arms was the size of most men's legs, and yelling to beat hell.

"This here soul," Ethan hollered, "is the best soldier they got in England. Ain't he pretty?"

We all bellered a laugh from down below as if our throats was lined with leather. I heard a good old hillbilly holler from a Verdmont boy and it sure made me righteous proud. The whoop got took up by a few more until we all give out with our own kind of a yip, and I bet them British never heard a noise as nasty.

Papa said once about noises, that it was the strange sound that could sour your soul, special if you hear it come at night. Well, if was night enough for us to whoop up good, the way the English go to war wailing their Scottish pipes, which according to Papa, scairt the pants off every army that ever got formed, Christian or heathen. Well, it was the Englishmen's turn to prick up ears to strange noises. And if a Verdmonter's whoop couldn't curdle the blood more'n any bagpipe, then my name weren't Able Booker.

"Looky this damn rat," said Ethan. "Boys, you like for me to drop him on his nog?"

For a breath or two, I sure thought Ethan Allen was fixing to let poor Delaplace fall, until Benedict Arnold leaned forward to lend a word into Ethan's ear. And then Ben shook his head as if to say don't drop the wretch. I heard Ira chime in, too, saying the word "ransom." With a mighty heave Ethan hauled Delaplace back up over the rail like he'd fetched a dead duck. Inside the bedroom, the woman was still screaming.

"Shut your pesky mouth," Ethan turned to her, "or I shall give you a bigger reason to scream over." He put his hand on his own crotch. Ira threw back his head and howled at the idea. So did we.

Nobody had let loose a shot. Except me.

Turning about, I retreated to where the man I wounded was stretched out in the grit. He rolled a bit, and it was certain he weren't very dead. English was all around us, their bare hands reaching up into the night, parading around in their white undergarments. As we was all mud-soaked, it looked like a scuffle betwixt a team of white and a team of brown. Bending down to touch one knee on the ground, I spoke to the soldier I cut down on. He moaned.

"I'm sorry," I said.

I don't know why I come out with such a dumb thing, as it sure weren't much of an easement to his pain. Yet the two words just sort of popped out my mouth, and I felt gratefulness that he weren't killed. It probably weren't his blame that Jake took the rope.

"Your shoulder's busted," I said.

Rolling his face, he looked up at me real strange, like he thought his throat was going to get cut. His hand pulled up as if to cover his face and ward off a blow. Then he seemed to read my face, guessing right that I'd not give him another helping of harm. He probable didn't know it was my gun that chopped him off the balcony. Until I told him so.

"You see, I just couldn't let you kill Colonel Arnold," I told him. "We ain't over here to kill folks. Honest." And come to think of it, dang if I knowed why we *was* here. Now we got the fort, what was we to do with the blame thing?

"What's your name, soldier?"

"Hawkes, sir . . . Private Andrew Hawkes."

"Can you sit up?"

He was as young as me, maybe younger. As I asked him the question, I felt another join us. I smelled Luke. The two of us, our arms yoked behind the back of Private Hawkes, pulled him up to a sit. He was bleeding some, but he weren't near to dying.

"Who . . . are you?" he said, blinking his eyes as if he was truly confounded.

"Able Booker."

"I'm Luke Shelby. We're of Verdmont."

"Where *you* come from?" I asked him.

"Scotland, and the town of Wee Burn."

"Your shoulder hurt?"

"Yes . . . yes, sir. I'm a bit woozy."

He was in white britches and a white blouse stained dark as the blood was seeping from his wounded shoulder. The sweet smell brought back the wounding of Luther Peacham. Well, if not for Jake, I'd at least evened the score for Luther, a wound for a wound.

"Is there a surgeon here?" I said to him.

"No . . . no surgeon."

"Best we git you patched up," said Luke.

"Can you stand?"

"I . . . believe so."

"Ready, heave!" I said, as we got Andrew's unsteady legs under him. He standing, but not without help at both hips. The shoulder was at a sag and his arm hung down real useless.

"I had me a broke shoulder one time," Luke told him. "Hurts a mite, but you don't die from it. Knits up quick."

We could read the pain on his face as we stood him, not knowing quite where to tote him off to. I was thinking I sure wish Mama was here to help set his shoulder and put him right. Then she'd give me the Devil for shooting him, and so would Papa. The eastern sky was bleaching into dawn, and I sure felt like going home. Just to milk Esther. I sudden had the want to hug Mama and tease old Phoebe, not to mention ask Papa's forgiveness for sneaking off twice in the same clock. Sure had been a long night, and I just wanted to lay up somewhere and snooze.

A soldier was walking our way that I recognized as Sergeant Joseph Ketter, the man who'd kicked away Papa's pipe and then made friends with us afterward. He'd stood opposed to Jake's hanging, and for that reason alone, I had liked the man.

"Thank you, boys," he said to me and Luke.

"It's his shoulder," I said.

"Let me have him," said Sergeant Ketter, who put his arms around the tottering Andrew Hawkes, "and we'll see he gets mended proper. You'll be fine, lad. Sound as a pound."

Hawkes limped off, held up by the brawny arm of Sergeant Ketter.

Both us colonials and the Regulars turned to watch them disappear inside a barrack door. For a moment, all were silent. I wondered if they were thinking the same thought I was . . . how wrong for Englishmen to war upon English. And I wonder how many Jakes it took to start it all; and if my father would take a side, now that the conflict was so near to home.

"Hey, lads! Rum!"

We heard a Verdmont voice call out, and turned to see a man I knew to be one Peter Sill carry out a keg of rum, to which a number of our Greenies run to. A companion of Sill's made a ram with his gun butt to break a stave and the rum flowed free. Another man come at a clank with a handful of dippers and tin cups. Men pushed and shoved to get a share of the drink.

"Come on!" said Luke.

"I ain't thirsty."

Truth be known, I was; but I'd a traded the whole durn keg for a dipper full of Esther's milk. And I was so tired out, I'd a swapped all of Fort Ti and every soul in it for a bite of Mama's breakfast and a nap. Luke was gone and then come back with a cup of the grog. He made certain I was watching as he let his rum wash down.

"That's poetry," he said, drawing a sleeve across his wet mouth. But his face read that his gullet weren't so keen on the sugary taste of rum as he'd have me believe. I'd had me a swig or two of rum, and it sure gives a man's inside a good boiling. Less I was froze to death or near abouts, I don't guess I'd hanker too hard for my next sip of the evil stuff.

"Good?" I asked Luke.

"Best I had. Think I'll go have me another, seeing as it belongs to old King George, him being too far away to matter about."

Our men were everywhere, busy as ants on a kicked hill, ducking in doors and coming out again with goods in their arms. One fellow run out into the morning light with a pillow and quilt, another with a rocking chair. I saw more than one Verdmonter with foodstuffs, a butter tub or a wheel of cheese. More kegs of rum got kicked in and dried up. Several of our boys was wearing red tunics that had belonged to the Redcoats. I saw a man with a drum under one arm and a bagpipe in the other. He laughed with a friend who appeared from out a door toting an armload of boots and shoes as well as a long bolt of muslin.

"Git yours, boys."

"Have at it all."

"More rum. More rum, lads."

Their voices sounded like the grunts of hogs at slop time. We were no longer an army but a pack of thieves, ransacking the fort like rats through a dump. Luke come back, drank more rum and shared it with me. There weren't much else to do so we filled ourselves on English drink, free from King George. My head was starting to spin. I wanted to sleep, but to close my eyes made the whole courtyard chase its tail like a mad cat. Hunger hit me a lick or two, but the drink that sloshed around inside me seemed to be claiming my stomach for its own. I wished I hadn't of took that last swallow. Luke's face was the color of June grass, and his eyelids at halfmast. He was still caked almost all over with dry mud. I reckon I didn't look a whit sharper.

"Able?"

"Yeah."

"I'm either fixed to cry . . . or . . ."

"Or what?"

"Or throw up."

He did. All over himself, me, his musket, and on the good soil of New York. It must of give me envy to see him do it, on account my next action was to do likewise. He puked and then I'd puke. We held on to each other as if it was all we had in the world to cling to. It sure was a sorry business, and felt as if I was losing my guts and both kidneys. It final stopped. Luke smiled.

"We're drunk," he said.

"Like a pair of skunks."

"Want another drink?"

"Not this year. And not maybe never. Rum's got to be a worse feel than smoking a cigar."

A woman screamed behind our backs. Not a cry of bother. This was the real article and both me and Luke heard the torment in her voice. Turning, I recognized the friendly woman who had showed Papa and me how to make candles six at a time. There was terror on her face as she motioned for Luke and me to come quick.

"My daughter," the woman screamed, as we run inside, "they got her in the backroom. She's only fourteen. Break the door. For the sake of God, break in the door!"

As me and Luke cracked through the wood, we saw a sorry scene. Two of our men were too drunk to do much damage, but they were holding a naked girl for a third who was more able to fill a function. The girl was crying. Lifting a chair up high, I brought it down hard on the back of the man who was trying to force the girl. The chair was heavy, and I guess I'd done enough farm work in my time to heft it and heave it with authority. He rolled to the dirt floor and lay stone still. Luke kicked one of the drunks under the chin, and as the third tried to rise, the bridge of his nose stopped a rung of the busted chair that I still could use as a bludgeon. It sure was a short scrap.

189

The woman ran to her daughter, lifting the crying girl up real gentle and held her head to her big breasts, rocking her to and fro until the girl's sobs had come to a rest. Luke and I sort of slipped out without saying too much.

"You hungry?" he asked me.

"Nope. You?"

"Sort of."

"Then go fetch yourself a help of grub. Me, I'm going to sit down and rest a spell. Meet me right here, cause I ain't going to leg one more step."

Luke left.

Inside, I could hear the big woman comforting her daughter. Here I had the chance to look at a naked gal and never took even a wink, it all happened so quick. I sure hoped nobody mean like them three ever got Phoebe cornered and tried to trespass her. I'd kill if the like ever happened to old Phoebe, or to Comfort, or any gal I knew. Closing my eyes, I went to sleep.

"Care for a cut of cheese?"

The voice woke me up right quick, and I looked up into a red tunic. My gun was across my knees, but empty. I never had got to give her a reload. Above the red of the tunic was the handsome face of Colonel Benedict Arnold.

"It's fair cheese," he said. "Want some?"

"Sure do," I said, suddenly empty. He cut me a slice off the quarter-wheel he carried. It sure was tasty. He read my enjoyment, and without my asking he cut me another.

"Thanks," I said, "sir."

"That is what I have come to say to you. Thank you, young master, for saving my backside."

We both laughed. "You're welcome, sir."

"Benedict Arnold." He extended a hand to me.

"Able Booker."

"How old are you? Hope you don't offend my asking."

"Seventeen, sir."

"Seventeen, eh? Well, were it not for you, Able Booker, I would not ever celebrate thirty-five. You're a Verdmont lad?"

"Yes, sir. We live crosslake from the fort. We're just farmers."

"You move quick enough when duty calls. Ever thought about becoming a lifetime soldier?"

"No, sir. But I guess going off to war would be preference to pailing a cow."

"Not to all. You have to be molded to stand the stink of it, lad. Here, have some more of this cheese. Take it all, in fact, home to your mother's larder." He handed it to me.

"We sure whipped 'em, didn't we, sir?"

"With hardly a shot."

"Girls could of done it," I said. "Why them British don't even know what hit 'em. I wager we could march on Boston and push every last Regular into the sea, if this is how well they fight."

"Son," said Colonel Arnold, "is this what you think the British Army really is?"

"Well, ain't it?"

"In no way is it. Fort Ti is manned by a shiftless pack of scum, outcasts and misfits, headed by a namby-pamby almost equal in competence to General Abercromby, the one who foolishly slaughtered his Black Watch not a mile from here."

"You mean . . ."

"Yes, just that." His fist opened to take a firm grip on my arm. "Listen, my lad. The British Regulars are the best in the world, and under a Gage or a Howe or a Burgoyne, if properly commanded, a platoon of them could have wiped out the lot of us as we came wading out of the swamp. Are you so removed from the real of things that you actually thought *you* fought the *Regulars?* Hell, man . . . the Regulars in Boston wouldn't spit on Delaplace and his crew of rejects. So hear me well and mark what I say to you. War is nothing like what you all fell into this day. British Regulars would mop the floor with half of us, and the rest of us would truly hang for treason."

"But we whipped 'em, sir."

"You caught a bunch of louts in uniform asleep in the morning mist. That's all we did. So if you have military aspiration, let me give you some advice to swallow along with your cheese."

"What advice, sir?"

"Train yourselves. Drill and march and fire your muskets until the barrels would sizzle eggs. Learn to reload on a dead run, because the whole business is willy-nilly upon us. Look at him."

"Who, sir?"

"Look at Ethan Allen up on that balcony. Thinks he sunk the Armada, to hear his bragging. He wouldn't know a real British Redcoat if it came up and bit his butt. Go home, Booker. Plow your field and drill, drill, drill."

"I will, sir."

"Thank you, Booker. You'll be a credit to your cause."

I watched Colonel Arnold walk away, I felt right proud that he said I'd make a soldier.

Chapter 19

I was still sick from the rum.

The lady who had made the candles and whose daughter we rescued come and give me and Luke apples to eat with our cheese, and a glass of cold buttermilk. It sure tasted better than the rum.

"Best we eat," said Luke.

The both of us sat a cannon barrel like we'd straddle the back of a horse, facing each other, eating more of the cheese.

"I ain't too hungry," I said.

"Me neither. But I heard it told that after you cough up a meal that it's best to eat and restore yourself."

"Who said?"

"My brother Will. He should know about how to scrape off the bottom of a good drunk, seeing as he swills enough for the three of us."

"How come he drinks so dang much?"

"He's married."

"Oh," I said.

"You aim to wed Comfort."

"Sure enough do."

"Soon?"

"Soon's the better. Sure wish I had a trade, besides chain. And I don't guess I want to farm it all my life. How about you?"

"Nah," said Luke. "Maybe I'll soldier with Ethan for a spell."

"Go north?"

"That's what the talk is. Hey, fetch me one more slab of that cheese. Ethan says we got to all stay banded to an army and tomorrow we go north and take Crown Point."

"How far is that?"

"Twenty mile."

"That's ten times two mile."

"Yeah boy, I jolly know what you mean. Them two swamp miles was enough to sell a soul. My boots ain't dry yet, and I still stink from the slime of the place."

"So do I," I said. My shirt had a foul smell to it, like it had been soured by the swamp water and no scrub of soap could again do it sweet.

"You coming north?"

"I don't cotton to."

"You sick of soldiering?" asked Luke.

"I sure am sick of something. Maybe it be the illness of listening to Ethan jaw it all day on how great a doggone general he is, and how he'll fix to writ a letter to the Continental Congress about how we took this cussed fort like a mouse from a cat."

"We ain't supposed to desert."

"Shucks on it, Luke. You and me ain't even supposed to *be* here. And we been stayed here all day. Good thing Seth Warner and that lot come, too, so we can say we're attached to his troop and not to Ethan's or Ira's. Who in the tarnation would care if we lit out for home?"

"Best we don't."

"You serious?"

"Sure am. Able, I seen them two sharpshooters who tag along by Ethan. All he's got to do is nod, and you and me would be shot before we even got to the lake."

"Maybe we made a mistake," I said, holding up my arm so my initiation scar would show.

"Possible did."

"Papa said that one time."

"Said what?"

"Well," I said, "the two of us was talking on things. Politics mostly . . . and he said that oft times it were a mite easier to get into a thing than get out of it."

"You sure he didn't mean Comfort?"

"Dang you, Shelby. Can't you never let an old dog die?"

"Sure, but this here is the first I ever heard tell that Mistress Comfort was an old dog."

"I swear if I don't lesson you."

"Don't get humored up. All the tease of it is on account I feel we're trapped into this Green Mountain Boy business and there ain't a clear way out."

"Papa was right," I said.

"He blessed was."

"I wonder what real soldiers do."

193

"They's a term of enlistment. But you can't lit off any time you dang well please."

"I know who'd know."

"Who? Seth Warner."

"Yeah, he might. But I reckon Colonel Benedict Arnold of Connecticut would know the certain of it, him being a regular soldier and all," I said.

"Let's ask him."

"I don't know where he's at."

"Seems he ought to be neighborsome, seeing as we're all in the same old fort."

"If I catch a looksee at him, I will. But for now, I reckon I'll just wait for dark, keep out of sight, and then head for home."

"How you fixed to git across?"

"Row."

"In what?" Luke's face was curious.

"One of them rear-guard boats that come the short way, after the fort got took. I seen a bunch of 'em when I was up walking the high wall."

Luke's face turned. Squinting, his eyes climbed up above the fort to where the flag pole was naked of cloth. "Somebody hauled down the Union Jack."

"Me," I said.

"You?"

"I got the old rag inside my shirt." It was true, as I felt the rough of it against my chest.

"You heard Ethan rant about that?"

"Yeah, I heard."

"He wants that flag to take home, as a spoil of war or whatever you call it."

"But he ain't to git this'n. It's mine. I fetched it off the pole and I aim to squirrel it away as a keepsake, if I want to."

"You mean it?"

"Certain do."

"Booker, you got more bowels than brains."

"I won't have a spate of either one if old Ethan finds it on my person."

"What you aim to do with it?"

"I got a use."

"Hang it over your bed?"

"Nope, not that."

"What then?"

"I don't guess to keep it very long for my ownself. Instead, it'd be a righteous thing to give to Jake's ma."

194

"Jake Cotter's mother?"

I nodded my head. "Yes, to her. Sort of to let her know that her son Jacob was a kind of hero, if you follow the mean. So she'll think for all eternal that little old Jake didn't die for nothing."

"Like he fired the first shot that took Fort Ti for the colony cause."

The way he said it, I knowed right off that Luke Shelby understood why I wanted the flag to go to Mrs. Cotter. It was a dumb idea, but at least to us it made a lick of sense. Not that it would measure up to take Jake's place, but it could possible ease the heft of his hanging like some outlaw. As I'd been a schoolmate of Jacob Cotter's, the flag of Fort Ticonderoga seemed little enough to give. Maybe his ma would hold it as a medal of her son's valor.

"I'd like to go with you when you give the flag to Jacob's mother," said Luke. "It's a good sentiment."

"You're welcome to come along."

"Thanks. I'm beholding."

"Maybe we're growing up, Luke."

"What makes you say so?"

"Just because. We started to care for people. You know, to feel the same hurt they feel."

Luke shook his head. "Nobody can do that. There ain't a soul on this good earth who can know the pain in a mother's heart who's had a son carted home dead."

"Not a soul."

"Along with the flag," said Luke, "I'll bring some flowers from Will and me to set on his grave."

"My father does that sometimes."

"Noah's folk got killed by injuns, true?"

"True. Back in 1745. He was only ten."

Luke nodded his head real slow, like he took to picture it all in his mind, the same way I tried to see it so I could better understand my pa's remembering.

"Able?"

"Yeah."

"Did you ever think you was about to die?"

"Sure did. Early this morn."

"Likewise for me. I wonder what Jacob thought."

"Just before hanging?"

"Yes. You were here, you and Noah."

"We were here. I reached out for Jake as them soldiers marched him by us on his way up to the gallows."

"Did he say anything?"

"He said . . . 'Pray for me, Able.'"

"Never knew old Jake ever heard of prayer," said Luke.

"But he meant it, Luke. You know the devil way his face used to screw up whenever he was up to clowning. Well, not that day. His face was . . . pure. Like he was newborn, or reborn."

"Says in the Bible we git born again."

"Must be true, on account I saw it on Jake's face. A sort of sweetness, like God already forgive him of all sin."

"I sure never heard *you* talk like this before," said Luke.

"Jake's dying hit me hard, Luke. It honest did. Not until now did I ever talk of it with nobody. A bit with Papa as we brung home the cold body, but not so much as to let it gush out. It's like I been holding my breath all these days, ever since the hanging."

"I think I know how ya feel."

"It's like a hatred I got inside me. Not up to a boil, just a simmer of resent I got against England. I want to get even for Jake, and git the bastard that put the rope on his neck. Somebody's got to pay a price for it, and it's got to be equal."

"Equal?"

"Yes," I said. "To hang Jake over a prank like hooking a cannon, that ain't fair. It ain't justice. But now the boot's on the other foot. Them British hanged Jake Cotter and now somebody ought to pay a full measure."

"Somebody's got to *die,*" said Luke.

"Right. Don't you agree?"

"I certain do. But who we gonna kill?"

"That's a rub. Can't just pick some poor Scottish lad and hang him from a nearby elm. I don't think I could hang Andrew Hawkes."

"The one you gunshot."

"Him. Shucks, he's sort of like you or me."

"Or Jake," said Luke.

"It'd be saying two dead boys is better than one."

"Don't reason out."

"Sure don't," I said. "I'd sell my worthless soul to Old Harry just to find that one Redcoat who said *hang Jacob Cotter.* I would hang that English devil, enjoy the doing of it, and laugh to beat hell to see his face go purple."

"Me too. But there's only one problem to that."

"What's that?"

"The way I see it," said Luke, "is that it'd be right and meet to hang the one who give the order. But if we hang the wrong man, say we hang somebody like young Hawkes, I'd feel like a mouse turd for the rest of my days. I sure would."

"So would I."

"Cut me another hunk of cheese."

"Take it all," I handed the whole blessed thing to Luke. "I'm ill of it. And I'm tired of forking this damn cannon. My arse feels like it's half iron. I'm so dogged sleepy I could crawl up the barrel and snooze. We ain't had no sleep."

"Yeah, we was up all night. Well, it'll be good training for you."

"How so?" I said.

"If you cotton to wed Comfort."

"Hush your mouth, Shelby."

"That there's a gal who'll keep you up all night and halfway through the morning. Why, I bet after a week in old Comfort's bed, you'll run to Ethan and beg to march at his side, through every dagburn swamp this side of Hades, just to rest up."

"That ain't likely."

"Besides, massive as he is, even Ethan ain't as big around to hug as Comfort Starr."

"You want that cheese to ram down your gullet?"

"Soft, son. I didn't mean no offense to your intended. Some fellows seem to preference a thin woman, and others go for fat."

My fist took a swing at his chin, but I missed by a mile and fell off the cannon. Luke spat a mouthful of cheese on me, laughed, and lit off like a rabbit with me after him. Under his arm was the rest of the cheese which I don't guess he was fixing to give up as his gut seemed so partial to it. He run through the dark of the arch toward the courtyard, me right behind. I'd a caught him for certain if'n Ira hadn't of caught him first.

"Cheese," said Luke in a puff.

Ira looked at the two of us, winded as we was, took the cheese from Luke and walked away. But then, thinking upon it, he turned to address us,

"You two got so much spirit to spare, go stack them muskets over yonder. Get a tool each and remove the triggers, hear? That's an order."

"Yes, sir," we said.

"Where'd you git this cheese?" Ira took a bite, between his blade and thumb.

"Colonel Arnold give it to me. For saving his hide, I reckon."

"That I saw," said Ira. "Good shot."

"Thank you, Ira."

"Thanks for the cheese."

"Ain't mine," I said. "Belongs to King George."

Ira smiled. "Plenty around these here parts used to be his'n and ain't no more. Noah know you're over here flirting with treason and Allen folk?"

"No, sir."

"I wager he does. That old moose don't miss much, if I know your pa."

"He don't," I said.

"You miss him?"

"Well," I said, "I don't guess either me or Luke is hankering for another battle right off."

"This weren't no battle," said Ira. "It were a pretty picnic, and the fort at Crown Point will fall the quicker. You boys game to go north?"

"All the ways to Crown Point?" asked Luke.

"Hah!" Ira laughed. "That just be the jump-off place. Boys, we aim to go clear to Canada, and push them British backsides into Hudson's Bay."

"Where's that?" I said.

"Away up north. So far up compass that the bloody English and their tax collectors'll never come south no more." Ira looked from Luke to me, as though he read our brains. "And they won't hang no boys like they done young Cotter, hear?"

"We hear."

It made me want to push his face in. A lot the Allens cared for Jake. They could of stopped it, but instead they let him hang in order to step up enlistment in the Green Mounties. Hell with you, Ira Allen.

"Where are your muskets, boys?"

"Back yonder."

"So's your arse, back yonder. Some soldiers you two make out to be. You'd lose your balls if they wasn't glued in your crotch. Go git them guns o' yourn and report to Seth Warner, hear?"

"Yes, sir."

Ira tossed the cheese to me, pretending to give my backside a swift kick which never did arrive. Somehow I liked Ira, but had to keep telling my own ears that he was an Allen, a probable enemy to my own pa and a past enemy to Comfort's. We went and reclaimed our muskets, ate more cheese, and sort of wandered around half-looking for Seth. What we really did look at was east toward Verdmont. The afternoon sun blessed the green valley and I could see the brown speck of home. I wanted to reach my arm over and touch Papa and Mama and Phoebe. Luke's face told he was thinking a like thought.

"We gonna search out Seth?" he asked.

"When we git good and ready," I said.

"You sleepy, Able?"

"Like a fresh pup whose eyes ain't open yet. You?"

"I'm right tuckered out."

"Let's go off someplace and snooze."

"We'll catch it."

"Seth thinks we're with the Allens, and Ira thinks we're with Seth's troop. We're free as a brace of birds."

"Don't you wish."

"Come on," I said.

Nobody was at the west gate. Not a soul. I saw Benedict Arnold and waved to him. I wanted Luke to see him wave back or throw me an easy salute like he done early, but I don't guess he saw me. He sure wore a smart uniform. Made me wonder if all them Connecticut officers looked as soldierlike as Colonel Arnold. For a moment I made the guess that Ethan was inside the officer barrack trying on uniforms. Not a one would girth him. He was too awesome.

For a few steps we stayed close to the outer wall so nobody would eye us as we worked our way north. Then, with the cheese in one hand and the musket in the other, I broke out a scamper for the trees. Luke run too, toting his musket and his horn.

Under the pines on the west hill it was cool as could be, in the shade and all, a right good May afternoon for a nap. We tried to eat more cheese, but the pair of us was full of the stuff. One more mouth of it and I'd turned into a curd. My throat still carried along an echo of rum, up from the stomach, a taste I couldn't spit out or piss away.

We lay down. I put my head on the flag, like it was a pillow. Never knew I'd miss that tick full of cornhusk that was uploft back at the Booker farm. I even wished it was Phoebe sleeping at my side instead of Luke. And to top it all, I ain't been gone much more than half a day. I wondered if Ben Arnold ever got lonesome for the face of family. He probable did, seeing as I could tell he was a human like the rest of us. It sure weren't easy to picture Ethan as a wee boy. I pictured his big body in a cradle, splintering the wood on all sides, and I most laughed at the image, even though my eyes was closed.

Luke let out a sigh.

"Able."

"I'm here."

"If'n I go off to sleep and say the name of Comfort Starr over and over, don't wake me up, on account you'll know what I'm up to."

I wanted to answer him back, or punch him a good one, but it all weren't worth the effort. All I wanted was to fall asleep for a couple of years. Chores were sorry enough, but war was more tiring. I was glad it was so quiet. Our war was over. Crown Point would fall into American hands, and then Boston and New York and them other places. The pack of Regulars would be so frighted, they jump in the sea and swim clear back to England. Wouldn't even stop to skin down to the white, the way Luther done. Wowie, that sure was a swim. How he ever goaded hisself into ice water for that long a swim is more than I'd ever understand.

Soldiering was poor aplenty, but it'd be worse to be a spy. A lot colder. I got to pondering how sticky hot it was to wade that old swamp. Up to our belts in the black and mucky, we was half wet and half sweat. Sure was relieving to know that the dainty nose of one Miss Comfort Starr was too distant for a whiff of Able Booker. I smelled like stockings at sundown, just one big stink; inside and out, thanks to the rum and the cheese. What a tincture, them two.

I wondered if Seth Warner was looking for us.

To heck with you, Colonel Warner, sir. Funny what he said about Ethan's army . . . more officers than beans. Seth weren't all bad. Suspect he'll be evil enough when he catches up to us. Well, let him do his darndest. Who cares? I got to git me some shut-eye. Crown Point was twenty miles north of right here; and if I know old Ethan, he's probable to ink a letter to Mr. Washington to brag on how his Boys waded twenty miles up and twenty back. Why them swamp rats of mine took joy in it, sir, Ethan will say. Can't keep a Verdmonter out of his muck and murk or he'll git homesick. Wading keeps 'em happy. Ethan's one regret'll be that a pen can't holler.

Sure wish Papa was along for the show. I can just see Noah Booker git ordered to wade twenty mile in a snake nest like the one we come through. Papa would shut one eye and squint the other.

Dog it! How in Hades am I to go home and face my folks? I got to do it sometime. Got to find the gumption to toe it to Papa and tell him why I run off instead of plow. He ain't going to be joyful about it. What makes it worse, he'll know I scampered out to aid Ethan's cause, which won't exactly please him some. Mama will side in, too, and give me what-for. And even Phoebe. Sure is going to be a hot home-coming. But I don't guess they'd swap it for Jake's. Just think, I'll say, I could of come home dead, and then think on how sorrowful you'd all feel. We ought to celebrate that I'm upright and kicking, so let's git out the cider jug.

Rum? No thanks. Got me a belly of that, and it sure is an illness. I got drunk, Mama. Luke did, too; but don't hasten to breathe it to his ma. Mrs. Shelby took a broom to Will, according to what Luke said. Hit his head again and again, his brains not being too healthy from the rum and packing an ache in the head. Ain't much worse than having a rumhead and getting whacked with a broom. A big woman, Mrs. Shelby. No wonder Will run off and married a wee wife. She can't hit as hard when Will empties the jug. Rum sure is a misery. I don't guess I was cast out to become much of a drinking man. Neither be Luke. He can throw up about as colorful as can I. Like we was two cannon.

Sure wish I could sleep.

Not far from my ear, I could hear Luke breathing slow and even. He was out like a snuffed candle. Was I to lay here and think all evening? It sure would be passable good to have a bite or two of supper. Made me wonder what Mama and Phoebe were fixing for themselfs and for Papa. Maybe it was ox meat. Something was certain wrong in a world when, to git by, you have to eat a portion of Simon. Yet it would of been sinful to waste all that fresh beef. I don't guess it bothered Simon, dead as he was. Even your own meat can't nourish back a lost soul.

I bet the Shelbys is out looking for Luke and already rode by the Booker place. They all talked and pointed and fret away the day. But I wager Papa just up and give the whole business a shrug as if to say if the young fools git hungered enough, they'll both leg it home like a loved-out hound.

What would my father do in an instance like I'm in right now?

He'd probable spit in old Ethan's eye and tell him where he could shove Fort Ti. Well, maybe that's what Thomas Starr done, and he ain't around to say different. Or to tell me to go soft when mixing it up with all them Allen brothers. I got to thinking on them mountain men and their long rifles, the two I saw at the hanging, the same pair they said sort of hung around to guard Ethan and to cut down a deserter who had a mind of his own. Them two was enough to scare Peter and Paul. Well, you can't make me believe that fewer than a handful of Greenies up and lit out, anytime they dang well pleased to do it. And you don't own Able Booker no way. Not you, Mr. Allen or Mr. Warner or Mr. Benedict Arnold of Connecticut.

Them boys from Massachusetts sure was dignity. Not a one of them mother's sons looted or tore up stuff; only *our* boys done that. And yet Colonel Arnold had a cheese. Well, what's a wheel of cheese? All them British is sure lucky it was Verdmont men who come in the night and not the red-devil Saint Francis. I don't guess there's a feel in the whole wide world as ill as to wake up in the darksome to hear the yelp of a stinking redhide, and realize that any odd moment one of them heathen would break through your own door. I don't guess I'll ever know how Papa's reason kept in one piece.

I know how scared I'd be. My britches would be as wet as swamp water and twice as smelly, if that were possible. Well, if old Ethan says wade to Crown Point, he can go by his lonesome. Maybe I'll be the rear guard, me and Luke. So far in the rear that they can all git to Canada before I even git north of Shoreham.

I fell asleep.

"Able. Hey you, Able, wake up."

It was Luke as he put a rub to his eyes. I saw him yawn which I knew would contagion me to do likewise. So I did. Yawned and stretched and felt my body gripe about how hard the earth was.

"What's the hour?" I said.

"Almost dark."

"You and me, Luke, we're gonna catch merry hell."

"From who?"

"From *somebody,* that's a certain. Ain't a living soul in the Mountain Boys that don't outrank the two of us like we was two specks of gunpowder."

"They got to catch us first," said Luke.

"Well, son, you know how simple that'll be. Them Allens all know the Booker place and the Shelby place, so I figure they'll come calling any hour they dang please and drag us off to a fire stake."

"Aw, go on."

"You ain't forgot that poor bastard they burned the night I got swore in."

"No, I ain't forgot. An unfortunate soul like that don't forget too easy," said Luke. He sat up, fingering the trigger house on his musket.

Just then I heard myself a noise. At first it give me one heck of a start, until the sudden that I warmed to right who it was. Turning, I saw her face. But even before we looked at each other, I sort of knew, even as I heard her bawl.

It was April.

She must of just been wandering around in the north meadow, north of the fort, free to enjoy the May grass. Hearing my voice must of rang some sort of a bell inside her remembering, so over she come to under the pines. Critters is curious.

"April," I said.

"Who the heck is that?" Luke looked puzzled and he rubbed his hair as if he took to clear his thought.

"Used to be our calf. Here, girlie."

April stood not much more than a spit away, looking my way as if she had the hanker to come to me but was feared of Luke.

"Come on, April." I held out my hand to her, but she still wouldn't advance no closer.

"Howdy there, April," said Luke.

With a nod of her head, she walked herself to me and I touched her ear. Somebody had notched her different than a Booker cut. Yet in a funny way she was still my calf. Mine and Phoebe's. As I put both my arms to circle her neck, resting my head up to the warm of her flank, I wanted my sister to be here, too. Old Phoebe would sure cotton to give a hug to April.

"We miss you, April," I said to her. It sort of brung back all we Bookers was, together in a family, the way homefolk was born to be. Her tongue sure was rough on my cheek. And still rougher on a memory.

I hoped Luke failed to mark my eyes.

Chapter 20

We saw the three men.

In the early dark, Luke Shelby and me was on our way back, entering the grounds of Fort Ticonderoga by its big west gate, when the three who'd tried to attack the young girl come toward us. I don't guess they knew us right off as we kept to the shadows.

"You loaded?" I whispered to Luke.

"Sure am. You?"

"No, but I'll bluff."

"Hey!" One of the three pointed at us, nudging the others to take note in our direction. We didn't say a word, but just kept on walking up the road, like we had intent to pass by all three of them louts without as much as a hello.

But they blocked our way.

We stopped. Doggone, I sure wish I'd reloaded my piece. Well, at least old Luke still had powder and ball. My fingers tightened on an empty musket.

"Them two," one of the men spoke.

"What about 'em?"

"They's the ones that busted up our frolic with the little missy and her fat old ma."

"You sure?"

"Sure enough to Jesus."

The three were in front of us. The man on the left, was the smallest of the three. Even in the dark, his britches was the color of sour cream. One stocking was up, the other wrinkled down about his ankle. The man in the center was the tallest, and I remember he'd wore a red vest, even though the light was too weak to see its color. The third man was heavy; thick legs and arms and almost no neck, as his round head sat his shoulders like a half-rot pumpkin.

"You two boys desert, did ye?"

"We ain't say," said Luke.

"We be officers," the tall man said.

"Yes, sir," I said, saluting. I give Luke a quick elbow in the ribs as my arm come up so he'd spark to the game and whip a salute as sharp as mine. He did, but we both knowed they weren't officers.

"What's your name, boy?"

"Ledder," I said. "Charles Ledder."

They took a step or two nearer to Luke and me. The tall one, Red Vest, seemed to be the best spoke of the lot, as the men at either hip let him handle the gab.

"You lads is supposed to turn your weapons over to us. That's an order."

"Whose order?" I said.

"I'm Ethan Allen," the thick man said.

"Shut up, fooly. We're to collect all muskets and stack arms back in the parade ground. A fact, we got sent to look for youse two bucks, on account you was missed at roll call. So we'll just take them two guns o' yourn, hear?"

"Soft," said Luke. His gun weren't pointed at their bellies, but it was on its way there, inch by inch. I was pleasured to note that the shabby threesome we faced toted no weapons. Papa once said that the danger that hurts is the one you can't see. So I watched six empty hands, expecting any breath to spot a pistol or a throwing knife. Against either, what would I do with a musket no load?

"What you got in your arm, boy?"

"Cheese," I said.

"You stole it."

I didn't answer the accuse. No need to. It was the cheese (or what was left of it) give to me by Colonel Arnold, and if them three wanted to question which cow it come from, they'd have to with no hand from me. I broke off three small hunks to toss their way. Thick Body dropped his.

"We're to pass by, sir," I said.

"Yeah?"

"We certain are," said Luke. "This cheese is for Ethan, and we aim to see he gits it personal."

"Right," I said. "I don't guess you want to stand betwixt Ethan and his supper, seeing as this here ain't no common cheese."

"What's so special about it?"

"Well," I said, holding up the cheese so they could see it, "the *lady*

205

that sends it to Ethan is special to *him*. So if I was you, best let the cheese go to the stomach intended for, which be Ethan Allen's."

Like we was two bulls (three, counting the big cheese) me and Luke walked by the men like they wasn't even there. Passing close to Creamy Britches, my gut got a griefy feeling he hankered to pull a knife and cut more than just a slice of cheese, but nothing took place. Them three fellows sure did stink. Figured I smelled no better. Red Vest muttered something as we scooted on our way, but its meaning got swallowed up in the night. Thick Body give a wee push to Luke, but it weren't enough to issue over.

"I owe him one," Luke said to me.

But we didn't look back, even when a small rock hit the top of my shoulder. If that was all they could do, other than commit a trespass on a girl, they sure weren't too harmful. I sort of hoped the one that flung the rock at me was the same chap I'd smacked with the leg of the busted chair, Thick Body. If it was, he already had an egg on his nog, and the score got even in advance.

We saw Seth.

Just as we ducked through the archway and out into the courtyard, there he was. As if he'd stood there for hours to surprise us in the dark.

"Booker and Shelby," he said.

"Yes, sir," I said. We both saluted. Trouble was, Luke was at my left hip. Carrying the cheese at my other, I brung up my left arm as Luke lifted his right. Our elbows whacked. Dang to near drop the cheese that was under my gun arm.

"Where you two been hid?"

"Back yonder," I said, "sir."

"We was so plum wore out from the frakus," said Luke, "we had to lay up and sleep for a short spell."

"A short spell? I been here since mid-morn and ain't seen hide nor hair. I was feared you got drownded in the crossing."

"Not us."

"What's that object, Booker?"

"It's a cheese, sir."

"Cheese?"

"Want some, sir? Me and Luke and Ira and Benedict Arnold can't eat it all." I figured being in the same breath with them other two wouldn't do us no harm.

"What make is it?"

"Just cheese. Here, have a morsel."

Seth cracked out a knife and cut himself a healthy slab. As he jawed it up, I was thinking what a Godsend this cheese turned out to be. A hundred uses. I sure would have to tell Colonel Arnold about its divers purposes, if he'd hold still long enough to listen. Some of the Massy boys run by, on their way to somewhere as they was all with muskets. I looked for Colonel Easton but he weren't among them.

"It's good," said Seth, not to notice the soldiers.

"Have some more."

"I will. Where'd you get it?"

"Colonel Arnold give it to me."

"He done *what?*"

"Honest."

"Booker, I wouldn't believe you or Shelby if you was both dying on the same Gospel."

"What's afoot, Seth?" said Luke as more of the Massachusetts men went by.

"Arnold's pulling out."

"Where to?"

"None of your business. Ethan's pulling out, too."

"Where's he at?"

"Upstairs. Been writing a letter for most of the day. Gits it all writ, rips it to a tatter, and begins anew. I wager the name of Benedict Arnold will appear in scanty count."

"Who's it to?" I said.

"A lady friend," Luke said.

"Watch your tongue, Shelby, or you may open your trap to only find it missing. It's a letter to the Massachusetts Council. And call me *sir*. We already got the downcountry boys to laugh our way, and calling us Verdmonters a bunch of bumpkins."

"We ain't bumpkins," I said.

"Both Able and me seen Skenesboro," said Luke.

"Lord help us," said Seth. "Lord help the Continental Army if this be a sample of its soldiery."

"Huh?" I said.

As my mouth opened, Seth Warner thrust in an orange sliver of cheese. He looked at us both, let out a big sigh of air, and walked away. Luke eyed me and shrugged.

"Must be the cheese," he said.

I smelled it. "Smells right to my nose."

"That's 'cause you and me odor so putrid, we'd start to reason a pigsty is sweet to compare. I'm hungry."

"Want some cheese?"

"Anything," he said, "but cheese."

"I don't guess I can gulp down even one more blessed bite of the stuff. What'll I do with it?"

"You could give it back to Colonel Arnold."

207

"He's headin' out."

"Maybe he ain't gone yet."

"Let's go look," I said.

"Best we don't run into Ira."

"He don't want us neither."

"If this cheese is gone wrong, we're going to have a passel of folks sore at us."

"I say if it's wrong, we feed some to them British officers and help thataway to win the war."

"Feed everybody this stuff and nobody'll be humored to do much fighting. I never knew so much a part of battle was trying to finish off a dumb old wheel of cheese."

My hand went to over my belly. I said, "I think the cheese'll win. Seems it turned against me."

"What say we look for Benedict Arnold?"

"I'm game."

Fort Ti sure did shine handsome, all aglow in the dark with candles burning at the windows. Although I did have no itch to live close to so many persons. Some of the men were still drinking rum. Others were watching a group of prisoners. I could hear Ira Allen shouting an order to some poor soul. It hit Luke's ear as soon as mine, so we turned to go the other way. We sat on a short rampart of stone.

No sign of Ethan.

We didn't see Colonel Arnold either. What we did see was men rolling up packs to travel north with. One man had what looked like a pewter candlestick the size of my arm, and he was trying to roll it into his pack. Then at his feet I saw its mate. They looked heavy; I pondered if he was fixing to tote the pair all the way north to Crown Point.

"Luke?"

"That's me."

"You ever see Crown Point?"

"No, and I don't hanker to. See one of them big old fally-down forts you seen 'em all. You s'pect that dull devil plans to pack them candlesticks forty mile?"

"He's simple."

"Like you and your damn cheese."

"Look you. Colonel Benedict Arnold give me this cheese for saving his skin, so I ain't about to give it up."

"Don't blame ya. That there cheese is probable as close as you'll git to a medal. Pity you can't pin it on your chest."

From somewhere up in the dark of the south barrack, a woman giggled through an open window. Her laugh sounded like she was in bed and under a goose pillow. Sort of muffled. It was followed by a Verdmont yelp of a good old boy from the green hills who I figured was having himself a time, as there was sweeter spoils than candlesticks. Or cheese.

"Let's git ourselfs a woman," was Luke's idea.

"Where?"

"They's bound to be some nearby. My father says that women follow an army like flies after a dying cat. What say we go find a hussy and have at it."

"Maybe we could git two."

"Yeah," said Luke, "and after the first go-round we could change off. You take mine and I'll take yourn."

"Sounds more like a barn dance."

"Fiddler, start the music." Luke tapped his foot on a flat stone. "And were it a barn dance, Booker, I can see you now."

"Doing what?"

"High-stepping with your cheese."

"I sure would like to take it home to my mother."

"Shucks, all you want is to fetch *yourself* home."

"Maybe so. I never been away from home before. It certain is a strange feeling, like I slipped my halter and can't steal back into my own barnyard. I even miss old Phoebe."

"I'm hungry. Instead of women, what say we seek out the cookhouse and tie into some vittles. I could eat a moose."

"Me, too. Them women'll just have to wait."

"You suppose they can stand it?"

Two men come out a barrack door carrying a brass bed. Both seemed to be drunk, and on the bed was a naked woman. Me and Luke just stared. The woman was screaming but she weren't really calling for help. Instead it sounded like she was inviting both boys to join her among the coverlets. In the candlelight from the windows, part of her pink body caught the squares of amber, turning her flesh to a crazy quilt of pink and yellow and white. I wanted to run over and jump on top of her and have myself a time. Just for the mirth of it.

From the way he was watching, Luke did too.

It made me wonder if Luke was still pure like me, or had he ever had at it with a girl. When he said he'd made love to Mary Comfort, I knew it was all in fun, just to bait me. But I still wondered if Luke had ever done it to some other girl. Somehow I felt like if he really did, he wouldn't tell. Oh sure, he'd kid about things he hadn't done, but not about the straight of it. Like I wouldn't spout him a thing about me and Comfort Starr. Narry a word, and I don't guess Luke would tell neither.

The two men were hollering at one another from opposite ends of the brass bed. One pointed east, the other west, and both couldn't of took one more gulp of rum. From their yells, I could tell they were Verdmont boys. The woman in the bed was English. Her laughter was light and giddy as if it come from far off. Then a third man come out the barrack. He was bare as a birthday, carrying armfuls of clothes of every description; some male and some female, britches and petticoats and also what looked like a corset. I had to rub my eyes to make me believe what I saw when he tried to dress himself in what appeared to be the lady's chest strap, or whatever that dumb harness was with the two white cups of cloth.

On the other side of us, a fight started.

Turning, we saw a Verdmont man and a Massy lock into each other and go at it like merry hell. One kicked the other. But the man kicked at caught the foot and bit the ankle. The kicker went down yelling for murder. As the biter jumped on him, they rolled closer to where Luke and me was watching. They smelled strong of rum. Of a sudden, the fight stopped as quick as it started. The biter looked my way, even though he was still on his knees in the grit.

"Want a drink?" He pulled a small bottle out of his shirt and handed it toward me.

"No more rum for me," I said, "but thanks all the same."

"Ain't rum," the man said.

"He don't know," the kicker said, who was lying on his back with his legs in the air. "He don't even know *what* it is. He just swallers first and ponders after. He'd drink a whore's bath."

The biter became a kicker.

Luke handed me the bottle and I took a sip, followed by three stout said.

"Gin," the kicker said. "And I'm the only drunk fool who has the taste for finery. Sure is unholy."

"What's gin?" I asked Luke.

"A new drink. I heard a man in Shoreham tell of it."

"What's it taste like?"

Luke handed me the bottle and I took a sip, followed by three stout gulps of the stuff. It sure was hot on the way down and got hotter with every pull. It was like swallowing a forge.

"Well," said Luke, "how's it taste to you?"

"It don't rightly *have* a taste," I said when I could finally talk, on account my gullet was afire. "It's more of a burn."

"Or a cut," said Luke. "Sort of like choking down a mouthful of knives and forks."

We handed the bottle back to the two fighters, and gave them our thanks. I couldn't of took another pull out that bottle if it'd meant I froze to death refusing. It made my head spin.

210

"Gin," I said, without no reason.

"What about it?" Luke said.

"Aim to remember the name."

"To buy some?"

"No. Just in case I git offered some again somewhere, so's I can light out and run a mile before I look back to say *no thanks.*"

"Make it two mile, just to be safe."

"Let's tote ourselves a walk."

"Better yet, let's go visit the filly on that there brass bed."

The woman was getting dressed. Looked like she was wearing one of the men's shirts. As she dressed she was singing, and it made me want to sing as well. I put my arm around Luke's shoulder.

"To hell, to hell with Benny Wentworth," I yelled out in a wrong tune.

The woman on the bed waved a pink arm to me and I waved back. She motioned to me, right friendly.

"Want some cheese?" I hollered over.

Luke busted out laughing. He dropped his musket. Falling to a clatter on the stone rampart, the hammer must of been forced the flint. The primer puffed in the pan to fire the main charge. When the musket went off I thought for a breath I'd been shot. Somewhere I heard the whack of the lead as it hit stone. Lucky it didn't kill a soul.

The woman jumped under the covers on the brass bed, and only her bare arse stuck up like two milky buns. With a shoe, one of the men gave her a stout lick on the fat of the cheek and she let out a muffled scream, like it come from the bottom of a well. The two men with the gin ran over and jumped on her. This sort of got the ire up of the two fellows who'd lugged out the bed to begin with. Somebody hauled off and give somebody's chin a lacing and in no time there was as fair a fight going on among the five men (the man who carried the clothes joined in) as you'd want to witness. The five men was all knotted up together like a mess of worms; kicking, biting and biffing out with their fists. Having a grand old time.

The woman yelled like she'd went mad.

"Hey," said Luke, "let's go grab her."

"I'm game," I said.

As I started to run toward her, the gin in my gut started its own fun. As we got to the brass bed, the woman was all wrapped up in the coverlets like a babe in swaddle, so as we picked her up, she had no idea it was Luke and me who was fixing to carry her off. Between the two of us, carrying her with bedclothes and all, she weren't too heavy. We run across the courtyard and into the shadow of the south barrack. She was full of kicks and screams, but mostly she was laughing fit to die.

211

Through the archway we went, into the black of the tunnel and then out into the moonlight. For some reason knowed only to luck, we had to head for somewhere and the way we picked was toward the small Wicker Gate, the wee entrance we'd all come through.

My breath was coming harder, and sooner or later I knowed I have to drop a woman, a musket or a cheese.

We were moving along right sudden, a corner of the coverlets hung down to drag along the ground as we run along. Luke was in front and had her by the head and one arm (from what little I could see of her) as I held her knees. But my foot stepped on a corner of the quilt, so down the three of us tumbled, down the little hill and through the gate. My hand hurt, and my shin took a bump on the stone. We was all snarled up in a heap. Something round touched my face, and whatever it was seemed to be soft and pinky sweet, so I kissed it. She giggled and wiggled closer.

"Hey! You down there!"

A voice that sounded like an officer's rang out from way back on the upper wall. Luke must of heard it, too, on account he got to his feet as I got to mine. A breath later we was at a full run, off into the dark, carrying all we had carried before plus a fresh supply of bruises. My knee hurt. Yet the pain was clearing the gin off my brains and I could suddenly think.

We ran east.

Ahead of us, down the hill, three torches burned by a row of small boats that Seth Warner and the rear guard must of come over on and beached. Two men with muskets was there, looking wide-eyed as we run their way at a full gallop, our arms loaded with weaponry and womanhood, not to mention the cheese that was somewhere in the blankets. I could neither feel it nor touch it but the smell said my cheese was still present. Closer now, I could read the bewilder on the faces of the two sentries who guarded the boats. Verdmont men, the both of them.

Beyond the boats was Lake Champlain, big and black and deep cold. On the farther shore was Verdmont and home. Had it been daytime, my dim eyes could have seen the Booker place. But not at night. Then why was I seeing it? Across the lake I saw my father's cabin, lit up like it was day. The north side of our house glowed like it was painted yellow. To the left was orange flashes of strong light, which meant only one thing.

Our barn was burning.

Chapter 21

"Who goes?" a sentry yelled to us.

We never stopped. And as we come closer to the two men, and into the torchlight, they leveled muskets our way. One man was taller than his partner.

"We're Greenies," yelled Luke between puffs, "so don't shoot us to bits."

It sure was plain to read on the faces of them two men that they weren't much joyful to be put in charge of keeping company down at the lakeshore with a bunch of boats. Not when (back up the hill at the fort) their comrades was into all that love, liquor and loot. And that was when my brain got a tolerable idea. We set the woman on the ground, on her hip, still wrapped in coverlets.

"Brung you boys a gal," I said.

"A woman?" They lowered the guns.

"An English woman. They're better than gin," I said.

"And nearsome as hot," said Luke.

"You lads ain't suppose to be down here," said the taller of the two.

"No, you sure ain't," said Shorty.

"Look," I said, "if you ain't decent about this, we'll take our lady-friend back to Fort Ti. We brung you fair company and you don't even affect us friendly."

"Well, now . . ."

"We're leaving. And we'll take her along," said Luke.

"Don't be hasty," said the tall one.

"You fellows had supper?" I said.

"Narry a bite."

"Want some cheese?"

"Yeah, sure do."

I tossed the cheese to Shorty whose face wore a hungrier look. In catching it, his musket slipped to his feet. The tall man looked down at the squirming inside the blankets, and laid aside his weapon. A pink leg thrust itself out, beyond the knee, to expose a full and fleshy thigh. She tossed away a corner of the quilt and we saw her smiling face. She held up a half-drunk bottle of what looked to be rum and giggled.

"Tope," she said. "Here's to gay old tope."

As Shorty dropped the cheese, Luke and me and our two muskets was into one of the boats and pushed off. The men stared at the woman who stood up and did a crazy dance, lifting up the man's shirt she had on until there weren't much left to imagination. I lay in the stern, Luke worked the oars. But our bow thumped against a rock, causing the tall man to turn and point at our departure.

"Hey! Come back here."

As the tall sentry reached for his musket, I give a cock back of the hammer on mine, even though my piece was still empty. In the still of the lakeshore night, it made a mean sound, and he figured I'd cut him down. He let his musket sink to the ground real easy.

"This cheese smells bad," I heard Shorty say.

"If'n you think that be bad," Luke hollered between oar pulls, "wait'll you smell that woman."

"Row hard," I said.

"Aim to, Able."

"Our barn's burning. Hurry."

Luke slid over. Side by side, with him working one oar and me the other, we felt the big rowboat hasten up. The three torches and three people back on the York side growed smaller and smaller, until only a threesome of what looked no bigger than sparks was left. What the two sentries was doing to the woman, (or she to them, more likely) weren't worth the mattering. As our bent backs was to Verdmont, I give my neck a quick twist to whip a look at our place. The barn was sure burning, and we could hear the distant crackle of flame. There was a slight breeze.

Our bow grounded.

Grabbing our muskets, we run east and up the hill. Under a rise in the land, our house and barn was no longer in sight, but I could see the yellow in the sky. We was both short of air from the hard pulling on the oars, but we run up the hill real fast. Now in view, our burning barn was a giant mass of twisted orange timber. I saw the black outlines of people, running between us and the light of the barn. We run hard. Coming close on, *five men* stood ahead, their backs to us as they watched the barn melt. The heat made them take backward paces in

214

our direction, and my face could feel the hot of it as we almost reached them. They never heard our steps.

"Burn, ya dang Tory!" a man hollered at the barn, his hands up to his mouth.

The barrel of my empty musket near to took his head off. He went down. Swinging the stock around, I caught a second man under the chin, and I heard the shatter of jaw bone. Just as he fell back, his face faded blank; and I saw the white roll of his eyes as I cracked his skull. A third man swung his gun at us. Luke fired. The ball hit the man's chest and he looked dead even before his knees jacked. The fourth man's musket pointed its little black hole into my face. He cocked it. I saw the jerk of his hand as he yanked the trigger back, but the hammer clicked forward. The noise said the gun was empty, which he'd forgot, but the click of the steel near about stopped my heart. Hot piss filled my britches as I saw Luke split the man's head with one swing of his musket.

But the fifth man's piece was ready. He fired at us. The noise sort of plugged both my ears as the flame from the muzzle stung my face. Beside me I saw a twisting mass of blood and bone that had only a moment before been the face of my dearest friend. The musket must of had a load of scatter shot instead of a ball. Looking down at the fallen body, I saw that from the shoulders up there weren't no Luke Shelby. From my hip I aimed my piece at the man and pulled the trigger. *Click!* But I jerked back the hammer and let it hit the empty pan. *Click!* Again I did it, as if I could reason to do naught else. *Click!* Like I was blind. *Click!* And to boot, deaf. *Click!* Over and over, I snapped a useless hammer at the man who'd killed Luke. I was coughing on the burnt sulphur. My eyes stung. His horn was reloading, pouring black powder down the barrel. Out of his mouth, he took a ball of lead and it followed the powder. From under the musket barrel, he pulled out the long thin ramrod. As he jammed in the load, the musket was already aimed at my belly. Yet I couldn't move. My feet seemed to be fasted to the ground by pegs. The rod went in and out, in and out, and then he pulled the rod from the muzzle. I heard footsteps but was too froze to even turn and see who was coming, and even after the lean body lighted on the man, I did not recognize the attacker. With both his hands on the ramrod, he drove its point into its owner, sticking the point of the rod through his neck and out again on the yonder side. In front, the rod was brassy in the noonlight; but from the back of his neck, the ramrod was scarlet and dripping. He couldn't scream. But from his throat come a gargle noise that was sorry to hear. His mouth bubbled out blood.

"Luke," I whispered to the dying man.

Luther Peacham jabbed with the man's own ramrod until he lay kicking in death. Only then could I move myself. Walking to where Luther was rolling off him, I aimed my musket at the dead man once more and pulled a dead trigger. *Click.*

"Able." Luther's voice was weak. His back was to the earth, one hand holding his gut as I knew he must have been hurting from his own wound of a night ago. With his other hand he pointed back at our burning barn.

"Able, your father . . ."

His lips tried to say more until he choked on his own agony. Luther's face was pale white. No more words would come, yet his frail finger pointed me toward the house and barn, only a few steps away. Turning to the barn, I dropped my musket and ran toward the giant fire. A mean whip of heat lashed my face, harder and harder the closer I got. Papa weren't anywhere to be seen. Neither was Mama or Phoebe. Opening the door to our cabin, one look told me there weren't a soul inside. I ran around back to get as near the barn as I could. The heat was sickening. Verdmont got turned to Hell.

"Papa!" I yelled. "Mama! Phoebe!"

My hollers were lost in the great roar of the burning barn. There was no going into the flames. Looking around on the ground, I saw no one, like the place was haunted by fire.

"Papa!"

I was yelling to myself, and even my own ears could not hear. It was as if I'd been struck deaf and mute. A bucket of water from the well would serve no purpose, so I ran around the pigsty and to the rear of the barn. Now I was upwind and could get closer to the snarl of the burning wood and hay. It was then I saw my father. He was coming near to out of the wagon door, hauling a burden under each arm. Whatever he held was burning. So was his hair and his clothing. He should have been screaming with pain, and yet his jaws was set together. Stumbling, he fell to his knees. I tried to reach him but the heat whipped me back.

I threw my body in the water trough.

Drip wet, I run inside to Papa. Somehow I hefted him up to his feet again, and out of the barn. As I half dragged and half toted him, my eyes was shut tight against the sting of the fire. My flesh was burning, water and all. Had my father let loose of his two burdens we could of got out faster but he'd took a firm purchase, arms locked around both in a grip I couldn't bust open. Hot gas filled my lungs.

Opening my eyes, it took me a breath or two to recognize that the two things he lugged at was Mama and Phoebe. Their clothes and hair was burned away. Yet he stood like a stock, clinging to the two black bodies, while he himself burned like a torch. I ripped away his grip on one and then the other and somehow pushed him into the watering trough. A steamy hiss rose up as his big burning body filled the bin, forcing the water to surge up over the rim because of his bulk.

For Mama and Phoebe, there was naught to do, as their black bodies was dead stiff. The stink of roasted flesh made me puke up the cheese and the gin and the rum. I could expel all but thought, the worst hurt of all.

Struggling, I got Papa's head up and out of the water so's he wouldn't dunk his lungs. Rolling him out of the trough, I fell myself into it to wash the burning off my skin that cooked me most all over. I sat Papa up, his back against the water bin to face a direction that he'd not be able to see the bodies of Mama and Phoebe. But then he turned and started toward them, crawling on his belly like a gunshot dog I'd seen one time, pulling himself along. All my strength couldn't stop him, not even the weight of my body on his hot back (which felt to me like a heavy hunk of cooked meat) could hold him from pulling himself along the earth until he reached his wife and daughter. An arm around each one, he lay panting, his soaking head burned bald and black, mouth open and sobbing into the grit of his land, and whimpering like a hurt animal.

As he wept, I held him.

"No," he said at last, his voice all twisted up like it had been tortured, soft as a sick child. "No, God . . . not again. Not never again."

"Papa." My head was down near to his as to touch him with my lips. "Papa, it's Able. Can you hear me, Papa? It's your son, and you're safe now. We'll make out, you and me. I'll be a Tory if'n you want. They can't burn us all, Papa. Not all."

"Molly," he said, "Molly." But there weren't no spirit in the name. I wanted to tell him not to call for his wife, or for his daughter. Not now, not ever again.

"Phoebe," he said, like he knew she'd not answer, her laugh ringing like a little bell. His eyes was closed, and his voice come out of his breast as if from afar off, up from a deep grave, like he knew he'd hear no reply. He coughed, like his heart was on fire. I felt like the whole world was black and burning.

"Grace," he called out. "Jenny, come quick. Injuns. My . . . gun." His hands dug into the soil, black claws, reaching for a gun that was nowhere about. His right fist closed on a hunk of May earth, damp from evening. Finding my arm, he rested the hunk of dirt into my hand, locking my fingers around it righteous tight.

"Able," he said . . . "hold our land."

His big body sort of kicked once, real hard, and then was near to still. Asleep, yet not asleep. He breathed his last, and come to his end. I let out a long sigh, like I'd held it up inside me, waiting for my father to die. Wanting to die myself.

"Papa," I said, "I pray Heaven is some like England."

My eyes darted from my father to Mama, and to Phoebe. I just sat in the dirt, looking from one to another, without the belly to rise. My thinking was also reaching out to take in Jacob Cotter and Luke Shelby. And dear old Simon. Somehow I wanted to say something to Mama, some personal words; and to Phoebe. Her death was the most bitter of all, as she weren't much more than a child. I'd not wake up another morn and see Phoebe in the uploft asleep at my side.

It would be hard to say how long I sat at Papa's side, doing naught but pondering on what to do first. Dipping my hand in the water trough, I washed some of the black off Papa's face, and then off my own. His body was wet and cold from the dunking.

Why were they all in the barn? Why? Why?

There were no answers to any of my asking. Verdmont had gone mad, neighbors burning a barn of neighbors. Although the five men were strangers. No neighbor could have harmed Noah Booker. Like the warriors of Iron Knife, they had come from afar off to burn and kill and make folks suffer. Well, they paid. Five lives for five. Three of us Bookers, plus Jacob and Luke. I wondered why revenge is so dear to a wounded mind. So I prayed the score to be even, all in balance, so I would not kill no more. Tory or Whig, English or American, all men would be welcome at the door of Able Booker. I put my head to the watering bin and washed the smoke from my face, and spat out the stench of burning. The water was usual sweet; but on this night, it bore the taste of dead and dying.

Why didn't they kill *me*, too?

I wanted to be dead so Luke could go home to his ma. He never got to kiss her good-by, he'd said. I never got to kiss him good-by, neither, and I almost wanted to. Good-by, Luke, you good old boy. So long, Jake. I wish for your sakes there's a coonhunt up yonder. Lifting my head, I looked at the sky and saw all the stars in the May night. I wonder, I asked the sky, if there's war up there. And why, Lord, do they wage so much war on Booker land?

Lowering my head, I opened my fist to see the ball of earth Papa had placed in my hand. A little hunk of Booker earth. First, it was old Israel's, and then Noah's. I wonder how long before folks will point to this clearing and say it be the Able Booker place.

Sorry, Papa, but it won't be English soil. If we can whip the Redcoats, words like Whig and Tory won't matter so much. And one day, we'll probable be a colony like New York or New Hampshire and we won't just be old Verdmont no more. Shucks, we could even be a country, like England or France. I hope it comes to be and righteous soon. Whether it be a newborn babe or a fresh calf or a new nation, birth is sure a bloody business. Why do we all have to git bore in so much pain? I heard Mama's scream when Phoebe come into the world, all wet and squinty-eyed. Mama was crying and Phoebe was, too. I'd saw tears on Papa's cheeks and felt 'em run down my own. We all had a good weep that day.

But now is not the time for grief.

Our barn was black and smoking. A beam fell. Small fires still rode the edges of the burnt timbers shaved thin by the fire. Tongues of orange licked here and there, which made me know how long I'd just sat a watch over my dead. Somehow I got up and walked toward the barn, trying not to see Mama and Phoebe, in a effort to remember the color of their faces and the shine in their hair. The tool shed had not burned, but the walnut handle of the spade was warm and the iron too hot to touch.

I dug three graves.

The markers would have to wait, but I would carve those in good time. Three black bodies got put to ground, and I spaded in the loose earth atop of each one. Verdmont is full of rock, both large and small, which made the job take a long time. Seven graves in all, now. Seven Bookers. Israel and his family next to Noah and his; all but me. My place would be there one day. With so much dying, it was now time for a lot of living, plus a stout measure of work.

My spade slapped the gravel flat on the last burial, my father's. Done. Well, Papa, you can't say I'm shirking from this day on. And I swear on your grave, sir, that no one else will. I vow to hold this land and to work it as hard as I shall work myself. I'll do it, Papa. Honest I will. And I'll marry enough chain to link Verdmont to Boston.

"Able."

I'd plum forgot about Luther!

Spade in hand, I run to the spot where we'd done in the five men. Bodies lay about. The five dead, and a headless Luke. I saw Luther Peacham still on the ground and trying to rise up. It was still dark and I welcomed not seeing no more death. The barn fire was near out.

"Luther, you sound?"

"Sound . . . as Continental money." His voice hurt.

"Which ain't very sound," I said.

"My stomach is on . . . fire. Did you find . . . ?"

He cut off his question, staring at the spade in my hand, the blade of which was frosted brown with fresh dirt. His face spoke his sorrow. It was plain he wanted to ask who I'd just dug a grave for, and he final did.

"Who?"

"All of them. Papa, Mama, Phoebe."

"I saw it, Able."

"How'd it start?"

"You have a cow called Festus, I believe."

"He's an ox. Fresh cut."

"Well, he was ill and distempered, according to your father, who shut him in the barn for the night. Phoebe was concerned, and begged to stay with him on a bed of straw. As the weather was clement, your mother allowed her. We were asleep, but heard the crackle of fire. Your father had yet to undress as he seemed to suspect some trouble. We heard voices and yelling. Shots were fired, but I think no one was killed or wounded."

"What about the barn?"

"As your father fired his musket and reloaded, your mother threw a shawl over her nightgown and ran into the night, I presume to the barn which was aflame. I went, too, albeit I was too sore and stiff to move with much alacrity. And I was yet half asleep. Your father shouted to your mother not to enter the barn, perhaps forgetting in his excitement that Phoebe was asleep inside it. Then I saw part of the roof structure collapse after your mother braved the flames. Your father threw down his musket and ran into the fire to save the both. And then you and your friend arrived. I am truly sorry, Able. Words cannot express my feelings, but I . . ."

His voice stopped, as he no longer seemed to know what to say.

"I tried to run to the barn and rescue whomever I could, Able. But by the time I reached the door, the flames repelled me. I lacked the courage to enter."

"You do not lack courage," I said. "All of this is my blame. I should of been here tending."

"Fault not yourself. Your father was a Tory, and you Bookers will not be first or last to suffer the consequences of loyalty. Whigs shall also burn. I do not condone it. In no way. Burning a barn or a house or even a fort proves nothing. God, my gut hurts."

"You saved me, Luther. When I saw Luke die, thataway quick, I was in a trance."

"I know, I saw it. No one heard me yell. I saw you and your companion down four of them. The fifth would have shot you dead. I made myself run."

"I owe you my life, Luther Peacham."

"And I owe the Bookers for my own. So help me, Lord, I swear to never remove the stitches in my abdomen. For as long as I live I will wear Molly Booker's thread in my body. This, I promise."

220

"Luke," I turned and spoke to the headless body. Closing my eyes, my mind went on seeing. I was too sick to even pray.

"Was that your friend's name?"

"Luke Shelby. He lives north of us, not far from the Cotters." I touched Luke's dead hand.

"He *lives,* you said, as if he were yet alive."

"In a way he sort of is. Can you stand?"

"I doubt it. My stomach smarts to a most dreadful degree."

"Let me help." I pulled him to his feet.

"Will you bury Luke and the others?"

"I'll hitch the ox and drag them five to the sump hole. Then I'll pack Luke to his mother."

"Your ox is dead, Able. Burned, I am sure. But while you were gone I heard a cow. And also the nicker of Pit. I know my horse. And of course you may use him."

"Is he really yours?"

"He truly is. I bought him near Middlebury."

"From an Allen."

"Yes." Luther's face was a question.

"My father knew."

"And he still trusted me?"

"He honest did. My father don't mark people with no tag that says Whig or Tory. He could befriend a Saint Francis warrior if'n he thunk the man was true."

"You Bookers are some family. I was rightly fond of . . . Phoebe."

"Yes. She fonded easy." It was all gone, all burned away. Then I took myself a slow look at the five dead men.

"Scum," said Luther. "You'll find vermin like that under every flag."

Reaching inside my shirt, I pulled out the Union Jack that I'd hauled off the Fort Ti flag pole. It was still wet, yet warm from the work of my body. I unfolded it to show Luther.

"The ensign of England," he said. "As a boy, how much I honored that flag. My old pa saw to that."

"And mine."

I covered Luke Shelby's body with the Union Jack. And if'n I'd had half a dozen I'd as well covered them other five. Looking at the smolder of our barn, I said, "It weren't his fight. It were mine, and not old Luke's."

"A fight belongs to all who wish to roll up sleeves and wade into it," said Luther.

"You still aim to be a spy?"

"If our forces will have me, yes." Luther nodded.

"Ever hear the name Benedict Arnold?"

221

"Yes. But I must confess I cannot quite remember where. Is he a spy?"

"No, he's a soldier. Colonel Arnold of Connecticut."

"You seem impressed."

"Sure am. Him and Ethan sort of split the command, so to speak. Your map was sure good, Luther. Me an' old Ethan studied it together. But like I was saying, if it comes to a real war, I reckon I'd like to serve under Colonel Arnold, about as well as anybody. Still, I don't cotton to do no more killing. To tell you true, Luther, there ain't another death left in me."

"Would your friend Colonel Arnold need an able, but now unemployed and slightly wounded, spy?"

"He might."

"Good."

"Just tell my name, and remember him of how I saved his skin at Fort Ti. Of second thought, just say I said a thanks for the cheese."

Together, the two of us limped slow toward our cabin. I toted the spade in one hand and half-carried Luther Peacham with the other. It was almost a toss up which were the heftier. The sky said it was wanting to be sunup. A new day that would bring me work to do.

I'd get some sleep, and then pack Luke Shelby home to his ma. And the flag to Mrs. Cotter.

Chapter 22

It was a June morning.

Tiny white puffs of clouds dotted the blue sky, like a trail of Indian sign. As if the Benefactor had writ a message in the heavens to bless this day forever. It was 15 June 1775.

"Are you afraid?" Luther asked me in a whisper.

"A mite bit," I said to him.

"Have a swallow from the jug that one of the gentlemen was kind enough to bring. It will sustain your courage."

"Can't. I don't want whiskey on my breath."

"I believe I understand why." Luther smiled.

"Maybe she won't come."

"She'll come. I have been a witness to the manner in which she beholds you, Able, and you have her bond that she'll not miss *this* day."

From the doorway of my cabin, we heard horses and voices. More people arrived in a wagon, the Wilkerson family from the town of Shoreham, a man and a wife and their five boys. One was my age, Benjamin. And then the Cotters arrived, from all directions; Henry Cotter and his family, Levi Cotter and his. And the Painters, too. Just about every soul in the valley come to our farmstead.

But no Comfort.

Levi Cotter moved like the big man he was; walking to me, shook my hand; and with his left, gave me a clump on the shoulder that could have near to fell a bear.

"You fixed to git wed, eh?" he growled.

"Sure am, Levi."

"Where's the bonnie bride?"

"Not here yet." I tried to smile.

"Aye. Changed her mind, no doubt."

"She probable did," I said.

He leaned close to my ear, and his words were already wet with what I got a whiff to be a mite stronger than cow's milk. "I hear tell you're to wed one them Starr gals."

"Yes, sir, I sure be."

"Which one?" There was a twinkle to his eye.

"Comfort."

Levi Cotter's old mouth twisted into a grin that was some removed from sanctity. His head give a few little nods up and down. "I sure wish I was you, boy." As he turned and trudged off to rejoin his wife and ten offspring, his old head was still nodding, as if to say that were he the groom this day, he'd give Comfort Starr a merry time under the quilts. Levi was a grandfather, and knowing that he still had the hanker made me feel right prosperous.

Luke's folks come.

Mistress Shelby put her hands around me to hug me hard, lifting up her face so's her cheek would cling to mine. Then she looked at me for a moment, as if she could see her dead son in my eyes. Henry Cotter's wife saw us and come to make us three. Reaching an arm around the both of them, it was like old Luke and Jacob Cotter was still among the living. They were both small women, almost birds, and the pair of them fit under my shoulders. They held close to me, not wanting to let go; as I was the last bit of their own sons they had left, and couldn't bear to surrender away the little that lingered.

None of the three of us said nothing. Narry a word. We just sort of held on, each to the other two. I knew they felt my loss of Mama and Papa and Phoebe. They still had part of their families, but knew I was alone.

"Good times," Luke's mother said at last. "You had some fair times together, you boys."

"I heard tell," Mrs. Cotter said softly.

"It ain't how much life," I said to them, "it's how much laughter. I reckon Luke and Jake and me got more'n our rightful share."

"Able," said Mrs. Cotter, "I'm happy you're to wed this day."

"And I," said Luke's mother. Then she sort of looked down at the ground we stood on, and then around and about us. "Was it . . . here?" I knew she was asking where Luke was killed.

"Over there," I said. "Right atop that knoll."

Three of us walked to the spot, facing west, looking over at Fort Ticonderoga. There was no British flag, no roll of British drums, and no Scottish pipes.

"You know," said Mrs. Cotter, "them British only give up a fort. I give a boy." Her body shook as she spoke the last four words.

"So did I," said Mistress Shelby. "And I'd willing trade all the forts ever built to bring him back."

"Ain't a tear left in either one of us," Mrs. Cotter touched the hand of her woman friend and neighbor.

We turned, looking at my new barn that both their men folk, along with other good Verdmont hands and salt had helped me raise. The timbers was so young and yellow they seemed happy to be part of the morning. Beyond the barn was a new ox, a wedding present I'd got yesterday from all the Cotters. He was black and white; and yet without a name, as there was no more a Phoebe Booker to do the job. I wanted to give my new ox the name of Prosper, but I'd wait until Comfort also had a say.

"We all lost," said Luke's ma.

"And we'll back our burden," said Mrs. Cotter. "No one's lost like Able. But today he wins a bride." She smiled up at me.

"Comfort's comely," said Mistress Shelby.

"Have a passel of children, Able."

"We will, I promise you."

"It'll be a cozy thought to know there's a fresh family close on, to work this land. Old Verdmont would be a haunted place without Bookers to neighbor with."

They both stretched up their faces, kissing me on both cheeks to once, and then strolled quietly away. I hoped they'd join the other ladies to be part of the gossip. But the pair of them seemed to be by themselves, as though they needed each other. Their faces stayed sad, like their insides wanted to break down into crumbs. Yet I knew they both would bear the hurt. Cotters and Shelbys don't bust easy. Neither do Bookers, or Starrs.

Luther had been making talk with the Wilkersons. Turning, he saw that the two women had let me be, so he come my way. He was walking better, now that a month had went by to help his healing; still with a limp, but not bent over like his gut was on fire. He weren't very powerful built, but Luther Peacham was sure some gent. If there was a fight to break out, you couldn't ask for a tougher character to put your back to. I felt like me and old Luther could lick half of Verdmont plus a bit of New Hampshire, and have some grit left over.

"How do?" he said, smiling.

"Like a teakettle most come to a boil."

"Remember what I told you, Able. Whatever you do, *don't* get nervous." With a gay toss of his head, he let out one of his best laughs. People turned to snatch the mirth of it for themselves. Those who hadn't heard his jest even laughed from the germ of Luther's chuckle. It sure was catching.

225

"You're a good old boy, Luther."

"I just enjoyed a drink of Verdmont whiskey," he said.

"Is that right."

"Yes. The man who offered it to me called it *corn*. I believe he referred to its humble origin."

"How'd it swallow?"

"Not so humble. Do you ever allow yourself a nip of that particular concoction?"

"Nope," I said. "I be a gin man."

"Gin?"

"Aye. You heard it."

"In Boston," said Luther, "they say that gin is hotter than Old Satan's spit."

"They couldn't of said a sorry a thing as that at Harvard College, could they? I presume that to be a fair and proper place," I said.

"Not according to Father. He contends that many a hard-earned pound of tuition money has been squandered by the young wastrels who attend."

"You were short on study?"

"Diliquent was the term my father used, not only to describe my actions but as a noun to befit the scholar himself. I believe my old pa has deep reservations on how much, or rather how little, education I absorbed at dear old Harvard . . until I was expelled."

Not knowing what expelled meant, I asked, "Is that where you took up the trade of being a spy?"

Luther laughed. "One hardly would find *Spying* listed in the formal curricula at Harvard College. To be a spy, my friend Able, all I needed was the basic qualification."

"And what might be that?"

"I'm just sneaky."

"No you ain't."

"But I am. Nothing excites me more than to pose as something I am not. And if one is a spy, you see, one can mask as a score of different personalities, in costume as well as character. You should see me as a little old washer woman. I wanted to have a go at the theater, but my father drew the line. He said that players were a louty lot, with morals as shabby as any bawdy house in Boston."

"I ain't never been near to a bawdy house."

"And from the brief exposure allowed me by your bride to be, meaning no offense as to the young lady's reputation, I see little reason that you will ever have need to go."

"Luther?"

"Your servant, sir."

"You aim to keep on in the spy business?"

"Perhaps. At least until I hang for treason. I do intend to seek out the chap you told me about, Colonel Benedict Arnold of Connecticut."

"He's some guy." I put my foot up on the hub of a wagon wheel, while Luther run his hand along the flank of a bay horse. It was going to be a hot day, and it felt as good to us to stand in the shade of an elm as it probable felt to Shelby's mare.

"Able, do you plan to continue with the Green Mountain Boys?"

"Only if the Regulars come this way. Doubt they will. Ain't nothing for'em in old Verdmont that would be worth the taking."

"I hope you are correct. You have offered enough." He looked over the horse's back toward our family plot, our little cemetery. "Seven," he said. "A pity, as this old world hungers for more folk like the Bookers. My heart is happy this day for you, Able. And I will sorely miss your company."

"We got an extra loft, Luther. Just on account Comfort and me are to be wed, don't mean you have to move on."

"I have abided here a month and more. My bones ache with work. Time I was on my way."

"You're welcome to tarry on. Don't know where I'd git a hired hand to cream a cow like you do. Esther will miss you."

"Tell her, good sir, I am grateful for the welcome. The cheer at your table is as warm as Esther's milk. Yet I am now full and can sop up not another sip. You and Miss Comfort merit the privacy of your own companionship. Pit and I shall trot south as soon as the ceremony's performed."

"I'll miss you, Luther."

"And I you. By the way, speaking of fair company, where is your buxom bride?"

"What's *buxom* mean?"

"Uh . . . it means bonnie. Full of body and limb. A nubile maiden, if I'm any judge. Ripe and ready, with eager arms and hospitable thighs." His face give a leer.

"You and your poetic stuff."

"I should have been a bard. My talents are far too abrim with artistry to be a spy. The tawdry trade of espionage is so lacking in both love and lyric. Spies are so bereft of grace." He did a quick dance step.

Our heads both turned as we heard the one voice in Verdmont that could have belonged to no one except the Widow Starr. It come from afar off.

"Whoa, ya dang fool demon!"

All heads twisted to the east, and we were rewarded. Around the bend in the road come a white horse, pulling a rig of screaming females,

227

the Widow Starr at the reins. Holding back the ribbons served only to excite her animal, spurring him to even a faster gait. Closer and closer they came, the horse at a dead gallop with no intent to slow down. His wild eyes rolled in their sockets and foam flecked his muzzle. A front wheel hit a bump, lifting the entire rig into the air. I prayed for Comfort's life and limb.

Everyone scattered.

The horse had no idea of stopping. And to make matters worse, the Widow Starr was standing up, yanking first one strip of leather and then its mate, in a feeble effort to turn her horse into some sort of circle that would hold down the damage to merely a few broke bones.

"Stop, you cussed heathen. Let loose o' that bit or I'll tan your rump, you rotten . . ."

The horse reared and stopped. Starrs tumbled atop one another, atop the horse, and onto the ground. But the animal stood stock still, snorted, and took the stance of a statue, like he'd been daydreaming in a pasture. I ran to the rig, as Comfort saw me and leaped, landing in my arms. She sure was *buxom*. I was off balance a bit as I caught her and so the two of us tumbled down in a heap. Yet I was too happy to hear the laughter. Comfort's white frock was all lace and handsome, and to hug her once gave me the all-overs.

"Where is he?" Widow Starr yelled.

"Who?" somebody said. "The groom?"

"No! The *preacher* we brung. Where'd he git to?"

"Hello, Able." Comfort's voice was yielding and soft.

"Howdo, Miss Comfort Starr," I said.

"Not for long," she said, sweet as hay.

The Widow Starr was yelling her head off, but as my arms were around her daughter, I didn't much care. We kissed each other. Ardent, Fruitful, Mingle, Propagate, and Nocturnal (the animal active at night) was all kissing both of us, both Comfort and me. They sure was pretty girls, and smelled like a jar of rose petals.

"We brung him from town!" screamed Widow Starr in a panic. "Where is he?"

"Reverend Staple fell off, Mama," said Mingle.

"Right at the mill turn, into a thicket."

"He fell *off?* Why didn't somebody say so?"

"We did. We all did."

"Couldn't of stopped that dang horse anyhow! But now we got no Reverend Staple. We got no preacher!"

No preacher! The words hit home, freezing my heart into a big hard lump. No minister would mean no wedding. And no wedding would mean that I'd not be in bed with Mary Comfort Starr this night. This night? Hell, all afternoon; as soon as all the company left. Soon as we could sneak ourselfs uploft.

"There's no preacher," some lady said.

"Quick! Go fetch poor Reverend Staple."

"Where?"

"Darn if I know. Widow Starr lost the poor soul on a bend. They say the man's deaf and near to seventy."

Everyone was talking all to once. Nobody seemed to know what to do. People were pointing back uproad toward Shoreham, expecting God's messenger on earth (Reverend Staple) to come limping through the trees and into view. He never come. I wanted to run all the way back and pick Reverend Staple up, and run home again with the old preacher in my arms. Anything, as long as it meant being wedded and bedded with my girl.

One of the Cotter boys rode north to look for the preacher. My heart sank. We waited. It come noon and the Cotter boy never come back. We ate. Some of the men drank. I looked with longing at Comfort and she at me. People was getting restless and shifty. Some had too many pulls of whiskey, and I felt like getting drunk myself. The words was on my tongue, ready to say, All of you go home, because there ain't to be no wedding. Not this day.

Hoofbeats were heard.

All eyes turned uproad to watch Christopher Cotter gallop into view. He looked hot and his horse was in lather. Before the gelding he rode come to a full halt, young Cotter slid off the saddle and come on a run to my side.

"Leg's broke," he said in a huff.

"Whose?"

"Reverend Staple. He got throwed clear of the Widow Starr's rig. I packed him into Shoreham to let Doc Pritchard have a look at his leg. It's sprain for certain. You ain't got no minister to say the words. You can't wed."

I was so doggone mad I could of got out my musket and shot that dangfool white horse of Starr's right in his poorly pate.

Luther stepped forward.

Holding up his hands for silence, he made his proclamation: "Friends," he said, "allow me to introduce myself. I am the *Reverend* Luther Boniface Peacham from the City of Boston, assistant rector of the Fifth Congregational Church."

The guests all muttered as if they was duly impressed. *I* sure was.

"I received my Divinity Degree from Harvard College in the true tradition of those revered recipients of that vicinity before me, such as

229

the Reverend Cotton Mather. And so, Master Booker, Miss Starr, and honored guests . . . you are indeed fortunate that *I* am present.

"A *preacher,* that boy?" someone asked.

"He said so, and of Harvard College."

"Weren't he the schoolmaster . . . ?"

"Yes, over to Fort Ti."

Once the rumble of questions and answers softed down a mite, Luther Boniface Peacham approached the Widow, bowing in a fancy and formal fashion.

"Mrs. Starr," he said, "now that you all have deliberated on my qualifications of the clergy, do I now have your blessing to perform the rites of wedlock for your daughter and the worthy youth who pleads for her hand?"

"Do it, boy. I mean . . . *Reverend.*"

At that moment I wanted so much more of Comfort Starr than just her hand, I near to leaped to the side of the Widow. But then I knew that a woman with six daughters weren't to be too fussy on who says the holy words, as long as they get proper said. Besides, old Reverend Staple could have mumbled a shoddy story and not a soul who stood witness could of told the difference. At least Luther would speak up to all congregated. And speak up he did,

"Join hands, Comfort and Able."

From behind his back, he produced a black-bound book. It was the Holy Bible, and it worked like a charm. Even the most doubting tongue (as to Luther Peacham's ministerial training) was stilled by its presence. The edge of the Bible had a rip in a certain place. I recognized it as our Booker family Bible that he had sneaked into the cabin to find and fetch. But the manner in which he opened it said to all present that it was the prim property of the Reverend Luther Boniface Peacham.

He cleared his throat, commanding attention. As he cracked open the Good Book, I prayed that it weren't the Songs of Solomon. If it was I'd a bust out laughing.

"To befit the solemnity of this occasion," said a sudden serious Reverend Peacham, "I shall read a passage from the Book of Ruth."

In my hand, I felt the fingers of the girl who would no longer be Mary Comfort Starr, soon to become Mrs. Able Booker. Her hand was small and strong, and clenched as if in the pain of a childbirth. My hand tightened upon hers, and we both looked at Luther's sober face. He was no longer jesting. Before continuing, he looked to and fro, from Comfort's face to mine as though he truly loved the pair of us, and was proud to unite us in wedlock. He then spoke.

" 'And Ruth said, intreat me not to leave thee, or to return from following after thee: for whither thou goest, I will go; and where thou

230

lodgest, I will lodge. Thy people shall be *my* people; and thy God, *my* God.'"

His words made me swallow. His eyes left our faces, looking beyond us and the gathering to the place where the seven Bookers rested in our land. He went on:

"'Where thou diest, will I die; and there will I be buried. The Lord do so to me, and more also, if ought but death part thee and me.'"

Tears ran down Luther's face. And when he spoke again, his voice was weak with affection.

"Mary Comfort Starr, do you take this man to be your husband, to love, to honor, to cherish evermore?"

"I do."

"And do you, Able Booker, take this woman unto wife, to love, to honor, to cherish always?"

"I do."

"Then by the Grace of God, and of his Holy Church, I bestow upon you the sanctity of marriage. And may our Heavenly Father long bless this unity. Able and Comfort . . . I pronounce you man and wife."

Luther hugged us both. My cheek felt the wet of his face. It all felt so doggone good, but I really didn't aware like I was honest married, but like I was still just old Able Booker.

Luther whispered into my ear. "Hey! I overlooked the part about the *ring*. Do you happen to have one?"

Fishing in my pocket, I brought up my mother's wedding band that I'd took off her hand before laying her to rest. Comfort held out her hand and the ring slipped on her finger, like it belonged there. I kissed her.

"Oh, Able . . . I am so blissful happy."

"And I, too."

Everybody stayed with us all afternoon and well into evening. It was near to dark when the last guest extended us a blessing and rode off. Luther Peacham packed up his duds, put the tack to Pit, and looked at the two of us. I felt as though we were his children. I couldn't say a good-by. I just put my fist on his shoulder.

"Luther," said my wife, "thank you for such a service. Every word was holy and heartfelt. I'm so grateful it was you and not Reverend Staple."

"May God rest his leg," smiled Luther, as he swung up onto Pit's back.

"It's hard to believe you're a preacher," she said, waving as he waved to us.

"Yes," he yelled, "it is."

Pit galloped off, heading south. And thus our friend Luther took his leave, and we were at long last alone.

In bed, a few moments later, Comfort was soft and pink, and about as *buxom* as a bride could be. We giggled in our joy, and the cornhusk beneath us crackled with its own crisp excitement. As we kissed in the darksome, I kept on pondering if we was really *wed*. Was old Luther Peacham really an honest-to-goodness minister?

Why study on that matter? Instead, I made Mary Comfort Booker my honest-to-goodness wife.

F